P9-CKC-779

FIRST IMPRESSIONS

"A lady never leaves her domicile without properly covering her head—a fact any English gentleman would know." The moment she spat out the words, she wanted to bite her tongue. This man would soon be a viscount and he could have her fired!

He surprised her by chuckling. "Well now, I've been accused of lots of things over the years, but being a gentleman was never one of them," he drawled.

The lout was laughing at her! "The reason for that is perfectly evident," she snapped.

"It appears to me, ma'am, that we've sort of gotten off on the wrong foot."

"You mean the one you repeatedly insist on placing in your mouth?"

He removed his boot from the edge of the fountain and turned directly toward her. She came only to his shoulder, hat and all. "For such a little bitsy thing, you sure do pack a Texas-sized sting."

"In Texas parlance, I surmise that means large."

"Yes, ma'am, everything about a Texan is large," he said in a husky voice.

TEXAS VISCOUNT

SHIRL HENKE

LEISURE BOOKS   NEW YORK CITY

A LEISURE BOOK®

October 2004

Published by

Dorchester Publishing Co., Inc.
200 Madison Avenue
New York, NY 10016

ISBN 0-8439-5243-1

Visit us on the web at www.dorchesterpub.com.

For all my loyal readers who have crossed the Atlantic with me and my American Lords. It's been a dandy adventure. Here's to continuing romance in England and America!

TEXAS VISCOUNT

Chapter 1

"Captain Cantrell, sir, you are out of uniform!" Theodore Roosevelt bellowed at the man standing buck naked beside the bed wherein a young woman with tangled dark hair huddled beneath the scant cover of a rumpled sheet.

Joshua Cantrell, whose sole accoutrement was the six-shooter clasped in his hand, quickly lowered the weapon as two burly Secret Service Agents trained their Colt Army specials on the Texan. TR dismissed them with a wave of his hand, leaving the trio alone in the garishly opulent room.

It was difficult to decide whose face was the redder, Cantrell's or that of his former commanding officer. Certainly Cece, Josh's companion of the evening, felt no embarrassment, but then Cece had been employed at the Trail Ride Saloon and Bordello far too long to be bothered by anything less than a full-fledged longhorn stampede down Main Street. Besides, she hadn't the faintest idea that the solidly squat man squinting fiercely through pince-nez eyeglasses was

1

the President of the United States, sworn in only weeks earlier after the assassination of William McKinley.

"Well, since I was already at attention when you came bustin' in, Colonel, should I get dressed now?" Josh drawled with as much sangfroid as he could muster, considering the circumstances.

"First, please ask the young lady to leave," Roosevelt snapped, turning his head to allow Cece privacy to slip from the bed and don the purple satin robe tossed on the floor beside her corset . . . and a welter of Cantrell's own clothing.

Roosevelt's face was definitely the redder of the two.

The whore looked at Josh for confirmation before complying. "I owe you one, darlin'," he said with a wink, fishing his wallet from his jeans and stuffing a wad of bills into the deep cleavage between her breasts as she belted the robe. With the Yankee intruder still staring steadfastly at a gas-lamp fixture on the wall, Cece flounced out the door, slamming it loudly in her wake, all the while cursing in Spanish.

Josh yanked on the well-worn pair of jeans and a cotton shirt while his former Rough Rider commanding officer paced back and forth across the carpet. The colonel had always had way too much nervous energy, to Josh's way of thinking. As he slid on his hand-tooled leather boots, he asked, "To what do I owe the honor, Mr. President?"

The frank bafflement in young Cantrell's voice broke into Roosevelt's tumbling thoughts. He snorted. "Still doesn't sound right. Call me Colonel. I'm used to that."

"I reckon it was pretty sudden, taking over when that madman shot President McKinley, but after being

'Your Excellency,' the governor of New York, I can't imagine you didn't figure to be president eventually."

"Eventually. Not last month—and certainly not under such horrific circumstances. You see those guards I'm saddled with?" He gestured to the closed door outside which his protectors lurked. "Damn nuisance. I'd rather take care of myself." He opened his jacket, revealing a Smith & Wesson hammerless .38 caliber revolver tucked neatly inside his suit pocket.

"Maybe those new Treasury fellows aren't such a bad idea, all things considered. There are safer places for you to be than in Fort Worth on a Saturday night, Colonel—not that I'm not glad to see you," Josh added. "Just surprised."

"And inconvenienced. My apologies for the young lady," TR replied dryly.

"You and I both know Cece isn't a lady, and you said 'for,' not 'to.' Your Yankee Puritanism's still showing, sir." Josh's grin was decidedly impenitent. This was not the first time his commander, a staunch Episcopalian and family man, had found his subordinate's morals wanting. "What can you expect, Colonel? I grew up in a place just like this. It's sorta homey to me."

"You might have had the misfortune to have been raised by soiled doves, but by Jove, man, you're a viscount now! You simply must learn to conduct yourself with decorum."

Ignoring the less-than-flattering comment about his upbringing—something he permitted from only a few men—Josh asked, "How the hell did you find out about that title business?"

"I have my ways. Springy's father was a long-time friend of your great-uncle's. He's informed me the old gentleman's beside himself over your refusal."

3

"Just because some passel of papers came from this Earl Hamilton—"

"Hambleton," TR corrected. "His title is Earl of Hambleton. Viscount Wesley is the courtesy title you'll assume."

"With all due respect, Colonel, I'm not assumin' anything," Josh replied stubbornly. "I'm no viscount. I'm a Texan."

"Lord Hambleton is the head of the Cantrell family, and you are his great-nephew and sole surviving heir. You have a duty to go to England. Good heavens, man, can't you see what an opportunity this is for you? You never knew your parents. Now you have a living kinsman who's searched for you for over twenty years."

"I haven't done too bad without any help these past twenty years on my own," Josh replied with a hint of defiance in his voice.

Roosevelt gave a rueful chuckle. "Yes, I know. While I lost my shirt in the cattle business in the Dakotas, you made a fortune here in Texas. Your prominence in Texas politics was what finally enabled the earl's agents to locate you. You could've been a governor yourself if you'd wanted it."

"My time in the legislature plumb cured me of political ambition," Josh replied dryly. "As to this nobility business, Cantrell's not that unusual a name. I can't rightly be sure it's even my own. Gertie and her girls may have picked it out when my mother died."

"Then how do you explain that ring?" TR asked, eyeing the distinctive gold and onyx signet Josh had worn ever since he was big enough to fit it on his finger. "That is the Hambleton family crest."

"Maybe one of Gertie's girls took it in trade and kept it for me," Josh replied.

"I'd never have believed it. You're afraid—afraid that you won't measure up. By Jove, that's it!"

Josh bristled. "I measured up by making my first million dollars in the cattle business before I turned twenty-seven. And you, of all men, should know I'm not afraid of anything."

"Of Spanish bullets, no. I'd never question your courage under fire, Captain. But you're afraid of meeting an eighty-year-old man. Your great-uncle's investigation was quite thorough. You're his heir."

"What if I am? Why should I go gallivanting across the Atlantic? Remember how seasick I was just crossing to Cuba? I have a business to run here in Fort Worth, a right big business. And, come to think of it, why do you care whether or not I become this count or viscount or whatever the hell I'm supposed to be? Seems to me, being president would give you more important things to worry about."

"Well, ahem . . ." Roosevelt cleared his throat and resumed pacing. "Perhaps this discussion calls for a bit of libation." He stalked quickly to the door and opened it, addressing the two large men waiting deferentially in the hallway. "Fetch up a pail of cold beer, if you please, Mr. Shane . . . or"—he turned to Josh—"would you prefer something stronger? What was the name of that frightful stuff you brought to training camp in San Antonio?"

"Who Shot John."

"Beg pardon?" TR said, blinking through his thick lenses.

"It's a brand of bourbon. The bartender knows," Josh said to the agent.

"Fetch it along. I'm sure the establishment will accommodate," Roosevelt commanded. The guard nodded and closed the door.

"Considering how abstemious you normally are, this must be good," Josh said grimly. "I know your Brit buddy Cecil Spring Rice is involved. How about that Anglophile secretary of state, John Hay?"

TR threw back his head and filled the room with booming laughter, revealing the set of incredibly large white teeth that had been the delight of editorial cartoonists for over a decade. "For one who purports to care nothing about what happens beyond your vast self-contained kingdom of Texas, you do know a considerable amount about Washington politics."

"Someone's got to watch the hencoop so the Repub—er, the foxes don't steal the chickens," Josh replied with a grin.

Roosevelt shook his head reprovingly. "Alas, ever the benighted Democrat."

"You didn't come here to convert me, Colonel. You know better."

TR sighed and resumed pacing. "No, I did not. Your political leanings are regrettable, but you may still serve your country in a unique way."

"What way?" Cantrell asked suspiciously. His instincts were humming. And he didn't much fancy the tune.

"Are you aware that Great Britain and Japan are presently negotiating a treaty? No, I thought not," he replied before Josh could even shake his head.

"But I can see the advantages of an alliance for both sides—and for America," Josh interjected just as a discreet knock sounded. He opened the door and accepted the bottle from the agent with thanks, then twisted the cork and took a long thirsty pull. Wiping his mouth with the back of his hand, he went on, "It's the Czar's interest in China that's got your back up."

"Most astute, Captain. Yes, since the Russians have

almost finished the Trans-Siberian Railroad, they can move troops from Moscow to Vladivostok rather more quickly than anyone in London or Tokyo would desire. They've always had designs on controlling the whole of the eastern Asiatic continent, which would menace British India, not to mention Hong Kong. And our own newly acquired Philippine Islands."

"Also play the devil with the other powers' China trade, wouldn't it?" Josh asked rhetorically. "The Japanese could provide a counterbalance to Russia . . . if you can control them." He slouched back in an overstuffed chair and took another pull on the whiskey bottle, studying Roosevelt closely. When he offered to pour a glass of the amber liquid, the colonel declined as Cantrell knew he would. Nothing stronger than beer or wine had ever passed his lips in the decade Josh had known Teddy, a nickname he knew the colonel detested.

"We can control the Japanese. I went to Harvard with an excellent chap, Kentaro Kaneko. He's highly placed at their court. I know what their objectives are in the Far East, and right now they coincide with ours—and with Britain's."

"What's that have to do with me?" The hairs on the back of his neck were standing on end now. He knew something was afoot, to bring Roosevelt halfway across the country, in secret, only weeks after he'd assumed office.

"A cabal of Russians in London is contriving to disrupt the negotiations between the British and the Japanese. There's even been an attempt to assassinate the Japanese minister, Hayashi. All hushed up, but if another is made . . . well, it will break the deal."

"So, let that prime minister, Salisbury, handle it. He's the galoot in charge over there."

Roosevelt gave a toothy grin. "You always did love playing as though you had no more brains than a balloon, but I saw through you in Cuba. That's why you're the perfect man for this job."

"What job?" Josh sat forward in his chair and set the whiskey bottle on the table.

Roosevelt paused, then leaned forward in his chair as well, fixing Cantrell with a steady gaze, made more penetrating by the thick lenses of his glasses. "A member of the royal family may be implicated. King Edward's brother Leopold's second son, George Clarence, a ne'er-do-well if ever there was one."

"From what I've read, the Wettins never had a shortage of those," Josh said dryly. "How's Georgie tied to the Russians?"

"He has a Russian mistress."

Josh whistled low.

"Yes, a pretty kettle of fish, isn't it? No sooner has this Jack the Ripper nonsense died down after the king's nincompoop son Albert Victor died, than they are faced with one of Edward's nephews possibly involved in high treason. Very touchy."

"Why rope and drag me into this fracas? I'm an outsider. There's nothing I can do. Hell, Colonel, I barely speak English, according to your Harvard friends. I sure as shootin' don't speak Russian."

TR smirked. "Ah, but you do speak Spanish."

"What in blue blazes has that got to do with anything?" Josh's head was beginning to spin, and it wasn't from the whiskey.

"You're considerably smarter than you let on. Just play the part of a ripsnortin' cowpuncher to the hilt. You possess a rare talent for espionage. Remember how you posed as a Spanish soldier and slipped into Santiago to assess their troop strength?"

Josh was forced to smile reluctantly. "I had to hold my arm across my left side the whole while so they couldn't see the bullet hole in the uniform. I was damn lucky my border Spanish was good enough to fool those drunk guardsmen. So now you want me to be a spy for the British."

It was not a question. Roosevelt didn't treat it as such. "And for the United States. Since the late war, we have a great deal at stake in the Pacific. I know you've never been one to shirk when duty calls."

Cantrell knew he was fighting a losing battle. Teddy was about to charge up another hill, and the devil take any man who got in his way. He sighed in resignation, but before he could negotiate some conditions, the president bucked him off another horse. "Lord Hambleton is your only living kinsman. He's eighty and in failing health, else he'd have made the journey here to Texas to convince you to become his heir. Springy says he's a grand old fellow. I think you should give this whole viscount thing a chance as well, Josh. There's nothing to be afraid of."

Cantrell stiffened. "I'm not afraid of any old man—I don't care if he eats a steer for breakfast every morning, hide and all. All right, I'll try to catch your assassins."

"Bully! Then let me fill you in on the details Secretary Hay's received from the British ambassador . . ."

Joshua Cantrell, soon to be the seventh Viscount Wesley and heir to the Earl of Hambleton, took a deep drink of whiskey and thought things over as Roosevelt talked. He had agreed to go to England. However, he had not agreed to remain there after the job was done.

"Sabrina, you simply must help me! This is the best position I've ever had. I should hate so to lose it," Edmund Whistledown implored his cousin. The cadaverously thin young man wrung his hands, ready to go down on his knees if necessary.

Miss Sabrina Edgewater sat primly on the edge of the well-worn Chippendale chair in her modest sitting room. She'd wanted to have all the furniture reupholstered but could not afford it on her modest income. And now here came dear, hapless Edmund, once again in trouble, begging her for money which she could ill spare.

"I saw him staring at this wretched suit the day he took me on as a clerk. And the tailor won't release my new clothing unless I pay him, and I can't do that until Friday next when His Lordship pays me. Crikey, Lord Hambleton will dismiss me without references if I appear in his office with frayed cuffs another day!"

Sabrina sighed as her young cousin suppressed tears. He'd always been an emotional boy, thin and frail, picked upon by the other boys in school. After his parents died when he was seven, he came to live with her family. She was fourteen then and had immediately become his self-appointed protector. As the eldest daughter of Squire Edgewater's large brood, she possessed, her father was fond of saying, the presence of a drill sergeant. Stern discipline worked well with her own wildly rebellious brothers, but she'd sensed immediately that the orphaned Edmund required a gentler hand.

She'd been redeeming him from tribulation ever since. Trouble seemed to follow her twenty-year-old cousin as naturally as mongrels chased a butcher wagon. Sighing, Sabrina asked, "How much will the tailor require for your suit?"

"Five pounds," he whispered in trepidation.

She sprang to her feet. "Five pounds! What did he make it of—wool or gold?"

"Well, you see, it isn't just the suit . . . I required a whole new wardrobe. The roof on my flat leaks, and during that storm last week every stitch I own—including my shoes—was utterly ruined." He paused a beat. "I'll lose my position, Coz."

"Very well, but I shall have to write a bank draft for such a large sum."

He brightened visibly, then immediately grew despondent once more. "Oh, but I have an assignment at eleven. That's why I'm supposed to be in good form. Lord Hambleton's dispatched me to meet the ship from America bearing his heir. I'd barely have time to change and be there if I can't pay the tailor immediately. See, His Lordship's coach is outside." He gestured through the shabby drapes to a handsome landau bearing the Hambleton crest.

"Then why did you wait until now to ask me, Edmund?" she retorted, struggling for patience.

His narrow face twisted as his pale eyes shied away from hers. "I . . . I know what a burden I've been to you, Coz. I tried to borrow the sum from some chums, but they're down on their luck, too."

"Then I don't know what I can—"

"Crikey, I have it! You can take the coach and meet His Lordship's heir while I cash your signed draft and retrieve my clothes. Then I can meet you at Hambleton House and escort Mr. Cantrell inside. You know ever so much more about dealing with fine gentlemen anyway. You've rubbed elbows with the peerage ever since coming to London."

"I don't know, Edmund. Meeting the earl's heir—"

"Oh, please say you'll do it. After all, you've had

11

dealings with Americans before and I have not. They're an odd lot, from what I hear."

"My only dealings were rather indirect. I was hired by Lady Rushcroft to tutor her granddaughter's young friend. I only met the baron quite by chance when she interviewed me for the position, and I must say that he was not in the least odd."

"There, you see. You'll know just what to do. The driver knows the ship's berth. The gentleman's name is Mr. Joshua Cantrell, soon to be Viscount Wesley," Edmund said, rooting through scraps of paper he dug from his coat pockets. He handed her the hastily scrawled note with the name and time on it, smiling pleadingly.

"Oh, very well, since there's no way you will be able to arrive in time," she said crossly, relenting as she always did with her baby cousin.

"You're an absolute trump, Coz! I shall be at Hambleton House by one, 'pon my honor."

Sighing as Edmund dashed off with her bank draft in hand, Sabrina walked briskly into her bedroom and selected her best hat and cloak. After all, one could not greet a gentleman such as Lord Hambleton's heir unless dressed properly for the occasion.

The wharves down the Thames from London Bridge were crowded with people and merchandise from around the globe. One had only to watch the varied parade of solemn Indians, ebony-skinned Africans and deferential Chinese to realize just how far the British Empire stretched. The stench of wharf rot was almost obliterated by fragrant spices from Ceylon blended with the pungent aroma of West Indian molasses. Over all hung the miasma of coal smoke belching forth from the factories and furnaces of British industry.

Sabrina never came to this part of town and was alternately awed and appalled by the contrasts of opulence and poverty that surrounded her. An emaciated beggar girl offering a grimy little fistful of wilted pinks for sale was almost run down by a young buck driving an expensive gig that nearly overturned as the nattily dressed driver swerved to avoid a cart loaded with melons.

Because of this terrible congestion, she was late. But a ship the size of the *Galveston Star* surely would not disembark passengers before she could locate Mr. Cantrell. According to the scribbled notes her cousin had given her, the gentleman was tall with black hair and green eyes. He would be wearing the Hambleton signet ring and looking for his great-uncle's coach near the foot of the gangplank. The driver assured her he knew the direction.

When they pulled up to the berth, cargo was being unloaded and it looked as if all the passengers had already disembarked. Sabrina bit her lip in vexation. It would serve Edmund right if His Lordship dismissed him. She scanned the crowd, searching for a tall, aristocratic gentleman, but the only tall, dark man she saw was well down the wharf, engaged in some sort of altercation with two ugly ruffians over the affections of a perfectly horrid-looking street doxy. He was dressed in some sort of fringed leather coat and the oddest boots with heels nearly as high as her own. That certainly was not Lord Hambleton's heir! Why, he looked positively shabby and dangerous.

"Let the girl go," Josh repeated as the skinny young prostitute huddled behind him, using a filthy handkerchief to stanch the blood from a blow delivered by her pimp.

"Whot's it to ye, bloody foreign bloke! Mitz is me gel, she is. You got no claim on 'er . . . lest ye wanna pay," the heavier of the two men said with a cunning leer that revealed he'd lost two of his front teeth.

Too bad he might soon lose the rest. "You were beating her," Josh said, realizing he was drawing a crowd, hoping it would include a member or two of the local constabulary. "Where I come from, men don't hit women."

"Then go back where ye come from," wheezed the little skinny fellow with the beaked nose. "Mitz's been 'oldin' out on ole Pepper. She's 'is preacher's daughter."

Odd slang, but Josh knew that it meant she was a whore. Young. Alone in a big city, frightened and hungry. Just like the girls Gertie had taken in at her place. Ones like his own mother. "You're not taking the girl," he repeated stubbornly. "I'll pay for her services," he added, reaching for his money clip, then thinking better of it with so many thieves and pickpockets surrounding him. Where the hell was that much-vaunted English law enforcement?

Before he could decide whether or not it would be wise to draw the Colt Lightning covered by his long jacket, the big beefy fellow with the missing teeth swung at him. His well-chewed ears gave further testimony to his time as a prizefighter—a bad one. Josh easily ducked the roundhouse swing and came in low and fast, landing a left-right combination to the tough's ample gut and face. Yep, more teeth gone. Oh well. He was poised on the balls of his feet, ready to finish the job, but then saw his opponent's greasy little companion pull an ugly blade from inside his filthy coat.

"Damn, now why'd you have to go and do such a fool thing?" Josh said, spinning around and kicking the fellow in his gonads. Beak Nose dropped the knife with a bleat and stumbled back, curled into a ball. Josh turned his attention to the bigger fellow, who moved in again, this time connecting with a clumsy right to his face. Hell, he'd have a beaut of a shiner, he thought as he quickly countered with another series of punches.

The little man Josh had kicked tumbled against an orange seller's cart, overturning it. Then the gap-toothed boxer stomped on a longshoreman's foot when Josh knocked him backwards, and suddenly the altercation erupted into a full-blown riot. Up and down the wharf, men began kicking and punching each other while street boys lifted purses from the unwary. Boxes and barrels smashed and tumbled along the rough planks, thrown by cursing, yelling men.

Mitz, the damsel in distress, vanished into the melee like fog evaporating on the Texas Gulf at sunrise. Her two keepers had been joined by a third fellow of equally unsavory looks, and the three of them closed in on the American with murderous intent.

Sabrina stood surrounded by cursing, shouting men of the lowest social order, utterly horrified that she'd been so foolish as to venture alone from the carriage to the gangplank. Somehow when the fighting had begun, the two footmen accompanying her had disappeared. She found herself being jostled by the odoriferous mob as she struggled to make her way to higher ground from which to view the scene in relative safety.

The gangplank. If only she could reach it and climb up to the ship! Surely Mr. Cantrell had remained aboard. How horrified he must be at the disgusting carnage below. Just as she placed her hand on the railing, a large, dirt-encrusted paw seized her wrist and yanked her back.

"Whot 'ave we got 'ere, eh?" he said in a coarse voice, his breath reeking of rotted teeth and stale cabbage.

"Unhand me, you ill-mannered lout!" Sabrina cried, trying in vain to jerk free. He was too strong for her, pulling her close to his body. As she thrashed and kicked, she could feel the sharp pull of her hat pin against her scalp. Her best Sunday hat tumbled to the rough planks and was quickly trampled, further igniting her fury. She pounded against the brute's chest with tiny gloved fists and used her pointy-toed shoes to good advantage, connecting sharply with one shin. He let her go with a snarled oath.

When she turned to flee, she could feel her hair pulling loose from its pins and flying out behind her like a banner. Her jacket was askew and the top three buttons on her high-collared shirt had been ripped away, revealing a shocking amount of bare skin. The ghastly fellow had even left filthy handprints soiling her pristine dove-gray skirt. How on earth could she face the new viscount looking like this!

Then directly below her, she heard a voice distinctly accented in that peculiar drawl spoken by Americans such as Lord Rushcroft. It was the tall ruffian who had started the whole melee, and he was still on his feet, swinging his fists with savage joy.

"Yeehaw! Haven't had this much fun since my first trail drive back in eighty-four," Josh yelled as he drove his fist deep into the boxer's gut, doubling him over. If only he could clear a path to the relative safety of the ship from which he'd so recently disembarked, he could watch over the pretty little gal he'd seen standing like a lost kitten on the middle of the gangplank. It would also be a good place from which to hold off his three adversaries.

Then he heard the shrill of police whistles. " 'Bout damn well time," he muttered to himself as he neared the narrow gangplank. The lone female stood midway up it, frozen as she watched him approach.

Must be some higher-class whore, from the cut of her clothes. He liked all that satiny-looking bronze hair spilling over her shoulders, and from his brief glimpse of her body, the curves were in all the right places. "Haul your little butt farther up the plank, out of the way, sweetheart," he yelled at her, but she didn't move.

Sabrina knew the accent. Unmistakably American. Subtly different from the Kentucky drawl of the baron, but it was Southern . . . or Western. A Texas drawl! No, it could not possibly be! Then the madman was set upon by the even more disreputable riffraff with whom he had been engaged. He pulled an enormous firearm from inside his strange-looking coat and brandished it as he backed up the gangplank, drawing nearer to her!

She shuddered.

"I wouldn't come any closer even if I was stump stupid like you fellers," Josh said in his broadest accent, trying to hold them off until the police arrived. But the little one he'd kicked in the nuts seemed to be egging the other two on.

"Whot ye afeard o', Pepper? 'E ain't gonna shoot. There's three o' us, Jake."

"Lordy, even stupider than a stump. This here's a

17

six-shooter. Want to start countin', you ugly little armadillo?" Josh asked, firing a round directly in front of the toe of Beak Nose's shoe. The trio backed down the narrow gangplank, stumbling over each other in their haste to escape. Josh kept his Colt Lightning trained on them as he climbed higher. Until he collided with something soft and sweet smelling.

The classy little whore with the bronze hair.

By this time police were swarming over the wharf, and the rioters vanished like roaches in a suddenly lit cellar. Still holding his gun in his hand, Josh turned to the girl—no, make that a woman. He judged her to be enough past twenty to know her way around, but the horrified expression on her face did not seem to fit. Well, if her protector had brought her to a rough neighborhood like this, he should have taken better care of her.

"You all right, ma'am?" he asked, reaching out to steady her.

She jerked away. "Will you please dispose of that . . . that firearm before you actually shoot someone," she demanded imperiously.

Josh grinned. "You're pretty as a paint pony on a sunny day, and that's no lie."

Sabrina only glared at the offending weapon, still more shaken than she cared to admit.

Before he could holster it, two police officers came rushing up the gangplank and seized hold of his arms. "Just give over the gun, lad," one said calmly while his companion held his nightstick at the ready.

"Josh Cantrell, at your service, officers. What in blue blazes took you so long?" He handed his Colt to the one who had spoken. "It seems like we had a little misunderstanding here."

"Looks to be a bit more than that, mate. Half the cargo on the pier's been smashed or looted, and you're the only fellow here."

"And the only one carrying a gun," his fellow officer added helpfully. "You're a Yank, right, lad? Me and Reggie here is going to give you a London tour. We'll start at the Thames Police Office. Lovely place, it is. Come along now."

As Josh argued with the two policemen, they escorted him down to the wharf. Sabrina backed away, unnoticed. Dear heavens, what was she to do now? They were arresting Hambleton's heir, and she and Edmund would be blamed for it, even though it was the dreadful fellow's own fault. The boorish oaf had started a riot, and she'd nearly been . . . well, it didn't bear considering what might have happened to her.

Sighing, she realized there was only one thing to do. She'd have to go to the police station and explain who Mr. Cantrell was to the authorities. And pray they'd believe her!

Chapter 2

Josh sat in the rear of the crowded stone dungeon that served as a large holding area for those recently arrested. It was immense and as cold as those ice caves he'd visited in the New Mexico mountains years ago. But where the Guadalupes were isolated and beautiful, this place was overflowing with men from the gutters of humanity. In all his years, even in the hellish jungles of Cuba, he'd never seen such privation. *And this the richest nation on earth!* he scoffed.

Old men with rheumy eyes sat silently in corners, staring at nothing. Boys covered with filthy running sores tried to steal crusts of bread from those too old or infirm to catch them. Scarred bullies knocked smaller men out of their way as they appropriated the most comfortable benches along the wall nearest the small, barred windows. Bad as the air outside was, it had smelled pristine compared to the rot and mold of this hellhole.

One bully boy with a glass eye and matted shoulder-length hair shambled toward Josh, obviously intending to deprive him of his seat. The Texan stared the man in his good eye and drew back his lips in a cold grin. "It'd be a shame to lose a second eye," he said conversationally.

The big fellow decided to remain standing.

Josh turned his thoughts to the colonel and wondered if his old commander would ever learn of his fate if the British justice system let him die in here. If he did, he vowed to come back and haunt the Republican Party for the next hundred years. Would his great-uncle, whatever his name was, even bother to inquire why he failed to appear? From what TR had said, the old goat had gone to considerable trouble tracking him down. Unless, of course, he found out it had all been a mistake, the real heir turned up and the earl promptly dismissed Cantrell from his thoughts. A right unsettling proposition all the way around, Josh thought ruefully.

Damn all Republicans and Englishmen to perdition!

But the immediate cause of this debacle, like most of the woes in his life, wore a skirt. First the poor beaten little whore on the dock, then that fancy piece on the gangplank. Mitz, he'd felt obliged to help because she reminded him of girls he'd known during his childhood. But the second female . . . well, she was another kettle of fish altogether. He'd seen that big brute grab her and watched her struggling as he fought his way across the wharf to her rescue.

What a marvelous little handful she was, swatting and clawing like a Texas wildcat! If he ever got out of here, he'd love to look her up and see if all that shiny hair felt as silky as it looked. He had gotten close enough to know she smelled sweeter than a spring prairie.

Suddenly his pleasant reverie was interrupted

when a loud screech of rusted metal followed by a re-
sounding clang indicated that the guards had opened
the gate. He could hear them ordering the prisoners
to stand back. He stood up. Being one of the tallest in
the crowd, he looked across the room, wondering
what would happen next. Then the guard who'd
stepped inside called out in a loud voice, "Mr. Joshua
Cantrell!"

"Well, I'll be double sheep dipped," he muttered,
not sparing a moment as he elbowed his way to the
front of the crowd. "I'm Josh Cantrell."

The guard looked at his bruised face and swollen
eye, the torn, filthy remnants of his buckskin jacket
and denims. "Yes, I do believe you must be. Follow
me, sir."

Once he was up the flight of hollowed-out stone
stairs and inside the office of the muckety-muck in
charge, Josh breathed a sigh of relief. If he'd made it
this far, could freedom be completely out of reach?
He studied the elderly man seated behind a battered
desk piled high with papers collecting dust. "Here's
the American, sir," the guard said with a cursory
salute.

The portly fellow behind the desk rose and crossed
his cluttered domain, smiling unctuously as he
bowed before Josh. "I'm sorry about the misunderstanding at the wharf, Your Lordship, that I am. The
earl's agent has just arrived to verify the report we received earlier. Of course, we couldn't credit it until we
checked it. Please understand. It is . . . er, rather unusual to discharge firearms into a crowd on the wharf
at noontime. And, considering the disturbance the
police were attempting to put down, well . . ."

"As long as I'm free to go, I'd be happy just to mosey out of here, if that's all right," Josh said with relief

when the man in charge nodded, that false, overly hearty smile still pasted in place. Then, touching his right side, which felt unbalanced, Josh added, "Oh, as to that firearm—it's a pearl-handled Colt Lightning, and I'd like to have it back. Sentimental value."

The old man appeared taken aback for an instant. "A gun? Sentimental value?"

"It saved my life in Texas and Cuba . . . and here in old London town, too."

Within minutes, his belongings were returned to him, including his money clip, which amazingly still held all but fifty dollars of what it originally contained. He waited while a guard was dispatched to collect his Colt and gun belt from wherever they'd locked them up. The fellow handed the weapon to him gingerly—didn't these bobby chaps even know how to shoot a gun? None of them seemed to carry them, which struck Josh as more than a little peculiar, considering how rough his introduction to the city had been.

Grinning, he thanked the police officer, buckled the gun belt around his hips and started to make his way out the door, where he'd been told the earl's carriage was awaiting him. He had ambled about half the distance when the clear, cultured tones of a woman's voice caught his attention. At once he knew it was *her*.

The classy whore on the gangplank.

She sat behind a desk, poised on the edge of a battered swivel chair like a sparrow ready to take flight, engaged in conversation with one of the minions of the law. Her hair was pulled up in some sort of knot at that delectable nape and she'd discreetly pinned her bodice closed, but he'd recognize her anywhere.

In the dark. Blindfolded. The faint essence of wildflowers wafted subtly toward him. Since the crowded room was filled with cigar smoke, volumes of dusty papers, mildew and just plain old grimy dirt, the aroma was probably his imagination. He was remembering what she smelled like from their encounter on the wharf that morning.

Pausing by the door, he asked one of the men in uniform, "That little gal over there." He didn't have to point, as she was the only female in the room. "You wouldn't happen to know her name, or address, would you?"

"Blimey, mate, ain't got no idea. We gets 'em in 'ere all the time. Mostly nights, though."

Just at that moment, as if overhearing them, she looked directly at Josh. Instant disdain flashed into her eyes, then was replaced by something else. Shock? Fear? Outrage? It looked like a combination of all the above, and he was damned if he knew why. All he'd tried to do was rescue her from that bully boy manhandling her. Of course, Mitz's pimps had followed him, and that had complicated the situation a bit, but she had no reason to react this way, blast it.

Shrugging, he nodded and winked, giving her a broad grin as he strolled out the door a free man. Somehow, he figured she'd be detained for a while. Served her right for being so uppity. Maybe next time they met, she'd be in a better mood.

Sabrina would have choked him with her ungloved hands if she'd not been so busy explaining how she'd become involved in the frightful mixup at the wharf. She had to be ever so careful not to get Edmund in trouble for missing his appointment to pick up the earl's heir. Of course, she could not imagine poor Edmund faring any better than she had after that wild

Texan started a riot! Her poor cousin would most probably have ended up in jail and she'd be here bailing him out anyway. And he would then most assuredly have lost his employment.

As things stood now, she had been afforded time to send him a message that he was to meet the coach here at the prison and escort his charge to Hambleton House. The driver and the footmen had miraculously reappeared like genies from a bottle as soon as the crowd dispersed, at least affording her the luxury of a ride to this odious place so that she could secure Mr. Cantrell's release. It had seemed to take an eternity, and all the while she stewed about harm befalling the earl's heir and Edmund losing his position in spite of her efforts.

Not that this entire fiasco was anyone's fault but Joshua Cantrell's. Well, perhaps her cousin was not entirely blameless either. But even if Edmund had been at the gangplank precisely when the viscount disembarked, what could he or anyone else have done to stop the wild man from accosting that dreadful fallen woman? And then he'd turned his attention to *her* and brought those waterfront cutthroats trailing after him.

They were all fortunate to have escaped with their lives. Still, she seethed at his sheer audacity in leering at her as he strode away in that rangy, loose-limbed way in which Americans seemed to move. He'd winked at her, too! Yes indeed, if she ever did have the grave misfortune to meet Viscount Wesley again, she would choke him. Bare-handed!

Abington Clermont Cantrell, ninth Earl of Hambleton, rubbed his hands with delight after reading the message. At long last, after a quarter century of fruitless searching, his heir was safely en route to his city house. He'd almost despaired of finding his younger brother's grandson. Indeed, he'd not even known that his nephew Charles had a son, only that he'd married and sailed off into the sunset like the ne'er-do-well he was nearly thirty years earlier.

At that time, Lord Hambleton's own son David was his heir, and David had two sons of his own. The succession seemed intact. But carriage accidents, consumption and influenza had taken their vicious tolls, leaving the old man but one slender hope. For all his nephew's profligacy—he was, after all, little better than a remittance man—it appeared that Charles's boy was a true Cantrell. Under the most appalling conditions, in the most primitive place imaginable, Texas—the old man shuddered just thinking about it—Joshua had made his own fortune.

Imagine. A self-made millionaire before he was thirty. And he'd started out life in a bordello where his poor dying mother had sought refuge after her worthless husband had gotten himself killed in some senseless duel. Or shoot-out, as those wild American cowboys called them. The earl smiled, stroking his handlebar mustache.

"I say, does something amuse you, my lord?" Wilfred Hodgins, his secretary, inquired as he placed a sheaf of documents from the Foreign Office on his employer's desk. Hodgins was fortyish with a receding chin which he hid unsuccessfully beneath a Van Dyke beard and a receding hairline about which he could do nothing at all. His keen dark eyes took in the reports on the earl's heir, and he smiled. "You're anticipating his arrival, are you not?"

"Most assuredly. I was also thinking that this

young hellion has much in common with the new American president."

"Oh, that Rough Rider fellow from the Spanish war?" Hodgins inquired politely. "I believe he was a cowboy of some sort, too."

"Yes, and to quote his worst political enemy, 'Now that damn cowboy is President of the United States!'"

Hodgins digested this bit of information. Since the search for Hambleton's heir had finally borne results, the earl had become quite an authority on American politics, a subject which both mystified and bored his longtime secretary. "Oh, in all the excitement over the viscount's arrival, you haven't forgotten that the Foreign Secretary will be here momentarily?"

"No, but I do hope we can keep the meeting brief. Joshua will be arriving shortly now, and I'm eager to meet the lad."

"I'm certain Lord Lansdowne will understand," Hodgins replied as a light rap sounded behind him. He turned to the door hidden behind a walnut panel, designed to conceal Hambleton's long association with His Majesty's government's spying network. Opening it, he ushered in the head of the Foreign Office.

"I see you're pleased with yourself, Hambleton," Lord Lansdowne said as he stepped inside.

Bowing discreetly to the two gentlemen, Hodgins left the room. The British Foreign Secretary walked over to the cabinet where the earl kept his liquor and, with long-accustomed familiarity, poured them each a snifter of fine cognac.

Accepting the crystal stem from his old friend, the earl sipped contemplatively. "Yes. You've heard of his arrival, then?"

"How could I not? Everyone in London has heard. The afternoon newspapers are full of lurid tales about his exploits at the wharf. It would seem he started a bloody riot. Are you quite certain he's the man for this assignment? Not to mention for the Hambleton titles?"

"Of course I'm certain. What could be better? He may appear a boorish American bumpkin on the outside, but he's a shrewd, war-toughened observer on the inside. That's why, after I received the complete dossier on him, I had Spring Rice put a bee in Roosevelt's bonnet."

"All quite convenient, I must confess, if the boy's as intelligent as you and that unorthodox American president claim he is," the Foreign Secretary said, tossing down his cognac and pouring a small refill.

"After your own experiences in India and Canada, you of all men should approve of Joshua, Lansdowne. He drove cattle from Texas to the Dakotas, riding with grown men when he was only eleven years old! By the time he was twenty he owned a ranch—"

"Which, according to the reports I read, he won in a card game," Lansdowne interjected dryly.

The earl waved that comment away. "The point is he held on to the land and filled it with his own stock, then began investing the profits. It's all here in black and white. Boy's quick as a whip and rich as a Romanov."

"And therein lies our problem. The always troublesome Russians. As Viscount Wesley, your heir will have many doors opened to him, but do you believe he can penetrate the inner sanctum of this cabal intent on assassinating the Japanese minister? Time is running out. If they succeed in killing Hayashi, we can whistle down the wind for a Japanese alliance."

"I know," the earl said, sipping his cognac. "But we

can't trust anyone in our own bloody government at this stage of the game. My grand-nephew is our last hope."

"Do you intend to tell him about your connection to the Foreign Office?" Lansdowne asked. "I would prefer you did not."

Hambleton nodded. "I see no reason he should be apprised of it at this point. His friend Roosevelt has already informed him of the, er, difficulty vis-à-vis King Edward's nephew. We will need an agent you trust implicitly to act as your intermediary. Whom have you selected?"

Lansdowne smiled like a Cheshire cat. "Michael Jamison. Young fellow who's proven himself most able. Third son of the Earl of Lynden. His grandfather had a distinguished career with us before inheriting the title. His grandmother was American, I believe, so they should have something in common."

Hambleton harrumphed. "If not for President Roosevelt's appeal to Joshua's patriotism because the Americans have a stake in this, he wouldn't have come to England."

"And you have an ulterior motive for involving him in this mission, eh?"

"It will all work out, my dear fellow. I'm certain of it if even half of what's written here proves true." He thumped the thick dossier outlining Joshua Cantrell's life history.

Lansdowne handed the earl a thick bundle of afternoon newspapers. "I'm afraid we may all of us have our work cut out if even half of what's written *here* proves true," he retorted.

The house was not much to look at, to Josh's way of thinking, but he was not about to voice that thought aloud to the nervous youth assigned to escort him to the earl's city residence. Edmund Whistledown looked as typically English as Josh could ever have imagined—pale with sandy hair and shoulders almost as narrow as his face. The lad seemed disinclined to talk and stuttered when Josh asked questions. All he'd done was repeatedly apologize for failing to meet the ship.

"I doubt it would've made any difference. Once I saw those scum roughing up that little gal, I'd'a waded in anyway," he'd replied with a grin, rubbing his skinned knuckles. "You wouldn't have been able to stop me."

Whistledown's only reply was an acute bobbing of his Adam's apple and an uncertain nod.

Not wanting the boy to feel any more guilty or uncomfortable than he obviously already did, Josh did not press him. They passed the duration of the ride mostly in silence.

The Hambleton city house was one of those tall, skinny stone buildings all lined up in rows, facing pruned-to-the-dickens little garden squares that the English seemed to set so much store by. Of course, since the Cantrell family had been living in it for hundreds of years, Josh supposed they were too attached to it to want to sell and build something a mite splashier. Like his place right outside Fort Worth. Brand spanking new, made of solid oak with a veranda all the way around the house, a forty-foot-long dining room, ten bedrooms and half a dozen water closets, thank you very much.

Of course, he seldom spent time there, since he traveled on business so much, but it impressed the hell out of visiting cattle buyers and bankers. He imagined wryly that the earl didn't have to impress anybody. Shoot, he didn't even have to work. Josh still had a difficult time wrapping his mind around that idea. Generations of folks—including his own kin—were so rich that they just sat around and sipped tea, or whatever Englishmen did. In America every millionaire he'd ever met, and in the past few years he'd met more than his share, all worked their tails off, whether they'd inherited their money like the Astors or made it themselves like Richard King or even old Jay Gould.

If His Lordship the earl thought he'd tether Josh Cantrell to a tea table, he had another think coming. He smiled at Edmund Whistledown and said, "Much obliged for seeing me here."

Then before the young man could do more than mumble, "You're most welcome, my lord," Josh jumped impatiently from the carriage. A footman, ready to open the door, stumbled backwards to keep from colliding with the striding American, and bowed awkwardly. Josh wasn't rightly sure whether the boy was embarrassed for failing to perform his job, or for the gauche Texan who didn't let him. Whistledown followed, almost skipping to keep up with his charge's long-legged stride.

Whistling, he bounded up the front steps, wondering how he would feel when he met his only living kin. He had no memories of either of his parents. "Garter" Gertie Greer had been the nearest thing to a mother he'd ever known. At the thought of Gertie sitting in some English parlor sipping tea, he broke into a broad grin. Now, that would be a sight to behold!

Would the old gentleman like him? What in the name of God would they have to talk about? Certainly not his real reason for being here. A note had been delivered to him before he disembarked from the ship. He was to meet a fellow named Michael Jamison sometime tomorrow. He would be contacted and informed of the details. This Jamison worked for the Foreign Office and would fill him in as to what was known of the assassination plot and Edward's nephew's involvement through his Russian mistress.

Women. Always trouble. An image of that bronze-haired spitfire flashed into his mind as the front door opened. Whistledown made his bow and scurried off, leaving Josh with a stern-faced man whose high starched collar looked about to choke him. The butler identified himself as Nash and extended his hand for Josh's hat.

Unable to resist, Josh shook it heartily. "Pleased as punch to meet you, Nash. Say, is that your first name or your last?"

The upper servant jerked back, then quickly recovered. "May I take your hat, my lord?" he inquired, ignoring the question about his name.

Obligingly, Josh shrugged and handed his battered Stetson to the butler, while he eyeballed the place. A lot fancier on the inside than he'd imagined from out front, he'd grant the earl that much. Huge mirrors with Louis XV gilt frames hung on either side of the entry foyer. Enormous sprays of flowers overflowing from Messien vases stood in front of the mirrors. The floor was polished marble, and the twenty-foot ceiling was hung with a crystal chandelier that glittered more brightly than pictures he'd seen of the crown jewels.

All this was definitely intended to impress visitors. But he wasn't a visitor. He was, by God, the earl's heir, and he'd be living in this magnificent mausoleum. Josh was not sure how well he'd sleep if his bedroom had a lighting fixture that size suspended over his bed, but he knew Gertie would have loved it. Personally, he'd rather have a mirror.

From the top of the curving staircase, the earl observed his young charge as Nash showed him into a sitting room. The boy certainly looked disreputable enough. The newspaper accounts of the brawl had been appalling. If the boy behaved half so badly, he'd never be received in polite society at all. That would put a period to presenting him at court, not to mention using him to ferret out those individuals plotting against an Anglo-Japanese treaty.

He'd take Joshua's measure and then decide what was to be done. Given the tendency toward exaggeration, even outright prevarication, in much of the press, their subject might be innocent of any misconduct whatever. The earl liked the boy's confident stride and the way he'd studied the interior of the house quickly, without gaping. If he was equally as adroit at judging people, the Foreign Secretary would be delighted. He would have to give Whistledown a good dressing-down about allowing Joshua to slip away and become involved in such a disturbance, but that could wait.

He descended the stairs and made his way to his study. After an appropriate interval, he rang for Nash to escort his great-nephew down the hall. In his limited experience with Americans, he'd found them to be notoriously impatient. It would do Joshua good to wait a bit. If he himself were the smallest bit apprehensive about this first meeting and the impression he might make on the boy, he would never admit it, even to himself.

Josh entered the dark, masculine room, impressed by the floor-to-ceiling shelves of books and the patina of age that gleamed from the wood-paneled walls.

The desk appeared well used, piled with papers much as his was at home, and the leather chairs looked inviting. The tall man standing in the center of the room did not. A thick silver mustache lined his upper lip, and his thinning hair was trimmed neatly with muttonchops brushed back so smoothly they looked as if nary a single hair would dare to move out of place. He was heavyset with bulldog jowls and shrewd gray eyes that missed little.

Josh could see him examining his ripped, dirty buckskin jacket and denims, swelling eye and bruised knuckles. "So, we meet at last, sir," he said, waiting for some cue.

"I must say, it's taken long enough. Welcome home." The earl stepped forward, and a broad smile suddenly changed his entire demeanor, tilting the mustache upward devilishly and making his eyes crinkle at the corners. He offered his hand.

Josh took it and they shook hands firmly. The earl's hands were large and fine-boned but soft, while his own were callused from physical labor. "I don't rightly know if this is home, sir," he said quietly. "Are you sure you got the right Cantrell?"

He'd seen no family resemblance whatever until the old man threw back his head and laughed aloud. "Oh, I'm quite certain, you young scamp! My detectives were quite thorough." He looked down at the ring on Josh's right hand. "That is the Hambleton family crest. Not too many of them floating about on either side of the ocean."

"From what I've heard of my father, he could've won it in a card game."

"Or lost it," Hambleton replied as his smile dimmed. "But he did not. I knew him well as a lad. He was a few years younger than you are now when he and his bride left England. Here is the family portrait he sat for when he reached his majority." The earl reached for a photograph amid the clutter on his desk and handed it to Josh.

The younger man paled as he peered at it, holding it as if he'd never let it go.

"Amazing resemblance, wouldn't you say?"

The face staring into the camera was his very own. Dark, slightly curly hair, square jaw, prominent nose and heavy slashes of eyebrow framing deep-set eyes that studied the world with heavy-lidded amusement. The wide mouth was sculpted, its smile revealing almost perfectly straight teeth whose only flaw was one slightly turned incisor.

"Any lingering doubts you're Charles James Justin Cantrell's son?" the earl asked dryly.

"How did they die—my mother—"

"I have the whole of it here," Hambleton said, touching the bound tome of reports. "But this isn't the time to digest so much."

"You know I was raised in a whorehouse in west Texas." It wasn't quite a question, more of a challenge.

"After your father was killed in a shooting incident, your mother was destitute and in failing health. She turned to the only place where she could find shelter for you."

"Gertie."

"Just so. The Golden Garter, I believe Miss Greer's establishment was called. You've risen far beyond such . . . er, humble beginnings."

"I'd never be ashamed to acknowledge Garter Gertie or any of the women who worked for her. They raised me," Josh said with quiet defiance in his voice.

"I assume that was the reason for this morning's incident at the wharf," the earl said, showing Josh several of the headlines: "Hambleton Heir Battles for Whore's Honor." "Texas Viscount Rides·to Rescue." "Lord Wesley Truly is Westerner."

"I knew what she was. Where I come from, it doesn't give a man license to hit a woman."

"Admirable. I agree."

Josh blinked. "You do?"

The earl smiled again. "We English may appear rather too formal at times, but we aren't ogres, I assure you. I rather imagine you could do with a hot soak to ease your battle wounds, and a change of clothing." He eyed his nephew's swelling eye and raw knuckles as well as the torn jacket. "After you're settled in, we'll talk more over a quiet dinner. Just the two of us."

"That sounds good, sir," Josh replied with a grin.

"Oh, Joshua, if you please, would you mind leaving the firearm in your room when you return? If it should discharge in the house, my staff would all die of fright, and good help is dreadfully difficult to come by."

"Well, I would say your position is quite safe, to judge by this," Sabrina crowed delightedly as she perused the note bearing the Hambleton crest.

"What does it say, Coz?" Edmund asked. He'd been trembling with dread from the moment the note had been delivered by the earl's footman. Was it his dismissal because the viscount had told the earl he'd failed to meet him at the dock? But why send it to his cousin's lodgings instead of his own? He breathed a sigh of relief when she beamed at him.

"The earl wishes to employ me!" she said. "I'm to meet with his secretary tomorrow morning at ten in the rose garden."

"Employ you how?" Edmund asked, puzzled.

"Eddie, what have I been doing to earn my living for the past seven years? He must want me to teach deportment to some kinswoman of his. He does not say whom." Sabrina considered for a moment. "I have it," she said with a snap of her fingers as her nimble brain quickly turned through the list of eligible young ladies coming of age for the spring season. "Sophia, I believe her name is."

"Oh, you mean His Lordship's niece Isadora's granddaughter? A perfectly horrid child," Edmund said with a shudder.

Sabrina laughed. "She can be nothing compared to that Liverpool steel magnate's daughter I tutored before her presentation at court last year. At least Sophia's of the peerage and has some idea of what's expected of her—and the knowledge that no amount of wealth will augment her status."

"Rich Cits are worse than the aristocracy?" Edmund asked. He'd witnessed enough snobbery and arrogance among the peerage to doubt her claim.

"Some are. The very worst thing is when someone who has made an excess of money believes a fortune entitles him to do and say whatever he wishes. Things simply are not done that way in proper society."

Chapter 3

Damn! Where does King Arthur sit?

The table was longer than the one in his dining room in Fort Worth. Amazing how much larger the earl's home was than it appeared from outside. The effect was elegant and intimidating at the same time. Light winked gently from a sterling candelabrum, and the fine china place settings were positioned so Josh would sit next to his great-uncle. A bewildering array of enough sterling flatware for a platoon of Rough Riders was arranged beside the plates. Half a dozen dazzling crystal goblets were carefully positioned, too.

But the size and opulence of the table and the room's furnishings were not what daunted Josh. The antiquity did. He sensed instantly that history had been made around this dining table. Sometimes such insights came to him out of nowhere, just like "blue northers" boiling up on the horizon. Normally he knew how to use the bizarre talent to his advantage,

38

but here, so out of his element, he was not at all certain what to make of it.

Did the old man do more than play cards at his club, attend balls and weekend at his country estate? From what little he knew of the British aristocracy, those were the pastimes of most of them. The exceptions were those who chose government service, but other than his hereditary seat in the House of Lords—not much work there in recent years—the earl was not involved in anything more serious than smoking fine cigars and drinking perfumy French brandy, as far as Josh knew.

He stood for another moment by the wide arched doorway, peering into the room. The odd feeling would not leave him. Shrugging off the mystery, he walked across the hall to his uncle's library. He knocked and was bade to enter.

As he walked in, the earl greeted him, smiling broadly as he took in his heir's appearance. "A bit of a facer you received there, but the swelling's already going down." Hambleton eyed Josh's clothing and made a mental note to send for his tailor posthaste.

"One of the servants was kind enough to fetch me some ice. It takes down swelling and soreness," Josh replied, flexing his knuckles.

"And you'd be an authority on such injuries?" the old man inquired with an amused lift of one eyebrow.

Josh's face reddened slightly. "A fellow once said you can't fry an egg without cracking it first. Same's true in the cattle business. The damn fools won't listen unless you crack a few heads now and then."

"Your president has said something to the same effect regarding politics, I believe," the earl replied dryly. "Shall we have a brief libation before we dine?"

He walked over to a long sideboard set with crystal decanters. "What would you prefer? French cognac? Scotch? I have an excellent claret from—"

"Much obliged, sir, but I never much cared for anything but good old American bourbon." He patted his jacket pocket, pulled out a slim flask and unscrewed the cap. "Who Shot John. Oh, that's the brand name," he explained. "Strong enough to peel the first couple layers off your toenails. Great stuff."

"I see," replied the earl, reaching for an empty glass as he poured himself a splash of cognac.

Before he could offer Josh the glass, his great-nephew upended his flask and took a long pull. "Ah, good stuff." He started to wipe his mouth with the back of his hand, but something in the earl's expression made him quell the gesture.

Startled by Josh's behavior, Hambleton raised his snifter in what he hoped was the universal signal for a toast. "To a new beginning here in England," he said gamely. Josh clinked his silver flask against the crystal and they both drank again. Perhaps he'd take a second splash, the earl decided as he drained the excellent liqueur in a single swallow. *Miss Edgewater will certainly have her work cut out for her*, he thought wryly.

"Dinner is ready whenever you wish it served, Your Lordship," the butler intoned gravely from the door.

As they filed into the dining room Josh had been inspecting a few moments earlier, he stuck his flask into his jacket pocket, not trusting to leave his small supply of the only drinkable alcohol in England unattended. He made a mental note to wire his agent in Fort Worth and order a shipment of several cases.

"I'm glad there's just the two of us tonight," Josh

said as the butler and a footman pulled out chairs and they took their seats.

"I thought it best for the two of us to dine simply on our first night," the earl replied, motioning for the consommé to be served.

"Mighty relieved you didn't have them seat me at the foot of the table or we'd have to yell to hear each other."

Hambleton chuckled. "True, but from what I understand about the home you built for yourself, the dining accommodations are . . . commodious as well."

"That's a horse of a different color, sir. See, Texans always yell at each other," Josh replied with a grin. "And it's smart not to let 'em get too close together when there's cutlery handy."

"Well, I'm happy to dispense with yelling, since my lung capacity isn't quite what it used to be," the earl replied with a chuckle, picking up his soup spoon and pausing to see if his nephew would follow suit.

"If you're wonderin' if I'll drink from the bowl, don't worry," Josh replied. "Got my mouth burned something fierce last time I tried it."

Hambleton resisted the urge to ask how old he'd been when that occurred. Instead he threw back his head and laughed. His nephew's table manners were not appalling, the earl decided as the meal progressed. Just a bit . . . inventive. Peas with the dessert spoon, bread torn in pieces to sop up the bernaise sauce. Practical ideas. American table decorum?

Somehow the earl doubted it. He also doubted that Josh lacked the wit to copy his use of utensils, he simply chose not to. Instead of draping his napkin across his lap, Joshua tucked one corner under his shirt collar. "Cuts down on the washing and ironing," he said by way of explanation, although he spilled not a speck of anything on it. Nor, the earl knew, had his nephew had to worry about doing his own washing and ironing for many years.

By the time Josh had plucked a ladyfinger of sponge cake whole from his serving of charlotte russe and used it to spoon up the Bavarian cream filling, Hambleton decided to call the young pup's bluff. "I realize, Joshua, that you were not overly . . . enthusiastic, shall we say, about coming to England. I understand it took an appeal from your old comrade the president to convince you to do so."

Josh pulled his napkin from beneath his chin and wiped his lips neatly, then grinned. "The colonel made it seem like you were at death's door and I had to 'do my duty'—those Harvard fellows are real big on duty."

"And you weren't the least bit curious about meeting your family?"

Josh eyed the flask he'd placed on the table, wanting a drink, but somehow deciding it would be strategically unwise to show such weakness at this moment. "Well, I had my business to consider. The livestock exchange in Fort Worth is a pretty busy place come fall. And . . ." he hesitated, then gave in and took a drink of Who Shot John before continuing, "I couldn't rightly believe I was related to an English earl. I thought it was some kind of mistake."

"And you're testing me by behaving as much the wild Texan as you think possible without getting yourself committed to the asylum or the zoo. Are you trying to provoke me into disowning you even after seeing that photograph this afternoon?" There was both warmth and amusement in Hambleton's eyes.

Josh cursed beneath his breath. "The colonel told

me I was afraid. Maybe he was right." He let out a frustrated breath. "Hell, I don't know, sir."

"I'm here to inform you in no uncertain terms, Joshua Abington Charles Cantrell, that I will not disown you if hell freezes over."

The old man's voice sure sounded strong enough for a Texas yelling contest. So much for the old devil being "too sick to travel." "Abington? The Charles is after my father, but—"

"The Abington is after me," the earl said, his stern tone of a moment ago now softened by a chuckle. "I suspect your father was trying to sweeten me up when he sent word from America that he was to become a father and a son would bear my name."

Thank the Lord I wasn't saddled with that moniker as a first name. "Why not name me after my grandfather?"

"Unlike you, my boy, your father was . . . how to put this delicately . . ."

"A remittance man?" Josh supplied, using the term applied to a young man who was such a social embarrassment that his family paid him a remittance to leave the country. The word left a bitter taste on his tongue, but it fit what he knew from Gertie about his mother's destitute straits when she'd come to the Garter. "I heard he was a gambler."

"And not as proficient as you at it," the earl added regretfully. "Nonetheless, you come from good stock; never forget that."

"My father was the lone black sheep. What about my mother?"

"Her father was a vicar, the second son of a baronet from Surrey. A fine and honorable house, the Kingsleys. I'm afraid they've all died now, but she was a lovely and loyal young woman who followed her husband on his ill-conceived adventures."

"I'm sorry I never knew her. Are there any Cantrell cousins?"

"I have two nieces by my now-deceased sister Alice, and they've married well. You'll like them and their husbands and children. Good girls, but only direct male heirs may inherit."

"So you're stuck with me," Josh said glumly.

"I'm considerably more than pleased with you, you young whelp, so do not assume I am offering you charity or scraping the bottom of the barrel to find one last Cantrell male! You've made a tremendous success of yourself with no help from anyone—and acting like a barbarian won't fool me for one moment. I know that any man who can acquire a fortune can learn drawing-room manners."

Josh grinned broadly. "You've never met Jim Hill or Jay Gould, else you wouldn't say that."

Ignoring the retort, the earl continued, "And do not assume either that you are doing me a favor because you've interrupted your business affairs to come here. Your president is quite correct about a man's duty, as I'm certain you're aware, else you wouldn't have volunteered to fight alongside him."

"What you're trying to say is that you're calling my bluff. But what if I'm not bluffing?"

The earl's smile was faintly amused now. "Oh, allow me to venture that I have every confidence you'll remain in England . . . at least for a while," he replied cryptically. "And while you're here, you'll require a few of the accoutrements of civilized society. My tailor will be here at eight sharp to take your measurements."

"You don't like my suit?" Josh asked, looking down at the chocolate-brown jacket trimmed with silver studs and dark green beadwork. "It's the latest thing in Fort Worth."

"No doubt," Hambleton replied dryly.

"But it won't do here?" The question was purely rhetorical. He knew his wardrobe as well as his manners had been a test of sorts to see if the old man would really accept him. Not that he was quite willing to confess as much at this stage of the game. But damn if he wasn't starting to actually like the old goat!

The earl eyed the flask sitting on the table as he rang for after-dinner cigars and cognac. "We'll have to see about smoothing over a few of your . . . rough edges. Indeed, they are egregiously jagged. I've employed a lady of impeccable credentials to teach you every aspect of drawing-room deportment. She has quite an excellent reputation, according to my niece Alvina."

"Deportment?" Josh grimaced as the earl selected an expensive Cuban cigar from the mahogany humidor a servant was holding. He recognized the aroma of his favorite smoke. With a grin, he took a cigar and allowed the footman to light it. "Beats the hell out of a chaw, I'll have to agree. Especially since I haven't seen any cuspidors around this place," he added with a grin.

"You and your teacher shall have a most . . . fascinating relationship, I suspect," Hambleton said with a chuckle.

Josh envisioned the old harridan as he blew out a stream of fragrant smoke. He'd met a few female reformers in his day—even faced down Carry Nation in a saloon in Pecos a few years back. That one had ended in a draw. Hell, after an ax-wielding six-foot Amazon with the strength of Hercules, how bad could one pale, scrawny ole English spinster be? He'd send her hightailing it in nothing flat.

Josh had been pinned and poked and had places on his anatomy measured in ways a Texas bordello madam wouldn't have dared try. After several hours and a small fortune spent with his uncle's tailor, he needed some fresh air and sunshine. Those were two things in real short supply around London. But in spite of the usual overcast of coal soot and phosphorus fumes, the sun, such as it was this far north, did its best.

He had time to spare before his first meeting with Michael Jamison, the agent from the British Foreign Office. The message had been delivered late last night just as he was drifting off to sleep. A fellow who was not one of his uncle's employees actually climbed in the second-story window of the sitting room off his quarters. Josh had nearly shot the damn fool before he identified himself and handed over a message from Foreign Secretary Lansdowne.

Rather melodramatic. He would not have thought the English would indulge in that sort of thing. At any rate, he was to ride in Hyde Park at one o'clock and this Jamison fellow would make contact. A ride sounded like just the thing, and he knew that Comanche, his prize blood bay stallion, would be as eager as he for a run. The crossing had not been easy on the horse . . . or for that matter on him either, although for vastly different reasons.

Suppressing memories of his wretched seasickness, he strolled toward the mews, taking a detour to view the gardens at the side of the house, where he could hear the soft burbling sound of a fountain. Being raised in dry country, the lure of free-running water had always fascinated him. He chuckled, remembering his first trip to New York and the champagne fountain Jay Gould had set up at a private party for his investors. Hell, he and that fancy piece Gould had fixed him up with had damn near drowned in the thing!

Just thinking about the incident made him acutely aware of how long it had been since he'd had a woman. Almost simultaneously, a vision of silky bronze hair, deep blue eyes and a haughty turned-up little nose flashed before his eyes. Lordy, what he wouldn't give to collide with that filly again. She was small but quite an armful, and she smelled . . . just like the fragrance emanating from behind the boxwood hedge.

Ah well, maybe one day he'd find her. Meanwhile, there was the fountain. He stepped into the maze of tall hedge, following the pathway's twists and turns in search of the musical call of the water. Why did the blasted English take such delight in making everything as twisty and complicated as possible?

Sabrina sat beside the fountain, gazing over the last blooms of roses, fast fading as fall overtook summer. What a lovely place this was. Her mother had grown roses in the small town in Kent where she had grown up. She'd always dreamed of one day owning her own small plot of land somewhere on the outskirts of London. It would house her school with plenty of room for gardens where girls raised in bleak gray slums could be introduced to the wonder of nature.

She inhaled deeply and dreamed. Ever since Dex had left for Africa seven years ago, she had had one goal in life—being headmistress of a school for young women from the poorest classes, those unable to pay the expensive fees she charged wealthy Cits and even the odd aristocrat, so that they might give their spoiled darlings the benefit of proper deportment. Not that she'd been unhappy with her teaching work. She was independent, earning her own way and beholden to no man.

Nor would she ever be again. Not after Dexter Goodbine. Ever since she'd arrived in London, alone but for her maid Katie, she had survived by using her only skills—a superb classical education, courtesy of her well-read father, and the most genteel of manners, courtesy of her mother, a baron's daughter who'd wed a mere squire beneath her station. Owing to her youth, Sabrina's first years in London had been lean, but gradually she had built an impeccable reputation and clients flocked to her. She saved every dime she could for her school. If not for Edmund, she might be within five years of achieving it.

Poor, dear Edmund. She should not think ill of him, since it was he, albeit most indirectly, who had probably been responsible for the earl remembering her for Sophia. She wondered why Mr. Hodgins had asked her to wait here in the garden. It really was rather irregular, but the note had been quite specific, and when she'd inquired at the door, she had been directed here. Odd.

From the second-story window overlooking the gardens, the earl smiled. As per his instructions to Hodgins, the very prim Miss Edgewater sat perched like a sparrow ready to take flight on the edge of the bench beside the fountain. He could see his greatnephew wending his way through the maze in her direction. With great subtlety, he'd casually mentioned after Joshua's ordeal with the tailor that his garden had quite a spectacular water display, a lure few men who'd spent time in the desert could resist. His four years in the sub-Sahara with Kitchener were one of the main reasons he'd had the fountain built when he returned home.

Joshua, he was certain, imagined some horrid old battle-axe carrying a heavy wooden yardstick with which to cosh recalcitrant students. From every report, the lady below was gracious and charming. She would put his nephew at ease and make the task of polishing his rougher edges a bit easier. Well pleased with his plans, he turned and headed downstairs to his office.

Sabrina heard footsteps behind her and turned to see *him* approaching. What on earth should she do? Or say? Had he mentioned to his great-uncle anything about Edmund's failure to appear and her having taken his place? Dear heavens, she was quaking in her boots like a green girl! *Get hold of yourself. Just remember, he may be an earl's heir but he's still an American ruffian. You can handle the likes of this lout. "Texas Viscount" indeed! Texas Visigoth would be more appropriate.*

But, of course, she'd never had to handle anyone like him before in her life, from Texas or anywhere else. His chiseled features were bold, what many women would fancy as quite handsome, she supposed. The swelling around his right eye was still visible, reminding her of the perfectly dreadful brawl he'd incited yesterday. He was even taller than she recalled, with broad shoulders and impossibly long legs made even longer by those odd boots he affected. There was something about the way he smiled that made her heart speed up rather than slow down, no matter how much she willed it otherwise.

And considering the leer in those smoldering green eyes, she most certainly did wish to maintain her composure. But before she could stop herself, the words burst out. "I see your manners have not improved since they released you from your cell. One might hope a few hours in such a place would have taught you better."

"Oh, jail doesn't bother me." He sidled closer, inhaling the fragrance of wildflowers.

"Because you've been in so many?" she asked sweetly.

He nodded, and a lock of hair fell across his forehead. "One or two back in Texas," he said with a twitch of a grin. "How about you?"

"I beg your pardon?" Sabrina stiffened angrily. "I have never been incarcerated in my life!"

He whistled low. "You sure do know some ten-dollar words. But unless my eyes are goin' bad on me, I'd swear that was you being questioned by those bobby fellows when I walked out of that jailhouse yesterday."

She almost blurted out that she had been there securing his release, but to do so would give away the fact that Edmund had not done it. "I was not a prisoner. I was a witness," she replied in her frostiest tone, which was difficult since he was moving much closer than she was comfortable with. If only he were not so . . . tall.

"Sure looked to me like you were in jail," he said with a grin, placing one booted foot on the edge of the bench where she sat.

Sabrina moved her skirt away disdainfully. Had the oaf no manners whatever?

"Have I stepped in something I shouldn't have?" he asked, looking down at his boot as he turned it sideways to inspect the sole.

Her face turned crimson. "That is no subject to bring up in the presence of a lady," she said, jumping to her feet and stepping briskly over to the water. He followed her, ambling in that loose-jointed way of his, and once again placed his foot on the lip of the fountain.

"My sincerest apologies, ma'am," he replied in a totally impenitent tone.

If not for the prospect of lucrative employment by the earl, she would have stormed out of the garden and never set foot in Hambleton House again. Swallowing her gorge, she nodded, praying that Mr. Hodgins would arrive immediately.

"You do look a lot different than you did yesterday. I liked your hair down," he murmured. "It's a real shame to hide so much of the beautiful stuff all knotted up under a hat."

"A lady never leaves her domicile without properly covering her head—a fact any English gentleman would know." The moment she spat out the words, she wanted to bite her tongue. This man would soon be a viscount and he could have her fired!

He surprised her by chuckling. "Well, now, I've been accused of lots of things over the years, but being a gentleman was never one of them," he drawled.

The lout was laughing at her! "The reason for that is perfectly evident," she snapped.

"It appears to me, ma'am, that we've sort of gotten off on the wrong foot."

"You mean the one you repeatedly insist on placing in your mouth?"

He removed his boot from the edge of the fountain and turned directly toward her. She came only to his shoulder, hat and all. "For such a little bitsy thing, you sure do pack a Texas-sized sting."

"In Texas parlance, I surmise that means large." What made him bring out such disdainfulness in her?

It was ever so ungracious, and if there was one thing Miss Sabrina Edgewater had always prided herself on, it was being gracious, especially to those less fortunate than herself.

"Yes, ma'am, everything about a Texan is large," he said in a husky voice.

Having no idea of his intended innuendo, she merely gave an indelicate snort. "Most particularly their egos. Perhaps Dr. Freud should have studied Texans instead of the Viennese."

"If ole Sigmund had, he might've reached some even more startling conclusions about why women envy men."

Sabrina blinked in disbelief that he knew who Sigmund Freud was, and astonishment that he had slyly raised the subject of men's genitalia! Now his comment about Texans and size made sense. The fact that she'd been the first to mention the controversial physician did not mollify her anger one whit. "You, sir, are an utter troglodyte, possessing the concomitant social graces of an ape!"

"More ten-dollar words."

When she started to whirl away, he could not resist reaching out and taking hold of her arm. "For a gal I found half dressed walking the waterfront yesterday, you sure do put on airs."

Sabrina slapped his hand away furiously. "Walking the waterfront!" she practically shrieked. "You believe I am . . . that I would . . . that. . . ."

She looked so damned adorable with steam coming out of her ears that his lust overrode his hearing—and his judgment. He pulled her into his arms and lowered his mouth toward hers, which was opened in a startled little "O." He knew she'd taste delicious . . .

He was going to kiss her! No man had kissed her

since Dex, when she was seventeen. Somehow she didn't think this kiss would be anything like that one. For one thing, her former fiancé had not opened his mouth as he pressed it to hers. Too late. The Texan had made contact—and what a contact it was. He cradled her head in one hand while his other arm pressed her body against his, practically lifting her off the ground.

His lips were warm and firm, brushing her mouth as the soft heat of his breath mingled with hers. She pushed her hands against his chest, but instead of beating on it as she intended, the shock of that sizzling kiss left them frozen, palms flattened against the hardness of male muscles. His tongue danced around the rim of her mouth, then plunged inside in one swift stroke, colliding with hers. He groaned and did it again, this time slanting his mouth for better penetration.

In some distant, hazy part of her mind, Sabrina knew her body was melting. That must be the reason she remained immobile, allowing this barbarian to take such unspeakable liberties with her person. In broad daylight. In the middle of Lord Hambleton's garden. Where his secretary would arrive at any moment. That last thought galvanized her motor abilities. She balled up her fists and pounded on his chest with one while the other aimed at his good eye.

Let the blighter have a matching set!

Her fist slammed into his left eye at the same time her pointy-toed slipper connected wickedly with his shin. He grunted and released her with an expression of utter bewilderment on his face. If not for the perfidiousness of his behavior and her horrifying reaction to his kiss, she might have believed he was unaware of having done anything improper.

Josh didn't know whether to cradle his painfully smarting eye or rub his aching shin. Being unable to do both at once, he simply stood there, staring in disbelief at the tiny bundle of wrath who glowered up at him as if he were Jack the Ripper. "Now, what in tarnation made you change your mind?" was all he could think to ask.

"You—you seize hold of my person and impose your unwanted advances upon me and then dare to ask—"

"Unwanted advances? You sure could've fooled me, the way you practically melted in my arms and opened your mouth like a baby robin waiting for a fat juicy worm. A woman like you ought to know how to refuse a fellow if she's not on the market," he added angrily. Damn, but his eye and shin hurt!

"Are you accusing me of being a . . . a *prostitute*?" She could hardly wrap her mouth around the word.

He crossed his arms over that impossibly wide chest and glowered at her. "Considering our two previous meetings were on the wharf and in jail, it seems right reasonable to me. My only question is, what the hell are you doing all decked out like a schoolmarm, sunning yourself in my uncle's garden?"

A curtain of red rage seemed to descend over her eyes. The nerve of the man! The colossal, unimaginable temerity—why, it made her so furious she wanted to strike him again. Before her judgment could rein in her temper, Sabrina slapped his face as hard as she could, wiping that smirk from it, but before she could beat a strategic retreat, he wrapped his large hand around her tiny wrist.

"Don't try that again," he said levelly, sick and tired of having a gnat of a woman thump him worse than that beefy pimp on the dock.

All he intended to do was stop her from inflicting further damage, that was the Lord's own truth. But the fool female jerked her hand away so hard that he lost purchase on the silk sleeve of her dress. She slipped from his grip and overbalanced, catching the back of her knees against the lip of the fountain and tumbling into the cool, bubbling water.

Sabrina landed with a loud splash, splattering water all over the impossible Texan. Since the pool was only a foot and a half deep, her soft derriere connected rather painfully with the cement bottom as her head dipped below the surface. She inhaled at least half the contents, or so it seemed to her as she came up for air, coughing and floundering. The final indignity was that her head was positioned directly beneath the urn in the hands of the Grecian god whence issued the steady stream of water.

Her hair was unfastened from its pins, plastered to her shoulders. Yet another of her three remaining hats was ruined, floating lazily out of reach, its feathers limply fanning out on the choppy waves. To add insult to injury, that Texas troglodyte was laughing at her as he leaned one boot on the lip of the pool and extended his hand, offering to help her out.

Hell would freeze before she accepted his help. She tried to stand up unassisted, but the bottom of the pool was slippery with algae. All she succeeded in doing was falling in over her head a second time. The Grecian god, another accursed male, continued raining water on her as she struggled to catch her breath and regain her balance.

Lordy, he could hardly believe how different she looked with that prissy dark blue dress molded to her skin. Every curve and hollow was accentuated. The silk had become almost translucent in the water. If not for all the foolish falderal females insisted on wearing, he would be able to see everything. But he could see enough. Lush rounded breasts stood at attention with nipples hardened into tiny points by the cold water. Sleekly rounded hips and calves practically begged for a man's hands to glide over them. And as for that bottom . . . well he could imagine sinking his fingers into the silky softness of it and pulling her against his—

"Good heavens, Miss Edgewater!" a voice exclaimed in horror. Angry that his delightful reverie had been interrupted, Josh turned to see Wilfred Hodgins scurrying across the garden. The first time he'd met the acerbic little man, Josh had thought he looked as if he'd been weaned on persimmons. Now his face was blank with amazement.

Not wanting his uncle's officious secretary to touch his prize, Josh stepped into the fountain and scooped up the struggling female, then gallantly set her on dry ground before Hodgins could reach them.

She rewarded her rescuer by shoving him so that he tumbled backwards into the water and coshed his head against the urn on his way down.

Chapter 4

The next thing he remembered was waking up with a two-quart Who Shot John headache as Wilfred Hodgins's agitated face faded in and out of focus above him. Lordy, the man had worse breath than a trail drover with a plug of Lucky Boy stuffed inside his cheek. The smell was enough to gag a buck maggot. Josh turned his face away and tried to take a deep breath, but the image of his attacker caught the corner of his eye just as he started coughing up water. She was as soaked to the gills as he, but he liked the way she looked with all that silk plastered to her curves.

Her step was more of a stomp as she vanished into the hedge, leaving him with the parting image of a perfectly delicious set of buttocks swaying gently in spite of her obviously furious departure. He wondered where she lived and how she'd get home in such a condition. "Give me a hand, man," he commanded the prune-faced secretary, who seemed frozen in myopic wonder, staring at his employer's heir through thick lenses perched precariously on the edge of his nose.

Hodgins complied, and Josh climbed out of the fountain. His custom-made boots squished with every step as he started after the virago who'd attacked him. By the time he caught up with her, she was standing forlornly on the street, shivering in the autumn breeze as she searched in vain for a hackney.

"You'll catch your death if you don't dry off," he said as he limped up behind her. When she whirled around furiously and raised her poor battered hat to use it as a cudgel, he backed off a step. "Whoa! I only meant to help."

"You've helped me quite enough, Mr. Cantrell, for one day. In fact, for the duration of my life should I live to be one hundred!"

"Not fair. Where's your British sense of fair play? You know my name and I don't know yours. What in tarnation were you doing in my uncle's garden?"

Sabrina clutched her ruined hat as if to swat him, but he made no move to come closer. Warily she watched the water drip in a steady stream off the tip of his nose. His second injured eye was beginning to match the first one, and a lump the size of a goose egg had begun to form on the side of his head.

She couldn't resist a smile.

"I don't see anything funny-looking about either one of us," he groused.

"You appear to have come out physically the worse from our encounter," she said, smirking, but then her expression darkened. "But considering that you have succeeded in decimating half my wardrobe in less than twenty-four hours, I have not fared much better. A viscount may refurbish his wearing apparel far more easily than a teacher."

"A teacher?" he echoed dumbly. "You don't look like any teacher I ever had."

"Considering your conduct, I very much doubt that you've had any—unless they wore bones in their noses."

"For a supposedly educated female, you have the wrong continent. That's Africa, not North America."

A large cluster of gray rain clouds began to darken the sky and the wind picked up, presaging a sudden autumn storm. She shivered.

"You need to come inside and dry off. At least let me find you a shawl or blanket to wrap around yourself before you go, Miss . . . ?"

He cocked his head, that devilish grin once again in place. She would not take the bait but turned instead and attempted to flag down a hansom driving by the corner. The cab never even slowed.

"No driver will stop for a passenger who looks so bedraggled—they'll figure you can't pay. Now, I can send you home in one of our coaches . . . in exchange for your name."

Damn the man, he could be charming—when he wasn't acting like a stag in rutting season! Well, she'd most probably lost the opportunity to instruct Sophia. There was little use in catching pneumonia and running up medical bills she could not afford, making the situation even worse. The fare over here had been expensive enough. Sabrina made a decision.

Looking up into his concerned green eyes, she said, "I am Miss Sabrina Edgewater, and I was requested to await Mr. Hodgins in the garden, where he was going to discuss engaging me to tutor Lord Hambleton's niece Sophia."

She was shivering again. He wasn't exactly warm himself since those clouds had taken over the sky, but that was not primary in his thoughts when she made her startling announcement. "What was a lady's tutor doing down at the waterfront—or at the jail?" he asked suspiciously.

Oh, wonderful. Now she'd gone and done it. How to explain without getting Eddie discharged? There was nothing for it but to bluff. "That was in regard to another teaching assignment with the sailing master's daughter. When you started that riot, I was mistakenly taken into custody. Once they verified who I was, I was immediately released, as you can see." She crossed her fingers in the folds of her skirts, a superstition her mother had scolded her for since childhood.

"First off, I didn't start that fracas—I was only trying to help out a little gal being attacked by some nasty galoots. Sorta like the one who came after you."

"I handled him. Just as I handled you." She made a point of looking at his matching pair of black eyes. "Green and black may be regimental colors, but they don't favor you," she couldn't resist adding.

He sighed. "Come on, Miss Edgewater. Let's get us both inside before we're frozen like that cussed statue in the fountain. I promise to behave." He raised his hands in mock surrender and sketched a bow, urging her up the steps into the house.

She could tell he did not believe her story about yesterday, did not even believe that she was a tutor. But the utter density of the oaf, to think that she was some lightskirt! Still, she was freezing, and it was far too great a distance to walk home even if she had been dry and warm. But Sabrina had overcome far greater obstacles than this. Besides, she'd never give the Texas troglodyte the satisfaction of succumbing to his charm.

Digging into her reticule, she extracted enough money for her fare home. "I believe you Americans have an adage, 'Money speaks louder than words.'" With that, she turned and began walking down the street, holding aloft several coins as another hansom driver turned the corner of the fashionable square.

Josh stood and watched her climb inside the coach. He started to scratch his head in bemusement but encountered the lump from his tumble into the fountain and winced. She was a damn fine-looking piece, but he was not altogether certain that bedding her would be worth the risk to life and limb.

"Let's hope this ride doesn't finish what the edgy Miss Edgewater began," Josh muttered to Comanche as he kicked the big bay into a brisk canter through the park. The pounding of his head had settled into a dull ache by the time he was scheduled to meet Michael Jamison. What he really wanted to do was lean into the stallion's neck and let him go full out, to blow away the frustrations of the past several days. And all thoughts of that maddening woman.

Could Sabrina Edgewater possibly be a teacher? His mind kept returning to her like a tongue worrying a sore tooth. She certainly was in the wrong places yesterday, but perhaps her story about the sailing master was true, although he was inclined to doubt it. He was good at reading people, and she'd been, to use one of her ten-dollar words, "prevaricating" about that. Still, her clothing was demure and conservatively cut, if one ignored the open bodice after the altercation at the pier yesterday . . . and the soaking this morning, he mentally added with a chuckle.

If she had been telling the truth about being summoned by the earl to tutor one of his shirttail cousins, then he'd acted like a perfect boor the way he had teased and flirted with her—to say nothing of grabbing her for that kiss. Yeah, that kiss . . .

"I say, you do keep up a good pace. Splendid piece of horseflesh. American quarter horse mixed with Arab barb?" inquired a dark-haired man nattily decked out in riding breeches and a bottle-green velvet coat as he pulled up alongside Josh.

"You know your horseflesh," Josh replied, nodding as he eyed the splendid chestnut thoroughbred the Englishman was riding. "Not many Englishmen are familiar with our quarter horses."

"My paternal grandmother was from Georgia. I've had occasion to visit your country, although I confess I have not been to Texas."

"I reckon you're Jamison?"

"Michael Derrick Jamison, at your service, my lord," the man replied with a quick smile that revealed a set of perfect white teeth.

"I'm not anybody's lord yet," Josh said flatly. "Maybe never will have to be if we get this mess with the Russians and Japanese straightened out. My president was right anxious about it."

"Was Mr. Roosevelt really a cow smasher before he became president?" Jamison asked incredulously.

Josh started, then threw back his head and roared with laughter. "You mean cowpuncher?"

Jamison nodded. "I stand corrected. I've never been west of the Mississippi. I found the newspaper accounts of President Roosevelt's adventures in the Dakotas as fascinating as those during the late war."

"The colonel was in the stock business right enough. I started out punching cows, but he bought his ranch right up front. I'm a stockman now, too. And I'll admit I've been a mite more successful at it than he was," Josh couldn't resist adding. "But then I'd be a disaster as president, so I guess you could say, every man has to do what he has the talent to do. That why you're a spy?"

Now it was the Englishman's turn to laugh. "An unsavory term but true, *alors*. I come from a long line of spies. My grandfather was an agent against Napoleon, and my father worked to deny British diplomatic recognition to the Confederacy." He looked over at Josh, realizing that Texas had been a part of that abortive rebellion.

"Don't worry. It was long before my time. As we say back where I come from, I didn't have a dog in that fight." Gertie hailed from Massachusetts and was a staunch Unionist, but he didn't particularly feel like sharing that with the Englishman. Jamison looked relieved.

All during their conversation he had unobtrusively been studying Josh's bruised eyes. When Josh finally looked directly at him, he reddened. "A souvenir from that set-to at the wharf yesterday?" he dared to ask.

"Only the right one. The other . . . well, I'd as soon not go into that." Now it was Josh's turn to feel his face flush beneath his tan.

"We'd probably be best advised to discuss the matter at hand before someone remarks on our being seen together," Jamison said briskly. He glanced quickly around the crowded park and then nodded to a wooded copse several hundred yards distant. "I'll meet you at the opposite side of those trees at half past the hour. Watch you aren't followed."

Muttering about tomfool secrecy and cow smashers, Josh meandered around the woods, returning the curious nods of fancy-dressed folks in carriages and dudes on horseback. He'd read the newspaper accounts of his arrival and would have bet the people expected him to incite another riot . . . or take a scalp or two before he left the park. Of course, playing the role of a wild and woolly dime-novel Westerner was what he was supposed to do. But being the resident yokel was getting to be a real pain in the . . . eyes.

"Reckon that fracas at the pier gave me a good head start on it," he mused with a chuckle as he rode to his rendezvous.

"You cannot be serious!" Sabrina almost dropped the teacup she was handing to Mr. Hodgins.

The secretary had sent word that he still wished to speak with her about the position in the earl's household. He'd asked permission to call at her home that afternoon and apologized for any inconvenience caused by the unfortunate accident at the fountain. Mollified and relieved, she had immediately responded that she would be delighted to receive him.

Until this. Steadying her hand, she managed not to spill the hot tea all over his pristine suit as she handed him the cup. "You wish me to tutor that . . . that is, Lord Hambleton's nephew?"

"That is correct, Miss Edgewater," Hodgins said, dabbing nervously at his brow with a handkerchief. He did not look pleased with her reaction, but the expression of disappointment quickly gave way to a placating smile. "Your credentials are quite impeccable, and Lady Rushcroft speaks highly of you."

I'd sooner teach a baboon to ride bareback in hell. "But I instruct young ladies in the social graces. I've never worked with a gentleman. It simply isn't done." *And he isn't a gentleman!*

"His Lordship understands your reluctance after the incident this morning, but it was a most regrettable misunderstanding. He urged me to assure you that the viscount will never behave in such a fashion again. He is an American, after all, and lacks, er, discretion."

He said it as if that explained everything. Perhaps it did . . . at least as far as Americans from Texas were concerned. Sabrina did not know, nor did she wish to find out. "Please convey my regrets to Lord Hambleton. I was led to believe it was his niece, not his nephew, for whom he wished to engage my services. While I should be happy to instruct Miss Sophia—"

"No. As of now, Miss Standish is studying at the Wilton Academy. Perhaps after she graduates in the spring, your services might be of use," Hodgins said unctuously.

Blackmail. Sabrina would have none of it. She shook her head. "I hate to disappoint, but I do have my other clients to consider. If I were to begin working with young gentlemen, well, you must understand how mothers might feel about employing me to instruct their daughters."

Hodgins was not happy. He was used to succeeding in any task the earl set him, but one look into Miss Sabrina Edgewater's stern blue eyes convinced him that this time he would fail. Perhaps Hambleton had an ace or two up his sleeve. He rose and bowed smartly to the squire's haughty daughter. "I shall convey your regrets to the earl. If you should reconsider," he added, thrusting a card into her hand, "you have only to inform me."

It will snow in the Congo first, she thought as she closed the door forcefully behind the pompous little man.

* * *

"Our worry is Albany's second son, George Clarence. Being Edward's nephew makes his liaison with the Russians most . . . embarrassing for the government," Jamison explained as the two men strolled in a small glade hidden by overgrowth while their horses grazed at opposite sides of the natural concealment.

"George is the son of the Duke of Albany, King Edward's youngest brother?" Josh asked.

Jamison studied the Texan with surprise. "Why is it that you seem to be one thing and are really quite another?"

"Just call me an enigma," Josh replied dryly. "Tell me about Georgie's Russian friends."

"You know about the Great Game?"

Cantrell nodded. "Britain versus the Russian Empire. Been going on ever since you fellows acquired real estate in India. You want to maintain the status quo, with the Royal Navy dominating the oceans. You've got the Russians blocked on the Bosporus. All you have to do is keep their ambitions in Manchuria and China in check. The Japanese can help you do that."

"I say, you are well informed." Jamison appeared delighted.

"I've read a book or two. Even polished up on recent English history during the voyage over." *When I wasn't hanging my head in a slop bucket.*

"Well, dear 'Georgie'—an apt name, by the by—is enamored of a Russian woman named Natasha Samsonov. Quite a beauty."

"Seems I recall that one of the king's other brothers is married to a Russian princess. What you folks have is too much inbreeding. Tends to produce stupid stock."

Michael threw back his head and laughed heartily.

"You're nothing if not direct—and truthful. All the royal houses of Europe have married their first cousins far too often."

Josh decided he could learn to like this shrewd Englishman. "For one of those stiff-upper-lip fellows, you're pretty outspoken yourself."

"When it suits me," Jamison replied cryptically. "Here's the dilemma in a nutshell. The Samsonov woman is quite a famous ballerina, employed by an English stage company here in London. But we've learned that she's involved right down to the tips of her red satin ballet slippers with a band of Russians who've supposedly run afoul of the czarina and been banished. They live lavishly in London."

"Sort of Russian remittance men?" Josh supplied grimly, thinking of his father.

"Not a bad analogy, but most Englishmen who find their way to America aren't dispatched to assassinate anyone—at least not by our Foreign Office. These Russian chaps are virulently expansionist. Nikolai Zarenko's father is a major shareholder in the Trans-Siberian Railroad. Sergei Valerian has a brother active in trade with China. They all pretend to be indolent aristocrats living as high-flyers here, but their real mission is to put a period to our negotiations with Japan."

"The president told me there'd been an attempt to assassinate this Hayashi fellow. I imagine if the Russians succeeded and could blame a member of the British royal family for the whole shebang, it would end any Anglo-Japanese cooperation in the Far East."

"Quite so."

"I still don't see where I come in." Josh scratched his head and winced again. Damn Sabrina Edgewater. He couldn't concentrate worth shucks, and it was all her fault.

"You're new to the London scene and will be invited everywhere. A Texas viscount is, after all, rather a novelty. Can you hold your liquor? We were informed you could."

Josh snorted. "I can imagine who told you, too. On the best day of his life the colonel couldn't hold more than two beers before he'd fall asleep. Not to brag, at least not much, but I can drink any dozen men under the table and walk away standin' straight."

"Perfect. That's your entrée to the Russians. They swill vodka like watered ale. Carouse with them. You might even find an opportunity to dally a bit with Madame Samsonov."

"Can she hold her liquor?"

Jamison shrugged and grinned. "Rumor has it, prodigiously. I suppose you'll just have to find out if you can keep up with her."

Jamison had been right about the invitations. They'd already started to pour in by the time he returned home that afternoon. Teas and balls, recitals and salons. Everyone who was anyone in London society wanted to meet the infamous Texas Viscount, Hambleton's scandalous heir. He began sorting through the heavy velum notes, discarding those that sounded too tame for the Russians' tastes, selecting several where he felt he might encounter them.

Although Jamison had told him the Russians had virtually colonized the Metropole Hotel on Northumberland Avenue, he decided that meeting them on neutral ground first might be the most natural way to infiltrate their inner circle. As he was making his choices, his uncle ambled into the room.

"I say, you don't look half as bad as you should, for

a man who narrowly escaped drowning this morning," the earl said with asperity. "What the devil possessed you to treat a woman such as Miss Edgewater so abominably?"

Josh looked up. "Let's just say we had a little misunderstanding. So, she really is a teacher and you were going to hire her for one of my cousins."

"You young scamp, I was going to hire her for you!"

Josh dropped the invitations . . . and his jaw. "For me?"

"Is there an echo in here?" the earl snapped. "If you'll recall from our conversation last night, I said I had employed someone to teach you sufficient manners so you could be received in polite society."

"You hired that . . . that girl? I was looking for some ancient crone with a stick up her ass wearing a frown to match. Come to think of it, except for the age, that description does sorta fit her," he muttered as an afterthought.

Hambleton allowed himself an ironic smile. "I imagined you'd have that preconceived notion, which was precisely why I allowed the two of you to meet informally. I was hoping you'd use some of that crude Texas charm on her. I fear she's been far too well apprised of the herculean efforts civilizing you will require. If I had the slightest notion you'd end up dumping her in the fountain—"

"She did a hell of a lot more damage to me than I did to her," Josh shot back, pointing to the fresher of his two black eyes and the lump on his head. "And she wasn't the only one who ended up in the fountain."

Hambleton rubbed his hands together and chuckled with self-congratulation. "The gel's half your size, boy. If she continues to hold her own this well, I cannot imagine anyone better suited for the job. It would appear I've made the perfect choice." *Yes, the perfect choice indeed!*

"Do they grow loco weed in London?" Josh asked in exasperation. "A female like that one is the worst choice on God's green earth for me. Anyways, she'd sooner eat a bucket of worms and turn up her toes than lay eyes on me again," he said glumly.

The earl's silver eyebrows rose as he studied his young nephew. "Then we shall both have to see to it that she changes her mind, shan't we?"

The ballroom was crowded, filled with ladies in brilliantly colored silks and bedecked with jewels that sparkled in every color of the rainbow, reflecting from the Duke of Chitchester's massive crystal chandelier overhead. Music and laughter wafted gaily on the warm autumn air as Sabrina inspected her charge behind the cover of a large potted fern in one corner of the ballroom.

"Now remember, Miss Forsythe, you are to dance no more than twice with Mr. Chalmers, no matter how he importunes you," she instructed firmly as she tucked an errant curl back into place and wiped a trickle of perspiration from one plump cheek. With soft brown hair and wide gray eyes, Esther Forsythe could be a pretty girl . . . if she would forsake bonbons and clotted cream long enough to shed twenty pounds of baby fat. But all the subtle hints and suggestions about ladylike portions had fallen on deaf ears so far.

"But I like Mr. Chalmers. His father is a marquess," Esther replied petulantly, sticking her lower lip out, another thing Sabrina had attempted in vain to change.

"His father is indeed a marquess, but he is the youngest of four sons and will never inherit. If you wish to enter the peerage, you must cast your sights on a first son." Heavens above, this child was as dense as iron. But, used to dealing with stupidity as well as spoiled tantrums, Sabrina kept her voice low and smooth as she adjusted the bow on Esther's shoulder.

"Is it one-two-three for the waltz?" Esther asked nervously.

Sabrina could see the girl mentally picturing each step in her mind. Esther had an unfortunate tendency to lose count and tromp on her partner's feet with distressing frequency. It was fortunate that her father was one of the wealthiest merchants in England, else she'd have men fleeing from her. All Sabrina had to do was see that she did not fall prey to a fortune hunter who would abuse the poor child.

"Do not count. Just follow your partner's lead and you shall do splendidly," she replied, giving Esther a winsome smile. "Now, here's your dance card. I believe Mr. Sheffield has the first dance." Sabrina pointed her in the right direction and the girl entered the fray, clutching the card like a medieval knight would clutch his shield in battle.

When the gentleman in question bowed and led her into the waltz, Sabrina stood watching with a pleased smile from her place of concealment. Mrs. Forsythe had fallen victim to one of her migraines tonight and requested that Sabrina see her daughter through the evening. She needed the extra money this night's work would bring, and so far all was going well.

Until a familiar voice behind her said, "So you really are a teacher. Got your work cut out for you with that one. Hope her daddy's rich."

Sabrina stiffened her back and turned to look up into the grinning face of "Viscount Wesley." She struggled to keep her tone civil. The bounder looked resplendent in black evening attire, the cutaway coat and perfectly creased trousers emphasizing his superb physique. His darkly tanned face contrasted dramatically with the pristine whiteness of his shirt. "I see the earl has set his tailor to work on your wardrobe. A formidable task for the poor fellow."

Josh looked down at his evening clothes and asked, "You don't think I could've picked these duds out for myself?"

She resisted a snort of derision. "Only if they were made of denim and trimmed with beads and bear claws."

He grinned. "I am right partial to Levi's and a little more trimming on my jackets," he said as he shot his cuffs and inspected the small ruby studs, matching those on his shirt front. "But if I had the right teacher, I expect I could learn better taste. You should feel it's your professional duty to help out a poor ignorant fellow like me."

"I see your uncle has explained the nature of the assignment he had for me. Has he also informed you that I turned it down?"

Josh shrugged, studying her simple blue gown. Plainly cut with a straight skirt and primly high neckline, it was unadorned except for a bit of white lace at the cuffs and collar. Her only jewelry was a cameo suspended on a thin silk ribbon at her throat. He wanted to pick it up and feel the warmth of her skin emanating from it.

"You consider me that hopeless? Or aren't you up to a real challenge? I'd be a lot more interesting than those pouty young girls." There was a dare in his eyes.

"I work only with young ladies—and they are not 'pouty.'"

"You didn't answer my questions. Guess I'll just have to show you how much help I really need," he said as one long arm swept around her waist and he whirled her from the concealment of the greenery and onto the crowded dance floor where a schottische was playing.

"Let me go at once," she hissed beneath her breath. "I'm not dressed appropriately to dance at a function such as this, and I was not invited in any case. I'm an employee of Mrs. Forsythe."

She tried to wriggle away, but he held on to her as he made big clumsy steps around the floor, narrowly avoiding bumping into people. He held her right hand in his left, pointing their hands straight out like the prow of a ship plowing through a stormy sea, dipping low, then high again with each giant step he took. She was dragged along with him, and unless she wanted to create an even more hideous scene, she could do nothing but pray for the music to end.

And stamp on his feet with her heels at every opportunity. But he was surprisingly clever at avoiding her ploy after the first tromp. "Why is it, Lord Wesley, that I suspect you of being less clumsy than you're attempting to appear?" she whispered furiously. "Please release me at once. I shall lose my position with the Forsythes."

"Then you'll have to come work for my uncle," he replied with a grin.

"I'll kick your bruised shin," she threatened.

"It's healed up, just like my eyes. You threatening to blacken them again, too?"

"How can I do anything with you holding me so tightly?" she muttered.

"A Texan learns to defend himself when he's no bigger'n a pup, Miss Edgewater. I underestimated you once and I don't figure on doing it again."

"You manhandled me," she snapped.

"Funny, but when the whole thing started, it didn't seem to me you disliked kissing me all that much." Lordy, she smelled like wildflowers—or was it roses? Her scent could go right to a fellow's head.

"You have a great deal of nerve."

"Where I come from, they call that self-confidence."

Sabrina could see that they were creating quite a stir. She wanted to vanish into the cracks in the brilliantly polished parquet floor. "Here they call it poor breeding."

"All the more reason I need help . . . teacher," he said as he swooped into another dizzying dip.

"I would sooner train an organ grinder's monkey!" Just then the music stopped. Sabrina's cheeks were flushed scarlet hot, not only from the exertion of the dance but her own utter humiliation. Had everyone heard her last words? She'd practically shouted them. Biting her lip, she wrenched herself free of his grip and fled to the sanctuary of the ladies' retiring room. He would not dare to follow her there . . . would he? With a Texas troglodyte such as Joshua Cantrell, it was difficult to know.

"I simply can't believe it, Eddy. This is the fourth client to cancel her daughter's appointment in the past week. At this rate of attrition, I'll be out on the streets within a fortnight," Sabrina said with mounting despair.

Edmund Whistledown sat across from her, sipping tea and munching on one of her lovely home-baked scones. "There, there, Coz, don't take on so. I'm sure you'll find new pupils. After all, there is no scarcity of boorish young Cits whose papas are rich as Croesus."

"Yes, but none of them are applying to me. And the excuses I've been given—why—why they sound almost as if they were rehearsed speeches someone told them to . . ." Sabrina jumped up so suddenly, her teacup rattled in its saucer sitting on the table beside her. "Could it possibly be?"

"Could what possibly be?" Edmund echoed as he stuffed another bite of scone in his mouth. Thin as a sweeper boy, he could eat his weight daily and never gain an ounce.

"The earl . . . or that perfidious Texas Neanderthal. I'd put it past neither of them—or both of them!" she said furiously, remembering the Chitchesters' ball last week and that arrogant lout's unconscionable behavior. She knew it had created talk when she danced with him, but given his behavior since arriving in England, she'd hoped people would realize the fault lay with him, not a proper woman such as she. One way or another, the viscount and the earl were conspiring to force her to do what they wanted.

They didn't know how stubborn Sabrina Edgewater could be.

Chapter 5

The Chitchester ball had been a good idea for more than one reason, Josh thought with a grin. Dancing the Texas two-step with Sabrina had been damn fine, but his main reason for attending had not been his fascination with the starchy teacher. Michael Jamison had sent word that one of the dissolute young Russians they'd discussed would be present. Josh had made contact with Alexi Kurznikov, who had enjoyed Josh's show with the prim tutor. One drink at the punchbowl—theirs well spiked with vodka—led to another. Within an hour of the time Miss Edgewater escorted her charge safely home, Josh had dear Alexi drunk as a skunk. The Russian count assured the Texas viscount that he was now his best friend.

This evening he'd agreed to meet Kurznikov, an amiable young fellow, at the White Satin Club, one of the dissident group's favored pubs. But first, he had to deal with a headache the size of the Tower of London. Seeing as how Russian vodka tasted like water from a horse trough, he couldn't for the life of him figure out how it could pack more wallop than a burro with a burr under its blanket.

While dunking his head in a basin of cold water, he vowed to introduce Alexi and his friends to the civilized amenity of bourbon. When he stood up and shook his head in a vain attempt to clear it, pain lanced all the way down his spine. The sudden movement also sent drops flying onto the shaving mirror in front of him. The face staring back at him looked grim indeed—black bristly beard, red-rimmed eyes with whites that looked as if they'd been coated with Tabasco sauce, hair standing up in spiky tufts.

"I say, what price head have you?" the earl inquired cheerfully from the doorway of the dressing room. If he disapproved of his nephew's overindulgence last night, it was not apparent from his mildly amused demeanor.

"If by that you mean how bad is my hangover, I reckon I've had worse . . . only I can't rightly recall when," he added beneath his breath.

"A good shave might help your appearance," Hambleton suggested.

Josh shuddered. "If you want me alive to inherit, I wouldn't suggest letting me anywhere near a razor for at least a week."

"One of the things you simply must accustom yourself to is allowing servants to assist you with grooming," the earl said. "Benton is an excellent valet and would be most happy to shave you. I've instructed him to lay out your clothing for the day . . . or what's left of it. When you're feeling a bit better, please come to the terrace for a light repast."

"That mean food?" Josh asked.

"You know it does."

"And you know I'm bright green. I'll only come if you promise not to eat in front of me."

"Agreed," the old man said and strolled out of Josh's quarters. He paused at the hallway door to say, "A pity you're so unwell. Cook has prepared a marvelous kidney pie."

"If I hadn't drunk a drop last night, just thinkin' about eating that coyote bait'd be enough to start me puking."

"We really must engage Miss Edgewater's services if you're to be received at court," the earl said, shaking his head as he turned to depart.

"The lady doesn't much cotton to me. I tried to make amends for what happened last week in the garden, but she's still madder than a scalded cat."

"Why is it you persist in trying to win her over, then?" Hambleton asked, pausing in the doorway.

Josh grinned. "I reckon she's a challenge. Anyone who thinks I'm that plumb hopeless has a lot to learn about me."

"I imagine you could convince her otherwise," the earl said dryly. He suppressed his chuckles until he was well out of earshot of his nephew. The boy was doing swimmingly. One evening with Kurznikov and he had a foot—no, make that a boot—inside the door of the snobbish Russian clique. Perfect.

Of course, as soon as matters became dangerous, Michael would take over and Joshua would be safely delivered from possible harm. There was no earthly way that the earl was going to endanger his nephew after spending so long to find him. Besides, he was growing to really enjoy the young rascal's wild Texas eccentricities. A pity Miss Edgewater would have to eliminate them.

Ah, yes, Miss Edgewater. A most formidable young

woman, who took no nonsense from her pupils. After reading her references, he knew she was the only one who could handle a Texas barbarian such as Joshua. He'd also anticipated that she might resist his rather unorthodox offer. But when the tenth Earl of Hambleton set his mind to a task, no one stood in his way. He considered the maneuvers he'd used to bring her to heel. Unfortunately, they had not worked . . . yet. But he had another ace to play.

It was obvious that Joshua would take delight in besting her by becoming a reasonably proper English gentleman. The earl could hardly wait to observe their war of wills. Congratulating himself, he strolled into the front parlor where the worst gossip in London, the Dowager Countess of Wiltshire, awaited him. When their conversation was complete, Miss Edgewater would work for him . . . or she'd work for no one in the whole of England.

Sabrina had not one single client left. And she knew who was responsible. Dare she confront the earl in his own home? Sabrina was growing desperate. If only Edmund could manage to pay her back some of the money she'd lent him, she might be able to hold on until the earl's interest in her waned. But her cousin seemed constitutionally incapable of saving a halfpence.

She sighed. The earl would only refuse to see her, or worse yet, grant her an interview and then smile benignly while protesting his innocence regarding her predicament. Her only recourse lay with the viscount. He had an appalling opinion of her morals, and, even worse, he upset her equilibrium in strange ways no other man ever had—a matter she assured herself had to do with his exotic background, nothing else. He was a . . . curiosity, an uncouth, utterly unsophisticated ruffian.

If the accounts she'd read in the newspapers were to be believed, he had actually grown up in some small hamlet in western Texas . . . in a house of ill-repute! Small wonder he could not discern a lady by her demeanor and dress. He was probably accustomed to seeing his women unclothed! She could still remember those coolly amused green eyes sweeping over her disheveled appearance on the gangplank of the ship . . . that lascivious wink he'd given her in the jailhouse. And the kiss he'd given her in the garden . . .

That was what made her hesitate to approach him. For one brief instant—well, perhaps more than just an instant, she was forced by her conscience to confess—she had allowed him to take utterly shocking liberties during that kiss. Closing her eyes, she leaned back in the large chintz-covered chair in her sitting room, imagining that moment when he'd held her and pressed those sculpted lips to her own. They were warm and mobile . . . and open! He'd actually dared to touch his tongue to hers. Sabrina could scarcely credit that she had even met him partway, allowing it. *Enjoying it*, an insidious voice taunted.

What she should have done was bitten it off!

He'd pressed her body tightly to his, enfolding her in powerful arms, cradling her head with his hand. Her breasts had been flattened against his stone-hard chest. Even now, that peculiar ache filled them, the nipples puckering into tiny hard points. She fought the urge to touch herself there, to examine what a mere memory could do. But, of course, she did nothing of the sort. Horrified, she practically sprang from the chair, small hands fisted into tight little balls as

80

she began pacing back and forth over the well-worn carpet.

Perhaps the good ladies of London were well advised to remove their daughters from her charge. Was she morally perverse? An unwholesome influence on young minds? No! She'd devoted her life to teaching upright Christian behavior as well as social graces to her pupils. This whole difficulty was the fault of one man . . . one dangerous, black-haired, green-eyed devil with a rogue's grin and a seducer's husky, melodic voice.

"Get past this, Sabrina. Take charge of your life. You've done it before when you were far younger and in more dire straits," she scolded herself. She strode into her bedroom to change clothes. Mrs. Collingwood went shopping at the arcade off Piccadilly the first Wednesday of every month. That was today, and the wealthy shipping magnate's wife had agreed to meet her for tea at a fashionable restaurant that afternoon to discuss deportment lessons for her daughter Martha.

"Just one new client," she repeated like a prayer as she dressed in her last good suit, a light-yellow linen with a frilly white blouse. The yellow straw flowers she'd sewn on the brim of her only remaining hat should match her outfit perfectly. "You can win over Mrs. Collingwood," she said sternly to her image in the mirror, giving her appearance one last inspection before setting out.

She arrived nearly an hour early, determined to take no chance that traffic might cause her to keep Mrs. Collingwood waiting. Besides, Edmund's birthday was next week and she needed to buy him a present. Thank goodness her family had sent a small amount to supplement her own meager contribution for the gift. As the youngest in the family, and an orphan, he'd always been everyone's favorite.

Sabrina browsed through the shops lining the arcade, searching for some item he could use. She was comparing handkerchiefs and trying to decide if her family's combined money was enough to have a pair of them monogrammed when a hatefully familiar voice sent a shiver racing down her spine.

"Buying your sweetheart a love token?" Josh asked, oddly peeved that she might indeed have a gentleman friend. He'd judged her to be near his own age, rather over the hill as far as English females in the marriage market were concerned.

Sabrina jerked around, holding a handkerchief in one hand while the other dropped to the counter for support. He looked utterly splendid, dressed in a conservatively cut suit of fine lightweight wool and a snowy white shirt. The paisley ascot at his throat picked up the dark-green color of his eyes, which were studying her with indelicate interest.

She refused to give him the satisfaction of craning her neck up to meet his gaze. Besides, it was safer not to be drawn into those laughing eyes. Already she could feel her pulse pick up speed like a locomotive on a downhill grade. "Whether or not I have a fiancé or am purchasing anything for him is certainly no business of yours," she snapped. "Please be so kind as to move along and leave me alone."

"Aw, I was hoping to get a lady's opinion on what monogram to put on my hankies," he said, giving her a blinding smile as he leaned one elbow on the counter directly in front of her. "I always went with JC back in Texas. Had a kinda nice ring to it, you know?"

She started. "Only *you* would have the audacity to

compare yourself to the Deity." The instant she blurted out the blasphemy, Sabrina froze with shock. How could she ever have thought such a thing? Why had this man made her say it? He provoked her beyond all reason.

Josh laughed, shaking his head. "Now, ma'am, I never would've thought of that," he protested. "I'm right surprised you did. No, you see, I was sorta thinking along the lines of using my full handle, er, name, since I found out I was called after my uncle. I have a whole mouthful of initials—Joshua Abington Charles Cantrell. What would you think of JACC?"

"Only that it's a pity you don't spell your last name with a K instead of a C. You could make a splendid acronym if you added an ASS on the end of it. It would suit you perfectly."

He threw back his head and laughed. "Girl, you are a caution. But I've been called worse things."

"And I'm quite certain you deserved every one."

Before he could reply, a small clock on the central counter chimed softly and Sabrina looked over at it. It was a quarter to the hour, and she would be late if she did not leave at once. How could she have been so foolish as to stand trading insults with this oaf? But the viscount did not appear to want her to leave in spite of her insults.

"The edgy Miss Edgewater. You have more prickles than a spiny cactus, but, you know, it's the funniest thing about those plants. They can thrive without any help under the worst conditions. No one, not even tough Texas longhorns, tries to mess with them . . . and every spring they have the prettiest blooms." He reached up and touched the cluster of yellow flowers on her hat. "Just about that color."

Somehow his hand trailed from the straw bonnet

perched on her head down to her cheek, where one long finger traced a soft pattern on her skin. "Like velvet," he breathed as his eyes met hers.

For a moment she could not move. She stood transfixed as their gazes locked. Were they both remembering that kiss? Sabrina was. This was insane. She turned her head and backed away. "I am late for a business appointment," she said breathlessly and darted past him like the craven coward she knew she must be. Hating herself for running, Sabrina did it anyway rather than let him touch her again. Besides, she did have to meet Mrs. Collingwood.

So intent was she on her headlong rush away from Josh Cantrell that she did not hear the distressed call of the clerk. "Miss, miss! The handkerchief! I shall summon a constable!"

Sabrina was halfway down the long concourse, her heels clicking on the hard floor as she walked as fast as her five-foot-two-inch frame could carry her. That was when she heard the shrill of a police whistle and an officer suddenly appeared in her path. She tried to step around him, believing he was pursuing someone behind her and she was impeding his progress, but he startled her by seizing hold of her arm.

"This the gel, Mr. Darby?" he asked the huffing clerk, who was pointing directly at her.

Well-dressed shoppers strolling through the large arcade stopped to stare at the altercation, women murmuring behind their gloved hands and children snickering until shushed by their mothers.

Sabrina looked from the burly policeman with an enormous handlebar mustache to the clerk who had been waiting on her. The handkerchief! She was still clutching it in her hand. She'd been so intent on escaping from that odious Texan that she quite forgot to place it back on the counter. "Oh, dear, there's been a terrible misunderstanding. I will certainly pay—"

"Oh, you'll pay right enough, missy. Off you go," the officer said, nodding to Darby, who snatched the handkerchief from her as if it were the Golden Fleece and she a slavering Gorgon.

"But, please, you must believe me, this was an honest mistake," she pleaded. Just then she saw Mrs. Collingwood approaching. Sabrina watched with a leaden heart as the lady's expression turned from puzzlement to incredulous indignation. Oh, to be invisible! The woman actually held her skirt out as she walked past, as if wishing to avoid contamination. There went Sabrina's last hope for employment. And it was all the fault of the swaggering, grinning lout who strolled up and placed his hand on the officer's massive shoulder in male camaraderie.

"Maybe I can help out with this fracas." He eyed Sabrina with ill-concealed amusement, watching her expression change from blind panic to seething fury.

"Oh, and who 'er you?" the man asked suspiciously. He was not actually a police officer but a guard hired by the arcade to catch anyone pinching small items from the shops.

"Well now, in a few days, depending on when the House of Lords gets around to it, I'll be Viscount Wesley."

The guard studied the tall man with the peculiar accent, taking note of his expensive clothes, but before he could do more than twitch his mustache, Mr. Darby interjected, "Oh, this is the Earl of Hambleton's heir. But I do not know this young woman." He eyed Sabrina as if she were a leper.

"Well, I do." Josh grinned. "You see, she works for my uncle and me." He let the words sink in, nodding to Sabrina. "Isn't that right, Miss Edgewater?"

Her eyes turned the color of a storm-tossed Atlantic. She itched to deny it. Almost shouted the truth to the high clerestory windows in the vaulted ceiling of the arcade. But she forced herself to return his nod woodenly. She'd go straight to perdition before giving him the satisfaction of uttering a word.

"I'll be right happy to pay for the doodad, and your trouble," Josh ventured as she jerked her arm angrily from the guard's meaty fingers. Josh wondered whom she'd punch first—him or the guard! As he fished several coins from his pocket, he was grateful that some color had returned to her face. She'd looked white as a ghost and ready to faint a moment ago, something he intuited Miss Sabrina Edgewater never did.

Anger burned through her as she watched the arrogant rotter hand Darby far more money than the miserable handkerchief was worth. "The price of that handkerchief—"

"Now, now, Miss Edgewater, let's not get all fired up over the little old mistake you made."

Rich men. They were all alike, thinking they could buy anything they wished, caring nothing for the dignity of those beneath them. She held herself in check as the clerk and the guard bowed and scraped to the viscount as if he indeed lived up to his initials.

As curious passersby began to drift away, the two of them were left standing alone in the center of the arcade. "You know you gave that man over twice what that article was worth. I shall repay you only for its true value," she said, then added stiffly, "but I do thank you for coming to my assistance."

He chuckled. "Lordy, you sound like you swallowed a sackful of hopping toads to get that one out."

When she started to stalk away, he quickly fell in step alongside her. If he'd touched her, Sabrina was not certain she could have kept from sinking her teeth into his hand, right down to the bone. "This entire debacle was entirely your fault," she snapped. "I said I will repay you—as soon as I find another client. Thanks to you, I've just lost Mrs. Collingwood's patronage."

"She the one who walked by looking like she'd just found out Jack the Ripper was really female?"

"You may make light of this, but I assure you, Lord Wesley, that I do not find it in the least amusing."

"What lucky fellow is this for?" he asked, handing her the linen.

She refused it. "Keep it. You paid for it."

"But you said you'd repay me," he countered. "Back where I come from, folks don't welch."

"If by that quaint colloquialism, you mean you don't believe I will make restitution, have no fear. Now please leave me alone, else I shall summon a genuine police officer," she said when they stepped into Bond Street.

"You could pay me whenever you want . . . real easy."

"If you think that blackmail will force me to become your tutor, you are most sadly mistaken."

"Nah, I was thinking along the lines of another kiss."

His suggestive tone unnerved her. "I'd rather kiss a cobra," she replied.

He swore softly, leaning against the wall of the arcade as he watched her stamp across the busy street and vanish into the crowd.

* * *

"I don't know what it is about that high-stepping little filly, but she sure does bring out the worst in me," Josh said glumly to his uncle that afternoon as they shared a late tea. Well, the earl was enjoying tea with sandwiches and pastries. His nephew had broken out a fresh bottle of bourbon.

A small smile touched the old man's lips as he observed the boy pacing across the carpet in the small sitting room adjacent to his office. "Miss Edgewater is an extraordinary woman. That's precisely why I intend to see that she becomes your instructor." He gave the bottle of Who Shot John a meaningful glance, and Josh capped it, then settled down in a leather chair across from his uncle.

"Considering that she and I get on like a sackful of bobcats, how're you fixing to do that?"

"It's only a matter of doing a bit of investigating of one's subject. Miss Edgewater has a life's dream." The old man stroked his slim mustache, waiting to see his nephew's reaction.

"Life's dream, huh? What's that? To see every male in England gelded?"

"Nothing so extreme. She wishes to open a school for indigent girls and educate them so they may aspire to bettering their unfortunate lot in life."

"Might have figured her for some do-good scheme." Josh grinned. "She'll do it, too. I'd bet my pearl-handled Colt on it, but how will that convince her to teach me? I don't think I'd look like much in a dress." He scratched the bristly beard beginning to darken his jawline.

The old man laughed. "Oh, she'll receive the funding for her school . . . after she accepts my offer."

"Seems to me she mentioned something about losing her last client this afternoon . . ." He let the words trail off as his grin matched that of his uncle. "When I first met you, I didn't think we'd have much in common. I'm beginning to change my mind."

White Satin in Josh's opinion was a horrible English misnomer for gin, which he found even more unpalatable than vodka. Instead of tasting like horse-trough water, it tasted like perfume. However, at the club named after it, the majority of the patrons were Russian. The only white satin in the place was the fabric in waistcoats and cloaks worn by bored aristocrats. From what he'd learned about the Romanov dynasty in general and this group of "exiled" princelings in particular, poor old Bertie's excesses were tame as salted-tail deer.

He was assaulted by the thick sweetish aroma of hashish hanging on the air the moment he stepped inside. Several musicians decked out in colorful peasant costumes were playing a lively Russian folk dance as drunken men wearing enough jewelry to sink a Newcastle coal barge wove their way around the crowded gambling tables. Here and there a scantily clad woman sat perched on some man's lap as he indulged simultaneously in a number of serious vices. The laughter was coarse and hearty, the language mostly French, which he understood well enough, and Russian, of which he knew nothing at all.

Scanning the room, he spotted Alexi and began to make his way to where his newfound friend was sitting at a table with three other men. Several large bottles of vodka were mostly empty, attesting to the group's jump on the evening. Josh had planned it that way. To add to his advantage, he'd used an old trick Gertie taught her girls: He'd drunk several ounces of cod liver oil to coat his stomach. He figured to have three hours before the alcohol ate its way through the greasy barrier.

After that, all bets were off. Lordy, he hadn't seen drinkers this serious since his first trail drive all the way from the Panhandle clean up to the Dakotas. Josh could feel the Russians watching him, some merely curious, others openly hostile. He waved to Alexi, who dumped a corset-clad young woman off his lap and stood up to embrace Josh in a bear hug that nearly cracked his ribs.

"Texas Viscount, my friend," Kurznikov slurred, slinging an arm around the taller man's shoulders. The Russian was dark with a full beard and a stocky build more suggestive of peasant than noble lineage. Presenting Josh to his companions, Alexi announced, "This is Lord Hambleton's heir, J-Jos Cantrell." The introduction ended on a hiccup.

Everyone laughed good-naturedly, but Josh could sense an undercurrent around the table. Not all the men were happy to see that their companion had invited an outsider into their circle.

One of the three was a coolly amused black-haired man with a blade of a nose and a high forehead, made to appear even more so by his habit of raising his eyebrows condescendingly. He was Nikolai Zarenko, of the Trans-Siberian Railroad interests. He made a comment in French that slurred Josh's background, saying the American came from God knew where in a backward wilderness, but Josh played dumb. Let them all think he didn't know the lingo and they'd talk freely in front of him.

Back when Josh was a green kid working in the Dakotas, an aristocrat playing at being a stockman, the Marquis de Mores, had taught him French. Already fluent in Spanish, Josh had discovered he had a natural affinity for picking up languages. He wondered how long it would take him to master Russian. Somehow, he doubted it would be as easy as French.

When everyone laughed and he joined in, it seemed he'd passed the test. Then they got down to some serious drinking. The others partook of the potent opiated tobacco, too, offering it to him. Having seen what hashish could do to a man, Josh pulled out a plug of Lucky Boy and bit off a piece, offering it around the table. After a taste, all but the intrepid Alexi declined to "chaw."

If I have to get sick, at least it'll be on something I know how to handle, he thought grimly as he spit in an ice bucket commandeered in place of a cuspidor.

After an hour or so, the door opened and a woman wearing a hooded ermine cloak, which looked ridiculous in the mild autumn weather, swept dramatically into the room. She was followed by an entourage of men, mostly in servants' livery. With a theatrical gesture that drew the attention of every man in the place, she threw back the hood and shook out a gleaming mass of ink-black hair. Her face was aquiline, its only slight imperfection a long, narrow nose. A female version of the man who sat next to Josh, Nikolai Zarenko.

As if answering Josh's unspoken question, Alexi whispered with tobacco-sour breath, "She's Nikolai's sister. Natasha Samsonov. A famous ballerina."

No mention of Mr. Samsonov. Apparently he was not considered of any importance in the grand scheme of things. She was, after all, the mistress of a member of the English royal house. *And trouble,* Josh thought as he watched her make her way toward them.

Perfectly arched black eyebrows rose above night-dark eyes as cold as chips of obsidian. Her mouth was generous, but her smile was not. She studied Josh as introductions were made, her glance bold and hungry while those black eyes swept from his crown to his boots and back, slowing ever so slightly at his crotch. This was not a woman with whom he'd like to trifle, even though she was a beauty.

Nevertheless, he bowed gallantly over her hand. "My greatest pleasure, ma'am."

"Not yet, my lord, not yet," she murmured in heavily accented English. Then she dismissed him and murmured something in French to her brother, too softly for Josh to make out.

The two moved quickly to a small table in a dark corner of the room while her retainers watched the crowd as if expecting a hoard of Cossacks to come galloping through the door brandishing sabers. A waiter, who obviously knew the lady's preferences, brought her a tall, slender crystal glass filled to the brim with vodka. She threw back her head and polished it off in one long swallow.

Yep, no female to mess with at all. Josh felt a cold shiver run down his spine as brother and sister put their heads together in earnest conversation. He'd give a good-sized herd of his best Santa Gertrudis cattle to know what they were talking about.

"She come here often?" he asked Alexi, giving his best imitation of a drunken leer. Not such a great stretch on the woozy part, considering how much vodka and chaw he'd consumed.

Alexi was faring even more poorly as he replied, "Only when her brother's here. Usually af'er her p-performances on T-Tues'ay nights."

Interesting. Josh studied the dark corner where they conferred, wondering how he might find a way to eavesdrop. Of course, if they spoke Russian, it wouldn't do him any good, but if they continued in French . . .

"I . . . I think i's time to go h-home," Alexi said as he toppled against Josh, nearly knocking the Texan from his chair.

Their companions around the table burst into raucous laughter. Resigned to playing the good sport, Josh hefted the heavier man to his feet and slung one arm over his shoulder. By now Alexi was looking quite green around the gills. As they made their way from the establishment to the cheering approval of the crowd, Josh could feel the cold black eyes of Natasha Samsonov boring into his back.

Chapter 6

The summons arrived three days after her debacle with Mrs. Collingwood. Sabrina had been expecting it. Her first impulse had been to tear it to shreds and return the bits to the earl, but innate practicality overcame her temper. Instead, she considered her options, which were grim indeed. Paying the past week's lodgings had taken the last of her savings. She had enough food in the pantry to last her through the weekend.

And not one single paying client.

That was thanks to the wily Hambleton and his infuriating nephew. She would not put it past the young rotter to have lain in wait for her at the arcade just so he could spoil her last opportunity for employment. When she calmed down, she realized there was no way he could have known that she was meeting Mrs. Collingwood, nor could he have predicted she'd be so utterly unnerved by him that she would rush out of a shop without paying for an article of merchandise.

Sabrina refused to consider why she always seemed to react to him in such an undisciplined fashion.

Having used her last pittance for Edmund's birthday gift, she was now faced with the humbling prospect of either returning to live with her parents in the Berkshires on the very limited income her father received in tenant rents, or accepting the earl's offer to teach his odious nephew how to conduct himself with decorum. Why couldn't a man of Hambleton's reputed intelligence see the utter hopelessness of such an endeavor? Joshua Cantrell would behave decorously the day Queen Alexandra rode stark naked through Hyde Park!

Biting her lip, she paced across the threadbare carpet, fighting back tears prompted by a combination of fury and failure. She was no nearer to achieving her dream than she had been seven years before. How naive she'd been to believe she could save enough money to open her school if only she worked hard. Perhaps such feats of pulling oneself up by the bootstraps were possible in America . . . if one were a man.

But she was English . . . and a woman.

A woman of principle, nonetheless. Sabrina stalked to the small broken escritoire, propped up by a book beneath one leg to keep it from wobbling. Taking pen and paper, she composed her reply to the earl's high-handed summons.

From his vantage point in the second-story window of his sitting room, Josh watched Miss Sabrina Edgewater march up the street, her back ramrod straight and her step firm. When she reached the heavy iron gate at the entrance of the Hambleton city house, she paused. Was there a fleeting hint of uncertainty in the set of her proudly pointed little chin, the crinkle of her brow, the quiver of those lush, kissable lips?

She was dressed in the same yellow suit she'd worn at the arcade, with that demure little straw hat with the matching flowers on it. As always, she wore no jewelry, nor did the plain tan slippers match her outfit. They were the same ones she'd worn every time he met her. Probably she owned a light pair for summer and a dark pair for winter. A woman of few frills. He imagined that her appearance had less to do with preserving her image as a no-nonsense woman of business than it did with the lack of funds to purchase more fashionable duds.

The little yellow daisies sewn around the edge of that jaunty hat spoke of a woman who appreciated pretty things and would have enjoyed wearing silks and laces, matching parasols, slippers and bonnets galore . . . if only she could have afforded such luxury. He would love to take her shopping.

Then she shoved open the black wrought-iron gate as if she were the Archangel Michael preparing to storm the gates of hell. "My imagination's playing tricks on me," Josh said with a sigh. There was far more of Athena than Aphrodite in this one.

Still, she fascinated him as no other woman ever had. She was not the most beautiful female who'd ever taken his fancy. The deadly Russian ballerina's features were more classically chiseled in icy perfection. As he watched Sabrina stride toward the front door, he chuckled aloud. The edgy Miss Edgewater could be pretty icy herself when she put her mind to it. But beneath that calm, poised and very English facade he sensed a warm, giving woman longing to be free of the strictures that she and society had placed upon her.

Sabrina lived by the rules. She was intent on earning her own living and right choosy about the way she did it. Well, that was fine with him. She could teach him to act like a gentleman . . . even if it killed both of them! Just thinking of the fun he would have deviling her during their lessons made him grin. One way or the other, he would have the prim Miss Edgewater in his bed and then he'd be the one giving the "lessons." Whistling, he strolled toward the stairs just as he heard Nash's sepulchral voice ushering her toward the earl's office.

When he heard her approach, Abington Clermont Cantrell smiled to himself. Yes, everything was coming together quite swimmingly. After this was settled, all he had left to do was introduce Joshua to Lord Chiffington's daughter and inform the boy that she was to be his future bride. Then he would let nature take its course. "Yes, swimmingly indeed," he murmured softly as Nash tapped on the door.

"My dear Miss Edgewater, please come in," the earl said in his most solicitous voice, utterly ignoring her stiff posture and the cool blue dare in her eyes. "Won't you join me for tea? I've had cook prepare some pastries as well as crumpets with clotted cream."

"I appreciate your kind offer, my lord, but as I indicated in my note, I've not come to enjoy tea. What I have to say may be better summed up if we refrain from the social niceties and get straight to business," Sabrina replied crisply.

"Nonsense. Nothing can be discussed any better while standing hungry than while sitting replete from a fine repast." He motioned for Nash to pull out a chair for the lady.

"This business can. I regret, my lord, that I must once again refuse your offer of employment."

"But you do not even know what my new offer entails," Hambleton replied, nonplused by her refusal.

Feeling at a terrible disadvantage when the earl acted so graciously, Sabrina knew she had to go through with the charade even if she had no intention of bargaining with him. She took the seat at a small Queen Anne table and watched as the butler poured two cups of tea.

"Lemon or cream?" the earl asked.

"Oh, she'll take lemon. I'd lay good money on it," Josh drawled.

Sabrina jerked around at the sound of his voice to find the tall Texan leaning against the heavy walnut door frame, arms crossed over that broad chest. He unfolded his long body gracefully and strolled into the room. Suddenly the large office seemed to grow smaller. "I might have known you'd be here," she snapped, then reddened, realizing how utterly rude that must have sounded to the earl.

Hambleton only laughed. "As a matter of fact, I hoped this young rascal might grace us with his presence, thinking he might aid my cause." He reached for a third cup and placed it at the side of the table without a chair. "Nash will fetch a seat," he said, knowing his nephew would do it himself.

Before the butler could move from his post by the tea service, Josh picked up a delicate Queen Anne chair with one hand and placed it beside the table, then slid into it. "Lemon, Miss Edgewater?" he inquired.

"As a matter of fact, I prefer cream," she said tightly. He gave her a knowing wink that his uncle could not see, but which spoke volumes to her in some odd, subliminal way. *What is he doing to me?* she wondered as he beat Nash to the punch again, pouring a generous amount of the rich stuff into her cup. In fact, she did prefer lemon, but she'd have choked before admitting he was right.

Once the three of them had been served tea and small plates filled with delicacies, the earl dismissed his trusted servant and inquired, "You wished to get right down to business, I believe, Miss Edgewater?"

Teacup halfway to her lips, Sabrina nearly sloshed the liquid over the rim as his direct gaze met hers. This was a formidable man. She must be most careful not to make him her enemy . . . if her disastrous encounters with his nephew had not done so already. "I believe that would be best. Please understand my position. I cannot teach gentlemen if I intend to continue teaching young ladies."

"The way I see it," Josh interjected dryly, "you have two problems here. First off, we both know I'm no gentleman." He did not bother to acknowledge the agreement he saw in her eyes. "Second, the way I hear it, you don't have any more young ladies to teach."

"And to whom do I owe that calamity?" she shot back, bristling at him, then attempting a more conciliatory expression when she turned to the earl. "My lord, being a spinster lady, I have no other means of survival if all my patronesses withdraw their charges from me."

If she expected a plea to soften the heart of such a shrewd bargainer, the lady was in for quite a surprise. Looking not the least bit sympathetic, Hambleton replied, "Ah, but your ultimate hope for employment is not in teaching wealthy young heiresses, is it, my dear Miss Edgewater?"

Sabrina carefully set her cup in its saucer and shoved away the crumpet spread with clotted cream. "What do you mean?" she asked, holding her breath.

"Only that you wish to be headmistress of a school for indigent young women," the earl said in a fatherly fashion.

Josh raised his eyebrows, and through a bite of flaky pastry asked, "Indigent? Doesn't that mean they can't pay for schoolin'? What kinda business plan is that?"

"I fail to see that it is an unrealistic or unrewarding goal. Not everyone expects to become rich, my lord," she replied indignantly to Josh. Then she turned back to the earl. "There are hundreds—no, thousands of young women toiling in factories and even starving in the streets because they lack the education to better their lot in life. If I could reach only a small portion of them—girls who are desperate to rise up and become self-sufficient in honorable professions—I would consider my life well spent."

As she spoke, Josh watched her face transform. The frosty anger was replaced by a fervent glow. Her eyes turned from darkest blue to sparkling sapphire, and her cheeks bloomed with delicate color. Even her lips . . . well, he'd better not pay too much attention to her lips or he'd end up ruining everything.

"And so you shall, my dear," the earl said in a kindly voice. "I believe we can come to an agreement which will achieve both your goal and ours."

Sabrina gave him a wary look. "How could that be?"

"Why, I will fund your school, of course. It will, I believe, take a considerable endowment to establish such an enterprise, am I not correct? Furthermore," he continued before she could do more than close her small open mouth, "I shall see to it that my friends and associates in the House of Lords give you their support as well. You will require a staff of at least a dozen, I would imagine. Teachers, maids, a clerk, a driver . . . after all, a lady such as you cannot just go about places such as Seven Dials and select candidates from the rookeries, now can you?"

This was so far beyond the modest one-woman operation Sabrina had imagined that it made her head spin. Why, she could . . . No! She stopped the fantasy, realizing that he was buying her as if she were some commodity, a piece of jewelry or rare book such as those lining the walls of this room.

Josh could see the warning signs. Her desire to achieve her dream was warring with her pride. And he knew Sabrina Edgewater had as much of that as he did. His uncle was overplaying his hand. Leaning back lazily in his chair, Josh made a show of brushing pastry flakes from his dark jacket as he drawled, "Oh, I wouldn't doubt Miss Edgewater'd have the nerve to walk straight into the gates of Hades if the notion took her. But there's one thing she's afraid of—me."

His green eyes were dancing as he studied her with unnerving arrogance. She fought the urge to fling the teapot at him and scald the most indelicate part of his anatomy. "I am not afraid of you, my lord. I merely find the idea of working with a 'gentleman' such as you"—she paused for the irony to sink in— "an impossibility."

"Why? I realize I'm plumb hopeless when it comes to knowing which fork to use and how to make polite conversation, but then, that's supposed to be your line of work, isn't it? If you can manage those rich fellows' spoiled little darlings, I can't rightly see how much harder it could be to teach me."

"Then you not only lack manners but intelligence as well," she snapped.

"Think of it this way," Josh said calmly. "I was so poor I couldn't buy hay for a nightmare—just like those girls you want to rescue. I made a fortune, but didn't have time to learn fancy manners along the way. Now I want to learn and you can teach me . . . unless you don't have the sand to try."

As the two antagonists sat facing each other, Miss Edgewater leaning forward with her hands clutching the table and Joshua leaning back like a big, indolent cat, the earl remained silent, immensely enjoying their exchange. His face, however, revealed absolutely nothing. As if they'd notice if he turned bright purple and fell to the floor!

"That is patently absurd," she shot back.

"Oh, I'm not so sure. Maybe it's not that you think I can't learn. Maybe you're so skittish because you think you're not up to the job."

The rotter dared to wink at her again! He was laughing at her, in secret so his uncle could not tell. But she could! Sabrina had never been so infuriated by one human being in her entire life. Not even when Dex had . . . no, she forced that unhappy memory aside. If not for that man she wouldn't be in this deplorable position. Now another wretched male sat facing her with a smirk on his face, as if he intended to see her flap away like a titmouse with a tomcat on its tail.

Well, if he believed that, he was sadly mistaken. She would have her school and she would teach this Texas troglodyte the rudiments of civilized behavior—if she had to bash in what few brains he possessed to accomplish it! Standing up, she met his mocking green gaze head-on. The earl at once stood up as manners dictated. The troglodyte took a deliberate length of time to unfold his tall frame and do likewise. Throwing down the gauntlet, was he? She smiled coldly and turned to the earl.

"My lord, since you have given me no other option, I shall accept your most generous offer. I will teach your nephew the rudiments of socially acceptable behavior. In return, you will support my school."

Hambleton nodded. "You have my word on it."

She extended her hand to the earl in a businesslike gesture.

But before he could shake it, the troglodyte reached across the table and seized it, practically wrenching her off balance as he raised it to his lips for a mocking kiss.

"Now you're talking my lingo, ma'am," Josh said, inhaling the delicate scent of wildflowers at her wrist.

She refused to meet his eyes, knowing he would wink again. Instead, she smoothly pulled away and nodded to the earl. "I shall report tomorrow morning at nine promptly. Please see that your nephew is ready to begin his lessons. I suspect it will require a great deal of time to civilize this . . . student."

Hambleton chuckled. "I could not agree more, dear lady."

Josh reached down for another pastry as she spun and walked stiffly toward the door. The natural sway of her slim hips held him spellbound as he bit into a crumpet heaped with clotted cream, which dribbled down his chin.

As his nephew wiped his mouth on a napkin, the earl smiled slyly. Joshua detested clotted cream . . . but this little mishap was only the beginning of his troubles. Only the beginning.

"We shall commence with the rudiments of table etiquette," Sabrina said as they walked into the dining room, where two places had been set at the earl's imposing table. She was utterly exhausted after spending the morning explaining the order of precedence and address to the lout. Why was it so taxing for any person with average intelligence to grasp that a duke preceded a marquess, an earl a viscount? Or that an earl's wife was not an "earless" but a countess? She shuddered at the memory of that blunder. The rotter was making mistakes just to fluster her. Well, he would not get away with it.

Josh had enjoyed teasing her and loved the way she blushed whenever he made her go over the boring lists of which titles outranked which, and who was to be paired up with whom, and in what order they would progress into a dining room. He'd memorized everything the first time she'd explained it to him, but letting her off that easy would not have been any fun at all.

The same bothersome array of crystal, china and flatware he'd used at his first dinner with his uncle were once again laid out. "There are enough fixings here to serve a couple of dozen folks. Seems a pure waste of dishes if you ask me," he groused, genuinely disgusted by all the dirty dishes some poor cook's helpers would have to wash.

"This is the manner in which people of consequence dine. You are now a viscount and must appear conversant with such details."

"Miss Edgewater, do you just naturally talk like ole Bertie's mama lecturing a stable boy?"

"Our late and present sovereigns should never be spoken of with such irreverence."

Josh shrugged. "Oh, I like ole Bertie well enough, but his mama didn't do right by him. Too much highfalutin' fault-finding."

"Her Majesty was a woman of the greatest moral rectitude."

"Did you learn all those ten-dollar words reading Mr. Webster's whole dictionary?"

Sabrina stiffened. "I most certainly did no such thing."

"Sounds to me like you chewed up and swallowed down every last page."

"Ten-dollar words, as you so quaintly call them, are the mark of an educated person, my lord."

Stroking his jaw and staring down at his boots, he appeared to digest this for a moment as they stood in the doorway of the dining room. "Here I thought an educated man was supposed to be able to make himself clear to anybody he met . . . and make them feel comfortable talking with him."

"What a quaintly American idea. But might I remind you that you are no longer in America? Here you are Viscount Wesley, one day to be the eleventh Earl of Hambleton. Colloquial speech, among other things, is simply not acceptable."

"No, ma'am, I reckon I learned that on my first trip to New York . . . to talk to some banker fellows about investing my money."

He was flaunting his wealth. This lout was not only a peer of the realm, by the accident of a very indirect succession, but filthy rich in his own right, while she had been born into a good family and labored diligently all her life. Suddenly Sabrina felt shabby in her one remaining decent day dress. Life was simply not fair, but that was that and she had a job to do, she scolded herself. "Discussing money during social occasions is considered déclassé."

"Oh, what should we discuss, then?" he asked.

"That would depend upon those present at a dinner. Social events, the weather, music and the arts are always suitable topics. Literature is an excellent choice. If you are engaged in conversation with an M.P., you might discuss issues pending in Parliament. But, of course, first you must begin reading so that you may grasp the complexities of modern society."

"You have a reading list in mind?" he asked innocently.

Sabrina nodded. "Certainly. For history, I would suggest Thomas Carlyle and Sir George Trevelyan."

Josh nodded. "Seems like I've heard a thing or two about them."

"I would also suggest a few of Mr. Shakespeare's plays. Perhaps *The Merchant of Venice* might be to your liking."

"I got more of a boot out of *Macbeth*. Now, his wife was a woman after your own heart. Portia's too tame."

Sabrina blinked, too startled by his revelation to acknowledge the implied insult in his remarks. "You've read Shakespeare?" she managed to ask.

"I liked *Lear* and ole *Julius Caesar*, but *Hamlet*, he was a little wishy-washy to my way of thinking. Carlyle would approve of the general but not the prince." He positively loved the way she stood with that delectable little mouth rounded in a small "O" of amazement. Only by exercising the greatest restraint was he able to keep from planting a kiss right on it.

"It would seem, my lord, that you are concealing a surprising amount of erudition behind a crude unlettered facade," she finally managed tartly. "It was my understanding that you never attended university."

"Shucks, ma'am, I never attended grade school. But one of Gertie's girls . . . er, employees, Miss Cynthia, had a fair amount of book learning. She taught me to read and do sums and such. After that, well, it sorta came natural to start picking up books here and there. Sam Bixby was a traveling peddler who came through Pecos every few months. He'd always bring me some books he took in trade. Not much call for history and playwritings in west Texas. 'Sides, I'd always sneak him a bottle of whiskey from Gertie's liquor cabinet in return. She knew I did it but she didn't care."

Sabrina digested what he was telling her, noting the faraway expression on his face as he spoke of what must have been a ghastly childhood. Yet he smiled fondly at the memories. Those green eyes were not mocking. Wistful, perhaps? *What kind of man are you, Joshua Cantrell?* For the first time since she had met him, she sensed an intelligence and a vulnerability she would never before have imagined.

"Then the newspaper accounts of your childhood are accurate?" she blurted out.

"You mean, was I raised in a bordello?" A harsh scowl replaced his softened smile. "Yes. I never knew my ma or pa. Gert and her girls were all the family I had, but they were good enough for me."

"I didn't mean to imply—"

"Let's just get on with dining like 'people of consequence,'" he interrupted, striding into the dining room and plopping down on the chair at the side of the table.

He looked for all the world like a petulant little boy who'd just been spanked for saying a bad word. She was not certain whether to be charmed by his protectiveness toward the unfortunates who'd raised him or chagrined at her own gaffe in asking about them. Sabrina couldn't believe she was having such unprofessional thoughts.

You are the tutor and he is your pupil, nothing more, she reminded herself. "We can only have our dinner

107

lesson if you first act like a gentleman and seat me. And remember," she added in her most pedagogical tone, "since you are the viscount and I your guest, you will sit at the head of the table."

Grudgingly he scooted back his chair, stood up and held it for her, muttering something about wishing for Aphrodite and getting stuck with Athena.

"My, even Greek mythology. I am impressed, Lord Wesley. Now let us proceed with dinner. First the soup course . . ."

Josh had learned enough by watching his uncle and the other men at his club to know how this exercise in dirtying dishes went. It was, after all, simple enough to watch which utensil and glass everyone else picked up and follow suit. But her curiosity about his childhood with Gertie and the girls bothered him in ways he did not want to admit. He was lucky Gert had taken him in, and he'd never be ashamed of them. What gave so-called "good women" like Miss Sabrina Edgewater the right to look down their noses at as fine a human being as Gertie Greer? And why the hell should he care what Miss Edgewater thought of his upbringing anyway?

When the young dark-haired maid Sally ladled out two servings of consommé, he couldn't resist. He'd act just the way Miss High 'n Mighty Sabrina expected him to. After all, he hated to disappoint a lady.

Sabrina watched in utter stupefaction while he picked up the bowl in both hands, pinkie fingers carefully raised as if he were holding a Sevres teacup, and swallowed a giant gulp of clear broth!

"Now, that's tasty." He wiped his mouth with the back of his hand. "But you might mention to the cook that adding a few beans and a chili pepper or two might give a little body to it. Know what I mean?" he said conversationally to the maid, who stood rooted like a sapling to the floor.

The young woman nodded dumbly, sending a pleading look in Sabrina's direction.

"Lord Wesley," Sabrina said in her most teacher-stern voice, "one never drinks one's soup!" She raised the soup spoon and dipped it carefully in the liquid, waiting for him to do the same.

"Aw, that way I'll drip on my shirt. Oh, well," he added in resignation, plucking his napkin from the table and tucking one corner into his cravat. "Uncle Ab told me not to do this, but if you insist on the spoon—"

"Please place your napkin on your lap. A man approaching three decades should have better dexterity than a boy of three years," she said in a dulcet tone.

Innocently he shrugged and complied.

After the remove, an aspic of salmon was brought out. Josh eyed it suspiciously. "This is one fancy notion I'll never cotton to," he said, shoving the jiggling platter back toward the maid, who again looked helplessly at Sabrina.

"Don't you care for salmon?" Sabrina asked, perplexed. Did Texans eat nothing but those horned cows?

"It isn't the fish, it's the jelly stuff it's smothered in. Where I come from, folks make it a practice never to eat anything that moves faster than they do."

"This isn't where you came from. This is England. And you will learn to appreciate aspic." By this time her toe was tapping beneath the table.

Josh could sense her agitation and fought the grin that was itching to break out like sunrise. Lordy, he was starting to get a real kick out of deviling this female. Manfully he used the right fork and took a few bites, after scraping away as much of the gelatinous coating as he could.

He was disappointed when the vegetable course did not contain peas, but in luck when he glanced at the glass Sally was filling with yet another variety of wine—red wine. Then she carried in the meat course, a crown roast of lamb with chop frills covering each rib bone. Carefully the maid placed the crown roast at the side of his plate for him to carve.

"I never much cared for red wine," he said, scooting back his chair. "That's why I keep something that goes better with a hunk of meat."

Sabrina watched as he stepped over to the sideboard and opened a polished door, taking out a half-empty bottle with a cork shoved into it. After using his strong white teeth as an opener, he walked back to the table and sat down with the bottle by his side.

"Now, let's see about this meat. No offense to the cook, but it looks kinda bony. That why they put these little mittens on the bones sticking out?" he asked Sally, who by this time just nodded dumbly, not daring to look in Sabrina's direction.

Sabrina watched in stunned horror as he ignored the carving knife and used his hands to tear apart the rib bones, separating the juicy meat of the chops into dripping hunks. He placed one three-rib slab on her plate, liberally sprinkling the tablecloth with pink splotches en route, then took another four ribs and plunked them on his own plate.

He looked at her and winked, then used the napkin on his lap to wipe his hands, saying, "Thought I'd forget, didn't you?"

Before Sabrina could form a response, he picked up the bottle labeled "Who Shot John" and took a generous pull, after which he replaced it by his side and tore into the rare lamb. He separated one rib from the others and tossed the frill on his plate, then commenced to gnaw the meat from the bone.

How dearly Sabrina wished to leap across the table and use that hateful napkin to strangle the life out of him! Better yet, seize that bottle of vile-smelling spirits and break it over his Neanderthal head! Suppressing those exceedingly unladylike although comforting visions, she said in the iciest tone she could muster, "You have made sport of me and this young woman quite beyond enough, my lord. We shall leave you to drink yourself insensate in solitude, since your company is too barbaric to be endured by anyone with a modicum of decent manners. When you are prepared to resume your lessons in earnest, you may apologize and perhaps—*perhaps* I shall return."

With that, she stood up, dismissed the red-faced servant, who went scurrying into the kitchen, and stormed toward the door.

Chapter 7

"Now don't take on like this. I was only funning, honest." Josh tossed down his napkin and stood up as Sabrina stomped out the door. Muttering an oath, he quickly followed.

"Your idea of humor would disgust the emperor Nero, my lord," Sabrina said when he overtook her in the foyer, blocking her path to the front door. "And you nearly gave that poor maid the vapors."

"Aw, Sally'll be all right. She knows how to take a joke. Only thing is, she was afraid to laugh because she thought you might fire her."

Sally. The chit was young and quite pretty. "Obviously, I have no authority to dismiss any of Lord Hambleton's staff and *Sally* knows it," Sabrina snapped, appalled at her sudden twinge of jealousy. She immediately quashed it. "As to my sense of humor," she quickly continued, "when something is genuinely amusing, I shall laugh. Perhaps the customs are different in Texas, but here one does not find

112

amusement at the expense of another. You were making sport of me."

Oh, I'd love to make sport with *you*, he thought, but he said, "That wasn't what I was doing. I was poking fun at myself. Well"—he hesitated and grinned— "maybe I was funning the way I thought you expected me to act, too," he confessed. "I apologize. Will you give me another chance?"

When he looked at her with that earnest schoolboy expression on his all-too-handsome face, those green eyes seemed to pierce right down to her soul. How could she refuse? *You need the money.* She assured herself that was the only reason she would agree. "If I do, I insist on your word as a . . . Texan that you'll try no more such shenanigans, but be a diligent pupil."

Josh put up his hands in mock surrender. "You nailed me, ma'am. Since I'm no gentleman, I could welch on that, but my honor as a Texan . . . well, that's another matter. I give you my word. No more jokes . . . at least none on purpose."

Sabrina looked uncertain for a moment, but the smile twitching at the corners of her mouth gave her away. She had bested him. And enjoyed it. "Very well. However, consider yourself on probation from here on."

He nodded. "Fair enough. We could go back and finish that lamb. I promise to use my knife and fork."

"I believe you've placed sufficient strain on the kitchen staff for one day. The afternoon might be more profitably spent working on drawing-room conversation."

"You mean you're going to give me another list—

this time of things I can't talk about in front of womenfolk?" he suggested with a grin.

"Among other things, yes. Your manners in the presence of ladies must be impeccable. For example, you must always see that a lady is seated before you take your own seat," she began, ticking off things on the fingers of her hand. "You should immediately rise when a lady enters a room, a matter about which you are not in the least attentive. When no servant is present to do so, you must always open a door and hold it for a lady. If the weather is cool, you should assist her in donning her cloak before going outdoors and in removing it when you reach your destination, if it is indoors."

Visions of "assisting" her in the removal of considerably more than a coat flashed through his mind as his eyes swept down her diminutive, curvaceous body. Josh could imagine the velvety feel of her pale English skin, flowing like silk beneath his caresses. He had to get a grip on his fancies or she'd be storming out of here again, mad as a rattler with the piles.

He extended his arm to her gallantly and said, "I reckon bowing and scraping for ladies is pretty much like eating dinner. Just watch how the other fellows do it and follow suit. I picked up a few things on business trips to New York and Chicago. Of course, even the richest Yankees can't match the English as gents, so I'll have to practice . . ."

His smile was enough to reduce her to a puddle of porridge. Gingerly she placed her hand on his arm and allowed him to lead her toward the front parlor. Sabrina knew she was treading on dangerous ground with this man. He was not only a foreigner but a member of the peerage, the likes of whom she had never before met. He was self-educated and proud, highly intelligent and possessed of a most unpredictable sense of humor.

And he exuded an aura of . . . what to call it? Untrammeled maleness? Wicked virility? No mere words did justice to the effect he had on her, always keeping her off balance. It must simply be his alien background. The more she learned about him, the better she could understand what made him behave as he did. Then she could deal with him as if he were any other man.

You know that is pure rubbish.

If the Texas viscount felt the faint tremor that passed from her hand through his coat sleeve, he did not reveal it as he ushered her through the door.

Instead, he smiled as he offered her a seat on the settle, hoping to join her there. Sabrina shook her head and sat instead on a chair across from it. "A lady and gentleman who are not affianced do not sit side by side," she said primly, struggling to keep her tone formal and instructive. But she knew he wanted to sit next to her, and that simple fact flustered her as she struggled to gather her scattered thoughts and begin another lesson.

If only he didn't fold himself into his seat with such negligent ease. His long legs stretched beneath the low table between them as he leaned back and grinned at her. She was so acutely *aware* of him. Each time he walked into a room, it seemed to grow smaller, filled with his Texas-sized presence.

And sexual aura. Sabrina felt her skin tingle as she suppressed the thought.

"Now, Miss Edgewater, what shall we talk about? Or maybe I should say, what *shouldn't* we talk about?"

The sly insinuation was not lost on her, but she stiffened her spine and ignored it. "I think it best if we simply begin conversing. I shall correct you as we proceed."

"Oh, I'd bet my best Santa Gertrudis stud bull on that," he said dryly.

"Perhaps when in an agricultural setting, the mention of . . . stud bulls would be appropriate, but not in a drawing room."

He nodded, not in the least chastened. "Well, it surely is a beautiful afternoon." He looked to her for confirmation. When she nodded approval, he continued, "The sun's shining to beat all, and the breeze is enough to cool the sweat—"

"Perspiration is not acceptable," she interjected.

Josh sighed. "This is harder than herding cats."

"We could discuss literature. Who is your favorite poet?"

"Ladies first. Who's yours?" he countered.

Sabrina smiled. "That is a difficult decision. Shakespeare's sonnets, Shelley, Wordsworth, Tennyson . . . but perhaps most of all Matthew Arnold. I particularly admire 'Dover Beach.'" Sabrina waited, wondering if in his eclectic readings he was familiar with this favorite of hers.

"A dark view of life and love. In fact, downright depressing."

"But the poet's words are vivid . . . and accurate."

He studied her with open curiosity. "A beautiful woman like you must've had lots of chances to marry. But you didn't. Why, I wonder?"

Sabrina cursed her errant tongue. She'd betrayed too much, mentioning that poem. This man was far too keen an observer of human nature. "That is a most personal question, and a gentleman never comments on the marital status of a lady," she replied.

He nodded at the rebuke. "You're right. None of

my business. As to my favorites . . . well, on this side of the pond, I'd have to go with Browning."

"I assume you mean Robert, not Elizabeth Barrett," she said.

"Most women swoon over her love poetry. You don't fancy it?"

"She's far too emotional. Maudlin."

Josh shook his head and grinned at her. "You're a hard woman, Miss Edgewater."

Sabrina could not resist returning his smile. "One who'll teach you to act like a gentleman yet."

They continued discussing various topics, with Sabrina interjecting corrections to his colorful speech wherever she deemed it appropriate. He accepted her instruction with good grace, finding that beneath her starch propriety she did indeed possess a sense of humor and bright wit. That combined with the delicious little package it was wrapped in made him even more anxious to lure her into his bed. She was unique. Independent.

Unlike so many fancy ladies he'd met since he'd become rich, she was completely uninterested in luring him into matrimony. Her standoffishness only heightened the challenge. Sabrina Edgewater was an enigma. Why would a lovely woman want to devote her life to educating indigent girls? Was her uniqueness merely the difference between more materialistic American females and their class-conscious English counterparts, or was there some secret hurt buried in her past that made her shy away from a conventional family life?

Eventually he'd find out. He was good at figuring people. That and plain back-busting hard work had made him successful in business. And business now concerned just two things—finding out how to stop the assassination of the Japanese minister and learning what made Sabrina Edgewater tick. Maybe the two could be combined . . .

As he walked her to the gate late that afternoon, the Hambleton carriage he'd summoned stood waiting. "I could pay for a hansom," she protested, but Josh had seen her walk up the street that morning and knew she could ill afford much in the way of fares for a public conveyance.

"Consider it a perquisite of working for Uncle Ab," he said with a grin.

"Do you actually call His Lordship that to his face?" she practically whispered.

Josh chuckled. "Sure. I think he likes it. He doesn't have much in the way of kin left. Just a few nieces who live a ways off and hardly ever visit. They have their own families to keep them busy."

"That must be lonely," Sabrina said thoughtfully, grateful for her parents, even though she did not get to visit them nearly as often as she would like.

"I have a favor to ask," Josh said as he dutifully opened the gate while the coachman jumped from his box and let down the steps to the carriage.

Sabrina looked curiously at him. "What is it?"

"Well, I have this invitation to watch a bunch of toe dancers tonight. Some fancy Russian bunch."

"Ballet?" Sabrina could not keep the excitement from her voice. "You mean the Saint Petersburg Company's production of *Swan Lake*?"

He looked glum. "Only time I saw a ballet was in New York a couple of years ago. I don't much cotton to watching a bunch of men tippy-toeing around a stage. Would you mind going with me? To sorta keep me out of trouble?"

"It wouldn't be at all proper for a viscount to escort

a tutor to such an elegant event," she forced herself to reply even though she would have given anything to see the world-famous Russian ballet.

Josh shook his head. He could tell by the glow in her eyes that she loved that fool toe-dancing stuff. "Always the proper woman of business. Just consider it part of my schooling. I know you attend balls with your young female charges. We danced at one, remember?"

"How could I forget?" She tried to sound cross at the awful spectacle they'd created, but failed. "But that is different. I remain in the background and merely encourage my students when they make their first outings . . . well, normally I remain in the background," she added with an accusing look that did not come off quite as sternly as she intended.

Taking her hand to assist her up the steps, he said, "I'll be by to pick you up at eight. I'll need a lot of encouragement to sit through this Tchaikovsky fellow's toe dancers."

"I don't know—"

"Remember, you're my teacher and I need help," he reminded her solemnly.

"That is blackmail, my lord," she replied as a tiny smile curved her lips and sparkled in her uncertain eyes. Her mind was already whirling with thoughts of whether she owned any dress that could possibly be suitable for such an occasion.

Sabrina stood in front of the mirror inspecting her gown. It was horribly old, one her mother had sewn for her trousseau over eight years earlier, but it was made of good quality silk in an odd shade of coppery gold that set off the highlights in her hair. She had been well taught by her mother and had reworked

119

the outmoded style, changing the trim and narrowing the skirt.

How greatly she would have appreciated Gilda's help at a time such as this, but her lifelong maid and companion had returned home to be with an elder brother who'd been taken ill several weeks earlier. She knew it was unseemly for her to live in private quarters such as this without a chaperone, but she could certainly not afford to hire a replacement for her old friend, who worked for little more than room and board. Well, it could not be helped. She was a respectable woman of business, and the only gentleman caller she ever allowed inside her home was her cousin Edmund.

Thinking of Eddy made her wish he would repay some of the money he owed her. Then she might have been able to make a few modest purchases to enhance her wardrobe, such as buying new slippers—or hats to replace those victimized by the viscount. Glumly she looked down at the scuffed toes of her only dress shoes, which did not match her gown. Well, a bit of polish and they'd simply have to do. In a darkened theater, who would see them anyway? Or notice that her grandmother's reticule was missing a few beads after years of use?

The Texan most probably would not.

Odd, but she'd begun thinking of him that way. A Texan. Yet he was also a viscount and the heir to one of the most prestigious titles in Britain, a man far above her station. "Don't be ridiculous," she murmured to herself. *You vowed all those years ago never to marry, and even if you changed your mind, he'd never consider a nobody such as you.* A man such as he was interested in only one thing from a woman like her. Once burned, twice shy.

Her ruminations were interrupted by the oddest racket. A strange puffing roar, almost like a train engine only not nearly so loud, followed by the neighing of horses and the angry cries of men on the street below. Sabrina went to the window and looked down. One of those new horseless carriages had just pulled up in front of the building and Viscount Wesley was stepping out of it!

The engine noises of the rumbling contraptions always frightened carriage horses and angered their drivers, although the sounds were becoming increasingly common on London's streets in recent years. But she'd never seen such a grand vehicle as the shiny white one he was driving. It had four wheels with elaborately decorated spokes and lush-looking black leather seats. Brass and chrome gleamed like newly minted coins.

In a moment he was knocking at her door. Swallowing for courage, she gave her hair a final pat and went to greet him. He stood there in a splendid suit of black kerseymere that fitted his tall frame with the perfection of fine tailoring. Every detail on his person was coordinated, right down to the emerald shirt studs that matched his eyes. She felt like a poor relation being escorted to a country dance by a rich city cousin.

Josh drank in the vision she made with her hair piled in a sleek pouf of some sort, accented simply by a sprig of fresh flowers. Her gown was an odd color that matched her hair, and the low vee of the neckline revealed considerable charms, although she wore only a tiny cross on a delicate gold chain. "You look pretty as an acre of pregnant red hogs," he blurted out before realizing how such a remark would be greeted by a teacher of decorum.

"My lord—"

"Let me try again," he interrupted with an engaging smile. "My dear Miss Edgewater, you look ravishing tonight. How's that?"

The smile, as usual, was contagious. "An infinite improvement," she replied as she turned to reach for her shawl. He dutifully helped her arrange it around her shoulders. Although he did nothing really indecorous, the slight touch of his hands on her bare skin was enough to send a shiver tingling down her spine. She quickly sought distraction by asking about his vehicle.

"I've never ridden in a horseless carriage before," she said breathlessly as they descended the stairs from her apartment to the street.

"Then you're in for a real treat—and it isn't a horseless carriage. It's a Daimler Mercedes 25/28 with a four-cylinder engine and chain drive. Designed by Wilhelm Maybach and named after the daughter of one of Herr Daimler's investors. Right pretty, isn't it?" he asked with obvious pride.

Sabrina had to admit it was. "Yes, I've never seen one like it. I've certainly never ridden in one. All that talk about cylinders and chain drives is way beyond what I've learned in books."

"The advances in engineering are made by hands-on hard work and . . . can I say it?—sweat." Josh whispered the word.

Sabrina laughed. "I suppose since we're discussing a horseless carriage, it's permissible."

"Ah, but there's that an old-fashioned term again. This is an automobile," he said as he opened the gleaming passenger door and helped her take a seat inside.

The leather was smooth as satin and amazingly

comfortable. She watched as he walked around to the front of the vehicle and whirled the starter crank, firing up the engine. Then he slid behind the steering wheel on the seat beside her. Even in an open carriage—no, automobile, she corrected herself—he seemed to take up all her space. "I would have believed a true Texan such as you would want nothing to do with anything that replaced his horse," she murmured.

Josh looked at her as if she'd just announced the world was flat. "Nothing will ever replace a fine horse, for riding pleasure or to work stock. But this is the future, complete with factories and assembly lines. One day everyone around the world will depend on internal combustion engines to get them where they hanker to go. That's why I invested in Mr. Daimler's company," he said as the vehicle moved forward.

She knew he was a wealthy rancher, but this side of Joshua Cantrell surprised her. "I had no idea you dealt in anything but cattle."

He watched the approach of several hansoms and allowed plenty of room before steering into the street. "I only made my first money in cattle. Once I bought the land and improved my herds, I started reading up on other ways to make money."

"How very American, my lord," she said with a mischievous grin.

"It's the Texan in me, I reckon. We always think more is better," he replied. Then studying her, he said, "When you smile like that, your eyes glow like a full moon on a clear winter night."

The compliment flustered her. "You're very kind, my lo—"

"Just between us, ma'am, could you call me Josh? I

get mighty tired of being lordshiped to death around the house. I've tried to get Nash and his staff to loosen up their starched collars a mite, but they won't budge."

"Servants would scarcely be comfortable in Christian naming a member of the peerage," she replied.

His green eyes turned dark as he said, "You aren't a servant."

"I am in Lord Hambleton's employ . . . and yours."

"As a tutor, not a maid."

She sighed. "You must understand the way our class system works. It's highly improper for employees and employers to become familiar. It can lead to all sorts of . . . difficulties."

"Especially if the employer and employee are a man and a woman?" He noted the heightened color in her cheeks and smiled inwardly. She wasn't as prim and indifferent to him as she wanted him to think.

"Especially, my lord." Her tone was emphatic. "Tell me more about your investments. What makes you so certain these automobiles will replace horses as basic transportation?" she asked as the engine sputtered and he worked a combination of mysterious hand and foot levers and instruments until the rough ride once again smoothed out.

"Speed, for one thing. Folks are always wanting to get places faster, and trains can only take them where rails are laid. This car has the power of thirty-five horses under the engine. It can go over fifty miles in an hour, and every year the speed increases." At the look of horror on her face as she clutched her hands to the seat, he laughed and added, "Don't worry. I'd never race it on a crowded city street—or ruin a lady's hairdo."

She watched as he drove slowly, keeping pace with the carriages around them. Now and again a horse would shy, but animals and drivers were getting used to the newfangled vehicles. They passed several other automobiles en route to the theater, although none were so grand and smooth-riding as the Texan's Mercedes.

"This is really quite exhilarating," she admitted.

Josh looked pleased. "Well, one day we'll take a spin in the countryside. Wear your hair down and I'll show you what this beauty can do." The image of Sabrina with her mane of bronze hair flying wildly behind her made his groin tighten.

She made a mock tsking sound. "Lord Wesley, a lady never appears in public with her hair unbound."

"Now, that's a fool idea if ever I heard one. Hair as beautiful as yours shouldn't be covered up with hats or tied up with pins. If we went horseback riding, you'd bounce that fancy hairdo loose quicker than I can . . . well, right quick," he hastily amended.

An amused light danced in her eyes as she imagined the word he'd intended to say. "Spit." It just popped out of her mouth before she could stop herself. Immediately, she covered her lips with both hands, horrified at what she'd done.

Josh threw back his head and let out a rich, deep chuckle. "Couldn'ta said it better myself, ma'am."

When they pulled up in front of the theater, Josh waited as the doorman assisted her from the automobile, then said, "Give me a shake or two to stable this out back and I'll be right with you."

Sabrina nodded. Then as he pulled away, she turned to the large posters at the front of the building. Most were of the famous lead ballerina, Natasha

Samsonov, whose photographs indicated that she was quite a dramatic beauty. Attending a performance of the Saint Petersburg Company performing currently in London had been a dream Sabrina had never imagined could come true.

And to ride in a horseless carriage besides! She felt like doing something she hadn't since she had been ten years old—throw out her arms and spin in a circle, giving a shout of pure excitement. How long had it been since she'd felt joyous and free? She gave herself a mental shake. Her life *was* as she had made it and she *was* free, she reminded herself. Free to come and go, to earn her own way, beholden to no man.

But you are beholden to the Texan.

As if her thoughts had conjured him, he walked calmly around the corner with two other men, one dark, stocky and short, the other taller, pale and thin. Both looked distinctly foreign. Although they were speaking English with French accents, she knew instinctively that they were Russian. How extraordinary that the viscount would be friends with them, for the Russian émigré community was notoriously snobbish and closed to outsiders.

Then she heard a woman's voice call out, and all three men stopped as a carriage pulled up beside them and another foreign-looking man jumped to the cobblestones. A black-haired woman stepped down. Joshua Cantrell's gallantry in helping her alight was faultless. Her beauty was unmistakable, even from this distance.

She was the prima ballerina Natasha Samsonov.

Chapter 8

Hell, what do I do now? Josh kissed La Samsonov's hand, which she had extended to him as if she were Catherine the Great and he a serf being offered the highest honor imaginable. She had to be the key to the leak of information from the Foreign Office, and he knew he could not pass up the opportunity to see what he could learn from her. But he could also see Sabrina from the corner of his eye glaring daggers at him.

"So, you are the wild Americain from Texas," Natasha said with a thick French accent. Without giving him warning, a pair of slender gloved hands pulled open his jacket to reveal his Colt Lightning in a shoulder sling.

Alexi burst into raucous laughter and Sergei scowled, but her brother Nikolai merely sneered down his long blade of a nose as if his sister's antics bored him.

"It is so! You do carry a six-killer," she exclaimed.

"It's a six-shooter, ma'am," he corrected her. "Made in America by ole Sam Colt." Josh was unnerved by the unnatural brightness of her cold black eyes. The idea of his being armed excited her—that and, he imagined, the simple fact that he was a foreigner from an exotic land.

"I have heard about your first day here in London, my lord Texas Viscount. After you watch me dance, we must drink good vodka and you may tell me all about this Texas."

"I don't much favor vodka. How about I bring some real Texas whiskey for you to try?" he replied with his most disarming grin.

She cocked her head as if considering, letting her gaze once more sweep over him from head to toe in that disconcertingly blatant sexual appraisal while the Russian men observed. Apprarently they were used to her behavior, but Josh was not. Even the most brazen harlots he'd met in cattle towns from Texas to the Dakotas were downright reserved compared to this imperious female. She would be no one to fool with. But he had a job to do. He'd promised the colonel.

"Come to my dressing room after the performance," she commanded and started to turn toward the side door where the performers entered.

"I regret I can't do that, ma'am," he drawled.

She turned, a look of disbelief on her beautiful face. The prima ballerina was not accustomed to being turned down. Josh smiled apologetically. "I have a lady with me and I'll have to see her home first. How about meeting at the White Satin after?"

A tiny smirk moved across her lips. "Very well. Bring your Americain whiskey and I shall taste it."

With that she swished away in a trail of gardenia perfume, Nikolai following behind her. Alexi and his companion Sergei congratulated Josh on piqueing La

Samsonov's interest. Somehow Josh didn't feel particularly lucky in that regard, especially when he drew near the spot where Sabrina waited. Quickly he made his excuses to the two Russians, who cast sultry gazes in Miss Edgewater's direction. Lordy, all he needed was to have her brain one of them with that little bitty beaded purse of hers and he'd be in a real pickle!

"You gave me to believe that you were not an admirer of 'toe dancers,' Lord Wesley," she said coolly as he drew near.

"Never claimed to be. More like the toe dancer's an admirer of Texans. Kinda surprised me. I only met her once a while back. Don't much care for her, though. A dangerous female. Reminds me of a hungry cougar," he said lightly as he tucked Sabrina's hand on his arm and escorted her inside the theater.

Somehow she intuited that his light words concealed some deeper meaning. "How did you meet those Russian gentlemen?" she asked.

"Oh, a friendly game of cards. One thing led to another and they took me to a drinking establishment a lady like you wouldn't know about."

"I should hope not," she murmured beneath her breath. The theater was lavishly appointed with royal-blue velvet curtains, Turkish carpeting in rich blue and maroon shades and an enormous crystal chandelier that filled the lobby with glittering light. Wealthy patrons dressed in silks and jewels laughed and chatted gaily, but the magic of her first trip to the ballet was gone. Stolen by the star of the performance . . . who had ensnared her Texan.

Her Texan?

Sabrina gave herself a mental shake. What on earth made her think of him as hers, for goodness sake?

The viscount seated her in the Hambleton box and took her wrap, laying it over the back of her chair.

"Very proper, my lord," she said politely. She could not help the icicles dripping from her voice.

Brrr. He could tell by her tone and the stiffness of her posture that she was jealous. He could not help but be pleased by the reaction. Of course, he had to meet with the prima donna tonight, and that wouldn't help his pursuit of Sabrina. "You sound colder than a blue norther sweeping down the Panhandle," he whispered in her ear, letting his breath caress the delicate lobe.

The warmth spread from her ear all the way to her toes, but Sabrina refused to give the rogue the satisfaction of detecting any reaction. Mercifully, the curtain rose on the first act of *Swan Lake* and Tchaikovsky's marvelous music filled the huge theater. She ignored her companion and concentrated on the stage.

Wilfred Hodgins arranged the papers on Lord Hambleton's desk with his usual precise efficiency. He had served the old earl for nearly two decades and knew exactly how everything should be done. That young pup Edmund Whistledown did not have the faintest aptitude for the work. Irritated, Hodgins checked the tall case clock in the corner of the room. As usual, the boy was late. It was after eight in the evening. His simple errand should not have taken more than an hour, and he'd been dispatched well before five.

"I take it Mr. Whistledown is tardy once again," the earl said as he entered his office.

"Do you wish me to discharge him, my lord?" Hodgins asked without betraying any eagerness in his carefully measured tone.

Just then a light tap sounded on the office door. At the earl's summons, Edmund entered, looking flushed and breathless. "My sincerest apologies for taking so long, Lord Hambleton, but there was a hackney accident on the bridge and all traffic was blocked. I did deliver the papers to Mr. Whitney just as I was instructed," he added eagerly.

Hambleton found it painful to watch the nervous youth shuffle from one foot to the other, like an overeager puppy trying desperately to please. He waved the youth away, saying, "As long as Lord Ashcroft's secretary has the trade agreement in hand before the marquess leaves for his grouse shoot, there's no harm done."

"You'll need to collect the signed documents on the morrow. Be here at nine sharp for any additional errands," Hodgins added as the youth backed awkwardly toward the door.

"Yes, sir. I will, sir."

"Need you be so hard on the lad, Hodgins?" the earl asked with a wry smile. "It would seem that I remember your being late a time or two when you started working for me back in . . ."

"That would be 1882, my lord . . . and it was only once. The day I broke my leg."

Hambleton cleared his throat, suppressing a chuckle. "Yes, I believe you're right. Ah, Hodgins, the first thing to deteriorate in advanced age is certainly not the mind, but 'tis a sad thing when it does nonetheless."

"Nonsense. You are every bit as keenly intelligent as you were the day I met you, my lord," Hodgins protested.

"Let us hope you are correct. Now, down to business. Lansdowne has asked that all those working on the Japanese matter meet with him tonight. I should have a draft of the alliance when I return. It will require some close study . . ."

Outside the door, Edmund stood, trembling as he pulled the crumpled note from his coat pocket and reread it once again. Pray heaven he could keep this position, else he'd be dead by the end of the week.

The White Satin was crowded by the time Josh arrived. It had taken him an extra hour to see Sabrina home first. He had not attempted to soothe her ruffled feathers by making up excuses for leaving her off directly after the ballet. She was far too clever and would have guessed that he was meeting the beauteous Natasha. Instead, he had offered to take her for a long ride in the country in the Mercedes. Of course, she'd refused, saying it was highly improper for a lady and a gentleman who were not blood kin or affianced to be alone in the middle of nowhere late at night.

He'd acted disappointed and tried to steal a kiss when they reached her apartment, but she'd bested him. Her elderly landlady sat waiting at the door. He would have bet his best cutting horse that Sabrina had asked her to do precisely that. Their good nights had been brief and proper.

As he entered the smoky dark club, he smiled to himself. If she had to trust old women to stand watch over her virtue, the proper Miss Edgewater must not trust herself. Tomorrow, maybe he would invite her for a horseback ride through Hyde Park. What could be more decorous than that?

His thoughts were interrupted by a loud rhythmic burst of clapping that erupted near the back of the large room. A circle about a dozen feet in diameter had been cleared and five men stood inside it facing each other with tall glasses of vodka tilted to their mouths, drinking as fast as they could. Alexi won the contest, polishing off his drink before any of the others. As onlookers and participants slapped him on the back in congratulation, it was apparent this drink was far from his first of the night.

When he spotted the tall American moving through the crowd, the champion called out, "Josua, m-my fren, come join ush!"

Wonderful. Josh could still remember how his head had ached after their last drinking session. At least this time he'd come armed with some good bourbon. Josh scanned the room for the prima ballerina, who was conspicuously absent. " 'Pears to me you've already proved you're the baddest Cossack on the steppes, Alexi," he said dryly as his companion enveloped him in a fulsome bear hug.

The icy blond Sergei Valerian laughed drunkenly. "Are you afraid to stand up with us?"

"Nope. I'd be more afraid of falling down with you about now. You fellows have a good running start on the evening, and it's not even midnight," Josh replied in jocular fashion.

"He's English. How could he hold his liquor?" Nikolai Zarenko sneered, coming up behind Josh.

"By act of Parliament I'm a peer of this realm, but by birth I'm a Texan. Nothing'll ever change that," Josh replied, seeing no sign of his antagonist's sister. *Damned if I'll get in a brawl for no cussed reason.* "I brought some real sipping whiskey. Instead of drinking fast, why not taste what we swallow?" he said with a big smile. "It's the custom back in America."

"Yesh, custom of t-th country," Alexi slurred, eyeing the bottle of golden liquid his friend was holding up.

"First we'd better sit down," Josh said, carefully assisting Alexi to a large table near the back of the room.

He poured shots all around and passed them to the Russians. All but Alexi eyed the colored liquor with its distinctive perfume suspiciously. Josh lifted his glass and took a sip, then smacked his lips in appreciation. Alexi gulped the whole thing at once. A good thing Josh had more than one bottle stashed in his Mercedes outside. He had a feeling he'd need them all before this evening was over.

"You drink like a woman," Nikolai said, placing his glass on the polished oak table with a loud thud.

Alexi hiccuped. "Unlesh tha woman's your s-sis'er."

Josh met Zarenko's cold dark eyes and took his measure. For some reason, the Russian was spoiling for a fight. Was his sister's attraction to Josh the reason? He gauged the reaction around the table. Three of their crew were already nodding off. Everyone alert enough to follow the conversation waited with avidly glowing eyes to see how the wild Texan would respond. No help for it. A fight.

"You just pissed in my hip pocket, Nicki, ole hoss. Now, just to show you what an easygoing son of a bitch I am, I'll let it pass . . . this time. Do it again, and you'll be pickin' your teeth up off the floor," he drawled in a deadly calm voice, then polished off his shot of whiskey and poured another round.

For a moment it looked as if Zarenko was going to throw the drink in Josh's face, but then a small white hand touched the Texan's shoulder and the overpowering scent of gardenias filled his nostrils. Natasha leaned over and purred, "Please do not use that six-killer on my foolish brother."

Looking up at her, he could see the warning light in

her eyes as they glared at Nikolai Zarenko. Josh patted her hand and smiled engagingly. "Why, ma'am, I wouldn't dream of discommoding a lady. May I offer you a drink of Kentucky's finest?"

"I thought you said this was Texas whiskey." She regarded the glass of amber liquid he poured for her.

"It is, but we have a deal with Bourbon County, Kentucky, to make it for us." He stood up and held her chair, scooting it in just the way Sabrina had taught him.

Like Alexi, she swallowed it down in one gulp, then looked up at him with a startled expression on her face.

"Tastes a mite stronger than vodka, doesn't it?" he asked with a grin.

"But it is good," she replied, her black eyes glowing as she held up the glass for a refill.

Before long he paid one of the barmen to go out to his car and unlock the trunk where he kept another three bottles of Who Shot John. He hoped the colonel and the British Foreign Office appreciated the sacrifice he was making for both of his countries.

The drinking continued for another hour, and one by one the participants began to fall to the wayside. Josh was careful to drink as slowly as he dared while appearing to keep up with the others. He acted considerably more inebriated than he actually was, listening to the drunken conversations around him, most of which were in French or Russian.

Although he had been studying Russian grammar and knew the words for Japan, treaty, minister and assassination, to mention a few, nothing he could understand was pertinent to the conspiracy. Then as Alexi slumped over the table and Josh and Sergei began to reposition their companion so he wouldn't tumble to the floor, some signal was exchanged between Natasha and her brother.

Pretending not to notice, Josh observed the pair move discreetly to that small alcove in the back. How could he position himself to listen? "I gotta bleed my goose," he announced drunkenly to the assembly, who laughed and exchanged a series of ribald jokes with him as he staggered outside.

After his first visit to this place, he'd checked the position of the windows and doors. He knew there was a small window just above the alcove where Natasha and Nikolai were talking. Praying they would follow the custom of all Russian aristocracy since the days of Peter the Great and speak French, he quickly made his way to it. The weather was unseasonably warm and the room filled with smoke. Every window in the place was open. Their voices carried in hushed whispers on the late-night air.

"I don't like it," Nikolai said in slurred French. "How do you know you can trust that stupid boy?"

"He has copies of the papers. You know there is no way I could obtain them through George. They have agents watching him and me all the time now. He's becoming suspicious about my interest in Japan. I can protest all I like about loving Kabuki, but he remembers talking about their Foreign Secretary's arrival while I was listening in the next room."

"Will he turn you out?" Nikolai asked worriedly.

Josh could hear the purr in her voice as she replied, "He's far too besotted for that, but I will have to be more careful in the future. As soon as his wife returns to their country seat, I know he'll have me move back in. That will make my work easier."

"We don't have time. She may not leave for weeks yet."

"That's why our Englishman is so valuable in the meanwhile. Pick up the papers, Nicki darling," she said with fond impatience. "They contain all the notes on the treaty prepared by the Foreign Office for Hayashi. We'll know what the British are proposing before Tokyo does. All you have to do is meet him in Hyde Park tomorrow at three."

She went on to describe a statue of Wellington where the exchange would take place. The British traitor was to be paid a moderate sum in exchange for the crucial information. Unfortunately for Josh, neither of them named the traitor or where he worked.

As the conspirators continued to talk, Josh heard the sound of drunken stumbling just around the corner and knew he could listen no more. Pretending to straighten his pants, he headed toward the approaching man. It was Sergei, weaving precariously as he unbuttoned his fly in plain view of the street. And he was about to make water on Josh's prized Mercedes! Cursing beneath his breath, Josh hurried to redirect the befuddled marksman's aim, then assisted him back inside.

When they took their seats at the table, Natasha and her brother were arguing sotto voce. Josh could tell by their angry gestures that he was most probably the cause of the fight. After a moment, she shoved back her chair and stalked toward the door, pausing only long enough at his side to whisper, "Later, *mon cher*." Glowering, "darling Nicki" followed her like a bodyguard protecting a very valuable person, which Josh imagined Natasha was.

Her access to Albany's son made her invaluable to

the conspirators. She also was obviously connected to the double agent in the Foreign Office. But how could Josh find out more if her brother watched her as close as a cow pony eyeing a maverick? Nikolai had undoubtedly forbidden her to have anything to do with him. But why? Josh was certain Zarenko had no idea he was anything but a loutish American who'd accidentally stumbled into the peerage. Perhaps he feared that a new lover might distract her from their mission.

Whatever else developed, at least Josh would learn who was passing information from the Foreign Office to Zarenko tomorrow at three. That was a damn good start.

"My intended *what*?" Josh croaked in a whiskey-roughened voice that matched the sandpaper inside his head.

"Wife, my good boy, wife," the earl repeated calmly as if explaining to a child.

"When I took on this job of viscounting, I was not fixing on getting married—least of all to some female I've never laid eyes on." Josh reached across the breakfast-room table and seized the silver coffee pot before Sally could reach it, pouring himself a hearty refill.

He'd been up half the night drinking with the Russians, pouring Alexi into his bed at the Metropole, and conferring with Michael Jamison until well past dawn. He was exhausted, hung over and out of six bottles of the only decent whiskey in the British Isles. Then his uncle summoned him to eat kippered herring at the uncivilized hour of ten in the morning and proceeded to announce that he'd picked out a suitable girl for him to marry!

"You must understand how things are done in families of consequence," Hambleton went on, stirring cream into his tea and ignoring the glowering outrage on his nephew's face. He'd fully expected the reaction. "The Marquess of Chiffington's daughter Eunice is a charming young lady. Just made her debut this year. Fresh as a spring breeze."

"I don't care if she's strong as a fall hurricane, I'm not marrying anybody. Why, I'm only twenty-nine," Josh protested, stabbing angrily into a pair of fried eggs—he'd be damned if he'd eat fish for breakfast.

"Precisely. As my heir, your duty to provide an heir for the Cantrell titles is long overdue. If you'd been raised here in England, you would have wed by the age of twenty-one."

Josh shuddered. "Hell, Uncle Ab, I wasn't even dry behind the ears then."

"Well, consider your ears dry as toast now," the earl replied, placing a generous dollop of marmalade on a perfectly browned piece of bread and popping it into his mouth.

Josh considered his options. Much as he was growing fond of the crusty old curmudgeon, he was damn certain not going to let his uncle pick him a wife, no matter if she was pretty as an acre of pregnant red hogs. Just thinking of that brought Sabrina's face to mind, and he grinned in spite of himself. If he ever did decide to marry . . . mind *if* . . . he might consider her.

What was he thinking? This musty, history-steeped English air was turning his brain to mush. He wanted to bed Sabrina, not marry her. Josh Cantrell had been as free and independent as a hog on ice since he was a tadpole. Gertie had always admitted that, even to him. Nosiree, if push came to shove, when this business with the Russians was finished, he'd just take the next steamer back to Texas and forget about being a viscount or anything loftier.

The earl observed the play of emotions passing over Joshua's face with positive glee. According to all reports, the boy was an expert card player, and could bluff magnificently in the business arena as well. But right now his expression was clear as glass. Of course, the earl was far more skilled at reading faces than most people on either side of the Atlantic. "Will you at least have the courtesy to meet the young lady and her parents next weekend? They've extended an invitation for us to join them at their cottage near Brighton. I assume your lessons with Miss Edgewater have progressed sufficiently so as to assure proper etiquette?"

What would it hurt? He was only stalling for time anyway while he and Michael Jamison solved this mess . . . and he had time enough to enjoy Sabrina. Josh wiped his mouth with his napkin, then said, "I reckon I can hold my own, but just to be certain, maybe we should bring my tutor along."

The earl appeared to consider that. "A bit unorthodox . . . but the marquess does have another younger daughter. I could inquire about having them interview Miss Edgewater for a position working with her. Once you've proven yourself a proper enough gentleman, her reputation will have to be returned to its previous pristine condition. My recommendations can undo what I did in securing her services for you."

The services Josh had in mind for Sabrina at that moment had nothing whatever to do with etiquette.

And the earl knew it.

What a perfect day for a ride. Josh had called her earlier in the day and suggested that she teach him the intricacies of assisting a lady while horseback riding, confessing he'd never even seen a sidesaddle until he came to England. Of course, she was still piqued with him over the previous night's debacle with the Russian ballerina, but she had taken a snide bit of satisfaction in refusing his offer of a midnight ride in his automobile and in having Mrs. Bretton waiting for them at the door.

The look of disappointment on his face had been quite comical. This was her job, she reminded herself. But it was still a perfect day for a ride. And riding was a luxury she had seldom been able to indulge since coming to London. Since many wealthy Cits had never ridden to hounds or, indeed, ridden horseback at all, she had now and then taught their daughters. This would be great fun.

If she was spending the afternoon with the Texan in the process, Sabrina preferred not to think about how much that added to her pleasure. She stood watching him as he led their horses out of the mews, a bay stallion and a dappled gray mare. The animals were magnificent, but her eyes kept straying to the man. He wore denim pants that seemed as if they'd been weather-softened to his long legs, and a pair of those odd high-heeled boots. His plain white shirt was open at the collar—highly improper, she had scolded, but she was happy he'd ignored her protest.

A bit of black hair peeked through at the base of his throat, making her breath catch when she imagined what it might feel like to touch it. He was hatless and his hair curled around his nape as he bent over to adjust a stirrup on her mare. Her fingers literally itched to brush through the black curls and feel the hard warmth of his broad shoulders. She watched with a

141

dry mouth while his muscles bunched and flexed as he worked.

Then he raised his head and smiled at her. "Cloudy's ready. Are you?"

She was a vision in a dark-green riding habit that set off the color of her hair. Of course, it was piled high in a bun, and a silly little hat with a green feather in it perched on top of her head. He imagined tossing it away and pulling the pins from her hair, then running his fingers through it, watching it fly like a banner behind her as she rode. Her reply broke into his erotic fancies.

"You may assist me in mounting, my lord."

Oh, yes, he'd love to do that . . . but not the way she meant. All he said was, "Just tell me what to do."

"Place your hands so." She illustrated, explaining how to give her a boost onto the horse's ridiculous little sidesaddle.

"That contraption still doesn't look safe to me," he said dubiously as he followed her instructions. What he really wanted to do was take her tiny waist in his two big hands and lift her up, but he knew that would elicit a rebuke. Sabrina lightly took her seat with practiced ease, holding the reins like a seasoned rider. He nodded in approval as he swung up onto Comanche.

"Ladies always ride sidesaddle. Even when they ride to hounds, which can become quite vigorous."

"Fool way to break your neck."

"Which, riding sidesaddle or fox hunting?" she asked.

"Both," he groused. "Dozens of grown men and women all chasing one little scruffy varmint, and they let a pack of dogs do all the work for them. Downright unsporting, if you ask me."

"You'd better keep that sentiment to yourself, Lord Wesley, else you'll not be welcome at any peer's seat."

"Speaking of country houses, are you going to go with me this weekend?" he asked casually.

"I suppose so. It does present a fine opportunity. If the Chiffingtons employ me, I'll soon have my reputation restored. I know how you and your uncle conspired to turn all my clients away. Even with enough money to open my school, I must be above reproach."

"Aw, I didn't have anything to do with that. Uncle Ab's the one with the devious mind," he protested as they rode toward the Wellington statue in the park.

As they circled in a leisurely canter around the tree-lined riding course, Josh noted that it was approaching three. Then he spotted Nikolai Zarenko dismounting from a beautiful black horse. He strode purposefully toward a· lone figure standing at the base of the statue. Nodding in greeting, he placed an arm about the slim Englishman's narrow shoulders, and the two began to walk as if they were old friends. Josh saw the traitor pass a sheaf of papers to the Russian, who quickly slipped them inside his jacket.

Glancing casually around as they rode, Sabrina admired the statue of England's greatest hero and wondered why her cousin Edmund was there walking with some strange man who looked vaguely familiar.

Chapter 9

Josh immediately recognized the skinny kid as the clerk who worked for his uncle. What did this green boy have to do with the Foreign Office? Uncle Ab was a member of the House of Lords, but from what he'd figured out, these days that was pretty much window dressing unless a peer became a cabinet member or worked in the government in some other official capacity, which he knew the earl did not.

He would have to learn more about this Whistledown fellow. Michael Jamison might know something . . . or be able to find out something. He would send word to the spy when he and Sabrina finished their "lessons." Tonight he had a command performance for dinner with the earl, just to be certain his dinner-table etiquette was sufficient to pass muster at the Chiffingtons.

Looking at the pensive expression on her face, he asked Sabrina, "What could be wrong on such a beautiful day—except for being rigged up on that uncomfortable contraption?"

She laughed. "This 'uncomfortable contraption,' as you call it, is the only way I've ever ridden."

"Then you have to let me teach *you* something—to ride astride." At her incredulous expression, it was his turn to laugh. "Women in America do it all the time, especially out West." His voice grew husky as he drawled, "There's nothing like riding flat-out across a sea of buffalo grass under a full moon with your knees wrapped around a galloping horse. You can feel the pounding power of every hoofbeat."

The vivid imagery was sexually arousing, as she was certain he intended it to be. Sabrina dared not look at him, but she could feel his gaze on her and knew her cheeks were flushed. "I suppose your Texas women wear britches and let their hair down."

"You've never known how it feels to let your hair down, have you?" He did not wait for her to answer. Her flaming face did it for her as she stared resolutely straight ahead. His voice was low, vibrating as he continued, "To have it flow like a banner on the wind while you lean over a pounding mount. Without that, you've never lived."

"I suspect a good many people have 'never lived' according to your definition," she replied dryly, at last daring to look over at the rogue. "But as to riding swiftly, I can manage that," she said and kicked the mare into a gallop, leaning low over the gray's neck as she took off.

Josh whistled low. "Girl, you are full of surprises," he murmured as he kneed Comanche into following her reckless ride across the manicured green. Considering how dangerous the sidesaddle was, she did manage to keep a smooth seat. His big bay quickly caught up to her small gray, and they rode side by side for a bit; then she reined in and slowed to a canter.

"You're a natural-born rider," he said.

Her smile was dazzling. "I take it that is quite a compliment coming from a Texan."

Her hair had come loose and a few pins stuck out from beneath her hat, which remained secured to her head. Wispy tendrils of shiny bronze blew across her face, and she brushed them away absently with one hand, then began to secure the pins holding her hair in place.

"Yes, ma'am, it is." His mouth went utterly dry when her upraised arms revealed the curve of her breasts as her jacket pulled open. The soft cotton blouse beneath could not hide the lushness of her figure. He could span her waist with his two hands, and if he judged rightly, her corset was not laced tightly. He was a very good judge of such matters after years of firsthand observation.

Sabrina could feel the tension humming between them. What was happening to her? Had she deliberately reached up to refasten her hair, even though she knew the frog holding her habit jacket allowed it to gape open? Her breasts felt suddenly tight, the nipples hardened beneath her chemise. Dear Lord, could he see the points sticking out through the well-washed layers of clothing?

When she quickly lowered her arms, he chuckled. "Lost your nerve, huh?"

"I have no idea what you mean, my lord," she managed to reply as she reined in and turned the mare away before finishing the job of fixing her hair. The mad ride had been a childish way of showing off for him, and now she chastised herself for it.

He gave her time to compose herself, leading Comanche in a wide circle before approaching her.

"Don't take on so. What's happening between us is pretty natural back where I come from."

By sheer force of will, Sabrina kept her face blank and remained superficially calm as she turned to face him. "Oh, and precisely how many viscounts in Texas carry on frivolous flirtations with their hired help?"

He looked innocently amused, a grin turning up one corner of his mouth as he replied, "I can't rightly say we have a lot of viscounts and such running around Texas, and I never heard it called frivolous flirtation, but men and women who're attracted to each other just naturally seem to strike sparks when they're together."

"We cannot be attracted to each other. It would be most inappropriate," she said stiffly. "Have you not absorbed anything about social class that I have repeatedly explained to you?"

"If a woman works for her living, there's no more shame in that than if a man does."

"I never said there was," she snapped.

"Then be proud of it. I always have. I started out with nothing and made my own fortune."

"This is not America. It is England."

"Just because I talk slow doesn't mean I'm stupid, Sabrina." He could hear her indrawn breath when he Christian named her. "I don't need a geography lesson."

"No, you don't. What you require most egregiously is a lesson in propriety. And at the moment, so do I."

He was pushing her too fast, but, damn, the woman made him crazy! "Now, don't take on so," he said soothingly

"I believe it's time I went home. Would you be so

kind as to convey my regrets to the earl about my inability to continue your lessons?"

"Oh, no, you don't. You're not backing away like some skittish filly. I know you have more sand than that, Sabrina."

"Do not call me that!"

"It's your name, isn't it? And mine's Josh. No one's around to hear us if we break a rule or two."

"You and your uncle used virtual extortion to force me to attempt the feckless task of civilizing you, but if I never again have another pupil, I don't care. I hereby resign my position." She kicked her mare into a gallop, heading back to the stables.

"Damn fool female," he groused beneath his breath as he followed her. This time she was riding even faster than before, recklessly cutting across rougher terrain, jumping a hedge and spurring the gray through a copse of alders. She was going to break her fool neck!

Sabrina could feel the sting of tears and blinked them back. She could barely see as she urged the little mare to race even more swiftly. All she could think of was escaping from him before something unthinkable happened. To use his crude Texas vernacular, the man could coax a buzzard off a gut wagon. The ghastly image made her cringe. A few short weeks ago, such a vulgar thought would never have entered her mind. Lord only knew what he could coax her to do!

Josh saw the gully ahead of them, partially hidden by some low shrubbery. He kicked Comanche into an even harder gallop toward the deadly abyss. If one saw it and was prepared to jump, a good horseman could accomplish the feat easily, but he knew Sabrina was not paying attention. She'd plunge downward and break her neck. He pulled alongside her, seizing Cloudy's reins in a tight hold as he wheeled Comanche into a sharp turn, bringing the mare with him.

But Cloudy's footing began to slip at the edge of the gully. As the horse struggled to keep from falling, Josh yanked Sabrina from the sidesaddle and swept her into his arms. For once he was glad for the silly thing. If her foot had been caught in the stirrup, he could not have pulled her free. Comanche wheeled around, allowing the mare to regain purchase in the crushed bushes and scramble to safety.

Josh held Sabrina tightly for a moment as both horses, winded and snorting nervously, calmed. His pulse was still racing, and he could feel her heartbeat pounding against his chest. Her hair had come unfastened and fell in a tangled cascade of silk down her back. He could smell the faint essence of wildflowers as she nestled her head in the curve of his shoulder.

Sabrina was amazed to feel his big body shiver as if he were afraid. Her bold Texan? Impossible. Or had he been that frightened that harm could come to her? She had endangered both their lives and those of two very valuable animals. Her own trembling was part terror, part guilt. How could she face him? Taking a shaky breath, she looked up, ready to apologize for her rashness . . . and found him smiling at her.

"I appear to be right hard on a lady's wardrobe. You've lost another hat," he said in a husky voice.

"Bother the hat. What I did was inexcusable. Please accept my apol—"

He silenced her with a kiss. It was quite different from that first sizzling one exchanged in the garden. He was exquisitely gentle, brushing his lips over hers like butterfly wings, pressing, withdrawing, teasing and caressing as he cradled her head in one hand and held her against him with his other arm. He pulled her up onto the saddle so she was seated across his thighs as he continued his mercilessly soft assault on her mouth. Sabrina could hear his low murmur, indistinct yet oddly soothing, as he pressed kisses around her mouth and on her eyelids.

"When I saw that drop-off and knew you didn't, my heart came near choking me, Sabrina . . . Sabbie, my Sabbie . . ."

She stiffened slightly.

"That's a child's name, and I'm a woman grown," she protested as he centered his mouth over hers once again. She should protest. This was utterly irresponsible, highly improper, deliciously wonderful.

This time she opened when his tongue rimmed the seam of her lips. Her fingers dug into the muscles of his arms as he deepened the kisses, slanting his mouth over hers with a more possessive abandon. They were both trembling, but no longer from the brush with death. This was something infinitely more dangerous . . . at least from her point of view.

She'd been hurt once before. How could she bear it again? Yet the magic of his kiss was mesmerizing. Her fingers trailed up his arms to his nape, then splayed into the thick night-dark hair curling around his collar. She pulled his head down to her, arching against him like a kitten being petted.

Josh could feel the pressure of her breasts against his chest and taste the delicate sweetness of her mouth. He was losing control, and he knew it but didn't give a damn. The ache in his groin was becoming unbearable. In a moment, if he shifted his weight—and it was imperative that he do so or risk injury—she'd feel very physical proof of his arousal beneath that delectable bottom of hers.

But she won't know what it means. At least he hoped she wouldn't, being a very prim and proper lady, and a virgin to boot. That very thought should make him want to let her go. But it didn't. He couldn't stop kissing her as long as she clung to him and returned his ardor. His dilemma was solved a moment later when the sounds of hoofbeats and laughing voices grew louder. A party of riders was drawing near.

Sabrina heard the noise but failed to register what it was until Josh gently disengaged from their embrace, planting a kiss on the tip of her nose as he smiled down at her. "I'd hate to ruin a lady's reputation," he said with a smile.

Idiotically, Sabrina found herself smiling back at him. "Even if you just saved her life?"

"Especially if I did, since I was the cause of her almost losing it. I didn't mean to spook you, Sabrina."

"Oh, my lord, but you do . . . you do," she whispered as he lowered her to the ground. He quickly swung off the big bay, who stood obediently still, reins trailing on the ground, while Josh walked over and gathered up the reins of the gray. Hungrily, her eyes drank in the grace of his long-legged stride, the strength of his sun-bronzed hands as he patted the mare, examining her for injuries.

Sabrina fumbled with her hair, knotting it into a bun and securing it as best she could with what few pins remained. Visions of those brown hands on her pale flesh made her knees go weak. She closed her eyes tightly and blinked, then steadied herself against the bay's saddle. What a fool she was, imagining all sorts of things that must never—could never be. Taking a deep breath, she walked over to him and took Cloudy's reins.

"I can ride now," she said in a voice that was not as calm and authoritative as she wished. In fact, it sounded more like a breathless squeak. Mercifully, the passing of the party of riders disguised her tone from him. Fortunate also that the party paid little attention to the two riders standing at the side of the swale.

Josh looked up at her pale face and glowing eyes. Earlier they had held the sheen of tears, then passion. Now he was not certain what he read in their sapphire depths. Could it be fear? Of him? Or of how she reacted to him? "Are you sure?" he asked dubiously.

"If the mare is not injured, *I* most certainly am not," she asserted, beginning to sound more like her old self. "Please give me an assist up."

"As my lady commands," he said, but instead of offering her his cupped hands, he did what he'd wanted to do earlier and placed his hands around her waist, lifting her like thistledown and placing her on the saddle.

"You know that was not the proper way to do that," she accused as she gathered up the reins, refusing to look at him.

Josh grinned. "Nope, but it surely was more fun than having that pointy little boot sole dig into my hand. I'll remember the proper way next time," he promised solemnly.

"Why is it that I don't trust you, my lord?" she could not resist asking any more than she could resist meeting his wicked green gaze. With that, she turned the mare and trotted sedately back the way they'd come.

Josh swung up on Comanche and followed her,

cursing horses, women and life in general. He knew he'd be well advised to pay more attention to what Zarenko was doing with that young clerk who worked for his uncle than to Sabrina Edgewater. But, damn it all, she was so much more interesting.

"She's his cousin?" Josh echoed incredulously. He felt as if he'd been gut-kicked by a pack mule as he stood in Michael Jamison's apartment late that night. A glass of his own bourbon sat untouched beside the bottle he'd brought along with him.

"Afraid so, old chap," Jamison replied. "They were raised together like brother and sister." He outlined Edmund Whistledown's childhood history. "When I received your note this afternoon, I made a few inquiries. Young Whistledown appears to have something of a gambling problem."

"At what?" Josh asked.

"Take your choice," Jamison replied. "Cards, horses. He's even been known to bet on the spring regattas. He loses. Frequently."

"And he works for my uncle, but that can't be the source of his information." Josh paced back and forth, combing his fingers through his hair. "How much would the earl know about this treaty with Japan? Parliament's not even in session."

Jamison knew about Hambleton's work at the Foreign Office but had been explicitly instructed not to disclose the fact to the viscount. "It's possible he may have a bit of information since he spends more of his time here in the city than he does at his seat in Suffolk," he hedged. "He's friends with several members of Lord Lansdowne's council. He might be a source that a man desperate for money could use."

"Like Whistledown?"

"I wonder if his dear cousin Miss Edgewater is involved as well," Michael said speculatively as he sipped his brandy. "She's also been most conveniently employed by the earl."

"No." Josh's voice was soft but firm. "I don't believe Sabrina'd do such a thing."

Jamison's eyebrow rose at the use of her Christian name, but he said nothing as his companion continued speaking.

"She's too inherently decent, too loyal."

"Ah, yes, but she's loaned him money. He made a payment to some rather nasty chaps at the Epsom racecourse several weeks ago. One might wonder where she acquired the funds."

"She's been saving to start a school. That's why she agreed to take me on—Uncle Ab agreed to pay for it if she'd teach me manners."

Michael almost choked on his brandy. "Teach you manners?" he echoed.

Josh's expression darkened. "What's so damn funny about that?"

"Nothing, nothing at all, old chap," Jamison soothed, smothering his laughter as he watched the Texan take a gulp of that dreadful American corn whiskey directly from the bottle.

Josh started to wipe his mouth with his hand, then stopped himself, grinning. "I reckon I am quite a tribulation to the lady." He paused thoughtfully. "I wonder if she knows her cousin's a sporting man? No," he answered the mostly rhetorical question. "If she knew he was doing anything so wicked, she'd skin him."

"Well, if she doesn't, the unsavory characters to whom he's in debt will do far worse, believe me. I

154

imagine the money Zarenko gave him was a god-send. Now, what I need to do is lay a trap to ensnare the Russians."

"How do you figure we can do that?" Josh asked, still shaken to learn of Sabrina's connection to this assassination business.

"We? No, no 'we,' my lord. You may keep an eye on the lady. I shall take responsibility for planting a bit of false information that will find its way to the earl . . . and thence to our Mr. Whistledown. If all goes according to plan, he'll soon be whistling at his own hanging. A pity the power of the Russian ambassador's office will keep the likes of Zarenko and his sister from joining our homegrown traitor."

"If you can't arrest them, what's the sense?" Josh asked in frustration. He hated the intricacies of diplomacy.

"We eliminate the seepage of information from our Foreign Office and send that whole nest of Slavic vipers back to Saint Petersburg. Good riddance," Jamison said, polishing off his brandy.

"Personally, I'd shoot Zarenko," Josh said, following suit with his whiskey. This time he remembered to use the glass. Sabrina was a good influence on him.

Lordy, he hated the noise and soot of trains. Josh would much rather have driven his Mercedes, but Uncle Ab was adamant about the unreliability of automobiles for long-distance travel. All arguments about the craftsmanship and roadworthiness of his vehicle were countered with arguments about the condition of English roads. The earl had finally pulled rank on him.

They were traveling by rail.

Josh stared disconsolately out the window of the private car his uncle had secured for their journey to the Chiffingtons' seat in West Sussex. For the past hour or so, the countryside had grown less and less interesting. From picturesque hills and quaint cottages, it had gradually changed into flat, sandy stretches, much like the southern parts of the Texas coast. He'd never much cared for the ocean.

But at least the view inside the plush car was much better. Sabrina opened the door and returned to her seat directly across from him. As soon as he saw it was she, not his uncle, he stood immediately. "See, I am learning my manners," he teased.

"I do believe you're capable of turning courtesy on and off like water from a faucet, my lord," she replied with only minimal exasperation.

"I'll be as well behaved as a Sunday-school teacher at a preacher's convention while we're at the marquess's. I figure if they see you can beat some culture into an ignorant cuss like me, they'll realize you'll do just fine for their daughter."

She ignored the teasing light in his eyes, wishing the earl would return, but he was absorbed in a chess game with a friend in the common car. He'd urged her to return and keep his "rapscallion nephew" company. What else was she to do but agree? It would scarcely work for her to confess her shocking attraction to that "rapscallion." Or his to her.

"You have been a challenge," she replied carefully. "I doubt I'll find Lady Drucilla Palmer a fraction so troublesome."

Josh chuckled. "It's right funny, you know."

Sabrina stiffened. Was he laughing at her? At what he considered the frivolity of her chosen profession? "What amuses you?" she asked defensively.

"We're both on display, sorta like a pair of heifers at an auction. Just to see if we're worth bidding on."

"Your crude livestock analogies will leave those in the aristocracy quite baffled, Lord Wesley, and those not baffled will be appalled," she replied in her best teacher's voice. She did not want to discuss why he was spending the weekend in the company of Lady Eunice Palmer, eldest daughter of the Marquess of Chiffington.

"It appears to me we're both being looked over to see if we're up to the jobs of work they have in mind for us—you to teach Lady Dracula—"

"Drucilla," she corrected with a twitch of her lips in spite of the uncomfortable topic.

"Yep, right, Drucilla. And me to measure up to being a marquess's son-in-law. Eunice." He grimaced. "Why do folks pick such fool ugly names?"

"You well know they are both classical Greek names."

"That's fine if you're a classical Greek. Plug ugly for a modern female."

"Drucilla means soft eyes, and Eunice means gloriously victorious."

He studied her with heavy-lidded eyes. "Aren't you just a fountain of information, Miss Teacher. Well, one thing I know for sure 'n certain. Lady Eunice Palmer isn't going to be victorious when it comes to catching me, gloriously or any which way. I don't figure on being hogtied into marriage, leastways when it's all been arranged before I even set eyes on the female."

"What if she's a dazzling beauty with wit and charm?" Sabrina could not resist playing devil's advocate. How else to make him realize that he would have to wed in the upper class someday?

"I don't care if she's as pretty as Lillie Langtry. I pick my own women," he said stubbornly, a dare in his eyes as they met hers.

"One is not always allowed to make choices in life, my lord," she replied gently.

"I am. Always was and always will. I was born in a bordello and raised dirt-poor, but I decided when I was a tadpole that I wouldn't spend the rest of my life drinking rotgut whiskey and cleaning out cuspidors."

"You still drink that awful whiskey." She could not resist teasing him or answering his slow grin.

"Why, ma'am, you just haven't learned to appreciate one of the finer things in life. Who Shot John isn't rotgut. It's pure bourbon."

"Now, there's an oxymoron if ever I heard one," she replied.

"Ever taste it?" he asked, leaning forward as he pulled out a flask concealed inside his jacket.

Her eyes grew huge. "You cannot bring that disgusting stuff to the Chiffingtons. They'll expect you to partake of their fine brandy after dinner."

"Who'll know if I switch that perfumy stuff for real whiskey?" he asked with a crafty expression on his face.

Sabrina found herself laughing out loud. "In all of your peregrinations across America, my lord, have you ever mastered what I believe carnival people call the shell game?"

"I've seen it. Nowhere half as hard as learning to palm aces," he replied with a grin.

Outside their car, the earl overheard their blended laughter and smiled to himself. His rogue of a nephew wasn't the only one who could run a shell game.

Chapter 10

The house perched like a great fat goose on a slight promontory overlooking the ocean. It was wood, painted a blinding white with the intricate scrollwork trim done in deep maroon and bottle green. Great verandas filled with bench swings and potted ferns encircled the sprawling edifice on all four sides. By the look of it, the Chiffingtons' "beach cottage" must have a minimum of a dozen bedrooms.

"I shudder to imagine the size of their actual seat if this is but the beachside residence," the earl said dryly as their carriage pulled up the front drive.

Josh looked curiously at him. "I thought you and the marquess were old pals."

Hambleton raised one bushy white eyebrow. "We attended the same schools and vote together on most issues in Lords. Until now, our friendship has been confined to London."

"But you have met Mrs. Marquess—er, the marchioness?" Josh corrected himself when Sabrina gave him a sharp look. "And her daughters?"

Noting the exchange, the earl replied, "Most certainly. Both are quite comely young women. You'll not fault the elder daughter's looks."

That oblique remark left both Josh and Sabrina to wonder if they would fault Lady Eunice for something else.

They were ushered inside the house by a bevy of servants. The majordomo had footmen working like ants, carrying their baggage to the assigned rooms, as he escorted them down a long hallway toward the back of the house where a veranda faced the ocean. Over the gentle lapping of waves in the distance, they could hear voices carrying down the hallway.

"I do not care if he is as rich as the czar! He's an American buffoon from some wild, backward place where they still scalp red Indians," a petulant young female voice pronounced stubbornly.

"Now, Eunice, do not take on so. I'm certain if he's Lord Hambleton's heir, he will be a gentleman," an older voice pleaded.

When Josh could see the two women, the mother was wringing her hands as her daughter paced, running one elegant white glove along the railing.

"Begging your pardon, ma'am. It was the Indians who scalped us, but they haven't done much of that for a few years," he could not resist saying as he made a courtly bow. The startled and hideously embarrassed Marchioness of Chiffington gasped and turned to face him.

"Oh, dear, that is . . ." Her words trailed away. She placed one hand to her throat, as if she could stop the deep red flush creeping up to her face. She was a thin, pale little woman with frowsy grayish-blond hair and delicate yet undistinguished features. "My deepest apologies, Lord Wesley—you are Lord Wesley, are you not?" she asked, looking over his shoulder to the earl for confirmation as Josh took her hand and saluted it.

"I'm afraid so, my lady," Josh said with a wink.

The earl nodded with a barely suppressed grin. "This young rascal is my great-nephew, Joshua Abington Charles Cantrell, now Viscount Wesley, late of Texas in America," he added, taking the marchioness's hand. "Now, don't you take on so. We all remember how it is to be young and impetuous, don't we? Allow me to present Miss Sabrina Edgewater."

"Ah, yes, the deportment instructor you spoke so highly of for my dear Drucilla," the marchioness said, seizing on anything to divert attention from her elder daughter's frightful gaffe.

As the earl soothed her mother, Lady Eunice studied Josh the way a hungry robin might size up an earthworm. Sabrina made her curtsy to Lady Chiffington, hiding her shock at the elder daughter's appalling manners, but unable to keep from glancing at her appearance. She was a beauty, no doubt of it . . . and spoiled rotten. In her years of teaching, both the aristocracy and wealthy Cits, Sabrina had seen what the combination of money and indulgence could do.

Eunice had inherited her mother's delicate features and pale coloring, but while the mother receded into the background, the daughter glowed like a polished gem. Her hair was as bright as spun gold, her eyes a turquoise more brilliant than the sea at sunrise. Each feature, from her tiny turned-up nose to her plump bow lips, was picture-perfect.

Lady Eunice appraised Josh's tall, lean body as if expecting some structural flaws to present themselves when he walked over to where she stood by the rail. "So you're the Texas Viscount. I've read about you," she said in an affected voice as if his wild antics had bored her in the extreme.

"Nothing good, I'd bet." Now it was his turn to measure her. Uppity as a cat and cold as a blue tick hound's nose. Her lips smiled but her eyes did not.

"I daresay, you are not what I expected."

"Oh, and what did you expect?" he drawled lazily, leaning one broad shoulder against a support post so that he towered over the haughty young woman. He used his other hand to open his jacket. "See, no hidden scalps. But I hate to disappoint. I do pack a six-shooter."

Eunice stepped away from him as if he were a madman. Josh couldn't help casting a quick glance at Sabrina to see if she was watching them. She was. He smiled inwardly.

"It is not acceptable for a gentleman to unfasten his jacket in the presence of a lady, nor is it at all acceptable to carry firearms," Eunice said in a horrified tone. Gone was the pose of bored sophistication.

"Well, it's real comforting that you know what's expected of a gentleman." He leaned closer. "Now how about what's expected of a lady?" he whispered. "I'm sure your sister and you could share Miss Edgewater's services."

"Oooh." Eunice's mouth dropped open as she appeared to debate the wisdom of slapping the grinning rogue. Then her outraged temper suddenly dissolved into an adoring smile. Giving Josh a wide berth, she sailed toward a tall, distinguished-looking man with windblown gray hair who was climbing the steps from the sandy beach below. "Papa! How was it?" she asked the gentleman attired nattily in sailing whites.

"Delightful as always, kitten. Wanted to make certain everything was shipshape for tomorrow's outing." He turned from his daughter to the earl. "How are you, Hambleton? So good that you could come and bring your nephew. Oh, and the governess, too," he added as an afterthought, dismissing Sabrina with a glance.

I can see where the little harpy gets it from, Josh thought as his uncle made introductions while Eunice clung like a limpet to her beloved papa's arm. Gazing out to the ocean, Josh could see a large sailing craft bobbing on the tide. *Please, God, no.*

As if in answer to his prayer, although the wrong answer, the marquess said, "I've made all the arrangements for us to have a smashing time of it. We'll take *The Lady Eunice Victoria* out for the day, sail over to Brighton and back, with a feast aboard fit for His Majesty himself."

Josh blanched.

Sabrina looked at him curiously, recalling some passing remarks he'd made about being indisposed while crossing from America. She could not resist a tiny smile as her gaze met his.

Witch. He mouthed the word silently to her while the others chatted excitedly about their day on the waves.

Catching some subtle exchange between the "hired woman" and the viscount, Lady Eunice suddenly became jealous. She was used to being the center of attention—even with men she spurned, and there had been plenty of them even before her debut. "You do sail, do you not, Lord Wesley?" she inquired with saccharine sweetness. "Or is there no ocean in America?" she added as a puzzled afterthought, looking to her father for an explanation.

"Oh, there's hundreds of miles of coastline in Texas

alone," he replied, wondering how anyone could be so stupid. "It's on the Gulf of Mexico."

"No one who's anyone goes to Mexico," Eunice replied as if that settled the matter for all time.

So much for the geography lesson, Sabrina thought with amusement as she again caught Josh's eye.

Then a timid young woman with her father's imposing height and rather plain features came from the house, practically hiding in the shadow of her mother, shoulders scrunched as if to make herself shorter. As she was introduced, Sabrina decided that if she had the opportunity to tutor Lady Drucilla Palmer, the first thing she'd work on was the poor girl's self-confidence. It was quite obvious that, being the ugly duckling, she was used to existing in the twilight while her breathtaking elder sister held court in the sun.

As they filed into the house for tea, Sabrina whispered to Josh in passing, "Smooth sailing."

Josh would have prayed for a hurricane but he figured he wasn't exactly in the Deity's good graces at present, and probably never would be. The day dawned bright and clear with a very brisk wind. He stood staring bleakly out the large window of his bedroom, watching the whitecaps boom against the sandy shore. Just looking at the swells made him start to sweat. No help for it. He would have to convince Uncle Ab to make up whatever excuse the old man thought would pacify the Chiffingtons.

The humiliating decision made, he headed toward the earl's room just as Hambleton stepped into the corridor. "Morning, Uncle Ab," he said casually. "Could I palaver with you in private?"

One white eyebrow arched. "If by that you mean

hold a conversation, certainly. I do wish you would master the English tongue, Joshua. It would make your life as a peer ever so much easier. Not to mention that of Miss Edgewater," he muttered to himself as he started to turn back into his room.

But before the earl could reopen the door, the sounds of an argument carried from around the corner of the long hallway. "Please, Papa, you know how sick I get. Please don't make me," Drucilla begged in a plaintive voice breaking with desperation.

"I'll not hear another word about your imaginary illnesses. The Palmers have been seafarers for generations. Why, your great-grandfather fought alongside Lord Nelson himself!" The marquess's voice was crisp and authoritative but bored, as if this family-history lesson had been delivered many times before.

"Oh, Gerald, she does tend to . . . well, you know," his wife interjected softly.

"You mean vomit like a puling infant. Say it," he replied irritably. "Small wonder the girl's such a weakling. Little doubt she inherited her mal de mer from you. Thank heavens Eunice is a splendid sailor, in spite of her delicate femininity."

" 'Delicate femininity' isn't quite what I'd call it," Josh muttered to himself as the argument was settled—in the marquess's favor, naturally.

Everyone would go sailing and that was simply that.

With a look of distaste on his face for the way the marquess had treated his wife and younger daughter, the earl motioned for Josh to follow him back into his room. "I believe I know what you wanted to discuss," he said. When his nephew did not respond immediately, the old man chuckled. "A bit of a pickle, isn't it?"

"If you ask me, it's more like a whole barrelful,"

Josh responded grimly. "Did you know about the marquess's hero being ole Lord Nelson?"

"When Chiffington issued the invitation for us to come to his seaside cottage, I feared he might want to take us out on his yacht," Hambleton admitted.

"Then why the hell did you accept? You knew I'll do the same thing poor Drucilla does."

The earl shrugged. "What was I to say? That my wild Texas heir suffers from *mal de mer*? No, dear boy, this is one situation which I fear you must master, for if you cannot, then the beautiful Lady Eunice Palmer will never consider you suitable. Most certainly, her father will not."

"Oh, she's beautiful, right enough, and just about bright enough to skip and talk at the same time . . . as long as the conversation is about her. I wouldn't marry that heifer if I was stranded with her smack in the middle of the Llano Estacado for the rest of my life," Josh said vehemently.

"Indeed? I rather thought she would appeal, as she's an heiress of some consequence and great beauty. Not to mention that the family name is sterling," Hambleton replied in a bland tone. "Ah, well, if you must find another lady who suits better, at least do me the courtesy of not offending the Chiffingtons any more than you're able to help doing."

Josh stood watching the earl's back as the old man strolled out the door with an utter lack of concern. He scratched his head, puzzled. "If I live to be older than one of those Galapagos turtles, I'll never understand the English." He sighed.

After mustering up his courage for the walk to the dock, Josh was surprised to see Sabrina decked out in a simple white blouse and skirt, her hair plaited in a fat braid that hung down her back. The wind loosened tendrils of bronze hair and whipped them about her smiling face.

"Good morning," she said, falling into step beside him, her slippers sinking into the sand as they walked.

Being in no hurry to reach the dock, he slowed to accommodate her. "What's good about it?" he replied.

"You might try some of these," she said, handing him a small sack. "I had poor Drucilla eat several instead of breakfast . . . which I noted that you missed."

"Don't even mention food," he muttered, looking inside the sack. "Crackers?"

"Sometimes it helps. I don't know why, but perhaps it acts like glue for one's inner parts," she replied cheerfully.

"I know better than to put anything in my mouth," he replied, recalling all too vividly the ten-course dinner he'd consumed the night before. Surely it was digested by now. They had eaten fashionably late, but he'd had nothing since arising.

"Suit yourself," she said.

"You're enjoying my misery."

She looked up at his accusing expression. "Why, not at all, my lord. You have not yet even begun to experience misery. My real sympathy goes to poor Drucilla. She should not be forced to do something that humiliates her."

He agreed, but he was damned if he'd let her know it. "But I should?"

"Shall I say you require an extensive diminution of hubris?"

"More ten-dollar words," he groused.

When they reached the dock, Josh placed one foot on the springy wooden planks and felt them give ever so slightly. He looked down the seemingly end-less distance to where a large double-masted sailing vessel bobbed and dipped vigorously on the waves. He would rather run a mile-long gauntlet of hatchet-wielding Comanches than walk those creaking planks to that boat.

Just looking at it pitch was bringing back the sweats he'd willed away earlier. The wind picked up abruptly. Even the elements were conspiring against him. If he could charge up a hill with artillery goug-ing holes the size of grizzlies all around him, why was he going all weak in the knees now? He glanced over at Sabrina, who was negotiating the rough planks as if she were on a ballroom floor, damn her sea-blue eyes.

"Here, take my arm. You might trip," he said, seiz-ing hold of her hand in what he hoped appeared to be a gallant gesture.

It did not fool her. She chuckled beneath her breath and waved to the earl and the Chiffingtons, calling out a warm greeting to the wan Drucilla.

The poor girl didn't look half as bad as Josh. He gritted his teeth and forced a jovial smile for the as-sembly. That was when he noticed that Uncle Ab was not with the others. "Where's my uncle?" he asked.

Chiffington gave a dismissive chortle. "Oh, he's not coming. My wife remained at the house to keep him company. He suffers from mal de mer, can you imagine?"

It's hereditary and the old goat didn't tell me! "Oh, I reckon I can imagine," Josh managed.

"Good morning, Lord Wesley," Eunice purred.

She was dressed in a spotless white sailing cos-tume, trimmed with navy blue piping. The skirt was inset with pleats, and the blouse had a fancy square collar in the back, which was blowing against her nape. Eunice had secured her hair beneath a jaunty straw hat with a wide brim to protect her delicate face from the sun. Navy blue ribbons trailing from the hatband snapped in the breeze. The ensemble was far more elaborate than the simple rig Sabrina wore.

"Papa feels sailing is a true test of manhood, but of course Lord Hambleton is quite elderly now and cannot be expected to exert himself," Eunice cooed, inspecting the slightly greenish pallor of the Texan's face. "Surely you are not afflicted by an illness of old men and young girls?"

Josh felt mad enough to chew barbed wire and spit fence staples. Impugn his manhood, would she? And worse yet, in front of Sabrina. "Nothing afflicts me, Lady Eunice," he replied, grinning like a shark. He gave Sabrina a hand as she climbed aboard, then vaulted over the side onto the deck himself. Willpower, that was all it took—that and holding on to the irresistible image of strangling the life from Uncle Ab when he got back on solid ground.

"Capital," said the marquess. "Then we're off!"

As a footman unfastened the last of the moorings, the would-be admiral issued crisp instructions to his crew and they began releasing the complex of lines that allowed the sails to unfurl and catch the wind. The craft rolled sharply to one side as Chiffington steered it away from the dock toward the open ocean. Josh planted his size-twelve boots firmly on the deck and refused to seize hold of the railing to keep his balance when no one else seemed to require such aid.

Once they made it away from the coast, the water grew a bit less choppy and the wind softened. Sabrina and Drucilla stretched out on deck chairs in the sun as they conversed. A bit of color seemed to return to the girl's cheeks as she responded to Miss Edgewater's questions. Eunice strolled about the deck, pretending to examine ropes and pulleys as she posed artfully, letting the breeze mold her clothes to the ample curves of her body.

Every sailor aboard the yacht was aware of her, although they dared to slip surreptitious glances only when the marquess was not looking. *That woman is more trouble than a prostitute at a prayer meeting,* Josh thought as he observed her exhibition. At least the diversion took his mind off the movement of the boat. Maybe there was something to that mind-over-matter ballyhoo after all. He decided he'd given the marquess's spoiled darling enough attention and walked deliberately over to where Sabrina and her charge were seated.

"May I join you, ladies?" he asked.

Sabrina looked up and smiled as Drucilla shyly nodded. He wore a dark brown jacket and tan twill trousers that were tailored magnificently to his body. His green paisley cravat, loosened by the wind, made the color of his eyes come alive in the brilliant sunlight. A lock of black hair tumbled over his forehead and he combed it back carelessly with one sun-bronzed hand. The sweating pallor of earlier appeared to be gone now.

A part of her was glad, yet a small, niggling voice in the back of her mind suggested how much fun it would be to see him brought low as he had done to her on so many occasions. Heavens, she was growing mean-spirited. And enjoying it, too. "You seem to feel better, my lord," she said with a smile. "Did you try the crackers?"

"Oh," Drucilla interjected, blushing beet red the

moment she emitted the exclamation. "D-do you suffer from seasickness, too?" she dared to ask.

He leaned closer. "Don't tell your pa, but yep, I sure do. It's nothing to be ashamed of, any more than catching a cold or breaking your a—arm when a bronc bucks you off his back." He looked at Sabrina, who was hiding a grin behind her hand as she nodded approval at his correction.

"My papa thinks it is disgraceful. I wish I were more like Eunice," Drucilla said plaintively.

"You're just fine as Lady Drucilla," Sabrina said firmly.

"But she's ever so much prettier and she can play tennis and sail and dance. I'm so clumsy."

"Beauty is a many-sided thing," Sabrina said carefully. "There is beauty of the soul and spirit—not to mention the beauty of a quick, bright mind. While the physical fades, the rest . . . well, those qualities you have for all your life."

"And don't worry about having two left feet," Josh added with a wink. "You just have to grow into 'em. It takes a while. When I was your age, I couldn't walk across a barnyard without stepping in— er, tripping over a twig. Tall folks when they're young are kinda like foals. You ever see a newborn horse?" he asked. When she nodded, he continued, "They get their legs all tangled up at first, but then as they get older, they learn to run like the wind."

"But it's not fashionable for ladies to be tall like gentlemen," Drucilla replied.

"Who says? Did you ever hear of Lillie Langtry?"

"The famous actress? Of course."

"I met her when I was about your age. She's right tall—taller than you are. So's that famous Russian toe dancer or ballerina or whatever they call her, Natasha Samsonov."

"Really?" Drucilla said, her posture visibly straightening as her eyes grew wide with delight.

Sabrina watched as Josh talked with the girl, drawing her out of her shell. He was utterly wonderful with children, had a natural way of explaining things in terms they understood. She almost forgave him for mentioning that Samsonov hussy. Almost.

The morning progressed smoothly although Eunice, noting that her supposed suitor was paying more attention to her wallflower sister and that nobody "governess" than to her, tried to lure him away by insisting he take a turn about the deck. It was difficult to refuse without appearing rude. Asking Sabrina and Drucilla to excuse him, he did as the lady commanded.

Her entire conversational repertoire consisted of talking about herself—her new clothing, the latest social affairs in London she had attended, even the suitors she had won. The only other subject worthy of consideration was her paragon of a father.

"Papa is the most marvelous sailor, isn't he?" she said as they reached the upper deck where the marquess stood at the wheel. "Have you ever taken the helm?"

"Well, Lady Eunice, considering that I lived hundreds of miles from the coast, that's one chore I never had to do," he replied.

"Oh, it isn't a chore at all. We have common seamen to do the hard labor. Steering is a skill, isn't it, Papa?"

Her father beamed at her, then turned to Josh and said, "I say, I would ask you to take the wheel for a bit, but it does take a special talent to hold her steady."

"I understand how you feel, Lord Chiffington. I sorta feel the same about my Mercedes. I reckon I'll stick to steering automobiles and let you steer boats."

The marquess's eyes widened in disapproval. "Automobiles?" he echoed. "Dangerous things."

"Papa doesn't approve of horseless carriages," Eunice interjected needlessly. "Personally, I think they're nasty smelling." She made a face.

Josh grinned. "A little smelly. Nothing compared to a stable . . . but then, that's why you have servants to clean up, isn't it?" he couldn't resist adding.

"Of course," she replied blankly. "Whoever would muck out their own stables?"

"Surely the better classes don't do that in America," the marquess said, horrified.

Josh shrugged. "I couldn't speak for folks born rich, but I earned my first cash money cleaning out stables."

"How unspeakably vulgar," Eunice said, wrinkling her perfect little nose as if she could smell a pile of fresh horse manure.

Just then Sabrina and Drucilla passed by below, engaged in laughing conversation. "I do hope the governess can do something with that girl. At least she's managed to hold down her breakfast," the marquess said with a sigh.

"If she does, it will be her only accomplishment," Eunice interjected snidely. "Drucilla's quite beyond help, I'm afraid. She can't dance or even dress properly."

"All the girl needs is time to grow up. She's only a tadpole," Josh responded.

Lady Eunice's expression was positively malicious as she looked at her sister. "She'll be as tall as a man before she's grown. Papa will have a terrible time finding her a husband."

"That's why I'm hiring that glorified maid to tutor her," he replied, aggravated.

Josh bristled at the dismissive insult to Sabrina. "Miss Edgewater is a highly educated lady who's fixing to start her own school."

"How dreadful to have to work for one's living . . . and to be a spinster in the bargain. At least Cilla won't have to worry about working," Eunice said.

Josh was beginning to dislike both father and daughter more by the moment. His devoutest wish was to get this weekend over with and return to London. Then he and Uncle Ab would have a serious talk about any further selection of matrimonial candidates.

As the sun reached its zenith, the marquess instructed the cook to serve luncheon below deck in the dining area. The old martinet even deigned to allow one of the crew to take the wheel while he played host at table. While they were making their way below, the wind began to pick up once more. Josh had been doing decently until then, above deck and distracted by conversation, even if some of it had aggravated him.

But once he stepped into the low-ceilinged dining area with its small portholes, that old queasy feeling began to creep up on him again. The horizon rocking from side to side through a round window was altogether more difficult for him to deal with than bouncing up and down on a bucking horse. At least when you fell off, it was on solid ground. Nothing aboard a boat was *ever* stationary.

The marquess took his seat at the head of the

cramped table and the others sat in their assigned places. Josh was at the opposite end of the table with Eunice at his right and Drucilla at his left. Sabrina was seated next to Chiffington, who began to discuss what she could teach his daughter. The cook served the first course, a lobster bisque, and everyone began to eat with relish.

Except Josh.

The aroma of sherry and heavy cream blended with lobster was definitely not a culinary delight when one was beginning to turn the color of the second course—assorted summer greens in vinaigrette. Shoving the soup away barely tasted, Josh manfully attempted a few forkfuls of the greens, but the pungent dressing made him immediately abandon that. Oh, for those crackers he'd turned down earlier.

"Whatever is wrong, Lord Wesley?" Lady Eunice asked. "You've scarcely touched a thing, just like Cilla. But then, we all know why she won't eat," she added with a smirk. "Do you not approve of our cook?"

"The cook is doing his job just fine," Josh managed, as he and Drucilla exchanged sympathetic glances. "Being raised in Texas, I reckon I'm just naturally more of a meat-and-potatoes sort of fellow."

"Ah, then the saddle roast of venison coming up should suit you perfectly," the marquess said as a huge chunk of beautifully browned meat was presented for him to carve. "Here, pass me your plate."

Josh looked down at the juicy rare slices of meat and felt the sweat beading on his forehead. He took a swallow of water. Then another. Somehow he had to get through this. Even poor Drucilla was managing to eat tiny bits from each course and hold them down. He cut a bite of venison and commenced to chew. All right. Another. He could do this. He *would* do this.

Josh smiled at Drucilla, and that was when he noticed her stash of crackers.

She returned his smile and passed him the bag around the corner of the table. He nodded his thanks and tried to extract a cracker without alerting Lady Eunice. But, dense as the mean-spirited little filly could be, she saw what they were doing and smirked. She was ready to make some snide comment when the ship took a sudden lurch and her wineglass filled with claret splashed onto the white linen tablecloth. Instantly she scooted her chair back to avoid soiling her fancy outfit. All the china and crystal slid gently across the table, tumbling several more of the glasses.

That's it. Josh's stomach went with them. He could feel it coming on and knew he had to do something immediately, but he was trapped opposite the stairway to the deck. To reach it, he'd have to climb over Eunice, the cook and a footman. He'd never make it in time.

Sabrina watched the tableau unfold with growing horror. Josh was green and perspiring awfully. Being below decks and surrounded by all the rich food smells must have triggered another bout of mal de mer. She started to slide back her chair and go to him, her napkin clutched determinedly in one hand, but before she could stand up, he reached over to Lady Eunice and yanked the wide-brimmed straw hat from her head. She let out a shriek and leaped up. Josh ignored her angry remonstrance as he leaned over, employing her hat in lieu of a bucket.

Sabrina thought it worked quite serviceably. A resourceful lot, Texans. *Now, if he would only clap it back on Her Ladyship's head!*

Chapter 11

The moon hung low and full like a pale golden ball hovering over the blackness of the ocean at night. The sound of the waves lapping onto the beach below kept Josh tossing and turning in bed until he threw back the covers and sat up, resting his head in his hands. What a damnable humiliation the day had been. He'd spent the duration of the trip hanging over the aft railing, doubled up, dry heaving. At least he'd walked off the accursed boat under his own power, refusing Sabrina's suspiciously solicitous offer of assistance.

Just thinking of what he was going to do when he confronted his uncle had been motivation enough for him to storm up the beach. When he reached the house, the old man sat on the veranda, placidly sipping a glass of port and chatting with Lady Chiffington. One look at Josh's grayish complexion and disheveled appearance led the earl to chuckle and nod in full understanding. The viscount had considered getting his Colt and turning the old buzzard into a sieve. If not for ladies present, he would have done it, too.

Hambleton had remained utterly nonchalant, but Sabrina must have seen the murderous look in his eyes, for she quickly placed herself between the earl and his bloodthirsty nephew until he reined in his Texas temper.

Sabrina . . . what an utterly unpredictable female she was proving to be. She, not the debacle on the boat, was the true reason he could not sleep. He cared nothing for Chiffington and his wretched elder daughter. And he'd made clear to the earl in no uncertain terms that any faint hope he might cherish of a marriage between the Lady Eunice and his nephew was dead as a steer in a slaughterhouse. Odd that the old man had taken the news with utter indifference.

Why the devil was his uncle not upset? He'd arranged this whole shebang. But then again, he'd known the marquess would insist on sailing and Josh would humiliate himself. It just didn't make sense. Josh stood up and paced across the softly creaking floorboards on bare feet, refusing even to look at the waves beating against the sand dunes. But that, too, bothered him. He'd never backed down from anything in his life.

"Damned if I'll let that water scare me," he muttered to himself and forced himself to open the french doors leading out onto the upper veranda. At once, the salt-laden wind ruffled his hair. As long as he was standing on dry land, it wasn't so bad, he thought.

Unable to sleep, he considered a walk along the beach. Maybe that was the first step in conquering his fear. Hell, he'd crossed rivers swollen to torrential tidal waves in spring storms back in Texas. He'd always been a strong swimmer. Maybe if he took a dip in the salt water, it might help him get a feel for the ocean.

That was when he saw her. Sabrina walked along the beach, a lone figure aglow in the misty moonlight. Her hair was down and blowing behind her as she faced into the wind, which molded her skirt and blouse against the curves of her body. Here was beauty without artifice. After Eunice's staged performance that morning, he found Sabrina's solitary walk far more appealing . . . and arousing.

Seizing a pair of jeans and a shirt, he began to dress quickly. In moments he was wading through the soft sand, closing the distance between them. Over the sounds of the ocean, she did not hear his approach until he called out to her.

Sabrina gasped, whirling around in utter surprise. "You're the last person on earth I ever thought I'd see here," she said, gesturing to the breakers slapping against the sand.

Josh shrugged as he fell into step beside her. "A fellow's gotta face his fears."

"Is that a Texas truism?" she asked with a smile. Somehow it felt natural to be strolling along together, even though she knew it was utterly improper for them to be alone this way.

"True anywhere, I reckon." She was dressed in the same simple white skirt and blouse she'd worn that morning, softened by many washings. Recalling the fixed-up older clothes she'd worn at the ballet, he didn't imagine she had much in the way of fancy dresses. But a woman who looked like Sabrina didn't need a lot of fancy duds to catch a man's eye. "I thought a lady never went out with her hair down," he teased.

"It was pinned up until the wind saw fit to undo my hasty work. Besides, I did not intend for anyone to see me," she answered carefully.

"Why are you out here alone, after midnight?"

It was her turn to shrug. "I couldn't sleep."

He grinned. "Me neither. Guess we'll just have to find something else to do."

She looked up at him sharply. "I have already found it—*walking*." She stressed the word.

"I was thinking more along the lines of talking," he offered. "Lookee, there's a seat for us, carved by the hand of nature just so we can get out of the wind."

Indeed, the sand dunes had been swept against a stand of tall brushy grasses, making a niche where two people could sit in seclusion, hidden from the house as well as protected from the brisk air. As if to induce her cooperation, the wind picked up, snapping her hair around her face and drawing goose bumps on her arms through the sheer fabric of her blouse.

When Josh took her hand and guided her to sit in the grassy enclave, she followed without protest. *This is most unwise*, an inner voice chided. Sabrina ignored it. The warmth and callused hardness of his large hand enveloping hers felt like magic. He took a seat on the soft sand and left a semi-decorous space between them as he urged her to sit beside him.

Once before, she'd gone out alone with a man on a moonlit night . . . with disastrous consequences. But somehow this seemed different. After all, she was older and wiser now. She had a career and would soon realize her life's dream—or at least what had become her life's dream after the girlish fancies of youth had passed her by.

She sat down.

As if reading her mind, he asked, "Why'd you never marry?"

"That is a highly personal and improper question for a gentleman to ask a lady," she responded reflexively.

"You're no old maid, Sabrina. But you are past the age when most females fix on getting hitched. And I know it wasn't because you never had offers. You're beautiful in all the ways that count. Inside as well as outside. You're smart, you care about people, and you can laugh at yourself, just like you told Drucilla."

Sabrina felt her heart warm at his words, which she intuited were genuine. "You were wonderful with that child today. She's been made to feel inferior and unloved by her own family. It's unconscionable."

"Tell me about your family," he said, intrigued as he watched the way her eyes glowed in the moonlight. Her hair fell like a silky cloak around her shoulders, wind-tossed and begging for his hands to comb through it. But if he tried to do that, he knew she'd bolt like a skittish colt. Besides, he found he really did want to know more about her—everything about her. That had never been true of his feelings for any other woman.

Her face lit up as she began to speak. "My father and mother live just outside a small village in Sussex. He's a squire with a modest income, and Mama's father was vicar of the local parish. They grew up together and were married by him. They've had such a wonderful relationship, a true sharing of their lives and dreams. It's what every girl wants, I imagine."

"But you didn't?" Somehow he doubted that that had always been true, given the dreamy expression on her face when she talked about her parents' marriage. Then a look of profound sadness flashed into her eyes. She quickly masked it, looking out to the shoreline.

"Oh, I did when I was seventeen."

"What happened?"

"He went to Africa. Dexter Goodbine was an admirer of Sir Cecil Rhodes and wanted to make his mark on the world, not settle for the life of a simple country squire. He'd always talked about it when we were growing up, but I never realized how much it meant to him. Especially after he asked me to marry him. I thought he'd given up on such fancies, but then an old school friend of his made a fortune in the diamond trade, and off Dex went. It was three days before we were to be wed."

"I'd say he oughta be roped and dragged behind a mule over a mile of sharp rocks, but he really did you a favor. Fellow like that would never have made you happy like your pa did your ma."

She looked back at him. "You're very perceptive. After recovering from the shock and embarrassment, I realized it was true."

"Just because he was a no-account doesn't mean there weren't other men," he said softly. Sabrina laughed but it sounded sad.

"I had other offers, but once a woman becomes older and wiser . . . well, let us just say none of them interested me. Sussex isn't exactly overrun with witty, charming young gentlemen who want their wives as outspoken as the Edgewater females tend to be. I became bored with them."

I never wanted another man . . . until I met you.

Her mind shut down, knowing the painful impossibility of that dream. Rather than dwell on it or on past betrayals, she continued with forced brightness, "As I had three younger sisters for whom my parents had to provide dowries, in addition to three brothers to be educated, it seemed best that I make my own way in the world. And there was Edmund to consider also."

"Edmund?" he echoed, feeling as if he were betraying her by prying into her relationship with his uncle's suspicious clerk.

"My young cousin, Edmund Whistledown. His parents were killed when he was seven. My parents took him in and raised him as if he were our own. I rather adopted him, since he was the youngest and I the second eldest in our large family. Poor Edmund was always being picked on by the older boys, my brothers and others at school. He was recently employed by your uncle. You may have run into him."

She went on describing Whistledown, and Josh admitted he'd seen him a time or two. It was obvious that she loved the fellow dearly and indulged him far beyond what was good for a man of nearly twenty. By that age Josh had survived two trail drives to the Dakotas and was saving money to buy his first beeves. But he was certain Sabrina had no idea that her darling Eddie might be involved in treason.

Wishing to change the subject, he asked, "Are your sisters married off now?"

"Not the youngest, Edna, whose health is frail. I fear she'll be with my parents and then my eldest brother for the rest of her life."

"You come from quite a brood. How many brothers?"

"Gerard, he's the eldest, will inherit our father's small estate, and Donald is in the military. Jeffrey followed Grandfather into the priesthood. He now tends the same flock."

"I never knew my family," Josh found himself admitting, something he rarely talked about. There was a quality about Sabrina that invited confidences, at least when they were alone together and she let down her very proper guard.

"Are the stories in the newspapers true?" she found herself asking.

Josh heard no censure or prurient curiosity in her tone, only quiet concern. "My pa was killed in a card game in west Texas and left my ma alone with a newborn. Seeing as how they were foreigners and all, the only one who'd take her in was Gert."

"The lady who ran the . . ."

"Bordello," he supplied. "No one ever accused Garter Gertie Greer of being a lady before," he added with a grin. "Gert was good as pure gold, though. My ma was sick even before Pa died. Consumption. Didn't matter to Gertie and her girls. They took care of her, and after she died, they raised me. I was a handful, but I never could put one over on Gert. She was the only ma I ever knew, except Rosie and Dolly. They were kinda like aunts, I reckon." He stopped short of mentioning Verla, Suzie and Lupe, younger recruits to the Golden Garter whose interest in a strapping fifteen-year-old had not been exactly maternal.

"What an extraordinary life you've led. Only in your United States could a self-educated man without connections go from poverty to such riches as you've earned."

"I only wish I coulda done it sooner. By the time I sold my first herd and got back from the Dakotas, Gert was gone. But she's got the damn biggest marble tombstone in all of Fort Worth. I was able to provide for Rosie and Dolly," he added, swallowing hard as he spoke.

Sabrina could detect the sheen of tears in his eyes

for a moment before he blinked them away. Without realizing it, she reached over and placed her hand on his. It seemed so natural to touch him, to offer understanding for his highly unorthodox upbringing and the loyalty he felt for those women.

He turned to her, and their gazes met. When he silently cupped her chin in his hand and tilted her head back, she did not resist. His mouth slowly drew closer to hers. And still she did not resist.

This was madness. They were all alone out here. There would be no officious servants to interrupt and save her from herself. If she wanted to be saved. The instant his lips touched hers, Sabrina forgot about the past, the future, all the rules by which she'd fashioned her life. This was now, and she wanted him to kiss her . . . wanted so much more than that . . . what she'd been denied long ago and would never be able to have.

Josh leaned over her, gently tasting her lips, rimming them with his tongue until she opened for him. But instead of plunging in, he invited her tongue to play, teasing it with the tip of his until she dared to dart it into his mouth, once, then once more. By that second time, the kiss was becoming far more hungry. He could feel her hands clutching his shoulders as their tongues dueled, entwining, withdrawing, dancing the dance of love.

Sabrina was melting. Suddenly the cool night air was heavy, laden with a spiraling heat that owed nothing to the weather and everything to the man whose clever fingers moved over the ridges of her collarbone and down the delicate vertebrae of her spine as she arched into his embrace.

She was so soft, so pliant, her mouth so sweet that he nearly forgot his resolve to go slowly. A virgin lady such as Sabrina could not be tossed on the sand like the experienced women he'd known all his life. She required special care. If he were not so desperate to have her, he would walk away. He *should* walk away. But he knew his need was all too quickly overriding his conscience.

The least he could do was go slow and make it good for her. He ran his fingers through her long, soft hair, murmuring, "Like silk," as he inhaled the faint fragrance of wildflowers on the moist salt air. He pressed kisses to her eyelids and moved down to her throat, where he could feel the furious beating of her pulse. His lips suckled the soft skin at her nape, and she gave a low whimper of pleasure, pressing her breasts against his chest and clinging to him, lost and eager.

He could not do this to an innocent! Gently he broke away and held her at arm's length, his breath coming in harsh pants as he whispered, "Sabrina, no matter how much I want you, I shouldn't take advantage of a lady like—"

She placed her fingers over his lips and shook her head, letting it fall forward. Her hair curtained her face so he could not read her expression, but her voice was a low, soft hum of desperation. "Please, Josh, don't think ill of me. I'm not what I seem." She raised her head and met his gaze with a plea in her eyes. "Why do you think I became a teacher of deportment—a paragon of propriety?"

His smile was puzzled as he answered, "Because being a vicar's granddaughter, you just couldn't help it."

"No." Her voice was flat. "I'm a fraud, even to myself. I've buried the past for too long. What happened between my fiancé and me was as foolish as it was wrong. Dex assured me that consummating our marriage vows a few days before the wedding was perfectly acceptable. That we were already married in the sight of God. I agreed.

"He left the next day," she whispered bitterly. "And you know the saddest part of all?" she asked with tears thickening her voice. "It was degrading and painful, but at least, mercifully, it was over very quickly.

"So you see, I'm not the innocent, nor the fine lady you and the rest of the world imagine me to be." She threw her head back, faintly defiant yet so painfully vulnerable that it tore at his heart.

Josh pulled her to him and held her in his arms, rocking her back and forth as he stroked her hair and murmured, "Sabrina, girl, you're plumb wrong. You are the finest lady in England and as innocent as a newborn lamb. That Dexter, whatever his name was—you're not to blame for what he did."

"I allowed it," she said softly.

He heard a faint flicker of hope in her voice and raised her chin so he could look in her eyes. "He took advantage of you, saying you two were married all the while he was planning to leave."

"Maybe he left because I—I couldn't please him." The words came out in a tortured whisper.

"It's up to a man to please a woman, not the other way around. Never let anyone tell you different . . . and if you want me to, I'll show you how right I am."

"I'm afraid, Josh . . . now that I've had time to think—"

"Too much thinking, even for as smart a woman as you, can be a worrisome thing," he drawled, letting his fingertips graze her temple and lightly brush back her hair. He waited, searching her eyes for assent.

Sabrina felt the fear and shame all jumbled up with

desire, a hungry inexplicable yearning that she had never felt before, not even with the man she'd believed she loved, the one she'd intended to marry, the one to whom she had given her virginity. After Dex's betrayal, she had seen the men who attempted to court her as shallow and self-centered. She'd told the truth when she said none of them were strong enough to engage her interest, but there was more to it than that. She was also afraid of being disappointed again.

Somehow she knew Josh could satisfy her desires. But he could also break her heart. There was no future for the daughter of a lowly country squire with Lord Hambleton's heir, even if the thought of marriage had crossed Josh's mind, and she knew it had not. But this was her one chance to know what it meant to be a woman in the arms of a man to whom she was desperately attracted.

There might never be another.

Slowly Sabrina reached up and placed her hand over his as he caressed her face. She brought it to her mouth and kissed his callused palm, eliciting a sharp gasp of pleasure from him. "No more thinking, Josh . . . only feeling," she whispered, her eyes imploring him.

"I'll make it as good for you as I possibly can," he murmured. Glancing around at the sand mounds surrounding them, he quickly slipped off his shirt and spread it on the ground, then laid her upon it.

She watched the ripple of his lean muscles and traced with her eyes the cunning pattern of dark hair on his chest, tapering down to the waistband of his jeans. She remembered how scandalized she'd been the first time he'd appeared with an open collar that gave her a tantalizing glimpse of what lay beneath.

Now she longed to touch him. When he leaned over her and lowered his head to kiss her, she placed one palm flat against his chest and, with her other arm wrapped around his back, pulled him closer. Her fingers curled into the springy mat as his lips brushed hers, teasing for her to open.

She did so and let the entrancing ballet of their tongues begin once more. He shifted positions over her, slanting his mouth and claiming hers, urging her to do the same for him. As the kisses deepened and grew hotter, his nimble fingers reached between them and unbuttoned her blouse. When one large, warm hand delved inside and cupped a breast, Sabrina's cry of pleasure was muffled in his mouth. She arched up when he teased the nipple into a hard bud with his fingertips, then repeated the seduction with the other breast.

Suddenly her chemise was too tight, her breasts aching and sending radiating pulses of heat down her body to her woman's place. His mouth left hers and she panted aloud, unaware of the little noises of pleasure she was making as he kissed and nipped his way down her throat, then used the tip of his tongue to draw a wet circle around one nipple, softly taking the tip between his teeth and biting it.

By now her hands were in his shaggy dark hair, pulling his head down to her as he moved from one breast to the other. "Help me," he murmured as he began to pull the chemise up from the miraculously unfastened waistband of her skirt. She raised herself up as he swept it over her head and tossed it aside. For her solitary walk along the beach, she'd not bothered with a corset. Now her bare breasts gleamed in the moonlight as he looked down at them with worship in his eyes.

"You are so incredibly lovely," he said, reaching out to cup the lush fullness of the pink-tipped mounds.

His hands lifted them and his mouth tasted them, drawing the nipples into his mouth and suckling one, then the other as she arched and writhed, falling back onto the sand. Her head tossed from side to side, spreading her hair across his shirt in a tangled mass as she lay swamped by the onslaught of sheer animal need. Her eager hands rose of their own volition and her nails dug into his back, pulling him closer, closer.

When he slipped one hand over the curve of her hip and pulled up her skirt and petticoat, Sabrina was unaware. Then she felt the heated thrill of his fingers as they danced lightly up one delicate ankle, over the curve of her calf and caressed the sensitive skin of her inner thigh. But the sheer batiste of her much-mended underdrawers kept him from reaching his ultimate goal. He retraced his path, this time slipping a soft shoe from one foot and massaging the instep until her toes curled. He did the same with the other before returning his attention to the center of her need.

Slowly and gently but with incredible dexterity, Josh unfastened and slipped down her skirt and petticoat together, then slid his hand inside the waistband of her underwear and splayed his fingers across her flat little belly. Heat, already singing through her veins, ignited between her legs as his hand gradually moved lower, brushing the tight curls at the apex, then cupping her mound.

"I have to undress you, Sabbie," he murmured between suckling caresses to her breasts and belly.

Panting, she assented, wriggling her hips as he slid down the rest of her clothes and shoved the petticoat beneath her buttocks to serve as a pillow. Then he rose up and looked down at her as she lay utterly naked before him. His eyes drank in the silvery moonlit beauty of curves and hollows, a perfectly formed female body, now heated with passion. "You are a wonder," he whispered.

Sabrina had never before been unclothed before a man. Her one sad experience had been performed with her skirts hastily shoved up and her undergarments pulled partially down. Dex had not even bothered to undress himself. She'd closed her eyes and wished only for it to be over. But now she was boldly hungry to see everything. She looked up into Josh's eyes and saw that he was pleased with her. Not impatient to get it over with, but genuinely pleased . . . even more, deeply hungry to devour her with his eyes, just as she was to see him.

Seeming to sense her silent wish, he knelt and began to unfasten the buttons of his fly. She could see the bulge in his jeans, indeed had felt the physical proof of his desire when he lay so close to her earlier. Her eyes dared to watch those strong, long-fingered hands as they worked the tight pants down his narrow hips and freed his sex. Now she could see the whole pattern of his body hair from its wide arc across the muscles of his chest narrowing in an arrow down his flat, hard abdomen and blooming around the long, hard staff standing out proudly as if inviting her touch.

Hypnotically, Sabrina reached up and dared to touch it, filled with wonder at the splendid beauty that the male anatomy could be. He flinched ever so slightly and she withdrew, but his hand encircled hers and brought it back, saying in a low, hoarse voice, "Please, don't be afraid."

"I—I thought I . . ."

His chuckle was low and desperate as he said, "You

could never hurt me, darlin', but I want you so much, even the slightest touch is sheer agony—and pleasure at the same time."

She was beginning to understand that as she let him guide her inexperienced hands to stroke and cup him. A pure thrill of power coursed through her when he gasped and bucked his hips helplessly. But then he pulled away.

"If we don't slow down, I won't be able to control myself," he said hoarsely, lying down on his side and pulling her to him on their makeshift bed of clothing. He drew her into another long series of drugging kisses, slow and languorous, then hot and hard. All the while his hands played over her body, making it hum with desire from head to toe. When he stroked her inner thighs her legs fell apart, opening in welcome. He murmured his approval and moved up to cup her mound again.

Sabrina whimpered when his fingers slid over the weeping flesh, swollen and pulsing with a hunger she could never have imagined. Now it was her hips that bucked in helpless entreaty as he stroked the small bud that seemed to be at the very core of her being.

It did not take long.

It took far too long.

She was not certain of anything except the sudden spiraling ecstasy that pounded through her veins, causing stars to explode behind her eyelids. She clung to him, quivering in the aftermath.

"That's what I meant," he whispered as he positioned himself to enter her still spasming body.

Ever so slowly, he slid deeper and deeper, letting her flesh stretch to take all of him. She was so sweetly tight, so wet and hot and responsive, unlike any other woman in his considerable experience. She was beyond compare. Sweat beaded his brow as he held himself in check, waiting for her. When she gave a small, involuntary twist of her hips he began to move from his fully seated position, withdrawing, then plunging languorously in, ever so gradually increasing the tempo.

Sabrina felt the heat building once again, the need . . . and now she knew the shattering wonder of what lay at the end of this estactic ordeal. But when she tried to move faster, he grasped her eager hips and slowed them, shaking his head.

"Hold on—making it last will make it better," he whispered as his tongue grazed the edge of her ear, then dipped inside.

On and on it went until they were both soaked with perspiration as the winds soughed outside the lee of sand that sheltered them. He murmured soft words of endearment and encouragement, feeling her body's signals that she was ready to slip over the abyss again. When she let out a small, keening cry and convulsed around him, he gave in and spilled himself deep inside her.

The second time was even more wondrous than the first, which had been pretty amazing, but coherent thought had long since fled. The contractions began to build, radiating from the core of her body where it was joined to his, spreading all the way to her fingers and toes. She felt his staff swell even more and his whole body stiffen and shudder as he pulsed life into her. When he collapsed on top of her, she held him in her arms and buried her fingers in his night-dark hair.

"If it got any better, I would die," she murmured dreamily as she moved her cheek against his raspy beard. Her fingertips glided, tracing circles in the bristles.

"It will get better, and you won't die. Trust me," Josh drawled, leaning up on one elbow so he could lave her salty skin with his tongue.

She purred like a kitten as he continued his ministrations, licking, caressing, suckling and teasing her until she could feel him once more hardening deep inside her. When he began to move again, she obeyed his command and locked her legs around his waist, arching to meet every swift, hungry thrust.

"Sometimes it's good when it's fast, too," he panted.

Sabrina agreed, although she was powerless to say so. She prayed for the night never to end.

Chapter 12

As Hodgins frantically took notes, Hambleton and Lansdowne discussed the impending arrival of the minister from Japan. They were seated in the earl's office with the hall door locked. This meeting was of the highest secrecy, and no one could be allowed to interrupt or even to see that the Foreign Secretary was present.

"This is confounded nonsense," the earl said impatiently, aggravated that his good mood from the weekend had been so rudely broken by these new developments.

"The Japanese are a stubborn lot, there's no denying," Lansdowne said, drawing upon his cigar. He studied the ash as he continued, "We tried as delicately as possible to explain that there would be risks if Count Hayashi made a public progress to St. James's Palace, but the Marquess Katsura said they'd lose face if his minister was slipped into London in secret."

"Pardon, Your Lordship, but Katsura is their Prime

Minister?" Hodgins asked. At Lansdowne's nod, he continued note keeping.

"Better to lose face than lose his demned arse," Lansdowne said irritably.

"The chances for the Russians to take another pop at Hayashi are damnably high." Hambleton sighed. "But I suppose there's no help for it."

"Have you anything on your nephew's Russian friends since he saw Whistledown slip the stolen treaty information to Zarenko?" At the earl's negative shake of his head, Lansdowne added, "Jamison's come up with nothing either, but I've assigned him to keep a close watch on both of them."

"My nephew is observing Whistledown as well as continuing to hobnob with Kurznikov and his circle," the earl said.

A sharp rap sounded on the door. At once Lansdowne stood up, prepared to slip away via the secret entrance. "Will you see to whomever it is, Hodgins? No one must know the Foreign Secretary is here."

"Very good, my lord," the servant said, quickly excusing himself.

Hambleton opened the panel, and the two men vanished behind it before Hodgins opened the door of the study. A small gaslight flickered on the steps leading down to the cellar. As the earl saw his guest out, they continued their conversation.

"At least we have an opportunity to send those damnable Russians on a false trail before the real arrival of the minister."

"I take it you've planted the scheduled arrival of the supposed ship?" Lansdowne asked.

"Tomorrow. If they receive that information from Whistledown—and we've given him ample opportunity to peruse it over the past few days—then they should make another attempt on the agent posing as Hayashi."

"If only we can capture one of the bastards and interrogate him. I have an agent whose father died at Balaclava who'd love to perform that service for king and country," Lansdowne said dryly.

"Are you absolutely certain of this, Mr. Loring?" Sabrina asked in the most no-nonsense tone she could muster. She stood in her front parlor, having taken the precaution of leaving the door ajar. After hearing what her unexpected guest had to say and knowing how her landlady enjoyed eavesdropping, she wished she'd forgotten about propriety.

The nattily dressed little man with the shiny bald pate nodded eagerly. "Yes, ma'am, I am. Mr. Whistledown owes me for his new wardrobe and hasn't paid one pence. When I threatened to go to his employer, he begged me not to. Said he'd lose his position, and then those bully boys from Epsom would kill him. But then I remembered you."

"Do you have any idea how much he owes in gambling debts?" she asked, wringing her hands as she paced.

The tailor shook his head. "No, but I know the likes of Frankie Bentham and Lorry Killian wouldn't bother with small change. It must be a lot. He was real scared, was Mr. Whistledown. I could see that much."

"Well, I have given my last sou to my cousin, thinking he was paying you while he was obviously using it for nefarious purposes. I cannot pay any more of his debts, but I do ask that you refrain from going to Lord Hambleton. Eddy's correct in assuming he'll be dismissed if you do, and then neither you nor I will ever recover what's owed us."

Loring looked at the determined gleam in her eyes. "What can you do, Miss Edgewater?"

"I shall start by paying a call on my cousin and getting the truth out of him," she said tartly. "Then we shall attempt to make some arrangements for him to repay you—and me!"

Josh was worried. He had followed Edmund Whistledown from his uncle's house early Monday morning after seeing him leave the earl's office. The young clerk met again with Nikolai Zarenko, and another exchange was made. There was no doubt that Sabrina's beloved young cousin was involved in a treasonous plot. But was the earl, as well? Had he dispatched the boy with the information, or had Whistledown stolen it?

How in hell did his uncle come by the sort of highly secret information the Russians were interested in? Something was beginning to smell like he was standing downwind from an outhouse on a hot day. Upon returning from Sussex Sunday evening, he had been briefed by Michael Jamison about some false information given to Whistledown. A ship rigged out to look as if it contained the Japanese minister would carry British agents lying in wait. He'd almost asked if his uncle was privy to this scheme, but something had held him back.

What if Uncle Ab was involved? Josh simply couldn't believe the honorable old gentleman he was growing so fond of could be a traitor. Unfortunately, he harbored no such doubts about Edmund's guilt. It would break Sabrina's heart. So would learning that Josh was working to place the boy in jail. How could he ever explain it to her?

He parked his Mercedes six blocks from Whistledown's modest lodgings, not wanting the automobile to alert the clerk to his presence. As he walked, Josh pondered his relationship with Sabrina. Everything had changed Saturday night on that beach, even if she refused to acknowledge it the following morning. She had spent the time closeted with Drucilla, and then made certain that the earl was present the whole time they rode back to London, giving him no time alone with her to talk about their feelings.

As he walked past street vendors and drays loaded with ale, Josh realized he could not have said for certain that he knew what his feelings were, much less what she might have told him in return. Did he love her? If so, did that mean . . . he shuddered at the very idea . . . that he should ask her to marry him? The only thoughts Josh Cantrell had ever given to marriage were those involved in avoiding it. After all, he was only twenty-nine. If he wanted to raise up a passel of children to inherit his wealth one day, there was always plenty of time for it after he'd sown more wild oats, fields of them!

But he was used to doing his "sowing" with women who knew how he felt and expected nothing more from him than a good time. Sabrina was different. He'd taken no precautions, which in itself was most unlike him. Normally he always used a condom. What if she was with child? With any other woman, that thought would have made him break out in a worse sweat than the prospect of a six-week ocean voyage. Somehow with Sabrina, the idea only brought a faint smile and a warm feeling crowding his heart.

Was he going plumb loco?

Sabrina stood frozen in the dense shade cast by an overgrown boxwood hedge at the corner of the block.

What on earth was Josh doing skulking about across the street from her cousin's lodgings? This was scarcely the sort of neighborhood frequented by the peerage. It was, in fact, somewhat dangerous for her to be here alone, but she had originally planned to have the hansom driver stop directly in front of Edmund's boardinghouse and let her out—until she saw Josh.

He was standing at the intersection of an alley across the way, deep in conversation with another man, also bearing the unmistakable stamp of aristocracy. Not wishing him to see her until she knew what was going on, Sabrina had ordered the driver to let her off around the corner. Then she'd walked back to observe the Texan and his mysterious companion. After a few moments, the fellow departed and Josh remained, as if he were spelling his companion. But for what purpose? Did it concern Edmund?

An icy surge of fear rippled down her spine. She had just learned a horrifying secret about her cousin, who had lied to her and taken money from her— money she could ill afford—under false pretenses. Edmund worked for Josh's uncle. What if his gambling debts had frightened the foolish boy into petty thievery? Nonsense. If so, the earl would simply have had the police arrest him. Perhaps this had nothing at all to do with Edmund.

Sabrina determined to wait and see. As she stood in the noonday heat, her thoughts skittered around the past weekend. Saturday night had changed her whole life. She was in love, desperately in love, with her Texan. Not hers, she corrected herself firmly. And not simply a Texan either. He was Viscount Wesley, and would eventually marry a woman of significant rank, when he found her.

An ironic smile passed fleetingly across her lips as she thought of Lady Eunice. No, Eunice would certainly not be his choice, no matter what the earl said, if that was any comfort to her. It was not. There would be many more eligible candidates waiting to ensnare Josh. A spinster teacher was merely a pleasant dalliance for a man used to charming women. His very skill as a lover attested to that fact. He had caught her at a very vulnerable time. The debacle aboard ship that day, his kindness and empathy for poor Drucilla, his perception about her own feelings—everything had conspired to make that one moonlit night pure magic.

Magic that could never happen again.

Oh, she knew well enough that he wanted to continue their liaison. If she'd ever harbored any doubts about her ability to attract a man—and she certainly had after Dex—he'd laid those fears to rest. She could thank him for that. The irony was that, now that she was certain she could have a normal relationship, she wanted no man but the one who was unattainable. Was it better never to have known paradise than to pine for it after it was lost? Sabrina thought about it. In spite of her heartbreak, that one glorious night had been worth the price of every lonely day for the rest of her life.

Besides, she would have other matters to fill her time after the earl provided her with the funds to start her school. But before she could reorder her life and begin implementing her dream of helping indigent girls, she would have to complete her assignment with Hambleton's charming heir. How ever would she get through it without succumbing to temptation again . . . and again?

That troubling thought was interrupted when she saw Josh slip out of the alley and start walking down the street. From her vantage point at the corner, she could not see the boardinghouse, but it quickly became apparent that Josh was following her cousin, who was climbing into a hackney he'd hailed. Before her amazed eyes, Joshua Cantrell, seventh Viscount Wesley, leaped nimbly onto the boot of the lumbering conveyance and pulled the canvas cover over himself.

Sabrina stood in flummoxed amazement until a fat woman carrying a market basket overflowing with leeks and carrots bumped her, nearly knocking her into the street.

"Watch where yer goin'," she snarled, waddling past.

What should she do? Wait for Edmund to return and confront him or go back home? It was obvious that her Texan would not be at the earl's city house for afternoon lessons. As she hailed a hackney, Sabrina reminded herself for the hundredth time not to keep referring to that rascal as *hers.*

The trouble he took following Edmund Whistledown was not worth the bump on his skull he'd received when he leaped from the hansom as it pulled away from Epsom. Josh gingerly rubbed his head. All the stupid young fool had done was to meet with a couple of plug-ugly characters whom Josh wouldn't have trusted to clean his cuspidor. The quivering clerk paid them a wad of cash, no doubt the same wad he'd been given earlier by Zarenko.

It was apparent from their menacing posture that Whistledown still owed more. How could Josh keep the young idiot from digging himself deeper into this manure pile? The boy was certain to take advantage of his access to the earl's office to pilfer more information and sell it to Zarenko. He sighed. It was probably already too late. If they caught the Russians aboard the boat tomorrow attempting to assassinate the man posing as Minister Hayashi, Edmund would be dragged down with them. He prayed the boy would not be with them, but, given his desperation, Whistledown might well fall into the trap he'd unwittingly helped set.

How will I tell Sabrina?

The thought plagued him on the way home. He would just have to deal with that when the time came. There was no chance Sabrina had anything to do with her cousin's treachery. But he still wondered about his uncle's role in the intrigue. Why did the earl have access to such secret information about the Japanese mission to England in the first place? As usual, Jamison had been evasive.

Josh wanted to be present when the trap was sprung. Michael had tried to convince him that he could jeopardize his camaraderie with Alexi Kurznikov and the others if he was present when they arrested the assassins. But he'd been adamant about participating in this little roundup. There would be plenty of time to continue ingratiating himself with the Russians if they failed to take the bait. Josh knew that meant he had to spend tonight drinking at the White Satin, when he'd far rather be motoring through the countryside with Sabrina.

With luck, once this mess was untangled, he'd have lots of opportunities to ride with her . . . and not always in the Mercedes either. He smiled at that thought as the hansom he'd hired dropped him off where he'd left the automobile. He cranked it up and set off for the Metropole. If he knew Alexi, he would already be ensconced in the hotel's elegant lounge with a bottle of vodka.

What Josh found instead was Natasha, who waylaid him in the opulent lobby. She was seated on a ruby velvet settee, surrounded by a gaggle of admirers, most of them young Englishmen ready to do her bidding. One was in the act of handing her a glass of champagne when she saw Josh from across the large lobby. He tried unsuccessfully to duck behind an immense potted palm, but her clear, high voice bounced off the tin ceiling, carrying around the cavernous space over the noise of murmured conversations and squeaky carts being pushed by weary bellmen.

"Why, if it is not my favorite Americain, the Texas Viscount," she said, rising and tossing off the glass of bubbling wine just as she did vodka, then handing it to the swain standing by her side as if he were a bellman. Apparently, Russians were anatomically incapable of sipping.

La Samsonov moved with the imperial grandeur of a Yankee clipper under full sail. The sparse crowd parted for her as if she were the czarina herself. Approaching him with both hands out, she seemed to invite him to take her hands and kiss them. Or did she intend to wrap them around his neck and kiss him full on the mouth? Her black eyes glittered as if she'd been partaking of hashish.

With a female as volatile as this one, Josh had no idea what was expected of him. He trotted out his most engagingly innocent grin as he took her hands and did a pretty good job of fancy-dan hand-kissing. "You're a sight to make a blind man see, Madame Samsonov," he said as she continued to grip his hands tightly. He could feel her heat through violet silk gloves and see the pulse that beat rapidly at the base of her white throat, revealed by the shockingly low cut of her gown, a dramatic concoction of dark purple and pale violet satin. Voluptuous breasts spilled out in milky splendor, adorned by an elaborate amethyst necklace whose lowest stone nestled in the deep vee between the globes.

Seeing where his eyes trespassed, she gave him a blinding smile. "You are so very charming. Original. Not like these stuffy English. And"—she hesitated for a moment, drawing out her teasing while she pressed the backs of his hands to her bare neckline—"I have learned that you own a horseless carriage."

Josh smiled ruefully. "I have a Mercedes."

Her smile turned instantly into a pout. "Pah, some Spanish woman can do nothing for you. You shall take me for a ride and I will show you," she purred.

It was a command he dared not refuse. He chuckled. "My Mercedes is an automobile, madame, not a woman."

She sighed. "I feel so foolish. But I also feel like riding."

Josh was certain that a woman as sophisticated as a prima ballerina who toured Europe would know about German luxury automobiles. She was not stupid like Eunice; Natasha was playing with him. But why? There was only one way to find out. He took her arm and said, "I'd be happy as a speckled pup with two tails to take you for a ride, Madame Samsonov."

"Tasha. My friends call me Tasha," she purred as they headed for the door.

As they turned, Josh caught sight of "Tasha's" brother scowling at them darkly from behind one of the palms. "Your brother looks like he's just run across a hornet in the privy."

She shrugged dismissively. "Nicki is always brooding about something or other. Forget him. The sun shines. The fresh air calls to me. Let us ride."

"Not much fresh air in London," Josh replied as a footman held open the huge brass door of the red granite hotel.

"Then you shall drive me to the country where there is fresh air," she said slyly.

As they drove through the busy streets, she studied him with intense dark eyes. He was a magnificent barbarian, no doubt of it. And Hambleton's heir. Her cabal was receiving more information now from her new source than from Albany's pale son, but both men bored her in the extreme. Poor sots. This Texan would be good in bed—she could always tell. He was as wild and reckless as she. Soon her assignment here in England would be complete and she'd be sent elsewhere. Tasha decided she was entitled to a bit of pleasure before that happened.

Neither the Russian nor the Texan saw Sabrina as she stood dumbly at the edge of Russell Square, watching the pair speed past. Trying to take her mind off her troubles, she'd spent the afternoon gawking at antiquities and was en route home. The wonders of the British Museum could not rid her mind of Edmund's gambling debts, or of the night she'd spent in Josh's arms. The last thing she expected was to see him with another woman, least of all the prima ballerina.

But she should have expected it, she thought bitterly. Had he not said to Drucilla that Natasha Samsonov was tall and beautiful? And she was. While Josh kept his eyes on the traffic, the raven-haired woman had her gaze fixed on his handsome profile as they laughed and talked. Oh, he was a charmer, probably en route to some trysting place where he would . . .

No, she could not finish the thought. It made her feel used and cheap. *Can you blame him? After all, you were no virginal miss when he seduced you,* she scolded herself as tears threatened. Sabrina blinked them back and kept on walking resolutely. She would go to the earl first thing in the morning and terminate her employment. If he chose not to bestow the munificent reward he'd promised for "civilizing" his nephew, so be it. She simply could not endure one more moment in Josh's presence.

Sabrina should have felt angry and humiliated, and she did. But she also felt betrayed . . . far more betrayed by her Texan than she ever had by Dex.

When the daunting butler Nash announced that she would be allowed to speak with the earl, Sabrina felt her stomach clench with an ache that had not left her since yesterday afternoon. She'd spent the night dreaming about Josh, seeing his green eyes dance with laughter, feeling the whisper-light caress of his mouth on hers, hearing the slow, intimate drawl of his voice as he crooned love words in her ear. Now it was over. So quickly, before it had scarcely begun.

Even though she knew that the breakup was for the best, she had secretly hoped for a few more nights in his arms before they were separated by station and . . . temptation. She knew how women responded to his exotic background, his charm and handsome face. There had been many before her and would be many after her. Even the glamorous ballerina was only a temporary diversion. Josh would marry a woman of rank and most probably continue having dalliances.

Especially if he ends up with one such as Lady Eunice, she thought with spiteful anger as she followed Nash into the earl's office. The elderly gentleman rose and smiled at her warmly.

"Good morning, Miss Edgewater. What brings you out so early? I'm afraid my rapscallion nephew is away from the house and not expected home until later in the day. I do hope he didn't forget a lesson you'd arranged?"

"No, we made no plans," she replied as she took the seat he offered her. Although Sabrina would have preferred to stand and quickly say what she'd come to say, it would have been rude to expect the octogenarian earl to stand while she did so. "But I did come to discuss my tutorials with the viscount," she said as she carefully arranged her skirts.

She's nervous and unhappy, Hambleton thought with a sense of foreboding. "What ever is troubling you, my dear young lady?" He leaned forward against his desk and studied her as she began to speak.

"I wish to terminate my employment, my lord. If you choose not to fund my school, I shall understand fully." She waited for the ax to fall, but was puzzled by the slow smile that turned up the corners of his mustache.

"Ah, so you've had your first lovers' spat," he said. "Not to worry. Joshua can be a trial, but—"

"Lovers' spat?" she squeaked with dawning horror. Surely he could not know . . .

As if reading her mind, the earl nodded. "Please, don't take offense. I could see by the way you and my nephew began that—"

Sabrina started to jump to her feet, ready to storm

from the room, when the door burst open and the mysterious man she'd seen with Josh yesterday appeared. His arm was draped over Josh's shoulder and he was supporting the viscount.

"You'll need to call a physician," the man said calmly as he gave the bleeding Josh a fulminating look. "The stubborn Texan refused to go to a hospital."

"It's just a nick," Josh said as he looked from his uncle to Sabrina. He removed his arm from Michael's shoulder and used the back of her chair to steady himself. "You do have the most incredible way of surprising a—"

She was out of the chair and on her feet in an instant, reaching out to him as the stranger caught him while he started to slide into unconsciousness. There was blood everywhere. "What's happened to him?" she asked as the man lowered Josh to the carpet.

"I told the young fool he needn't be there, that you could handle it, Michael," the earl said, ignoring her question. "But being one of those wild and woolly Americans, he had to be in on the hunt. How bad is it?" the earl asked in an amazingly calm voice, although his face had turned ashen as he rang the bellpull to summon help.

Sabrina knelt beside the man the earl called Michael as he pulled a small knife from his pocket and began to cut the sleeves of Josh's jacket and shirt, slicing upward until he revealed a long, ugly gash that had soaked his jacket in blood. "Must have nicked a big vein," he said as if discussing the weather. "I wanted to take him to St. John's after everything was finished, but he insisted it wasn't serious."

"You'll need to stop the bleeding at once," Sabrina said, reaching over and taking the knife from him. She used it to cut a long strip of her soft cotton petticoat and applied pressure with a wad of cloth. "Hold this while I wrap it," she commanded, placing Michael's hand over the pulsing wound.

"How did you learn medicine?" the earl asked just as Nash came scurrying into the room to announce that he'd already sent for a physician, having seen the condition of the viscount when he was brought in.

"I was second eldest of seven children, three of them boys, not to mention my very accident-prone young cousin," she replied as if that were explanation enough. "Now, this looks as if it came near shattering bone. Although Gerard, Donald and Jeffrey did grievous injury to themselves growing up, I've never seen such an ugly, deep furrow. What happened?" she repeated, leveling piercing blue eyes on Michael.

From behind her, the earl replied wearily, "It would appear, my dear, that he's been shot."

Chapter 13

"First I puke in a woman's hat, then I faint dead away. Some damn fine way to impress a lady," Josh groused as Sabrina leaned over him with an expression of concern. He looked around and realized he'd been moved into his room and lay on his bed. Someone had removed his clothing and bandaged his arm, which ached like hell.

"I hardly think passing out from loss of blood would qualify as fainting, my lord," Sabrina replied soothingly, placing her hand against his uninjured shoulder to keep him from sitting up.

"Hell, I've been shot a lot worse and managed to stay awake."

"So I noted by the plethora of scars adorning your body," she said tartly, then could have bitten her tongue when a lazy grin replaced his chagrined expression.

"Did you now?" he drawled.

"Dr. Maynard asked that I remain to assist him when he examined your injury. His examination was more extensive than I'd bargained for. You've led quite an active life, Lord Wesley," she replied primly as she pulled the sheet higher, trying to cover more of his disturbingly enticing chest. Whenever she was around this man, she blurted out things far better left unsaid.

"Oh, so now I'm bein' 'lordshiped' again, even when we're alone together." His voice was low and intense. He'd make her get over her protective sense of decorum, one way or the other.

"You are a viscount and I am a teacher. The differences in our stations will never change." It came out more like an excuse than a statement of common sense as she'd intended it.

He treated it that way. "The hell with stations. I was raised in a bordello and made myself a millionaire. Titles be damned. I desire you, no one else. I thought after Saturday night you'd be convinced of that."

Sabrina drew back. "You need not dissemble, my lord. I saw you with Madame Samsonov." Heavens, that sounded jealous! His grin widened once more, indicating that he knew it. "I have no claim whatever on you. If you wish to cavort with every dancer and actress in London, it's of no moment to me."

"Now, why don't I believe that?" he asked rhetorically. "You have my word that I'm not in the least interested in that female—at least not in the way you think," he added, wondering how he was going to soothe her ruffled feathers and at the same time conceal his true reason for associating with the icy Russian beauty. "I'd sooner mate with a praying mantis. Did you know the females eat the males after?"

He decided that actions were probably better than words. Before she could frame a question he could not answer, he seized her hand, rubbing tiny circles around the racing pulse of her wrist with his thumb. He'd always found that a good gauge of a woman's feelings.

Sabrina tried to jerk her hand free but he pulled her closer, using his good arm to force her to perch on the edge of the bed. "I'm not in the least interested in your new inamorata, praying mantis or no," she lied. "In fact, I was just giving my notice to your uncle when you interrupted bleeding all over the carpet. Did some jealous lover shoot you?"

"You're the one who's jealous, and there's no reason."

"Oh?" She succeeded in pulling her hand free and fairly jumped to her feet. Damn the man, he was beguiling her again. What she needed to do was place some distance between them . . . and find out what on earth was going on. "Then who shot you? And why were you skulking around my cousin's lodgings yesterday?"

Josh sighed, trying to shift his fuzzy brain into a higher gear, but it was stuck somewhere between first and second and he was too tuckered out to engage the clutch. He tried to reach up to her, but when he shifted his weight on the mattress, his injured arm shot fiery pain all the way to his fingertips. He muffled an oath as he fell back against the covers.

"Now look what you've done. If you're not careful, you'll start the bleeding again," she scolded, examining the wrappings on his arm.

"You patched me up, didn't you?" he asked, vaguely recalling her instructing Michael and bandaging his arm before he'd gone down for the count. No question she still cared about him. Before she could reply, he gave a low moan and closed his eyes. Might as well play-act up a storm if it would keep her sitting beside him so he could smell that faint essence of wildflowers and feel her thigh pressing against his side. Lordy, the woman went to his head faster than a double shot of bourbon at the end of a hard day's ride.

Sabrina murmured to herself about male foolishness and felt his forehead to see if he was starting a fever, one of the things the physician had cautioned them about after examining the wound and commending her on stopping the bleeding so efficiently. Josh felt cool enough, but touching him made *her* feel feverish. The man was a womanizer and would break her heart. If she had any sense at all, she'd stand up and walk away.

She leaned closer.

And drank in his face while those devilish green eyes were closed. His black lashes lay against the windburned tan of his cheeks, the square cut of his jaw was faintly bristled with beard, and the sculpted beauty of his lips looked so inviting. How could she ever forget the way he'd employed them, kissing her until she was breathless, a mere bit of clay for him to form for his own designs?

Then she felt his good arm encircling her waist and pulling her forward as he murmured softly, "I'll die if you don't kiss me, Sabbie." Somehow she found her mouth drawn to his. Unable to resist, she pressed her palms against his bare chest and opened her lips as he raised his head to meet her in a searingly gentle kiss that gradually grew deeper, hungrier.

Only the sound of the earl clearing his throat in the open doorway broke the spell. Sabrina shot from the bed as if launched from a cannon before Hambleton sauntered into the room, looking amazingly well pleased, considering that his sole heir had just experienced a brush with death. She knew her cheeks must be flushed and her clothing mussed, but she refrained from calling further attention to herself by straightening her dishabille.

Instead, she stood very still and studied the elderly gentleman as she said, "I must be going. The physician seems to feel the viscount will recover, although you must instruct the servants to watch for fever."

Before she could make good her escape, Hambleton replied, "Tut, my dear young lady. You have proved a far better nurse than any of the servants. I'd prefer that you remain to care for my nephew."

"But I'm not a nurse, I'm a teacher of decorum, and this is most . . . indecorous," she replied, hating the way her fair skin and frazzled nerves betrayed her.

"Nonsense. The boy's been shot, and you knew how to stop the bleeding. Dr. Maynard said so himself. No higher recommendation than that. You'll stay. I've sent for your clothing and such. A bedroom's been made ready for you . . . directly next door." He motioned imperiously to the doorway connecting this room with the adjoining one.

"That's a right good idea, Uncle Ab," Josh drawled. "You never know when I might take a fever. I've been prone to overheating ever since I was a tadpole."

Sabrina looked from her "patient" to her employer. Her *former* employer, she reminded herself. But she knew that if she walked out of here, her dreams of founding a school would be forever lost . . . as was her heart. What more could happen? She was already in love with the Texas viscount. Although she could not hope for a permanent relationship with him, this would be her only opportunity to be near him before he went on with his life.

"Very well, I shall remain for a day or so," she

replied primly. She could use the time inside Hambleton House to learn what Josh and his mysterious friend had been doing that had led to a shooting.

Edmund Whistledown stepped from the earl's office with a sheaf of documents in his hand to be delivered to Whitehall posthaste. He was surprised to see Sabrina standing at the end of the long hallway with a look in her eyes that could only spell trouble for him. "Hullo, Coz. I heard you were staying to tend to the viscount. Awful business," he ventured as she drew near in a no-nonsense stride.

"We need to have a word, Eddy," she said, indicating he should follow her into a small sitting room across the hall.

"Er, His Lordship's secretary gave me these papers. I'm off to Whitehall—"

"I do not give a fig if you're off to be knighted. Into the room, Edmund."

Shoulders slumping, he followed, allowing her to close the door firmly. When she turned to face him with her arms crossed over her chest, foot tapping steadily against the polished hardwood floor, he knew he'd been found out. She waited for him to confess. He could never win when Aunt Mildred or Cousin Sabrina cornered him this way.

"Crikey, Sabrina, I'm sorry about all this mess." His complexion, already sallow, turned an even paler shade as he said, "Those chaps from Epsom didn't . . . they didn't—"

"No, I was fortunate enough to be spared that indignity," she interrupted coldly. "Mr. Loring came to visit me, hoping I would pay a bill I already gave you money for. He explained about the way you've been using my hard-earned funds . . . and lying to me in the bargain."

"I . . . I didn't mean to, but if I'd told you about Epsom—"

"I would have been appalled by your folly, but I wouldn't have left you to be beaten to death by fellows such as Mr. Loring described," she replied.

His Adam's apple bobbed as he swallowed repeatedly, hanging his head. When he spoke, his voice was so low it was barely audible. "I was ashamed. You're right, I was a real ragger at the racecourses. You see, I won at first, and then when I lost, I thought it would only be a matter of time before my luck changed again."

"But it never did." Her comment was not a question.

"I was that scared, Coz. Bentham's man Killian, he's off his onion. He'd as soon slit a man's throat—"

"Spare me the gory descriptions. I have sufficient imagination to envision what would have happened to you. All the more reason to tell me the truth. Do you owe them more?"

His head hung even lower. "Well, I paid Bentham a hundred seventy—"

"One hundred seventy *pounds*?" she echoed incredulously. That was far more than what she'd lent him. "Where did you obtain such a large amount of money? Surely you aren't reduced to stealing from your employer," she whispered, horrified as a guilty expression she remembered well from childhood settled over Edmund's narrow face.

"No, I've stolen nothing from His Lordship," he answered her uneasily.

Sabrina could tell when he was evading the truth. "Then how did you come into a small fortune such as that? No one else in our family has anywhere near that kind of income."

"It's a long story," he replied with some petulance.

"Sit down. We shall take all the time necessary for you to assure me that you are not a thief."

Edmund sank onto the chair she pointed to and commenced wringing his hands as he spoke. "This buck I'd seen a time or two at Epsom and Sansdown, he came up to me and asked how I was doing one day when I was on my way to work. He'd given me some good tips on horses before, when I was winning." His voice faded but then he continued, "I explained how I was really down on my luck. That Bentham and Killian had threatened me. He said there was a way I could earn some quid really fast. Since I'd already borrowed more than you could afford to lend me, I jumped at the chance."

"To do what?" she asked, one hand clutching her throat, half afraid of his answer as she realized why Josh must have been following him. Had her Texan been using her to get to Edmund? She suppressed the thought and concentrated on her cousin's reply.

"Deliver papers, that's all. I'm a courier. It's real respectable, Coz, honest it is."

But when he explained how the "courier system" worked, Sabrina became distinctly uneasy. "Allow me to get this straight. A man cloaked in darkness hands you a packet of papers, and you in turn take them to a rendezvous site and slip them to some foreigner. Do you know neither man?"

"Well, I couldn't see the chap who's given me the papers, no. He meets me behind the Golden Hind Inn—you know, the pub near my lodgings. It's always dark in the alley. And the buck I give 'em to, well, he's a Frenchman. At least he talks like one. Tall and has black curly hair."

"I saw you in the park with him several weeks ago," she said. At the time she'd thought something about the scene had been off, but she hadn't been able to put her finger on what. If only she could remember what the other man looked like, but it had been too great a distance and she'd paid more attention to Edmund than to his companion. Then too, she'd had other things on her mind . . . such as nearly breaking her neck and Josh's kisses. Suppressing those thoughts, she asked, "Can you recall any details about this fellow?"

"Oh, he's a real buck. Dresses to the nines. Maybe he sounded more German than French," he added as an afterthought.

"What makes you think that?"

"He sometimes says 'da' instead of oui or yes."

"Edmund, Germans say 'ya,' not 'da,'" she replied with a sinking heart. "'Da' is Russian for yes."

His eyes grew huge and the Adam's apple bobbed again. "Crikey, and our government is put off about them building a railway to some ocean or other, isn't it?"

"A bit of an understatement," she replied tersely. "What explanation did these French-German-Russians give you for the secrecy if all you were doing was acting as a business courier?"

He hesitated again until Sabrina resumed tapping her toe. "They told me I was working for our government—in an unofficial way," he said with a sigh. "That some French businessmen wanted to build a canal in Central America and they wanted to stop them. I was sworn to secrecy."

It made sense. Edmund had been made to feel important and was given badly needed money while he believed he was doing some dashing deeds for king and country. Now she was the one who sighed.

"This is bad, isn't it, Sabrina?" he asked glumly.

"Perhaps not. Do you know where this fellow from the racecourses can be found?"

"Not even his name. And I haven't seen him since he put me in touch with the chap I meet in the alley."

"I was afraid of that. We shall just have to find out what's in those documents and turn them over to the police. When are you supposed to receive your next 'assignment'?"

"I don't know. A note with the time on it just appears under the door of my room at the boarding-house."

Nothing but frustrating dead ends. Sabrina studied her cousin, whom she had practically raised since he was a sickly child. Was he telling her the truth now? Or was this another fabrication to buy her cooperation? Sabrina simply did not know.

"Very well," she said carefully. "As soon as you receive another note, let me know immediately. Speak of this to no one, do you understand?"

He nodded, seemingly relieved to have placed the burden on her slim shoulders once again. "You're an absolute trump, Sabrina. I know you'll get us out of this," he said brightly.

"Us?" she echoed, raising one eyebrow.

After dismissing Edmund, she paced about the sitting room, trying to figure out how to proceed. Although he did not believe it, Edmund's employment by the earl had to be connected to the quagmire he'd been drawn into. Josh, too, was involved in this tangle in some way. What could the old man and his nephew be doing? Surely they were not spies in the pay of the Russians?

She dismissed the idea as too preposterous to consider. But Russia was a traditional foe of England, and tensions between the two governments had never really dissipated since the Crimean War over a generation ago. Coming from America, what would Josh have to do with this Old World rivalry? Perhaps some secrets lay hidden in the earl's office.

"As long as he insists I remain here and tend to his precious heir, I'll avail myself of the opportunity to do a bit of snooping," she murmured to herself, beginning with finding out why said heir had been shot—and by whom.

Josh felt greatly restored after a hearty supper of roast beef and potatoes. Cook had first prepared consommé and a bit of that nasty fish in aspic, but he'd sent Benton back to the kitchen to demand real food, not catfish bait. He'd even threatened to dump the hot soup over his valet's head if the poor servant did not do as he was told. Nothing brought a man up to his full strength like a good chunk of Texas—or, he conceded—English beef.

He'd not seen Sabrina since their encounter at his bedside earlier in the day. Gazing speculatively at the adjacent room, he considered that she'd be sleeping there in a short while. Or not. He grinned, wondering what his uncle was up to. If he didn't know better, he'd swear the old goat was matchmaking. First, he'd arranged for her to tutor him, then set up that fool weekend with the Chiffingtons, knowing full well that he'd disgrace himself in front of the marquess and his darling daughter.

With Sabrina there to comfort him.

Josh grinned. What a night that had been. And tonight would be even better, thanks to his uncle, who'd seen to it that she would be next door. First he'd have to be certain he was up to the night's exertions. He sat forward and carefully swung his long legs over the side of the bed. Then, using his good arm, he reached for the brocade dressing robe lying on the chair. He winced at the long stretch but managed to snag a sleeve and reel in the slithery garment, but before he could put it on, the door opened.

"What in heaven's name are you doing?" Sabrina asked as a startled Josh quickly bunched the dressing robe over strategic parts of his anatomy. Then, seeing who it was, he smiled in that slightly off-center way that made his eyes—and her heart—dance.

"Why, Sabbie, I was just getting up to stretch my legs, sorta work the kinks out, you know?"

"What I know is that you have lost way too much blood to be cavorting about without assistance. You have no reason to leave that bed," she scolded.

He watched her standing in the doorway as if she might turn tail and run. "You and I both know I have every reason," he said, casting a glance toward the adjacent room she would use tonight.

"Even if I were to permit it—and I hasten to add I will not—you're far too badly injured to . . . perform," she finally managed, her face heating up to match the fire in her heart—and other places she refused to think about.

"Close that door and come here, Sabbie. We'll see how well I can perform," he said in a husky voice. His eyes willed her to obey, but he had no idea what he'd do if she refused. After all, he wasn't about to win any foot races.

Sabrina stood transfixed. The need—no, she admitted, the desperate hunger—for his touch held her in thrall. If she possessed one iota of sense, she should turn and walk away. After all, he couldn't very well chase after her.

"I've asked you not to call me Sabbie," she said, frozen in place as their eyes met and held.

"Somehow 'Miss Edgewater' doesn't seem to work anymore. What do you want me to call you?" he asked reasonably, standing up and slipping into the robe, giving her a glimpse of his naked body as he did it. He heard her tiny intake of breath and smiled inwardly. But when he tried to take a step toward her, the room started to spin. He grabbed for the bedpost and hung on for dear life.

"Damned if I'll pass out at your feet a second time," he muttered through gritted teeth, lurching toward her.

Sabrina was frozen during the brief interval it took for him to reach her. She only realized how badly off balance he was when she saw the dazed expression on his face as he reached over her shoulder and shoved the door closed. He tumbled against her, pinning her rather uncomfortably between him and the sharp edge of the door frame. The knob prodded in a most indelicate place. And her tailbone hurt like the very devil.

"If you don't release me, I shall cry down the house." She was angry and afraid for him all at once.

"If I do release you, I'll fall down myself," he whispered in her ear.

His breath tickled her ear as his tongue lightly circled the sensitive inner shell. Sabrina could scarcely draw her breath as he began to nuzzle her neck. His hands pressed against the door, steadying him as he continued his sensual assault. She was trapped, and the heat of his body was starting to send messages to her body, overriding what her mind was saying. He pressed kisses onto her eyelids and inhaled the scent of her hair, murmuring how sweet she always smelled, then centered his attention on her already parted lips.

"Like plump, juicy strawberries in spring," he said as his mouth slanted over hers and plundered inside.

Her reply was to encircle his waist and dig her fingers into the hard muscles of his back. She surrendered to the kiss, letting it build and intensify, loving the way the heady warmth of it radiated through her body until everything started to melt. The world went away as they stood entwined. Her breasts pressed against his chest and the ache in her nipples rippled downward, pooling deep in her belly. His hips rocked against hers.

Finally, when his mouth disengaged from hers long enough to take a desperate, panting breath, she said, "If you persist in prodding me from the front while that doorknob does the same at the opposite side, I fear permanent injury, my lord."

Josh felt the chuckle build from deep inside him until it rumbled through his body. "Woman, you are a caution, and that's the Lord's own truth," he managed to choke out as he eased himself away from her without lowering his arms, which still imprisoned her. The injured arm hurt like hell on a hot afternoon, but he was too preoccupied to notice until he shifted his weight slightly to his left.

An involuntary grimace of pain betrayed him. Seeing it, Sabrina pulled his right arm over her shoulder and helped him toward the bed. "You should not be up yet," she scolded.

"Darlin', I've been 'up' ever since I kissed you. The

question, seems to me, is what are we going to do about it?"

It was not a question and she knew it as she began lowering him back onto the wide mattress. Instead of letting go of her arm, he pulled her with him and they both tumbled backwards. Somehow he managed to land on top. As his mouth brushed hers, she murmured, "At least the bed is softer than the door frame . . ."

"Now you're only poked from one side," he whispered.

"You're vulgar for a viscount." Sabrina didn't sound particularly concerned about the character flaw.

"Darlin', I'm vulgar for a Texan."

"You need more lessons," she murmured dreamily, burying her hands in his thick, black hair.

"Never said I wasn't quick to learn."

Chapter 14

Josh braced his weight on his good elbow and reached over to cup her breast with his injured hand. The pain lanced up his arm. "You're gonna have to be real gentle with me. I'm an invalid," he whispered as he massaged a tiny circle around the hard tip he could feel through the layers of her clothing. "You have too many duds on. In my condition, I can't get you out of them, so . . ."

When he lay back flat on the bed beside her, she started to sit up, a concerned expression on her face, saying, "You're in pain."

"Oh, God, yes, the swelling's unbearable." He yanked the tie of his robe loose with his good hand and flung the garment open, revealing his pulsing erection.

"Oh, my. It must be," she whispered, unable to keep from staring at the splendid maleness of him—proof that he was indeed ready to perform. But how could he if he couldn't support his weight on his arms?

In answer to her unspoken question, he drawled, "I

have a plan. First, will you get undressed for me, please?"

"Since you asked so nicely," she agreed shyly, not sure she could do it. "Is this Step One of your plan?" The light outside was fading rapidly but still it was considerably brighter than moonlight. Could she actually strip off her clothing while he watched her? Sabrina took a deep, shivery breath and fumbled with the buttons running down her blouse. As the sheer cotton gaped open, revealing the deep vale between her breasts, she heard him gasp.

Not daring to look at him, she unfastened the cuffs, then worked at the belt of her skirt, pulling it free. But there was still so much clothing in the way. Unlike their first lovemaking, this time she was wearing a corset and a full array of undergarments, right down to stockings and garters.

She hesitated.

He coaxed.

"Slide the blouse from the waistband and get rid of it. Let me touch them."

Her breasts responded as if he were speaking directly to them, the nipples puckering even tighter, the ache deepening. She obeyed, pulling the blouse free and peeling down the long, fitted sleeves, tossing it onto the floor as she sat beside him on the bed. His right hand cupped a breast through the sheer lace of her chemise, and she could not muffle the soft moan his caress elicited. He moved to the other breast, lifting it in silent praise, then rubbed the palm of his hand across both of them until her nipples protruded brazenly.

"Now, pull that soft covering over your head," he instructed as he lifted the edge of her chemise and allowed her to complete the task, revealing her corset-clad waist with breasts peeping over the top. The nipples were rosy and puckered as the sheer fabric grazed over them before floating to the floor beside the bed.

Josh didn't know how much longer he could wait. She was unused to undressing in front of a man, and that rig she wore would take some time to undo. He did what Americans were noted for. He improvised. "Okay, that's enough of Step One of the plan. Now for Step Two," he whispered hoarsely. "Climb aboard, darlin'."

Sabrina was amazed when he lifted her thigh and placed it over his hips so that she was straddling him. "W-what are you doing?" she asked, frankly puzzled and a bit uneasy.

"Just raise your skirts, love," he instructed calmingly, tugging at the bunched fabric on his right side.

"Oh!" She quickly caught on, freeing her other knee of the skirt and petticoat, baring her legs. The clothing became wadded at her waist. But she did not notice because his hand slipped over the curve of her hip and glided upward, caressing the sensitive skin on the inside of her thigh. He moved unerringly toward his ultimate goal. Nimble fingers found the front fastening of her underdrawers and slipped inside the narrow placket, pulling it open, reaching her heat.

How slick and sweet she was, how wet and ready for him. He watched her lashes fan over her cheeks as she arched against the persuasion of his hand, letting her hips rock as he caressed. Although he'd never cared for the confounded things, her corset emphasized the tininess of her waist and lifted her breasts like an offering. He drank in her soft whimpers of pleasure as he brought her to the brink and watched as she tumbled over it.

When the storm of ecstasy had passed, Sabrina's eyes fluttered open. She was dazed yet still aware of his staff pressed against her inner thigh, unassuaged. "How . . . what . . . Oh, dear . . ."

"Shhh," he murmured. Sweat beaded his face as he used his left arm, but he ignored the pain, positioning her hips over him, then pulling the placket of her drawers open and guiding himself to paradise.

When she felt the scalding heat and hardness rubbing delicately against her, Sabrina was lost, hungry all over again, bold and shameless in her wanting.

"Ride me, darlin'," he pleaded.

She sank onto him in awe, feeling him fill her, buried to the hilt. When he arched up, his hips bucking beneath her, she caught the rhythm and began to raise, then lower herself on him. *Ride me.* Mindlessly, she did just that, falling forward, her hands eagerly bracing against the hardness of his chest, fingers buried in springy dark hair. He pulled her closer, raising his head to suckle at her breasts, his mouth wetting the hardened nipples that protruded over the top of her corset.

He murmured words of praise, of encouragement, of love, but they were both so wildly inflamed by the passion consuming them that neither was aware of the latter. Sabrina sobbed and convulsed, peaking once more, her body clenching fiercely around him until she felt him stiffen, swell and shudder in perfect sync with her. They rode to the end of the rainbow together and then, gently, ever so slowly, came back.

Sabrina lay collapsed, limp as a rag doll over his chest, her hair spilling around his shoulders, pins scattered across the bed. He felt a pin poking his left side and moved to dislodge it, only to let out a hiss of startled pain. At once she raised herself up and looked down at him, her face now cast in twilight shadows.

"Are you . . . did I . . . hurt you?" she finally managed to ask.

He smiled crookedly, using his right hand to lift a silky coil of hair and rub it between his fingers. "Not you. Those hairpins. They're sharp as a fresh-stropped razor."

She looked around the badly rumpled bed in dismay. Her skirts were bunched around her waist and her stocking-clad legs straddled his hips. She even had one slipper still on her foot! Dear heavens, what an absolute trollop she must appear!

"Now, don't go and get all huffed up on me," he said softly. "Sometimes, making love with your clothes on isn't too bad . . . you think?"

She dared to meet his gaze, and the warmth of it brought an answering smile. He made her feel at ease, comfortable, as if this was the most natural thing in the world for both of them. "If you're fishing for compliments on your American ingenuity, I cannot but give them. Your plan was very well executed," she said boldly. How utterly different this was from the fully dressed, hurried coupling that awful time with Dex.

As if reading her mind, Josh said, "I never want you to feel used, Sabrina."

She said nothing, pushing to the back of her mind other ways in which a man might use a woman, in which he might be using her to get to Edmund. But tonight was for herself and her lover. No one else. Tomorrow would come soon enough.

"We have to get you out of that uncomfortable contraption," Josh said. "Turn and sit on the edge of the bed with your back to me so I can unlace you."

Doing as he asked, she could not resist saying, "You appear to have had considerable practice with female unmentionables."

"As far as I'm concerned, there's nothing unmentionable about a beautiful woman like you."

"I'm scarcely a great beauty like La Samsonov," she said, shamelessly testing the waters.

His hands never broke their smooth motion as he continued unlacing her corset. "I've never made love to her. And you're every bit as beautiful, just in a different way. She's cold as a blue norther. You're warm as a summer day," he murmured as he freed her from the corset and corset cover. His fingers massaged the reddened marks as he placed delicate kisses down her vertebrae.

Sabrina felt the magic of his mouth and let go of her jealous concern about the Russian woman. It was so difficult to think when he was near, doubly difficult when they were together in bed. A soft laugh bubbled to her lips. "No man has ever called me warm before," she said.

"Only because they're too afraid of your sass to see beyond it to the real you . . . bright, warm, ready to laugh. That's important, being able to laugh," he added. " 'Specially at yourself. Never pays to take yourself too seriously."

"Ah, but as Hambleton's heir, you will require gravitas," she said, only half teasing, as if trying to remind herself of the gulf between them.

"The grave part comes fast enough for everyone. Thing is, a man and a woman have to enjoy life while they're able."

"You know I wasn't talking about a grave," she scolded as he tossed her corset over the side of the bed.

Ignoring her comment, he said, "Now get rid of

those skirts and stockings, then climb in bed beside me where you belong."

Sabrina complied without protest, snuggling in his open arms as he spooned her against him and pulled the covers up.

Josh lay awake early the next morning, watching Sabrina's slow, even breathing. Lordy, he was getting in deep over his head. He'd never in his wild amorous life spent a whole night actually sleeping with a woman. He paid them and sent them on their way, or went off on his own. But here he was, like a lovesick pup, mooning over how her eyelashes curled like dark fans over her cheeks and the way her lips almost parted as she smiled in her sleep.

Yup, this was bad. Or good. Damned if he knew which. The only thing he did know was that he wanted to keep her with him for as long as he could imagine. The thought of losing her made him feel hollow as spunk wood inside. Was that love? He was damned if he knew that, either. But until he did, there was no way Miss Sabrina Edgewater was leaving him, even if that meant he had to lasso and hogtie her like a prize heifer!

She did care about him, that he knew. He rubbed his aching arm, recalling how concerned she'd been about the injury. She was a cool, competent nurse, a no-nonsense female who didn't get all fluttery at the sight of blood. He smiled, recalling that she'd said growing up in a family with three brothers had been like being raised by wolves. Her wit was sharp and self-deprecating, much like his own, a rare trait. One he had not encountered since leaving Gertie and her girls. Sabrina seemed to understand how he felt about them, too.

But she didn't understand about Natasha Samsonov, of course, and he couldn't blame her, even if he was secretly pleased at her jealousy. There was no way he could explain to her why he spent time with the pesky Russian toe dancer. Just thinking about Natasha made him frown as he slid from the bed. The colonel owed him a lot for making him put up with that scary female.

She'd insisted on driving his Mercedes that afternoon and damn near wrecked it before he seized control of the wheel to keep them from careening into a hay cart. Then she'd turned her wrath from the hapless cart driver to him. The lady was used to getting her way, and had quite a temper when she didn't.

He had not learned anything from her that would be of use to Jamison, but perhaps yesterday's trap would provide some information. One assassin had been taken alive. They might get enough out of the fellow to stop the Russian conspiracy. That would suit Josh just fine. This spy stuff was more dangerous than bulldogging an ornery longhorn. The other would-be assassin who'd escaped was the one who had winged him.

He had to reach Michael and find out what the government agents had learned from their captive. And, once and for all, he was going to find out just where his uncle fit into this whole diabolical tangle. He reached for a shirt with his good arm, then realized that Benton would be along any minute "to assist His Lordship in dressing." Sabrina had to be in her room before his valet discovered her asleep in his bed. Josh didn't give a damn what the snooty valet thought, but he knew she would be humiliated by servants' gossip.

With dismay he looked around the bed at their

clothing, strewn everywhere. Just as he started to gather up an armful of skirts and female unmentionables, a sharp rap sounded on the hall door. He cursed beneath his breath.

"Good day, m'lord. I've brought hot coffee from the kitchen, just the way you like it." Benton's nasal voice carried from the other side of the door, the tone implying how unsuitable strong black coffee, without at least the civilizing complement of cream, was as a morning beverage. English gentlemen drank tea.

Josh tensed when Benton tried the door, but fortunately, he'd remembered to lock it last night. Putting a finger to his lips as Sabrina sprang upright in bed with a look of horror on her face, he answered the valet. "Much obliged, Bent, but I'll come down directly for that coffee. Right now I feel like spending a little more time on siesta."

"His Lordship the earl has asked to speak with you as soon as you're up and about," Benton replied stiffly. "Please ring when you require my assistance in dressing."

"That'll be the day petunias sprout in hell," Josh muttered as he watched Sabrina trying to slip from the bed, using the sheet for covering as she reached for the "unmentionables" he held bundled in his arms. Her face was as pink as sunrise when she met his laughing eyes. "He's gone. It's all right," he soothed.

"Please, Josh, give me my . . . er, garments," she implored, her eyes darting from his devilish look to the outside door, as if Benton and all the other servants were going to mount an attack and break it down at any moment.

"Well, at least you used my handle. No more 'Lordshipping' me," he said, offering her the bundle but holding it just far enough away that she had to let go of the sheet to reach it. He could read on her face the urge to stamp one small bare foot in frustration when she realized his ploy.

"You're taking advantage of me," she said crossly, wiping sleep from her eyes.

"Appears to me that if I am, it isn't exactly the first time. 'Sides, I've already seen everything there is to see . . . not that I don't want to see it again."

"You are an utter . . ." Words failed her as she felt the edge of the sheet sliding away. While offering the bundle with his good arm, he surprised her by using his injured one to snatch the sheet away. •

"Now we're even," he said with a grin.

She clutched the clothing in front of her body while he stood completely naked in front of her. The only difference was that he remained calmly unconcerned about his nudity as he began picking up her remaining clothing and adding it to the growing pile in her arms. The night's rest had obviously done him a world of good. The pallor and weakness appeared to be gone as he moved gracefully around the room. Her eyes were drawn to the muscles rippling across his broad back, the way his long legs bent with clean economy as he knelt to pick up her slippers and then stood again.

"Here you go, Cinderella," he said with a lopsided grin, placing the slippers on top of the teetering mound.

He knew he was a beautiful specimen, confound the man. She could not keep her eyes averted to save her life. "Cinderella is a good appellation, since it's past midnight and my magic wanes with daylight," she managed.

"You haven't turned into a pumpkin. Far as I can

see, you look even better in daylight." His eyes swept from her tousled hair down to her trim ankles and dainty little bare feet.

"You know perfectly well it wasn't the girl but the coach that turned into a pumpkin," she retorted with some sass.

"Yep, but I didn't expect you to turn into a mouse like the footmen in the story."

"I do not lack for courage, Josh, but I must leave before your uncle comes upstairs after you. I doubt you can fob him off as easily as you did your valet. That does not make me into a 'mouse'!" Now, how the devil was she going to cross to her room without affording him a full view of her bare backside?

As if reading her mind, Josh reached over and tucked the skirt around her fanny, managing to caress a rounded cheek as he did so. "Just trying to help a lady," he said with an innocent wink.

Sabrina exited and closed the door behind her with as much dignity as she could muster, which was not a great deal considering how red her face was . . . and how her derriere tingled from his touch.

When Josh entered his uncle's office, the old man was seated behind his desk, sorting through a sheaf of documents. He looked up at his nephew with a very serious expression on his face. In fact, Josh would have said the old man had aged another decade overnight. "You look like a fellow who's been on a nine-day bender. What's wrong, Uncle Ab?"

"Thank you for the compliment, my boy," the old man said dryly as he waved Josh into a chair. "The elderly are ever so grateful just to be reminded that they still breathe. You, being a young and disgustingly resilient Anglo-American, appear little the worse for your encounter with a bullet yesterday."

"I've been shot at a time or two during the war in Cuba, but there I knew who the enemy was," Josh replied, wondering when the old man was going to ask him why he'd been shot. He had some dim recollection of his uncle telling Michael that he should have stayed out of the fracas yesterday, as if the old man knew all about it. He leaned back like a good poker player, which he was, and waited for the earl to lay out his cards.

Hambleton sighed. "All right. I might as well explain the whole of this tangle, although I'd hoped, for your own protection, that it wouldn't prove necessary."

"You work for the Foreign Office." It was not a question. "I think you'd better level with me, Uncle Ab. I suppose you know the colonel—President Roosevelt—asked me to look into this mess for him?"

"Yes, I did. In fact, it was I who recommended to Salisbury that he request help from your old comrade in arms. Short of crossing the Atlantic myself, it was the only way I could be assured you'd accept your position as my heir. The situation here obviously precluded such a voyage on my part, and I must admit you are admirably suited for the task at hand," Hambleton added with a touch of pride in his voice.

Josh studied the crafty old man. A grudging grin spread over his face as he replied, "I reckon we have even more in common than I first thought. You did just what I'd do in your position. But, speaking of your position, just what the hell is it you do for Salisbury and Lansdowne?"

"I've been an advisor to His Majesty's government

237

on matters of espionage for most of my life. No one outside the Prime Minister and the Foreign Secretary have ever been apprised of that," the earl replied.

"Until someone started trying to kill the Japanese minister and you figured they were getting their information through you somehow?"

The old man nodded. "Very astute. At first we assumed it was Albany's son, which was correct. He was a pawn used by his mistress, but when we saw to it that he could no longer access the negotiations with the Japanese, the Russians still had a source of highly secret information that led to near disaster. Yesterday's fiasco proved that. Whoever is behind this fell into our trap because of what was learned from here," the earl said angrily.

"I wondered why Michael was so close-mouthed about how they'd laid the trap for Whistledown," Josh said. "Hell, he wouldn't even have told me about it if I hadn't agreed to spell him in following the kid. I gather there's no doubt he's guilty. What did the Russian we captured yesterday say about it?"

"That is part of the conundrum. You see, the villain was killed before he could talk. Our agents had taken him to a location known only to the Foreign Secretary, Michael Jamison and me. Somehow, one of their agents slipped in and slit the throat of his fellow conspirator, then escaped."

"And there's no way in hell they could've known where to look for him unless they got the information from here?" At the earl's grim nod, Josh continued, "Then it has to be Whistledown. I watched him pay off some bully boys at the track on Monday, and he owes them more."

"Michael Jamison informed me about the lad's

gambling and its possibly treasonous results. Regrettable, most regrettable," the earl said.

"You don't keep secret information lying around, I know. How did the dumb kid find out where the prisoner was being taken?"

"That is what I have been pondering. It's possible he overheard my discussion with Mr. Jamison after you'd been taken upstairs. He was here, and the household was in such an uproar over your being shot that no one, alas, including me, was as alert as we should have been."

Josh pictured Sabrina's reaction when this all came out. Damn the fool boy for his stupidity! "Are you going to arrest him now or wait?"

Outside the door, Sabrina held her breath, anticipating the earl's reply. How could Josh have used her so shamefully? And poor, foolish Edmund would pay for all their sins. When she heard the earl say that he had sent for the no-longer-mysterious Mr. Jamison to take Edmund into custody, she slipped away, biting her lip in anguish. Somehow she had to get Eddy away before he was apprehended. Then the two of them would prove he was merely a cat's-paw, not a traitor.

At least that was what she prayed they could do.

As to the pain of Josh's betrayal, she would not consider it until her cousin was safe. Maybe by that time it would not hurt so badly. But she doubted that her heart would ever stop aching.

"Crikey, Sabrina, they have to believe me! I didn't—"

"Will you be quiet and come with me before it's too late," she hissed, practically dragging the boy toward the servants' entrance. "Now you will go straight-away to the Berkshires. Mama and Papa can hide you until this whole disaster is sorted out. I've scraped to-gether enough money for train fare, but we'd best hurry," she continued as they slipped unobserved from the house and down the alley behind the mews.

In the hansom to the railway station, Sabrina quizzed the white-faced Edmund about how he'd been drawn into the conspiracy, beginning with his "friend" from the racecourses whose name he still could not recall, if he'd ever known it.

"They were using you from the start, drawing you into betting by offering false information about win-ning horses. I can see that now," she said thoughtfully.

Edmund sat glumly silent as she skewered him with a penetrating blue gaze. "How much more do you owe those racetrack ruffians?"

He swallowed in misery, his Adam's apple bob-bing. "I don't owe much more," he whispered hoarsely, struggling hard to keep tears at bay.

"Perhaps it's good that you're still in debt."

"Why?" he cried.

"The Russians don't know you've been compro-mised yet, only that you still need money. Perhaps if I act quickly, I can find out who has been stealing the information. I believe I can identify the Russian I saw with you in the park. The lot of them live at the Metro-pole Hotel, if the newspapers are to be believed."

"Oh, Coz, I can't have you going off to spy on Rus-sians by yourself. That's far too dangerous. I'll go with you." Before she could refuse, he pressed on, "I'd recognize the chap anywhere. You only saw him from a distance one time. You'll need my help . . . just as I need yours," he finished, red-faced.

Sabrina considered that as they drew near their

destination. Perhaps Eddy was right. She'd had only a passing glance at the tall, dark-haired man, while her cousin had met him on numerous occasions and could spot him in a crowded place like the Metropole. "Very well, you shall come with me, only long enough to point him out. Then it's off to the Berkshires with you before you vanish into some secret place about which only the Foreign Office knows."

Edmund's Adam's apple quivered again, this time not with shame but with terror.

Chapter 15

When their hansom pulled up in front of the Metropole, neither Sabrina nor Edmund saw Josh observe them alight and pay the driver. He sat in the shadows, leaning back against the squabs of the cab he'd flagged down to follow them. He was numb with shock. Edmund he would have expected to run, but not Sabrina. She simply could not be involved in this whole ugly business.

Then what on earth is she doing here, walking calmly into a nest of Russian assassins, if she hasn't been hired by them? a persistent voice whispered. Having no answers, he combed his fingers through his hair in confusion and despair.

It entered his mind that he'd never asked his uncle about why he'd selected Sabrina to tutor him. Was it because her cousin was already in his employ? Or did he and his Foreign Office associates already suspect Whistledown's involvement and want to use her to get to him? Or was she a British agent herself? Figuring all this out was as twisty and rough as riding a sunfishing bronc. Just thinking about it made Josh's head ache . . .

But not nearly so much as his heart.

Reluctantly he climbed out of the coach and followed them into the hotel lobby.

"Do you see him?" Sabrina asked her cousin as they stood beneath the shelter of an enormous potted palm. Edmund peered around it, his eyes scanning the ladies and gentlemen strolling across the lobby en route to breakfast.

"No. Maybe he sleeps late," he offered.

"From what I've read of the Russian aristocracy, they stay up all night and sleep all day, like vampires." She chastised herself for not having thought of that before. She and Edmund might cool their heels here until sundown before that man appeared . . . unless. "Perhaps what we need to do is infiltrate."

Edmund looked uneasily at his normally sensible cousin, not liking the sound of her proposal. "Infiltrate what?" he asked in a squeaky voice.

Sabrina bit her lip as her gaze skittered around the cavernous lobby and into the airy lounge adjoining it. "You stay here and keep watch on that doorway." She pointed across the lobby to a door from which a bellman had just emerged, resplendent in maroon and green livery.

"Crikey, why?" Edmund's eyes bulged out more than his Adam's apple as he swallowed nervously. He definitely did not like this.

"I'll signal you when the way is clear. Wait here until I return."

He nodded unhappily as she strolled across the foyer and down the hall to the door from which she'd seen the bellman emerge. She opened the door and disappeared behind it. Servants could pass unnoticed through a building. If this hotel operated like the one where her spinster aunt Hannah worked, it would facilitate the plan formulating in her desperate mind.

It did.

After slipping down the narrow, uncarpeted hallway, trying each door along the way, she netted her loot—two uniforms, a maid's costume for her and a bellman's for Edmund. So thoughtful of the establishment to clean and press a range of sizes in this sewing room, where rips were mended and stains removed from the expensive livery. Bless Aunt Hannah, who had been the best seamstress in the Berkshires before she came to London to earn her way.

Sabrina quickly changed into the maid's uniform and returned to the lobby. She signaled to Edmund, and groaned inwardly as he furtively darted toward her. If only no one saw him.

Someone did.

Josh stood behind a wide pillar, watching the scene play out with mounting confusion. What the hell was going on? Now Sabrina had on a chambermaid's uniform and she had ducked behind a door with Edmund. Josh's conscience warred within him. He should grab Whistledown by the scruff of his scrawny neck and haul him back to the earl, but that would mean dragging Sabrina along. Somehow, he just couldn't do it.

Not if there was a chance she was innocent. He wanted to believe that—needed desperately to believe it, like he had believed while growing up at Gertie's that one day he'd be a man of property. If Sabrina and her cousin were involved with the Russians, why all this ruse? They would just walk up to Zarenko's room and transact their business. No, there had to be another explanation. Josh intended to find out what it was before he took the cousins into custody.

When he attempted to enter the door they'd used, a bellman stopped him, explaining deferentially that this way led to the servants' stairs. Returning to the lobby, he bribed a clerk to give him Zarenko's suite number.

Josh knew the cousins had no money to offer bribes for information, even if they knew Zarenko's name. Then he went up to the second floor and hid in the alcove near Zarenko's suite. It wasn't long before he heard Sabrina's precise yet soft voice around the corner. He ducked behind a fern as they passed the intersecting corridor, then followed them.

How would they locate the Russian? Sabrina stopped a young maid carrying a scrub bucket and inquired which floors the Russians occupied.

"Why, the lot of 'em stays right 'ere on the second," she said, giving Sabrina a curious look. "Say, I never seen you afore," the girl added suspiciously, squinting at Edmund, who shuffled nervously behind Sabrina.

Josh was amazed when Whistledown, now in a bellman's uniform, seized the maid's work-reddened hand and kissed it. "We be new. This 'ere's our first day."

He went on spinning a charming tale in an improbable cockney accent that quickly had the maid giggling, her face as red as her hands. A surprisingly slick dude, Sabrina's beloved young cousin, Josh thought, wondering if Edmund was good enough to have fooled Sabrina as easily as he did the scrub girl. Somehow he doubted it. He waited to see what they would do once the maid departed, buckets sloshing as she rounded the corner.

At the rate Sabrina and Edmund were going, the Japanese minister would be cold in his grave before they found their quarry. They knocked on the doors of the first four suites, all occupied by women. With a grimace of amusement, Josh imagined La Samsonov's fury if she had been awakened by a pair of mere servants. He had to give Sabrina credit for ingenuity. The prim "chambermaid" asked to speak with the guest about a complaint from the suite above them. Too much noise late last night. Whistledown stood officiously beside her, as if offering his dubious protection.

Finally, the seventh try brought them to Zarenko's suite. His servant, who spoke virtually no English, attempted to explain that his master had not yet arisen, but the more he insisted in a polyglot of French and Russian that he would not disturb Zarenko, the louder Sabrina and Edmund's voices grew.

At length, a cursing, reeling Zarenko, still in his cups from an all-night debauch, appeared at the door, threatening to take maid, bellman and his own valet and bash in their skulls if they were not silent at once. Josh noted the way Edmund carefully averted his face, hanging his head down to conceal his identity. Drunk as the Russian still was, Josh doubted that Nikolai would have recognized his own sister Natasha, much less a nonentity such as Whistledown.

A great flood of relief washed over Josh as he listened to them make their excuses and begin a whispering conversation as soon as the door slammed shut in their faces.

"That's him, Coz!"

"Yes, he does look like the fellow I saw with you in the park that day, although I doubt I'd have been certain without your confirmation. However, it is now time for you to take the train home and wait until I can straighten out this tangle."

"This might be dangerous, and it's all my fault. I'm not leaving you," Edmund said manfully.

"Don't be even more foolish than you've already been, Eddy. If you are arrested, they'll likely arrest me, too, for being with you. And then where shall either of us be?"

"B-but what can you do?"

"I shall wait for that odious drunkard to leave his quarters. Given his condition, I imagine I'll have time aplenty to change my clothing, eat a hearty luncheon and take a nap first," she replied crisply. "Then I'll follow him and learn who the other conspirators are and what they are doing with whatever information you gave them."

"I don't—"

His protest was cut short as they made their way toward the end of the hall and a hatchet-faced man in bell captain's livery stalked toward them, calling out, "I say, what are you about? Lollygagging while there's work to be done. You—" he jabbed a finger into Edmund's chest—"see to transporting Lady Landenham's portmanteau downstairs. It must weigh at least five stone. Harry cannot manage it without assistance. She's in 314. Get on it now," he added impatiently when the young "bellman" hesitated.

"And you," he said, turning to Sabrina when Edmund had moved off toward the servants' stairs, "you're needed to clean up the mess in the suite at the end of the hall. One of Madame Samsonov's servants requested assistance."

"Assistance?" Sabrina echoed dubiously as her mind raced to find a way out of this tangle.

The cadaverous man towered over her as an expression of thunderous disapproval slashed across his downturned mouth. His breath reeked from rotten teeth. He spoke as if to a half-wit child, saying, "The lady was indisposed from overindulgence. The noisome mess will ruin a perfectly good Turkish carpet if it is not scooped up and scrubbed off immediately. Then there's the matter of the bed linens, as well," he added with a sniff of disapproval. "Damned Russians."

Sabrina paled. If it had been some poor soul genuinely ill, she would not have hesitated. But a drunkard . . . and that odious woman whom Josh had taken riding to boot! "I will rot in Hades before I lift a finger to—"

"You will do as you're told immediately or I will take you to Mr. Hasmettle and have you dismissed," he interrupted, seizing her arm and jerking her toward Samsonov's suite.

Josh grinned as they approached the door, but then decided it would be best if he took a hand before both he and Sabrina lost track of dear Eddy. "Hey, there, you in the general's suit," he called out to the bell captain in the loud tone of a nouveau-riche American. "I need that there little filly to help me unpack my duds." He strutted up to Sabrina, who stared at him gape-jawed as she jerked her arm angrily free of her captor's grip.

The look in her eyes was murderous, but it was obvious to Josh she could not decide on whom to vent her fury as she looked from the protesting captain and then to her rescuer. Josh grabbed her other arm just as the bell captain let go, and whispered in her ear, "It's me or the puke, darlin', take your pick."

"Please, sir, I'm certain you don't want this female. I was just about to dismiss her for impudence. I shall summon another maid. What is your room number?" the captain asked.

"This here filly will do right enough . . . if you take my meanin'." He gave a lewd wink to the man and peeled a large banknote from the roll in his pocket.

The bell captain's eyes lit with greed as he seized the money, bowing obsequiously. "Very good, sir. Very good indeed."

Josh grinned. "I sure hope she is!"

As the smirking bell captain bowed and scraped his way down the hall, Josh was left with a spitting-mad Sabrina. "Kiss me and make it look good," he commanded, lowering his mouth to hers. He could feel the stiff resistance in her body as he claimed the kiss.

That avaricious lump of greed who called himself a bell captain watched for a moment, then slipped down the servants' stairs. The instant she heard the door close, Sabrina stomped down with her heel on Josh's instep.

"Ow! Now, why'd you have to go and do that?" he asked, hopping around on his uninjured foot. "It's not time for my dance lessons yet."

"What are you doing here, you . . . you lying, deceitful, conniving—"

"Whoa, now," he interrupted her tirade. "It seems to me if anyone's been deceived, it's me—by your darlin' Eddy. Not to mention my own uncle," he added beneath his breath.

"You used me," she burst out, suddenly realizing to her mortification that tears were stinging her eyes. She blinked them back as she went on the attack again. "You were never interested in me—just in entrapping poor, foolish Eddy!"

He dodged her little fist as she attempted to plant it with surprising force in his stomach. "This isn't the time or place for this palaver. I can't afford for Zarenko to find me here."

"I suppose that's the villain to whom my cousin delivered those documents," she said, suddenly deflated. She was a fool to think even for one moment that a viscount would dally with a spinster teacher if he did not have an ulterior motive. She'd actually believed he found her desirable. *Fool, fool, fool!*

"Dammit, Sabrina," Josh said, placing her arm around his and starting for the stairs, "you're meddling in something that could get you killed."

As opposed to breaking her heart. "I will not stand by and watch my cousin be imprisoned for something he was duped into doing. This Zarenko—"

"Would kill you or Whistledown quicker than a frog would swallow a fly. We have to find your cousin and take him—"

"Oh, no! You're not taking Edmund to be interrogated by your friends in the Foreign Office. I overheard what happened to the last fellow they had in their care!" she cried.

"I wondered why the two of you took off so sudden-like," he mused as they began descending the steps.

Midway down, they encountered a young gentleman escorting an elderly lady in puce satin. Son and mother gaped at the obviously well-dressed man who held on to a mere chambermaid as if she were his wife. As they passed, the gray-haired lady muttered something about the impudence of servants, the moral decline of the upper classes, and whatever was the world coming to?

"I have to change clothes," Sabrina whispered when they were out of sight. "That's where we'll find Eddy—but I'll cooperate only if you promise not to turn him over to the authorities before hearing us out." Did she dare trust him? Sabrina had no idea, but she did have a choice. Once she and Edmund had their clothes back, they could slip away from Josh.

She needed time to think, to formulate a plan. At least they now knew the name of the Russian agent. Then another thought struck her. "I heard the earl mention that the mistress of a member of the royal family was involved in some assassination plot—it's Natasha Samsonov, isn't it?"

Josh sighed in capitulation. "You're smart as a treeful of owls, aren't you." It was not a question. "That female is, if anything, even more dangerous than her brother, who, incidentally, is Nikolai Zarenko whose daddy owns a big chunk of the Trans-Siberian Railroad."

They were at the bottom of the staircase and starting to draw curious looks before Josh realized he had to let go of her. The moment he did, she hissed, "I'm going to change clothes. I'll bring Edmund out to meet you as soon as we're ready to leave."

Josh grinned. "Now, why don't I believe you?"

"Because you lied to me and judge others by your own standards," she snapped back.

He let her go, watching the starchy way she walked across the lobby, like a queen shooing aside courtiers. There wasn't a man alive with the sense of half a brick who'd mistake her for a servant. If ever a woman acted to the manor born, it was Miss Sabrina Edgewater. But that didn't mean he could trust her to keep her word. Not when she was playing mother hen to her favorite chick, Eddy Whistledown.

Josh figured he had about five minutes to find the servants' rear entrance to the hotel.

* * *

"Come on, Eddy, don't dawdle, else you'll have to worry about another sort of neckwear," she scolded impatiently as he fussed with his cravat. "If we don't slip out the back door quickly, I'm certain the viscount will come searching for us," Sabrina chided in frustration. Heavens above, she'd managed a whole row of buttons down her back in half the time! "Do you want to be turned over to the earl, who believes you've stolen secret documents and betrayed your country?"

"Of course n—" he protested as she practically dragged him from the small room and down the hall.

The sunlight was bright as they burst through the door into an alleyway strewn with refuse from vendors' produce carts. Edmund nearly slipped on a slimy, well-blackened banana peel as they looked around, getting their bearings. "I think we should go that way," he said, pointing left.

"I think you oughta head my way," Josh drawled conversationally as he emerged from behind a large wagon loaded with beef for the hotel kitchen. "What? Not glad to see me?" He shook his head in mocking reproof. "Sabbie, Sabbie, what am I going to do with you?" His eyes lit up devilishly at possible answers to the rhetorical question. "And here I saved you from having to clean up after Natasha. Drinking vodka like she does, I bet she can geyser up like Old Faithful."

"You should know, my lord, being intimately acquainted with the toe dancer," she snapped, then quickly scolded, "and as oafish and crude as ever."

He grinned. "Did you expect a change in the five minutes since you last saw me? But I reckon more lessons might help."

"I'm surprised you'd trust me to give them, or do

252

you intend to come to my prison for instruction?" She arched one eyebrow and fixed him with a cold stare.

"I don't think you're a spy, darlin'. As for your cousin here, I'm not so all-fired sure."

Looking as if he'd just swallowed a goldfish, Edmund stood frozen as he listened to their exchange, which was too intimate by half in spite of Sabrina's addressing the viscount properly. The American certainly did not return the courtesy, an infraction for which he had seen her deliver many a set-down. Then he dared to glance at Sabrina and saw something soft and vulnerable flash in her eyes. But perhaps it was a trick of the light, for she blinked and it was gone.

Edmund tried to move protectively in front of her, braving the viscount's wrath as he protested, "I say, my lord, you can cast aspersions on me but not—"

Sabrina thwarted his grand speech by stepping forward and pushing him to the side. "I can handle this matter myself, Edmund."

Stubbornly he moved in front of her once more. "As the man of—"

This time Sabrina held on to his arm with amazing strength as she stepped around him again, but before she could utter a word, Josh broke into laughter, saying, "You two got the makings of a good vaudeville act there."

"Will you both stop this instant!" she practically shrieked, stamping her foot, which unfortunately landed in a pile of slimy lettuce. If Josh had not reached out and steadied her, she would have fallen.

"Easy," he said gently as she jerked her arm angrily away.

Regaining control of her emotions, she said in a cool voice, "I was going to return, my lord, once I saw my cousin to safety. Edmund is not guilty. He, too, has been used quite shamefully."

The barb struck home. Josh winced. "Now, that's a downright nasty remark. I've never used you for any reason, Sabrina, but this isn't the place to palaver on that."

Once again, Edmund interposed himself between his cousin and the tall Texan. "I say, you may be a viscount, sir, but you cannot address my cousin so familiarly." He swallowed hard. "I shall be forced to take measures—"

"Oh? What measures would those be?" Josh asked, skewering the skinny youth with cold green eyes as he revealed his Colt Lightning concealed in a shoulder holster.

"Stop picking on poor Eddy, you great Texas bully," Sabrina said, planting her hands on her hips as she stepped menacingly toward the viscount.

Edmund placed a restraining hand on her arm. "I say, Coz, as your only male kinsman present, it is incumbent upon me to—"

"Shut up, Eddy!" both Sabrina and the aggrieved viscount yelled in unison.

Edmund nearly swallowed his tongue.

"Come on, let's go," Josh said, ignoring the boy as he shook his head at Sabrina. "We'll sort this mess out, and then I'll decide what to do." With that, he signaled a hansom driver who had just turned into the alley, and the vehicle lumbered to a stop, narrowly missing the side of the butcher's wagon. Josh opened the door and indicated they should climb aboard.

"Only if you promise to give us a full and impartial hearing," Sabrina said stubbornly.

"I've never been able to be impartial about you,

darlin'," he murmured. "But I'll listen to the boy's story."

Grudgingly she allowed him to assist her into the coach, unconsciously noting how polished his physical manners had become, even if his vocabulary remained sadly lacking in social graces. Edmund jumped aboard like a frightened jackrabbit.

Josh gave directions to the driver and then joined them. As the hansom rumbled down the street, he leaned back, stretching his long legs in front of him, brushing the side of Sabrina's skirt as she perched on the seat across from him with her cousin at her side. "Now, begin at the beginning. And this better be good," he said, affixing his most daunting Texas glare on Whistledown.

Natasha Samsonov reclined on a fainting couch, languidly sipping vodka with ice. Normally she preferred not to dilute her liquor, but last night she'd foolishly overindulged and this was the price she had to pay. She had a performance tonight, and if this did not relieve the damnable ache pounding in her temples, she doubted she'd be able to go on.

At least the servants had finally finished fussing over the inferior furnishings in this wretched English hotel and left her in peace. If only that wretched Englishman would do the same. Just thinking of him made her take a deep swallow of vodka. A pity no one ever witnessed her greatest performances, pretending to be madly in love with that fool. He was even more repulsive than Albany's son, but since that source had been discovered, they'd been fortunate to find someone even closer on the inside to feed them information.

Her hopes for the Texas viscount had been dashed

as well. He could have been ever so entertaining, but he turned out to be quite impossible. No man had ever dared speak to her the way he did! And all over some silly horseless carriage. Once their mission was accomplished, the czar would reward her. She would buy herself one of those German vehicles and race it across Saint Petersburg!

Her pleasant reverie was interrupted by a rap on the door. That would be her tiresome brother here to lecture her about last night. As her maid admitted him, she finished her drink and set the glass discreetly behind the couch.

Nikolai Zarenko stormed into the room, his lip curling with disgust as he looked at his sister's pale face and bloodshot eyes. "They nearly captured me, we had to risk our best assassin to silence Vassily, and all you do is drink! How did this happen? I believed you when you said the old fool was besotted with you."

"He is, Nicki, he is," she said, wishing he'd lower his voice but knowing that if she pressed him, he'd only yell louder to punish her.

"The information he gave us led me into a trap!"

"All the better we arranged things as we have, but I am certain he did not deceive me on purpose. After all, if he did, he would risk exposing himself . . . and losing me," she said, running her fingers through her waist-length black hair and twirling a curl idly about her fingers. She shuddered in revulsion, thinking of what she would have to do to get the information they needed.

"We have only a few days before the treaty is signed. You must learn when and where Hayashi will really arrive. There is no time for another blunder,"

Zarenko said darkly. "That treaty must not be signed, and the English royal family must be disgraced!"

Natasha sighed. "I know, Nicki, I know. Finding out about the Japanese minister's arrival will be simple. Allowing that pig to rut on me is the difficult part."

"You could always close your eyes and pretend he's your virile Texan, not an inept old Englishman," her brother said nastily as he pivoted and walked through the door to his suite.

She threw the half-full vodka bottle at him but missed.

Chapter 16

The earl decided that bringing Sabrina and Edmund to the city house might alert Russian agents that the jig was up. Instead, he smuggled them into a private room at his club, the only way acceptable for a lady to set foot on the premises. The very old-school men's club reeked of masculinity. The walls were covered with dark green paper and the woodwork was dark teak. The furniture was massive, and the paintings on the walls, all of hunting scenes, were outnumbered by pieces of antique armament.

Josh sat in one of the large leather chairs across from his uncle as Sabrina and her cousin laid out the details of how Edmund had come to be duped by the Russians and an English traitor in their midst. Hambleton's face remained expressionless as Sabrina prodded Edmund and elucidated when he was unclear. Whether or not the earl believed them, Josh had no idea.

I'd hate to play poker with him.

When they had finished talking, the old man

leaned forward, placing his elbows on the desk and steepling his fingers, deep in thought. "Very interesting," he ventured at length as the silence in the room thickened.

Josh could sense the old man's mind working as Edmund fidgeted nervously in his seat. Damn fool kid was acting guilty. Then again, for all Josh could tell, maybe he *was* guilty. On the other hand, Sabrina sat perched on the edge of her seat, back ramrod-straight, as cool as if she were serving tea for a deportment pupil. But he could see in her eyes that she was afraid for the boy.

"If someone at the Foreign Office or in your establishment is guilty, what better way to cover himself? Whistledown is a natural-born sucker," Josh ventured.

At that insult, Sabrina turned angrily in her chair and glared at him. "That is most unkind."

A grin tugged at his mouth. "But you didn't say it wasn't true."

Edmund merely hung his head in red-faced misery.

"I think it's monstrous that we've been drawn into this—this conspiracy under the basest pretenses," she said, addressing the earl. "We've been lied to and duped and made to look like fools. How can we prove to you that we're innocent?"

Josh knew she was really speaking to him. Did she actually believe he'd made love to her because he wanted to lure her cousin into a trap? He started to protest, but a quick gesture from his uncle made him subside. There was a decisive look in those cool gray eyes as the old man spoke.

"Perhaps there is something you can do. Edmund, you say you still owe over a hundred pounds to those ruffians at Epsom?" Hambleton inquired as he jotted the names the boy had given him on a slip of paper.

Josh knew the earl would have Michael investigate them as soon as this interview was over. Edmund swallowed, eyeing Sabrina uneasily as he nodded.

"Excellent. Then the Russians know you're still desperate for money."

"But what does that matter?" Josh asked. "Zarenko knows the kid's been exposed. You had agents trying to catch him when I told you I'd found him."

"Quite," the earl replied with a faint hint of a smile. "But if Mr. Whistledown here is half the actor you've given me to believe he is"—Hambleton nodded to Josh—"then he could slip into the Metropole and accost Nikolai Zarenko, insisting he's in dire straits and has some pilfered information for sale to the highest bidder."

"You mean, something he swiped from you himself before he turned tail and ran?" Josh asked, seeing the possibility.

Sabrina, who had already thought of the same ploy, cleared her throat and said, "With half the government searching for him, it would be more believable if he were to appear in disguise."

The earl nodded to her. "Capital, m'dear young lady, capital."

"S-Sabrina, I'm not sure I could—"

"Nonsense. You can and you will," she said firmly.

"Just think of it as another act to wheedle money from your cousin," Josh suggested innocently, even though his remark drew a sharp look from Sabrina. Edmund, docile as a lamb, nodded but said nothing.

"Quite," Hambleton agreed, fixing the young man with a level gaze. "Now, here is what you shall do . . ."

Sabrina watched as Edmund climbed down from the hansom in front of the Metropole. Twilight was near, adding a vague sense of menace to the already foggy, drizzling day. If she had not watched Michael Jamison disguise her cousin, she might not have recognized him herself—until he began to speak, of course. He wore a blond wig and neatly trimmed chin whiskers, which blended convincingly with his pale complexion and light blue eyes. Small wire glasses perched on his nose, and his emaciated body had been padded to add the appearance of another thirty pounds.

Everything depended upon his ability to convince Zarenko that he had been able to steal an itinerary for the Japanese minister from Lord Hambleton's office before he had escaped one step ahead of British agents. It was quite apparent that the Russian conspirators already knew about the earl's position vis-à-vis the Foreign Office and that the British wanted to apprehend Edmund. But could her young cousin act well enough to fool Zarenko after the earlier assassination trap had failed?

She was forced to admit that Eddy certainly had done a superlative job of deceiving her. *Just as Josh had.* No, she must not think of that now. It hurt too much despite his protests. How on earth could he expect her to believe that his attraction to her had nothing to do with the assignment given him by his friend the American president? She was twice a fool if she thought he had seduced her because he found her beautiful and desirable. Her conscience had been stricken enough when she admitted to herself that she was willing to settle for an illicit affair.

After all, she was in love with the bounder.

That might have mitigated her guilt if he'd had no ulterior motives for making love to her. Now, however, she felt used and shamed. The worst of it was that this time the pain was ever so much greater than it had been with Dex. That was the final irony. No use mulling over something she could not change, Sabrina reminded herself. Edmund was in harm's way tonight, and he had to be her primary concern. Once this whole tawdry mess was cleared up, she would use the funds the earl had promised her to open her school and get on with her life.

Still, a niggling uneasiness plagued her as she rode back to her quarters. The plan was for Edmund to wait in the lobby tonight and approach Zarenko, whose name he supposedly did not know, insisting that he had come to the well-known residence of expatriate Russians in London in hope of finding the man who had paid him for documents. When Edmund was in dire need of money, she knew how inventive he could be with her, but she was, after all, his elder cousin who had practically raised him. A dangerous character such as Nikolai Zarenko was quite another matter. Edmund worked his charms best on women . . .

That gave her a sudden start. *Natasha Samsonov is Zarenko's sister*. Josh had told her that. She recalled that night at the ballet when he had left her at the theater entrance while he parked his automobile. He'd returned with a group of Russian gentlemen, and then the prima ballerina and her brother had arrived. Zarenko! Small wonder he had looked familiar to her that day in the park. Josh's assignment explained why he was out driving with the haughty Russian beauty. Or was that merely wishful thinking on her part?

Sabrina was not certain, but she knew that the woman had to be deeply involved is this nefarious plot. She tapped her nails on the armrest and thought. By the time the cab pulled up in front of her home, she had reached a decision. If the trap Edmund was baiting failed, not only was he in danger from the Russians, but also from his own government, which might believe he was guilty of espionage and send him to prison—or even, heaven forbid, execute him!

She would take a hand. Her cousin was not the only one who could don a disguise . . .

Michael and Josh waited outside the hotel as darkness gathered. From their vantage point across the street, they watched the comings and goings of the wealthy and powerful of Europe, most especially the large number of Russians. Alexi came rolling out around nine, already well on his way to total inebriation.

"Beats me how that man can stay on his feet," Josh said. "His liver must weigh fifty pounds."

"Do you believe he's one of the conspirators or just friendly with them?" Jamison asked, idly glancing around the scene as the rotund little bear of a man stumbled into a carriage and took off.

Josh shrugged. "Well, Alexi is pig simple. Folks back home would say he thinks fat meat isn't greasy, but that doesn't mean he couldn't be used by Zarenko and Natasha."

Jamison chuckled. "Ah, the lovely Natasha. What a woman." His dark blue eyes lit up. It was obvious what he was thinking.

Josh looked at him. "Why was I picked to cozy up to her? Didn't you want the job?"

"Oh, I did. The sad fact is, my friend, that she could drink me under the table. Who knows what state secrets she'd pry from me then?"

Josh threw back his head and laughed heartily.

Jamison joined him; then when they drew the

stares of several passersby who noticed them loitering in the alley, he said, "Careful, we'll give ourselves away," but his amusement was scarcely tempered. "That woman drinks like a fish. Of course, if reports from Hambleton are to be believed, *you* can drink like a thirsty camel."

"Don't know about that. I never drank with a camel, but I do know it takes a heap of endurance to match Tasha. The trick is not to drink vodka. I brought my own bourbon."

"An allowance she'd make for an American, but not for a mere Englishman," Michael replied dryly. "Since my drink of preference is good strong tea, I doubt she'd be enchanted."

Josh snorted. "It'd do her good to join you. If that bell captain wasn't exaggerating about how 'indisposed' she was last night, she spouts like a beluga whale. Sabrina nearly got corralled into cleaning up after her." He smiled at the memory of rescuing her.

Something in the tone of his companion's voice made Jamison turn his keen gaze on the Texan and note his quiet smile. *Love smitten.* He smirked. "So it's Sabrina now, is it? You said you caught her and Whistledown dressed up like hotel servants, but I expect there's more to the story than that . . ." His voice trailed away, inviting Josh to volunteer more if he chose.

He didn't.

The silence was broken when Sergei Valerian came out and jumped into a hansom, accompanied by two men neither of the watchers knew. "Well, have they fallen for Whistledown's tale or not?" Michael wondered aloud, knowing they had to make a swift decision. "We know that Valerian's part of Zarenko's inner circle."

"Right hard to tell. There are more of those Russians than ants on a Texas ant hill. I'd rather wait for Zarenko."

Jamison sighed. "Knew you would," he said as he sprang forward and began trotting behind the hansom as it started to pull away. As soon as the bellman who'd waved down the vehicle turned his back, the agent jumped nimbly onto the boot and concealed himself.

Josh waited for another hour, wondering if he dared to go inside and check on Whistledown. He hoped to God the fool boy hadn't decided to bolt and run. It would go hard on him if he did. He wondered if Zarenko would take the bait. Once burned, a critter just naturally stayed off a hot stove. Still, they'd made the documents look authentic. Hell, they *were* authentic, since his uncle had procured them from the Foreign Office himself!

But the secret meeting between Lord Lansdowne and Count Hayashi would be attended only by Lansdowne, who was willing to risk his life to trap the culprits. Amid much fanfare and incredibly high security, the Japanese minister would be presented at court the day after tomorrow. The actual meeting to finalize the treaty and sign it was scheduled to take place the day after that.

In the documents signed by Lansdowne that Edmund was trying to sell, the meeting was supposed to be tomorrow night. If they caught Zarenko and his agents, the lot of them, including one famous toe dancer, would be deported. They'd find themselves on the next boat for Saint Petersburg trying to explain to their government why they'd failed in their mission . . . if they got the chance to explain.

If Zarenko took the bait.

Shuffling to his other foot on the hard cobblestones, Josh considered what might happen if the Russian did not fall for this gambit. Sabrina's cousin might be in really big trouble. So might Count Hayashi. Sighing, he headed toward the side entrance to the hotel to see what was going on.

On the second floor, Sabrina slid the key in the lock and turned it until the heavy door swung open. It worked! When she'd taken the skeleton key from the peg board in the hotel manager's office, she could not be certain it would unlock every guest suite.

She slipped into the darkened room, having waited until Natasha and her personal maid had left for the theater. There was a performance that evening. She should have plenty of time to search the suite. But what was she searching for? Sabrina wasn't sure, but knew she'd recognize anything that might prove useful if she found it, providing that it was written in French, not Russian.

An hour yielded nothing but armoires bursting with French couture clothing, boxes glittering with jewels, and a sizable cache of Russian vodka concealed inside a dressing table. She was about to give up when a tiny edge of a slip of paper lodged between the upholstery on a settle caught her attention. Carefully she pulled it free. The crumpled remains of a love note carelessly tossed aside from the looks of it. The prima ballerina must receive hundreds of them, not to mention more substantial tokens of esteem such as the baubles overflowing her jewel cases.

Sabrina quickly perused the protestations of undying love and a tryst arranged at "our usual place" and was about to replace it when she noticed the crest embossed on the expensive vellum—the House of

Wettin! It was signed "Georgie," no other identification, but she remembered that conversation she'd overheard between the earl and Josh. The Royal Duke of Albany, the king's younger brother, had a son named George Clarence. His Majesty's own nephew was the one unwittingly giving secret information to the enemy!

What an embarrassment for the government if this ever became public! Surely there must be more letters, being held to incriminate the royal family once the Japanese minister was assassinated and the treaty between their countries abrogated. Sabrina continued to search for another hour but found nothing. Perhaps if Natasha's brother was the man in charge of this whole scheme, he was keeping the love notes from the foolish man.

Dare she risk searching Zarenko's suite? Remembering the ugly menace of his drunken, twisted expression, she took a deep breath. Yes, she could do it. She had to do it for Eddy. Satisfied after inspecting her job of straightening Natasha's quarters, she headed for the room down the hall and once again set to work. This time she had a better idea about what to look for.

She found all sorts of notes and papers, some written in indecipherable Cyrillic, some in French. Nothing she could read was incriminating, mostly bills from various merchants. Like his sister, Nikolai enjoyed living extravagantly, especially considering that he was purporting to be an expatriate disowned by his own wealthy family. When the sitting room yielded nothing, she began a search of his bedroom. Finally, hidden behind the headboard of the elaborate canopy, she found a bundled packet of letters.

"Oh, I've hit the jackpot!" she exclaimed, then realized she was beginning to sound like Josh, using American vulgarisms. No time to chastise herself about that now, not when she had a packet of love notes from a member of the royal family addressed to his darling Natasha. What a fool George Clarence Wettin was, fancying himself in love with someone who was using him!

What a fool she was for the same reason.

Sabrina tucked the bundle in an ample pocket of the shapeless maid's uniform she'd "borrowed" again and started toward the door. That was when she heard a key turning in the lock and the sound of Nikolai Zarenko's voice on the other side . . .

Josh sat in the lounge, nursing a glass of the nasty warm foamy stuff the English called beer, observing the crowd. Zarenko had emerged from one of the small private parlors off the main lobby and headed upstairs a few moments earlier. Josh hoped that meant he'd been waylaid by Whistledown according to plan. He debated on following the Russian, then decided it would be better to find the boy.

Just then Edmund slipped furtively from the same place as Zarenko. Judging by the jubilant expression on his face, the ruse had worked. Josh hoped the fool kid had been better at concealing his real emotions from Zarenko.

He shoved the beer aside and made his way through the press of opulently dressed people to intercept Whistledown. As he sidled up to the boy near the front door, he took his elbow in an iron grip and whispered, "I take it your play-acting worked."

Edmund nearly jumped out of his skin until he recognized Josh. "Crikey, you gave me a fright! I thought that Russian bounder had changed his mind and come to slit my throat."

"He went upstairs. Come on, I'll get a hansom and you can tell me all about it."

In moments they were inside a dank, musty-smelling cab headed toward Hambleton House and Edmund was babbling excitedly about the performance of his life. Josh would guess the boy had been a natural-born liar since he was in kneepants. Whistledown pulled a wad of cash from his pocket and waved it in Josh's face.

"He went for the whole of it! Oh, he was suspicious at first, mind, but once he saw the papers signed by Lord Lansdowne and recognized the signature, he believed me. I assured him they wouldn't be missed until at least the day after tomorrow. I held out for enough to pay everything I owed at Epsom—just as His Lordship told me to," he hastily added.

Josh exhaled. Perhaps this would work out all right after all. He sat turning over plans about how he and Michael could seize the Russian agents tomorrow night. Of course, that left unresolved the issue of who had been stealing information from the earl's office. An English traitor was still on the loose. But at least they could send his paymasters packing soon.

His ruminations were interrupted when Edmund asked ingenuously, "Do I get to keep the money?"

By the time Michael arrived at Hambleton House, Josh and the earl had already begun formulating how the trap could be sprung. Looking up as Nash announced their visitor, Josh asked, "What was that polecat Valerian up to?"

"A waste of my time. Just another drunken orgy

with some of his companions. They ended up at the White Satin again. I lurked about for a while, but there was nothing to be gained. La Samsonov graced them with her presence briefly, but her brother never arrived. I hope that means he's taken the bait?"

"Quite," the earl said. "He's already seen enough stolen official documents to recognize Foreign Secretary Lansdowne's signature. Obviously, he does not read Japanese, but I'm given to understand the forgery of Count Hayashi's pictogram was accurate enough. He paid young Whistledown for the information."

"Where is the boy? I cannot trust him," Jamison said worriedly.

The earl chortled mirthlessly. "None of us dare. He's upstairs, secured in comfortable quarters with two footmen guarding him until we decide how to proceed."

"I believe he's too dumb to come in out of the rain, but not a traitor," Josh said, more because he hoped it was true for Sabrina's sake than because he completely believed it. The fool kid was one hell of an actor.

"Which leaves us with a problem. Who is the mysterious fellow who gave Whistledown the earlier documents?" Michael asked as he paced across the carpet.

"We will deal with that matter after we've sent the Russians into exile," the earl said firmly. "Right now the paramount issue is the signing of the treaty and the safety of the Japanese minister. He's to be presented at court in only two days."

"Yes, with his paymasters gone, perhaps this spy will find other employment," Jamison said, but Josh could tell he was not satisfied by Hambleton's words.

Josh was not certain he was either, and that worried

him. He did not want the boy upstairs to be guilty . . . but he didn't want his own uncle to be either.

Please, not Uncle Ab . . .

Josh was too restless to sleep, worried about the whole mess he'd been caught up in because of a debt of honor to his old commander. When he'd agreed to come to England, he'd never expected to give a hoot about any fancy nobles, folks who never did a day's work in their lives. Now he had come to love the shrewd, testy old man who was his closest blood kin. Surely he had not been blinded by that fact. Could his uncle be a traitor?

The more he turned it over in his mind, the more worrisome the possibility became. Hambleton had hired Edmund and Sabrina both. What if it was only to use them? His uncle had dismissed the problem of discovering the traitor while he sent Michael out to capture Zarenko and a bunch of Russians who would only be deported for their crimes. Josh had insisted on going with Jamison. Of course, the earl had argued against allowing his heir to endanger himself by participating in the arrest, but Josh had been adamant. At length, the old man had given in. Was it because there would be no danger? No capture because the Russians would be warned it was a trap?

"It doesn't make sense," he muttered to himself as he poured two fingers of Who Shot John into a glass and took a swallow. The earl was richer than he was, and Josh had been well into making his second million when he'd been summoned to London. If the old man didn't need the money from the Russians, what other reason could there be for him to betray his honor and his country? The answer was simple.

There was none.

Josh commenced to pace in bare feet, polishing off the bourbon and pouring a refill. Maybe when they caught Zarenko, they'd find out the truth. That would not only relieve his own mind but clearing her cousin would make Sabrina happy as a pig with its snout in the slop bucket. Edmund had written her a note, explaining that all had gone well and telling her not to worry. One of the earl's servants had been dispatched to deliver it to her lodgings as soon as they'd arrived at Hambleton House and found she was not there.

Josh assumed she had decided to return to the safety of her own space. "Runnin' scared, darlin'," he mused with a chuckle.

Sabrina. She had slipped under his guard and gone straight for his heart . . . a target he'd believed impervious to marriage-minded females. The idea of getting hitched still made him itchy, but he knew that was the only way he'd get to keep her. What an uproar it would create if the Yankee heir to the glorious Hambleton titles took a country squire's daughter to wife. The thought of it made him grin.

But he was getting ahead of himself. First they had to catch the Russians and wait for the dust to settle after this all-fired important treaty was signed. Then he'd tell his uncle what he intended to do . . . that is, if Sabrina ever forgave him for his deception. Somehow, he figured he could convince her to do that.

Just thinking about the nature of that "convincing" made his body stir. He began wondering if there was any way he could get past that old harridan who ran the lodging house. Maybe there was a drainpipe he could climb or a trellis, or he might toss pebbles against her window until she opened it.

"Nah, that's a damn fool idea that only works in

storybooks," he muttered, disgusted with himself for being as lovesick as a calf who'd lost its mama. The hell with it, he was burning up with need! Josh started to unfasten his robe. He'd dress and go do whatever it took to reach her.

Then he heard a faint ping against the windowpane. A second one. He crossed the room, mystified and a bit edgy about the bizarre coincidence. Someone was tossing pebbles against his window. He peered below, trying to make out the figure in the misty moonlight.

Chapter 17

It was Sabrina! Josh rubbed his eyes in amazement.
Then a slow grin spread across his face as he slid
open the window and ducked his head out. "You
have this Romeo and Juliet business ass-backward,
darlin'. It's real sweet, but don't you think the door
would've been easier?"

Sabrina clutched the bundle of letters in her hand,
resisting the urge to throw them at the arrogant oaf.
If not for their vital importance, she would never
have come here, she assured herself for what seemed
like the hundredth time. "The door is locked, and
it's late. I have to give you something of a critical nature, but I don't wish to alert the household staff.
Please come down," she said with as much confidence as she could muster given her near brush with
disaster.

Something in her voice indicated that she had not
come for the reason he'd foolishly hoped. Josh could
not make out her face, but he could tell she was excited. "I'll be right there. Don't move."

He slipped down the rear servants' stairs and out the back door into the garden at the side of the house. High stone walls surrounded it, and the brick pathways were shaded from the misty moonlight by the low-hanging branches of willows and pin oaks. The heavy air was warm and moist with the promise of rain as he approached the spot where she'd stood beneath his window.

He didn't see her. "Sabrina?"

"I'm here," she replied in a small voice, materializing from behind a wisteria bush. "I—I didn't want anyone to see me lurking about and call the police."

"Always sensible," he said as he drew near. "Now, what's so all-fired important that you're out alone in the middle of the night to deliver it to me?"

"Love letters—"

"Oh, darlin', you shouldn't have," he said, bending down to kiss her.

Sabrina fought the urge to smack the grin from his lips. "From the Duke of Albany's son to Natasha Samsonov," she said, gritting her teeth. She shoved the bundle beneath his nose.

Josh nearly dropped the letters. "How in Johnny blue blazes did you get ahold of them?" He pulled her into his arms, suddenly frightened half out of his wits. There was no way she could've done this without considerable risk.

He wore nothing but a silk robe. She could feel his heart pounding as her hands pressed against his chest. Her own heart was pretty erratic as well, and not only because of the danger. "I decided that searching her suite while she was performing might prove worthwhile. You'll recall how simple it was to obtain a maid's uniform. It was equally simple to pilfer a skeleton key."

"Sneakiness must run in your family," he said with a sigh, planting a light kiss on the tip of her nose.

"Will you be serious, Josh? You know what these letters could mean to the Russians—how they could employ them to create a horrible scandal in the press and humiliate the royal family," she said, pressing her hands against his chest until he released her.

"And you found them in Natasha's suite?" he asked incredulously, glancing at the fistful of papers.

"Well . . ." She had always been an abject failure at prevarication. "No—that is, I found a small piece of one. With the Wettin crest on it. When I couldn't find any more in her quarters, I searched her brother's and—"

"You went into Nikolai Zarenko's lair alone!" He would have yelled at the top of his lungs if all the breath hadn't been squeezed out of his body. "Do you have any idea what he would've done if he'd caught you in his suite, tearing the place apart?" Now he *was* yelling.

She shushed him. Before she could utter another word, she was back in his arms.

"This calls for something to drink—something wet and strong and I don't mean tea," he said as he scooped her up and began walking toward the house.

"Your arm—you'll reopen the wound," she protested.

"My arm's fine. Just a scratch," he said, kissing her into silence.

Before she knew it, Sabrina was carried stealthily up the rear stairs. Josh moved silently on bare feet, taking the steep wooden risers two at a time until he reached the second floor. He did not put her down until they were safely behind the closed door of his room. As she slid from his arms to the floor, she felt as breathless as he—and she'd not exerted a bit of energy climbing the steps. She watched him take a bottle of whiskey from the small library table across the room and pour two shots into glasses.

"Here, drink this. I think we're both going to need it," he said, handing her one as he tossed down the other.

She shook her head. "I do not require strong spirits to fortify—"

"Yes, you do. Go ahead. Fortify yourself," he commanded, his green eyes skewering her fiercely.

Sabrina attempted to emulate him, taking a fulsome swallow . . . and began coughing fiercely the moment the powerful stuff hit the back of her throat. Josh patted her back while she blinked back tears. "Th-that b-burns," she finally managed to accuse between coughs.

"I didn't intend for you to toss it back like a Texas drover at the end of the trail, darlin'," he said with a hint of a smile.

She didn't know if her face was red from the strength of the vile corn whiskey or from embarrassment. "I was merely trying to get it over with as quickly as possible."

"Try sipping it," he suggested as he led her over to a comfortable-looking settee that filled one wall of the large, masculine room.

She tried not to look at the rumpled bed from which she had most probably awakened him. Instead, she carefully arranged her cloak, preparing to sit down.

"Here, give me that thing. It's wet from the fog," he said, pulling the tie at the neckline so the cloak hung open, revealing the maid's uniform she still wore.

Before she knew it, he had peeled the damp garment off her, tossed it across a chair and was taking a seat beside her. Sabrina tried to scoot away from the heat of his thigh, but could not manage it with the glass in her hand. When she tried to set it on the table beside her, he placed his hand over hers and guided the glass to her lips. He put his arm around her, and his robe gaped open so that she could see the curly black hair of his chest . . . and knew that she was lost.

"Now finish it." His voice was soft now, under control after his angry outburst downstairs. Damn, the woman frightened him . . . in more ways than one.

"This is taking advantage," she said, already feeling the warm glow building in her belly from the first swallow of whiskey. Still, she took another sip. "Perhaps this is not as bad as I first thought. If one imbibes slowly." He nodded in encouragement. Before she knew it, the whole glass was empty and her head felt light as air. She had to focus to understand what he was saying.

"How did you find these?" Josh had untied the packet and was sorting quickly through the foolish protestations of undying devotion addressed to "Darling Tasha" and signed "Georgie."

"I told you. I searched his quarters just as I had hers. They were hidden behind the headboard of his bed in some sort of secret compartment. I suppose I was fortunate to stumble upon it."

"You were just plain dumb lucky he didn't catch you," he groused.

"Oh, but he did," she blurted out. Curse that whiskey! Why had she volunteered that? *Perhaps because you're still frightened out of your wits . . . and you're inebriated,* a voice in her head teased.

Josh's heart missed a beat as he pulled her into his arms. "How the hell did you get away? He could've killed you! He would've—" He broke off, unable to let himself think of what might have happened. "Tell me how you escaped," he demanded, his voice hoarse with fear.

"Well"—she moistened her lips, still unable to quite believe the whole of her adventure—"he thought I was the new chambermaid, come to turn down his bed. He . . . he asked me for a sweet." Her face reddened.

"A sweet?" he echoed, not liking where this was going.

"One of the mints the maids lay on the pillow after they turn down the covers. But, of course, he didn't mean just that."

"Go on," Josh encouraged, touching her face gently, trying to keep the killing rage that burned inside him from showing. If Zarenko had touched her, he'd die hard . . . Texas hard.

"He started to . . . to press unwelcome advances on me. I imagine the bounder has taken advantage of dozens of poor, defenseless serving girls over the years," she said darkly, warming to her story in spite of the fright Zarenko had given her. "He laughed when I tried to push him away, and then he pulled me onto the bed." Josh stiffened and muttered a curse. Feeling his anger, she said quickly, "That's when I coshed him with the brass samovar on the tray beside the bed."

"You what?" he asked, torn between relief and laughter.

"I hit him over the head with a very large, heavy teapot," she replied tartly, rubbing her wrist. "And probably sprained my arm doing it. He fell backward against the pillows, unconscious. Dear heavens, I hope he was unconscious! Do you suppose I could've killed the wretch?" she asked as the thought suddenly occurred to her for the first time.

"His head's too hard," Josh replied, thinking that when he finished with the bastard, Zarenko would be dead anyway, so it really did not matter. "Even if you had managed to kill him, you'd a done a patriotic thing for king and country. Just think of England," he said, with a grin as he cupped her chin in his hand and gazed into her troubled blue eyes. "You are a wonder, but I don't want you taking any more chances, gussying up in disguises and getting into scrapes. Promise?"

When he eyed her uniform, Sabrina explained, "I was in such a rush to escape that I fled the hotel without my own clothing."

"Where did you change—in the same place as before?" he asked. When she nodded, he dismissed her fears. "I'll send a servant over in the morning to return this and fetch your duds," he said soothingly.

"Oh! I still have the key. I took it from the manager's office."

"Aren't you just full of surprises." His voice was amused now. "Imagine, a fine, educated lady like Miss Edgewater pinching keys and play-acting. I can't believe Zarenko'd mistake you for a maid."

"I'll 'ave ye know me da's a preachin' man, 'e is. An' I be a good girl, sor, I swears it," she replied in a convincing cockney accent.

"I see that a talent for the stage really does run in your family. You're better than your cousin," he said, chuckling in admiration.

"Eddy! Is he all right? Dear me, in all the excitement, I utterly forgot about him! Did he convince Zarenko to pay him for the false documents? Where is he?"

"He did just fine. Zarenko took the bait. Now we have to see if the trap works this time. Right now, Edmund's asleep at the other end of the hall with two footmen spelling each other to be sure he doesn't give us the slip until the dust settles."

"You still don't trust him, do you?" she asked apprehensively.

"I trust you, darlin'. And that's all that matters. If you're so all-fired sure he's innocent, then I expect he is," he said, trying to soothe her with his voice as he caressed her face. Then he gently wrapped his hand around the back of her neck and drew her closer as he lowered his mouth to hers for a kiss.

She knew she should not have drunk that whiskey. The thought flashed through her spinning head as the last of the bourbon settled in her belly. She knew the heat spreading through her body had less to do with the restorative power of spirits than with the nearness of Josh Cantrell's lips. Those magic lips that were brushing hers, the tongue rimming her mouth until she gave in and opened breathlessly.

Josh murmured her name as he deepened the kiss, cradling her head in his hand, pressing her gently against the soft, overstuffed back of the settee. His body settled over hers and the swell of her breasts brushed his bare chest. He reached down and let his fingers play with the sensitive nipples. Even through layers of clothing he could feel them beginning to harden into points. She tasted of whiskey, his prim lady who never "imbibed"—whiskey and that unutterable sweetness that belonged to her alone. He groaned when her tongue danced with his as she returned his kiss passionately.

Sabrina could feel his fingers as they deftly began to unfasten the buttons of her uniform, starting in the middle so he could reach her breasts. Once he had opened a wide enough space, he slid his hand inside and continued his maddening assault, pulling down the thin cover of her chemise and using his thumb to circle the aureoles until she felt the sweet ache, now so familiar. The world went away as she seized a fistful of his hair in each hand and arched into his kisses and caresses with fierce passion.

Her hands roamed over his shoulders, shoving his loose robe down, baring his sun-darkened skin and sinuously rippling muscles. She felt him shrug the robe off and realized he wore nothing beneath it. Sabrina was so hungry to feel, to touch, to taste this man. Even if he betrayed her, even if he could never love her, never offer her anything more than this . . . this was enough. More than enough.

Josh laid her across the length of the settee as he slid from the side of it and knelt before her, all the while continuing to rain kisses over her face and down the slim column of her throat while his hands deftly worked on getting her out of the maid's costume. Fortunately, it buttoned down the front. Unfortunately, her corset was laced down the back. But he was nothing if not resourceful, even when confronted with a confounded contraption such as this. He slipped her chemise over her head, then laced his fingers in her heavy hair, gently lifting the pins so they scattered, allowing her hair to fall in a cascade of bronze silk over her shoulders.

Just looking at her made him ache with desire. He lowered his mouth to her collarbone and nipped and licked at the delicate skin covering it until his tongue touched the furiously beating pulse point at the center. Then he moved lower to the swell of her breasts, nuzzling them as his hands gently brushed aside the lace cups covering the lower halves of them. He took one in his mouth and heard her gasp as he suckled it with firm insistence before using his teeth to lightly bite down on the distended nipples, first one, then the other.

She felt the jolt of fire shoot from her breasts, radiating outward until every inch of her body burned from it. A long, slow moan escaped her lips as the heat licked deep in her belly, pooling lower at the juncture of her thighs. As if knowing exactly what she felt, he slid his hand beneath her skirt and caressed her leg, moving unerringly to the ultimate destination. He cupped her mound, pressing the sheer fabric of her underdrawers over the wetness where she ached to be filled. She squirmed, bowing her body up into his caress.

Taking advantage of her move, he pulled the drawers over the lush curve of her little buttocks and peeled them down her legs. "Now," he whispered in a labored voice, "let's get rid of the rest of your clothes. I need to see all of you, Sabbie."

He began by removing her slippers, a well-worn black pair she'd chosen to match the maid's outfit. Sabrina had never felt a man's hands on her feet before. He squeezed her toes, then massaged her instep, his large palm fitting into the arch while his thumbs pressed on nerves she'd never imagined existed on the ball of her foot. She purred with pleasure as he moved from one foot to the other, repeating the process.

Her lashes fluttered closed, then opened again. In spite of the languid pleasure his touch elicited, she wanted to watch his naked body move while he made love to her in this slow, unexpected way. His eyes met hers as his hands began to roll down her garters and stockings, kissing the sensitive skin of her inner thigh, bending her knee and gliding along her calf. One much-mended cotton stocking flew to the floor. He worked on the second one.

She was burning up. Her hand reached out to him and he took it, bringing it to his lips, biting softly on the tips of her fingers. The rasp of his teeth over the pad of her thumb made her cry aloud. He leaned over her and silenced her with his mouth. His hands grew more urgent now, matching her own desperation as he began to unbutton the waistband of her petticoat. She sat forward, helping him by pulling off the long sleeves of the uniform and shoving the whole mass down so he could wrest it away.

As he threw the dress and petticoat on the floor his eyes swept over her. "You are the most beautiful woman ever born," he whispered in awe.

Sabrina could not believe her own boldness, here in a fully lit room, allowing her gaze to move down his body while her fingertips glided from his chest, following the narrowing pattern of his body hair over his navel down to the jutting proof of his desire. He arched his hips and his staff prodded her thigh, scalding her with its heat. A sudden sense of power, generously fueled by whiskey, led her to wrap her hand around his sex.

Quickly his hand covered hers, moving it up and down, stroking as he bucked. Josh felt his control slipping and knew he had to do something quickly. He unpeeled her hand, murmuring, "You're too good at this, darlin'."

She had enjoyed the feeling of velvet over steel, the heat of him in her hand, and felt bereft when he pulled free, but when he reached out to her, she went into his arms, melting as her bare flesh pressed

ightly against his. They knelt on the carpet in front
of the settee, kissing and caressing. She was oblivious
to everything but the need to sink into his skin, to
own, even for a little while, every inch of him, body
and soul.

When he lifted her buttocks and urged her to wrap
her legs around him, she complied, opening herself
for his penetration. Perspiration beaded his face as he
slowly glided into her heat. She placed her arms
around his neck and clung to him, helpless in the
bliss of joining, greedily tightening her knees at his
sides to hold him fast. Her tongue darted out, licking
the salty sweat from his face and neck, biting and nip-
ping as he'd taught her while they rocked together in
ageless rhythm.

Sabrina could feel the crest coming so swiftly she
could do nothing but surrender to it, letting her body
clench and unclench in hard, panting spasms as he
stiffened and shuddered his own completion deep inside her. When they tumbled to the floor, still joined
together, he cushioned her with his body, letting her
lie on top of him as he looked up into her eyes. His
hands were filled with her breasts, suspended like
small, perfect pears, ripe for his tasting.

She watched as he pulled one to his raised head
and began to suckle it. "Yes, yes," she whispered
softly, shaking her loose hair around him like a curtain. Bracing her hands on either side of his head, she
arched into his caresses, letting the fire rekindle. "Oh,
osh, please . . ." For what was she pleading? That he
make love to her again? She knew he would, for his
body was already hardening inside her.

That he love her? She knew he would not . . . could
not . . . but for this golden moment suspended in
time, it did not matter. She loved him enough for both

of them. The heat, the giddy rush of pleasure radiating through her body, overtook her and she cried ou
her love, unaware of what she was saying as sh
neared the pinnacle once more.

Josh could hear her soft voice, hear the hot, desperate longing that he, too, felt, the need to possess, t
melt into one perfect whole with her, the hunger tha
seemed only to grow the more times he loved he
Loved her. Yes, he loved her—was *in love* with he
and in spite of his vow not to fall into the trap, h
knew it was too late.

His Sabbie had already caught him.

After the shattering climax, they simply lay in eac
other's arms, panting and soaked with perspiratior
murmuring indistinct love words, awash in conten
ment that transcended speech. Finally he untangle
them and scooped her into his arms, carrying her t
the bed. He felt the silk of her hair slide over his ches
as he inhaled the faint scent of wildflowers and sati
ated female. Tonight he would get a good night'
sleep after all, he thought with a peaceful sigh.

Sabrina awakened feeling suddenly cool and looke
across the bed. Josh had just slipped from beneath th
covers and was stretching, arms raised over his head
She studied his long, lean body, broad shoulders an
back, his tight buttocks and long legs pale in the din
morning light. His black hair was spiky from
sleep . . . and other activities that had mussed it dur
ing the night. Just thinking of that brought new hea
coursing through her. What a splendid sight he
Texan was! She allowed herself the luxury of th
dream in the half-wakefulness of the early hour.

Downstairs she could barely make out the chimin
of a clock, striking six times. Why was he rising s

early? To leave her before she could ask embarrassing questions or importune him about his intentions? What had she revealed during their long night of making love and sleeping together? Good heavens, did she talk in her sleep? The thought brought her into full wakefulness, but she feigned sleep as he moved silently across the floor, gathering up their scattered clothes, placing hers in a neat pile by her side of the bed.

Sparing her from servants' gossip, no doubt.

And sparing himself from any danger of being trapped into a debt of honor to marry her? No, that was not true. If he worried about that, the night after he'd been shot should have laid his fears to rest. She could have made her presence known to Benton, but instead she'd slipped silently back into the adjoining bedroom. As she would do now, as soon as he left.

Are you afraid to face him in the morning light? The question taunted her. When she had brought him the letters last night, she had known the risks to her heart. It would have been prudent to wait until this morning. Yet she had come anyway, knowing on some unconscious level that she would spend one more night in his arms. But soon this would have to end.

After she'd found out he was using her to trap Eddy, she should have refused to speak to him ever again. Of course she had not done so. All he had to do was smile that lopsided way and fix those dark green eyes on her and she was beyond all reason. Sabrina knew she would have to pay the price. She'd already paid it.

Her heart was his.

"You can stop playing possum now," he drawled in a softly amused voice. "I know you're awake."

She blinked. "How could you tell?"

"Your eyelashes are too long. They flutter. And you're not breathing regular," he said as he finished buttoning his jeans and sat down on the edge of the bed beside her.

"How can I when you're looming over me like this?" she asked with no particular alarm in her voice. In fact, it sounded rather dreamy.

"Like this?" he echoed, leaning down to kiss her quite thoroughly. When her arms came up about his neck, he climbed back onto the bed. "How the hell am I going to meet with Michael if you keep leading me into temptation?"

He didn't sound particularly alarmed either as he bared her breasts and watched the cool morning air pucker the little nipples into nubs. His appreciation of the lovely sight was interrupted by a rap on the door. "You asked that I awaken you, m'lord," Benton's voice intoned from the other side of the door.

"Lordy, that man's like a social disease. Can't get rid of him," he whispered to her, planting a quick kiss on her nose before he called out, "All right, Benton. Go fetch me some coffee, if you please," he added quickly, not remembering whether he'd bothered to lock the door last night. The pesky valet was learning not to barge in and start dressing him as if he were some department-store mannequin, but Josh didn't want to take any chances.

"You have a meeting with Mr. Jamison?" Sabrina asked.

"Yep. We're taking turns watching the goings-on at the Metropole. I'm pals with a couple of the Russians now, which makes it easier for me than for him, since all he can do is stand outside in the bushes."

"You're going to discuss the trap Eddy lured them into, aren't you?" she asked.

"We have to make plans. And I have to get those love notes to a safe place."

"Won't you give them to your uncle?" she asked innocently.

Josh hesitated. "If we keep them here, whoever's working for the Russians could steal them back once Zarenko finds out they're gone."

She sensed some evasion in that answer but decided to say nothing. "As long as they aren't used to embarrass His Majesty's government," she said. "Might it be best to just burn them?"

"I'll ask Uncle Ab," he replied as he pulled back the covers, exposing her naked body to the chill. She gasped and started to leap from the bed, grasping for her undergarments. Josh gave her derriere a light swat, chuckling as he said, "Better get into your room next door before Benton comes back."

"But I'm not staying there anymore," she protested.

"Uncle Ab left it ready for you. You came back last night because it wasn't safe at your place after you found these," he said, holding up the packet of letters. "There are clean towels and all sorts of female falderal the maids put there for you. Just rumple the bed, then freshen up and mosey downstairs for breakfast. Edmund will be down whenever he wakes up."

Sabrina nodded, realizing that was all she could do. There was no way she could slip from this house filled with servants without someone seeing her, and the attempt would cause far worse gossip than following his advice. Lord Hambleton had insisted she remain as his guest while she was supposedly giving Joshua instruction in behaving as an English gentleman.

Rather more like he's been giving me instruction in . . . behaving in other ways, she thought to herself as he walked out the door, whistling. The bounder.

Then she remembered Eddy. He was here, and he'd be afraid of what was going to happen if the trap he'd instigated did not work. That worried her a great deal as well. Perhaps she'd go and quiz him about what had transpired with Zarenko. Just remembering her brush with that brutal man made her shiver. She hoped she'd bashed in his brains.

Such bloodthirsty thoughts! Josh was beginning to rub off on her in more ways than one. Repressing that disquieting thought, she quickly dressed and went in search of Eddy to find out just what had happened the night before.

Hambleton worked diligently at the small lock for several moments, kneeling on the hard wooden floor behind his desk. He stopped for a moment and shifted his considerable weight, trying to favor the left knee where the worst of the pain was. He should have laid a rug here before getting down, he thought sourly. "Getting too old for so many things," he muttered almost wistfully to himself.

After a few more turns with the tiny brush, he pulled it out, then inserted the key. When he removed it, a grimly satisfied smile curled his mustache but did not reach his eyes. This was the final test. "Tonight I'll know whether you pass or fail," he said as he pulled himself up into the large chair behind the desk.

He sat rubbing his aching knees, deep in contemplation of what his next move would be.

Chapter 18

It took several raps to rouse her cousin from a sound sleep. He came to the door appearing rumpled and dazed, rather the way he had always seemed to look as a small boy. He was wearing a brocade robe of such good quality, and such ample size, that she judged it must have been loaned to him by the earl. It hung in folds sufficient for him to double it around his thin body as he fumbled with the belt.

"Good morning, Eddy," she said, briskly, stepping into his room.

"Wha-what are you doing here, Sabrina?" he asked, combing his fingers through baby-fine wisps of hair that nevertheless contained a stubborn cowlick.

"I'm here to discuss your mission last night," she said, pulling the bell rope to summon a maid. "I see we'll need some good strong tea to wake you up, first." A footman appeared immediately at the door, inquiring what she needed. Sabrina told him and he quickly went to do her bidding, leaving a second man still loitering in the hall. She was worried.

"Crikey, it's barely dawn out there," Edmund moaned, peering out the window at the hazy orange ball rising over the horizon.

"Well past time to be up and about. You are still in the earl's employ, are you not?"

He shrugged disconsolately. "Your guess is as good as mine. After the Texas viscount fetched me back here, His Lordship put me under house arrest last night. Guards at the door and all."

"So I noted, although they're discreet about it," she replied, biting her lip. He was a prisoner, not an employee. "That isn't likely to change unless Jo—the viscount," she quickly corrected herself, "and his associates foil the Russian plot and capture Nikolai Zarenko."

Edmund was too disgruntled and sleepy to take note of her slip. Just then a knock on the door brought a morning tray with tea and biscuits. Thanking the maid, Sabrina served up a cup of the strong, fragrant tea heavy with cream, just the way he'd liked it since he was a lad back in the Berkshires. "Now drink," she commanded, offering him the biscuit plate and marmalade, then allowed him time to refresh himself and finish waking up. As a boy Eddy had always been the last one ready for school or church.

She sipped a cup of tea, gathering her thoughts as she waited, then spoke. "Tell me everything about your meeting with Zarenko."

He popped the last half of a biscuit slathered with marmalade in his mouth and chewed, then dabbed with a napkin as he swallowed. "Not much to it, really. I did a crack-up job of acting, Coz. Everyone said so."

He looked as pleased as he'd been when he was selected by his instructors to play Bottom in *A Midsummer Night's Dream*. "I imagine the Foreign Office saw to it that you had authentic-looking information," she ventured. Eddy still was not taking this seriously enough.

"The documents the earl gave me looked like the real thing. That Zarenko chap thought so." He gave a visible shudder. "Odd duck, that one. Crikey, he made me nervous. When I met him before, he never said much, just took the papers and paid me, but this time . . ."

"What did he say?" she asked apprehensively.

The euphoria of last night's success began to wear off under Sabrina's acute questioning. Edmund started to sweat. "Well, he asked me a lot about how I'd located him. That seemed to bother him. But I said just what the earl and the viscount told me to say— that I knew the Russians mostly stayed at the Metropole and I was hoping to find him before I had to breeze out of town."

"He must have believed that, else why would he have paid for the information?" she mused as she paced the floor. Something about the whole encounter did not feel right to her. It had been too easy. A man as experienced and vicious as Zarenko surely would not leap at a second trap after narrowly escaping the first one. She wondered if Josh and Lord Hambleton felt the same way. And what about that spy, Michael Jamison?

"Oh, Zarenko paid me all right, but he warned me not to leave the city." He snorted in disgust. "As if I could, cooped up here. I'd be in high clover if they let me go to Epsom to pay Frankie Bentham."

Sabrina turned. "Why would he care if you left? What exactly did he say regarding that?" she asked.

"Well, I dunno, Coz." He scratched his head as if rubbing his cowlick into a new configuration would help jar his memory. "Something about another source who'd know about the meeting. He didn't exactly say it to me, come to think on it, just jotted a note on the margin of the documents in some funny scripty writing—Russian, you know—and muttered it to himself in English."

"Did you tell the others this last night?"

He paused. "No, I didn't think of it and nobody asked."

Were all men idiots? "He's going to verify your information with someone who knows when the Foreign Secretary will really meet with the Japanese minister. The mysterious man who gave you the papers before!"

"Then they'll know it's a trap . . ."

"And not fall into it," she said, drumming her fingers nervously on the tabletop as her mind whirled.

"I'm still in trouble, am I not, Coz?" It was a rhetorical question.

When Sabrina came downstairs, the earl had gone to a meeting with some associates from the House of Lords and Josh was off with Jamison. Thoroughly vexed, she decided to leave a note for the earl on his desk, explaining what she suspected, then take action on her own. It had been Josh's assignment to coax information out of Natasha Samsonov, but the two of them had had some sort of contretemps and she would no longer see him. He and Michael were concentrating on her brother instead.

But Sabrina was certain that Josh's hard-drinking "toe dancer" was the Russians' source for double-checking the information Eddy had sold them. It was only logical. She had been the one who'd seduced Albany's foolish son. Perhaps George was still privy to what was going on. Or perhaps the lethal lady had found another man who'd sell his soul for her favors.

Sabrina hired a hackney and headed to the Metropole to wait. There was probably no cause to rush, since the prima donna seldom rose before noon. In this case, Sabrina devoutly wished she would. The trap was set for tonight, and time was running out. She had to find the secret agent working for the Russians before the earl and Josh concluded that Eddy had betrayed them.

Taking a page from the disguise Jamison had given her cousin, she had selected an old black silk day dress and purchased a new hat her budget could ill afford. But the expense was essential, since the hat had a heavy veil that would conceal her face. Otherwise, Zarenko might catch sight of her. He would remember her none too fondly from last night. Just thinking of his wrath made her stomach clench. Then again, if she was fortunate, he would still be abed nursing a terrible headache.

If Josh or Michael Jamison were anywhere about, she could not spot them as she sat in the lounge of the Metropole, watching the grand staircase for La Samsonov's appearance while pretending to sip from a cold cup of tea. She hoped that to anyone observing she was a guest in mourning, waiting for a male family member to escort her outdoors.

By noon, the waiters in the lounge were beginning to give her suspicious glances, wondering why she remained alone at the table for so long. Of course, being well conditioned to think that a respectably dressed woman in mourning should not be disturbed, they said nothing to her. But what if one of the Russians overheard them speculating about "the widow"?

She debated leaving the sanctuary of the hotel and waiting out on the street as she'd seen Josh do, but that left a woman alone in a highly visible and vulnerable position. Just as she was beginning to think she was drawing too much attention, Natasha Samsonov came sweeping down the curving stairs with her maid trailing behind her.

Sabrina tossed some coins on the table and made her way to the front door just as an expensive carriage pulled up and the ballerina climbed inside. Quickly hailing one of the many public conveyances waiting outside the hotel, Sabrina instructed the driver to follow at a discreet distance. He gave her a fish-eyed look, but when she offered him extra money for his trouble, he spit a noisome wad of tobacco into the gutter and nodded sharply, whipping his horses into a smart trot.

Drat Eddy, he was costing her a fortune in hansom fees. And this on top of the huge amount he already owed her! To add to her woes, the ride was long and circuitous, as if Natasha were trying to avoid being followed. Several times Sabrina had the driver stop and put down the step as if she were going to get out; then while she pulled in the step he quickly leaped back onto the box and caught up with the Russian's carriage.

Twice she was certain they'd lost it, but by the time they reached Mayfair, the carriage was in sight again and pulling into an alley. Sabrina paid the driver, then slipped down and made her way on foot. Surely it could not be . . .

But it was.

The carriage had stopped at the mews behind Lord Hambleton's home. Her heart pounded. Josh had suspected from the first that someone employed by the earl was guilty of selling stolen information. Now she was about to learn who it was!

She watched as the ballerina, now as discreetly veiled as Sabrina herself, slipped from the carriage, leaving her maid behind. She glanced about, satisfied that no stablemen were in the mews, then walked through the open gate to the garden at the side of the house. How well Sabrina remembered that garden and her encounters there with Josh. She forced aside such thoughts and concentrated on following her quarry undetected.

Whom could she be meeting in broad daylight in the middle of the earl's topiary? Sabrina was pleased with the prospect of being able to eavesdrop through the shrubbery and hear whatever they said. But that was not to be. By the time she reached the edge of the wall and slipped inside, the Samsonov woman had vanished. Carefully, Sabrina prowled around the fountain, taking every pathway through hedges and around the willow trees. No sign of the woman.

Where on earth has she vanished? I'm beginning to feel like Lewis Carroll's little Alice.

Not a sound could be heard beyond the gentle trill

of water and birdsong. Surely even if they were whispering, Sabrina would have caught some slight noise, but there was nothing. Discouraged, she took a seat on the bench where she'd had her first disastrous encounter with the Texas viscount. Pulling back her veil, she rubbed her temples in frustration, considering the possibility that Natasha had slipped out the front gate and had another coach pick her up, but no. She would have heard the horses' hooves. The quiet residential street had remained silent.

Surely the haughty Russian would not have set off on foot down the street. A well-dressed female walking without escort would have been noticed by someone. She had to be in the house, but how had she gotten inside from the walled garden? It simply did not make sense, unless the Russian was capable of black magic. Well, she was a witch, of that there was no doubt, Sabrina thought grimly.

Just then she heard the soft rustle of taffeta. Natasha was approaching. Sabrina leaped up and darted behind a hedge, holding her breath as she peered through the greenery, grateful for her dark clothing, which would not be readily visible. La Samsonov's brilliant scarlet cloak floated out like a bird of paradise as she whisked out the gate and past the mews. In a moment the sound of her carriage taking off echoed down the alley.

Sabrina feared that La Samsonov had met someone inside Hambleton House who would know that the Japanese minister was not going to meet the Prime Minister tonight. Eddy was in the soup for sure unless she could find out who it was—and how these secret assignations took place. There had to be some kind of secret passage from the garden to the house. It was the only possible explanation this side of the supernatural. Where to begin looking? She started toward the side of the garden wall from which Natasha had returned but the sound of voices interrupted her.

Two stablemen returning from their midday meal strolled from the kitchen to the mews, discussing how fast the viscount's big bay stallion could run if he were entered against the Caruthers's line at Epsom. Then a gardener greeted them, saying he was going to sharpen his shears and prune the boxwoods in the garden. She could hardly risk being caught by servants returning to their afternoon chores as she crawled about in the shrubbery!

Although the spy must be a house servant, the outside help too were part of the gossip chain that included those higher in the hierarchy. Also to be considered was the ease with which anyone on the second or third floors could see out into the garden through the east windows. She would have to continue her search after everyone had retired tonight, under cover of darkness.

"Do I look Japanese?" the slightly built agent in a ceremonial kimono asked nervously as he adjusted the elaborate wig on his head.

"Do I look like Genghis Khan?" Michael joked as he surveyed with misgivings the theatrical makeup he'd applied to make Calvin Firth's eyes appear Oriental. Any close scrutiny would reveal his Caucasian ancestry.

The poor devil wasn't even really a Foreign Office agent, but merely a clerk who worked on secret documents for Prime Minister Salisbury. He'd been asked to volunteer for this dangerous assignment because he approximated the size and build of Count Hayashi. Calvin Firth had no field experience whatever.

"It'll be as dark as the inside of a dog in that carriage," Josh said, sensing how spooked the fellow was. He couldn't blame him. "As soon as we spot the Russians, a dozen agents will bulldog and hogtie 'em before they know what's happening."

Jamison reviewed the route for the agents sitting calmly around the large table in Lansdowne's office. They would send the unmarked government carriage from Buckingham Palace along Pall Mall at precisely ten that evening. It would pass around the east end of St. James's Park to the dark, narrow confines of Downing Street, heading toward Whitehall.

"The best case would be for them Russians to attack the carriage from the park, which will be deserted by that time. With two of us concealed inside and others following closely, we'd capture them without exposing Mr. Firth to gunfire as he alights from the carriage on Downing. However, the street is, as the viscount has said, narrow and poorly lit. Since it provides two means of escape for the conspirators after their attempted assassination, it might be the most likely place for them to strike. Remember, they know the route, the time and the destination. Doubtless they've sent men to examine all possibilities by this time. We must be prepared for any eventuality. Are we all clear, gentlemen?" Jamison asked.

Josh watched him, cool and professional, as he fielded questions from his men and then informed each agent of his precise placement along the route. This was quite a different kettle of fish from the colonel's charge up San Juan Hill. Cantrell was glad the Englishman was on his side. Jamison had taken sole responsibility for the failure of their first subterfuge and the subsequent death of the prisoner. He had no intention of allowing Zarenko and his companions to escape a second time.

Josh, as a member of the peerage untrained in espionage, was not officially supposed to participate in the exercise. But without him they would never have learned about Zarenko's and his sister's roles in the plot. He insisted on going along, and there was no way even Michael could prevent him from being there. Josh had a vested interest in catching the assassins. It would prove that Sabrina's beloved cousin was a befuddled innocent, not a guilty traitor.

It would also prove that Uncle Ab had nothing to do with Russian spies.

The night could not have been better suited to Sabrina's purpose if she had arranged it with the Deity. Thick clouds scudded across a waning moon and a light drizzle had begun to fall when she slipped undetected from her room. The household was asleep, except for Josh, who was out trying to capture Zarenko and his henchmen with Mr. Jamison and the other agents. The earl had gone to his club and was not expected back until very late.

She tried not to think of the danger her love might be in if they did foil an attempted assassination. The last trap had ended with a bullet slashing through his arm. What might happen this time? But if she was right about Natasha Samsonov's role in the conspiracy this afternoon, then Josh and his companions would be in no danger at all.

Poor Eddy would be the one in trouble, and he was still under guard upstairs. She thanked heavens that the footmen paid no attention to her when she said she was going downstairs for some warm milk and intended to sit in the library and read because she could not sleep. They'd exchanged knowing smirks, certain she was worried about the viscount, who'd vanished on some errand unknown to them.

After Josh had been injured and the earl had insisted that she spend nights here, giving her a room adjoining his heir's, she'd known the servants would gossip even if nothing happened between them. But of course, something most certainly *had* happened between them. She only hoped that the rumors would not spread outside Hambleton House. If they did, she would lose the position Lady Chiffington had offered instructing Drucilla, which was her only hope of regaining her formerly impeccable reputation as a teacher. Even with the money the earl had promised for her school, she could not hope to establish it if respectable people believed she was a woman of loose moral character.

But I am *a woman of loose moral character*.

As she let herself out the kitchen door, Sabrina tried not to think of a future without Josh Cantrell . . . her Texan. But he wasn't her Texan; he was a viscount who would marry as his station dictated and leave her behind. The thought was so wrenching that she nearly dropped the small kerosene lamp she was carrying. Once beneath the shelter of the trees, she could light it if necessary.

Focusing her mind on the task at hand, she made her way carefully down the wet steps to the backyard and headed toward the garden gate. After stumbling on several uneven bricks, she almost decided to light the lantern. Surely the stablemen were all asleep above the mews. No, they were too close. She dared not risk it. After a moment more, her eyes adjusted to the darkness. Feeling assured, she slowly opened the heavy iron gate, whose hinges were always oiled so that it made nary a sound. Lord Hambleton's staff was extraordinarily attentive to every detail inside and outside his city house.

Why would a man so punctilious about his affairs hire a boy as unreliable as Eddy? The question had been niggling in the back of her mind for some time. And why had he chosen her to tutor his nephew? He suspected, as did his servants, that she and Josh were lovers. He'd hinted at it rather openly just before Mr. Jamison had interrupted them, carrying in a wounded Josh. She was beginning to sense a very disquieting connection between this conspiracy and the earl's mysterious motives for employing her and Eddy.

All the more reason to find out what the Samsonov woman was doing here and how she'd found her way inside the house. Lord forbid she'd come to see Lord Hambleton. Josh would be devastated if he'd crossed the Atlantic just to find that his only blood relation was the traitor the American president had sent him to uncover.

It scarcely seemed credible. Lord Lansdowne's clever Mr. Jamison would surely have suspected the earl if there was any reason to do so. Who was she to doubt a man who was the confidant of kings and prime ministers? Eddy's life, and perhaps her own, hung in the balance, she reminded herself. For good or for ill, she had to learn the truth.

Sabrina methodically worked her way along the wall, shoving aside bushes and running her hands over the damp roughness of the stone. She almost missed it. A tiny crack, far too straight to be the result of natural settling on the ground, was concealed behind a large weeping fig bush. Sliding her fingers into the crevice, she ran them up and down, encountering a slight resistance that immediately gave way. When a narrow doorway soundlessly glided open, she gasped and jumped back. Somehow she'd triggered a hidden latch.

I've found the White Rabbit's hole!

Inside was stygian darkness. Glancing nervously around the deserted garden and up at the windows overlooking it, she detected no one. Sabrina swallowed hard, forcing back the prickle of uneasiness that had been building ever since she'd set foot in the garden. The matches would not work even though she'd been careful to keep them dry. Fumbling nervously, she tried again. Finally one flared to life and she lit the tiny lantern as she stood inside the shadow of the door.

A narrow flight of stone steps wound their way downward to some unknown destination. She had read about hidden passageways used during the English civil wars centuries ago to hide rebels and religious dissidents, but this was Mayfair in the twentieth century, and Hambleton House was certainly not old enough for such a thing. As she followed the stairs, she examined the walls and steps, realizing that they appeared smooth and new. No wear from countless people over years of use. This passageway must have been constructed in the recent past.

By whom? And for what purpose?

The stairway ceased its descent and began to rise again. If her sense of direction was not utterly off, she was now beneath the ground level of the house. In a few minutes she had climbed sufficiently to be at the first floor of the house . . . and at a dead end. A solid wall faced her once again. She held up the lantern and began to examine it.

What lies beyond this?

Josh crouched down in the darkness of the alley, smelling the noisome odors of garbage blending with bilious phosphorus fumes from a waterfront factory upwind. They had been waiting for over two hours since Calvin Firth, disguised as Count Hayashi, had entered the small room on Downing Street. No attempt had been made to shoot him during his ride from the palace to his destination. Their last slim hope was that the Russians were being extraordinarily cautious and waiting until he came out from his "meeting" with Lansdowne, who had been cooling his heels inside all this while to no avail.

"I imagine the Foreign Secretary's pacing a hole in that splintery floor," Michael whispered.

"At least he's not squatting in this piss hole," Josh replied. "Smells bad enough to knock a buzzard off a gut wagon."

Jamison chuckled softly over his friend's colorful American idiom, then stiffened as he observed the door across the street opening. "Our Japanese minister's coming out," he said, preparing for action.

Josh, too, tensed, as both men scanned the narrow street. There were agents on the rooftops of several key places, and men posted on Whitehall and in St. James's Park. If a shot rang out, there would be no escape for the assassins this time. But Firth made his way to the waiting carriage, his figure silhouetted in the lantern light, without incident. He climbed inside and the vehicle took off. Josh and Michael waited until the sound of the horses' hooves died away. The carriage would retrace its route back to the palace.

Finally both men stood up, greatly disheartened.

"If Zarenko'd taken the bait, it would appear reasonable that he'd have tried here or in the park," Jamison said.

"And we'd have heard the hullabaloo from here. Damn it all to hell!"

"He paid Whistledown for information he did not use," Michael said, rubbing his chin speculatively. The glint in his eyes was hard and cold as steel.

A chill rippled down Josh's spine.

Sabrina tried the same tactic she had employed on the outer door. At first it seemed not to work, but when she reversed her search to the opposite side, she encountered the same kind of latch. It clicked open, revealing a beautiful walnut panel. She stepped into Lord Hambleton's office, recognizing immediately his massive desk and the bookcase-lined walls around it. A secret passage into his inner sanctum! She speculated over what it signified.

Such a device made sense if he held clandestine meetings with high-ranking members of the Foreign Office. But what had Natasha Samsonov been doing here this afternoon? That was the disturbing question. Sabrina set her lantern on the floor so the light would not shine through the narrow crack in the heavy velvet draperies drawn over the front window. Did she dare to search an earl's private office, especially one so highly placed in the government? If so, what should she look for?

Not having the slightest idea, she began to go through the papers on his desk, then the drawers, being careful not to disturb anything. There were all sorts of scribbled notes about legislation pending or proposed for the next session of Parliament, reports from the factor who managed his estates scattered all about England. Nothing at all amiss for a peer of wealth and standing.

"I would never have suspected you possessed the nerve to break into a peer's home," snapped a nasty voice. "I should have known better."

Sabrina whirled around to confront the familiar figure standing at the doorway to the secret panel. The first thing her eyes fastened on was the pistol in his hand, pointed directly at her. In his other hand he held the note she had penned that morning.

"So you're the White Rabbit," she said.

As he advanced toward her, he stared at her as if she were a complete fool.

"Of course I am!"

Chapter 19

Josh and Michael took a hansom to meet the earl at his club after the debacle on Downing Street, per Hambleton's instruction. En route both men were quiet, deep in thought about why the trap had failed. It was obvious that Zarenko had known about it. If Jamison believed the earl was involved, he said nothing, but, considering that Josh himself was worried about the possibility, it made for a grim ride indeed.

"I shall hate to report another failure to Lansdowne and Hambleton," Michael said as they approached the heavy oak door.

Josh broke stride. "The Foreign Secretary'll be here?"

Jamison sighed. "I'm afraid so. With Hayashi arriving to discuss the final version of the treaty tomorrow, this was our last hope of averting a diplomatic catastrophe. I fear Lansdowne will ask the Prime Minister to cancel the reception at court. Your uncle's opinion on such a delicate matter will definitely be considered. Lansdowne certainly will be here. It wouldn't surprise me if Salisbury himself didn't put in an appearance."

Gloomily they followed the footman who had admitted them as he led them down a long maroon-carpeted hallway to a private room where they would be interrogated by the highest-ranking men in the government. "After this shindig is over, maybe I should see if my old pard Alexi and his pals are at the White Satin. Things usually get lively about this time of night," Josh ventured.

Preoccupied, Jamison nodded.

Salisbury was not present but Lansdowne was, just as Michael had guessed. The distinguished gentleman was a whipcord-lean outdoorsman of vigorous middle years. His hairline had receded, but he sported a luxuriant mustache in compensation. Like his friend the earl, he exuded a sense of quietly restrained power. The Foreign Secretary broke the silence the moment the door was closed by the footman. "Wesley, it is indeed a pleasure to finally meet my old friend's heir." He extended his hand, and Josh clasped it in a firm grip.

"I don't reckon your pleasure's gonna last all that long, my lord," Josh replied.

"I take it you were unsuccessful," the Foreign Secretary said, observing the expression on his best agent's face.

As they discussed the situation, Josh studied his uncle. There simply was no way the old man could be guilty of treason. *But who—*

"I say, Joshua, you're in a brown study. Do share your opinion with us," the earl said.

"Oh, I was just thinking of everyone who works at Hambleton House. More folks than it'd take to drive a herd of beeves clean up to Alaska."

"You're assuming that the leak of information comes from your end, not my office," Lansdowne interjected, his keen dark eyes fastened on the American. "We have cut off all information available to Albany's pup, but I do have a small hand-picked cadre of men whom I trust implicitly . . . perhaps too implicitly." Abruptly switching his attention from Josh, he asked Michael, "What do you think of Piltcher?"

Before Jamison could reply, the earl said, "I've been turning over the problem since we discovered young Whistledown was involved. The boy's a fool, no more capable of this sort of intrigue than is my cousin Ludlow, who was perhaps the most plodding man ever to be ordained in the Church of England."

"If not Sabrina's cousin, then who?" Josh asked.

The Foreign Secretary and his agent both waited for the earl's reply.

"I may know when we return home. In fact, I suspect I shall be quite certain," he replied in a subdued tone.

Sabrina fought to breathe through the heavy wad of cloth stuffed in her mouth, bound tightly in place with a scarf. Another scarf covered her eyes. If only her heart would stop racing. She was alone, in stygian darkness, rocking back and forth on the floor of a badly sprung carriage as it bounced toward heaven knew where. She had no idea what he was going to do with her now that she had unwittingly discovered him. In fact, she had no idea if he was even aboard.

After binding and gagging her, he'd pressed a cloth soaked in some vile liquid to her nose and mouth. Ether. She remembered nothing from that horrible moment in the library until she awakened in the carriage. At first she'd been terrified that her roiling stomach would rebel and she'd aspirate because of the gag, but by sheer force of will, she'd fought to subdue her body's natural urge to purge itself of the drug. Her head still ached, and every time she attempted to move her cramped arms and legs, dizziness assailed her.

There was little room in which to move anyway. The carriage was a small closed conveyance with both doors locked. She'd tried kicking at the one nearest her feet, but could do nothing to open it. Then she'd struggled to turn around in the narrow space between the seats and kick the other door. Equally useless. The driver had ignored the racket, never slackening his breakneck pace.

Where are they taking me? And what will they do to me when we arrive?

Such thoughts would only lead to more panic. Sabrina could not afford that luxury. She was utterly on her own. Well, that was scarcely a new experience, considering that she'd come to London to make her own way seven years ago. If she had succeeded by brains and determined self-discipline once, she could do so again. All she had to do was to use her mind to outsmart her enemies. She concentrated on breathing deeply.

Judging from the silence outside and the muffled sounds of the horses' hooves, they were somewhere in the countryside. Perhaps if she feigned illness from the effects of the badly administered dose of ether, she would find an opportunity to escape once she was taken outside the confines of the locked carriage. Pretending to be ill would not take great thespian abilities, she concluded, considering how wretched she felt.

Suddenly the carriage jerked to a stop, causing her

to hit her head against the seat. She could hear voices speaking a polyglot of French, Russian and English, mostly French, which she understood.

"Why did the fool send her here?" Natasha Samsonov demanded imperiously after the driver had made a halting explanation of some sort in Russian.

"After tomorrow our Englishman will have outlived his usefulness." The voice of her brother, Zarenko. Sabrina shivered, wondering what he would do once he recognized her as the "maid" in his room. Had they realized yet that the love letters had been stolen?

"The woman also has no usefulness. She is a pest to be disposed of immediately," Natasha said.

"Not so quickly. I want to find out what she knows. How did she find her way to the secret entrance?" Zarenko issued some sharp order in Russian and the door of the carriage opened.

Rough hands seized hold of her and she was flung over a massive shoulder and carried like a sack of potatoes. In a few paces she was inside some sort of shelter. The blindfold was removed, revealing the scowling face of Nikolai Zarenko looming over her.

Sabrina blinked, trying to accustom herself to the bright light issuing from a kerosene lantern on the table beside which she had been seated. Her captors were ringed around her—Zarenko, Sergei Valerian and Natasha Samsonov, whose eyes had an unnatural onyx glitter that frightened Sabrina even more than the menacing man who spoke to her.

"So we meet again." Zarenko massaged the side of his head, where a reddened mark was visible at the hairline. Of course he remembered her!

"You know this meddlesome female?" Valerian

asked in a bored voice, as if his companion's amours •
held not the slightest interest for him.

Zarenko ignored him. "Now the mystery is solved.
What did you do with Wettin's letters, my dear?" His
almost genial tone was in contrast to the brutal way
he grabbed her chin and tore the gag from her mouth.
"You are an English spy. Where are the letters? I
promise it will go far easier for you if you tell me."

Her mouth felt as if it had been glued closed, and
her throat was parched and sore. Sabrina forced herself to ignore Natasha's penetrating stare and concentrate on the man interrogating her. When she spoke,
her voice was raspy but firm. "I am no spy, merely a
teacher employed by the earl."

"And whom were you teaching in my hotel suite,
hmm? Dressed in a chambermaid's uniform." One
big hand took hold of her hair and pulled on it hard,
bringing tears to her eyes from the stinging pain.
Then he used his other hand to close off her already
aching throat until she coughed and gasped for air.

"You will tell him. They always do." Valerian stood
at the opposite side of the room, pouring himself a
tall glass of vodka.

"Oh, do be quiet, Sergei. Let us do what we do
best." Natasha's voice was husky with excitement.

"I am not a spy," Sabrina repeated stubbornly.

"But you were searching my quarters—for Wettin's
billets-doux?"

"No. I knew nothing about them." A lie but she
hoped a forgivable one.

"You took them. What did you do with them?"
Natasha said, gliding closer, her long nails curved out
like claws, close to Sabrina's face.

Steeling her courage, Sabrina met the pitiless

black eyes and replied, "I turned them over to British authorities."

Valerian cursed and downed the rest of his vodka. Zarenko slapped Sabrina so hard her ears rang and bright lights flashed before her eyes.

"I don't believe her. She's involved in this up to her eyebrows," Natasha said, using a nail to trace the delicate arch of Sabrina's eyebrow. "I wonder, can a teacher find employment if she's blind?" she mused, pointing two fingers directly at her prisoner's eyes.

"I no longer have the letters. They are with the government. Most probably destroyed by now," Sabrina said, lowering her lashes so as not to meet the daggerlike threat from the Russian woman.

"She's probably telling the truth about that. The evidence is too damning to keep," Zarenko said angrily.

"Then let me kill her," his sister replied.

Sabrina held her breath as the three conspirators argued.

Lord Lansdowne had departed from the club for an urgent meeting with the Prime Minister. Salisbury would not be pleased to learn that their Japanese treaty was still in jeopardy. By the time the earl, Josh and Michael arrived at the town house, the city was starting to come to life. As they passed street vendors and clerks en route to work, the three men in Hambleton's carriage maintained a tense silence, each deep in his own thoughts.

When Nash opened the door for them, Hambleton asked, "Has Hodgins arrived yet?"

"Yes, m'lord. He's in the kitchen taking his tea as usual."

"Please ask him to join us in my office. You, as well, if you please."

314

Bowing diffidently, the butler nodded. "Very good, m'lord." He walked briskly down the long hallway to the kitchen at the rear of the house.

Mystified, Josh and Michael followed Hambleton. Nash and the earl's secretary quickly joined them. Instinctively, Josh felt for his Colt, concealed inside his jacket and noted that Jamison was doing the same with his Webley. They stood on either side of the door as the two men approached the earl, who paced at the large window behind his desk.

"Would you be so good as to show me your keys to my desk?" he asked both men.

The Texan and the agent exchanged puzzled looks, both still wary as Nash reached without hesitation inside his pocket and produced a key. Hodgins took a moment to fumble through the numerous pockets of his suit, then did likewise. The earl held one in each hand, comparing them

"Very good. You may go, Nash," Hambleton said. Then he turned to his private secretary, who had been with him for over twenty years. As soon as the butler closed the door, the earl fixed Hodgins with weary gray eyes and asked, "Why did you do it?"

Hodgins drew in his receding chin in indignation. "Do what, m'lord?" He cast an uneasy glance at Jamison and the viscount. Both young men were poised on the balls of their feet.

Hambleton held out the keys he'd taken from Nash and from his secretary. "Pray examine the evidence, my dear fellow. You will note that Nash's key is clean. Yours is stained blue."

Hodgins put on his glasses and squinted at the blue cast on the edges of the key. "It must have rubbed against something in my pocket," the secretary said.

"Only if you are in the habit of carrying pure blue

pigment inside your good suit jacket," Hambleton replied.

"Pure pigment—like for paint? That stuff never dries," Josh said as Jamison nodded grimly in understanding.

"You were the one who verified that young Whistledown's information was a trap. I deliberately kept that knowledge from you, but when Zarenko sent someone to ask you about it, you went to the only place I might keep such sensitive documents and found precisely what I had left there."

"You set a trap inside the trap," Josh said as he breathed a huge sigh of relief.

If Michael Jamison felt the same, he concealed it completely. "How much did the Russians pay you to betray your country, Hodgins?"

By now the thin little man was chalk-white and perspiring profusely despite the cool morning air. He ran one ink-stained hand over his thinning hair and slumped against the bookcase. "I know nothing about this," he protested in a thready voice.

Before anyone could question him further, Edmund Whistledown burst through the door with Nash and the two footmen-cum-guards trailing behind him. "I tried to stop him from interrupting, m'lord," the butler said apologetically.

The earl nodded, then turned to Edmund. "Now what is so urgent—"

"Sabrina's missing! I knocked on her door and the latch hadn't caught. Her room is empty, the bed unslept in. I've searched the house. She's vanished without a trace."

Josh placed one hand on the boy's shoulder and turned him around. "None of the servants saw her this morning?"

"No. They"—he gestured to the footmen—"they saw her late last night. She said she couldn't sleep and was going to the kitchen to warm some milk and read in the library. Nothing's been disturbed in the kitchen or the library." He nodded to the men, who had helped him search.

As Josh peppered the three with questions, Hodgins pressed the latch to the hidden panel and started to draw a small Adams revolver from his pocket. Jamison was on him before he could raise the weapon, knocking it from his hand. He seized the trembling man and threw him onto the desk top, holding him by the scruff of the neck, his face pressed against the wood. "Now, why is it, old chap, that I suspect you know what happened to Miss Edgewater?"

The sound of Josh's Colt cocking directly against Hodgins's temple filled the large room. "Talk, or so help me God, I'll blow your brains from here to that wall," he said in a deadly voice.

Jamison pulled Hodgins up so Josh could center the large-caliber pistol between the secretary's bulging, terrified eyes. As the two men were dealing with Hodgins, the earl dismissed Nash and the footmen, instructing them to question the rest of the household staff in case anyone had seen Miss Edgewater since last evening.

"Why did you do it, Hodgins? You've been my right hand for twenty-one years."

"T-twenty-two," his secretary stammered. "I-I did not do it for money. It was for her. She's wealthy. We were going to live in Paris . . ."

"You're going to live in a hoosegow—if you're lucky—and that's only if I get Sabrina back," Josh said.

"He means the Samsonov woman," Jamison said,

shaking his head. "You fool, don't you know she used you the same way she used the Duke of Albany's son? Who, I might add, is younger and considerably better-looking than you, not to mention a shade richer himself."

"What did you do with Sabrina?" Josh repeated, growing more desperate with each passing moment.

"I turned her over to them. My last . . . duty for Tasha's brother was to fetch all the documents in the private folders," he said, moistening his thin lips nervously as he glanced at the locked drawer that had revealed his treachery. "I knew you were at your club, waiting to hear about the trap you'd set."

"One that you knew would fail," Hambleton said with a downturned mouth. "How did you encounter Miss Edgewater?"

"She left a note for you earlier in the day, saying she was suspicious of Tasha. I only found it after"—Hodgins's face turned from white to red for a moment—"Tasha came here . . . to verify whether Count Hayashi was meeting Lord Lansdowne last night. I . . . we . . . well . . ." He cleared his throat nervously.

Josh could well imagine "Tasha's" wiles, seducing information from this piteous fool in exchange for sexual favors. "Sabrina followed her here, I'd bet on it. She'd do anything to save her cousin."

"Somehow she found her way to this office through the secret passage," Hodgins admitted.

"She must've gone out to search the garden late last night. Then you followed her into the office. Am I getting it right so far?" Josh asked. The barrel of the pistol never wavered from Hodgins's nose.

"Y-yes. I took her and the papers to the end of the alley, where Tasha's carriage was waiting. Tasha was that upset and said I couldn't come with her now.

That first she'd have to deal with the woman."

"Sabrina would never go willingly with you and climb into a carriage with that Russian rattler," Josh said. "What did you do to her?"

"I only used a bit of ether, then carried her. Honestly, I did not harm her," Hodgins quickly blurted out.

"But you knew your darling Tasha would harm her plenty." The menace in Josh's voice was bowstring-taut.

"Where would she take Miss Edgewater?" the earl asked.

Hodgins closed his lashless eyes as if preparing to die as he swallowed, shaking his head. "I have no idea."

"I just might," Michael said. "My men have been watching the comings and goings of the Russians for some months. Besides living at the Metropole, this group has a small, private hunting lodge in the north of Essex, not far from the coast."

"A perfect place for making good their escape by sea after they assassinate Count Hayashi," Hambleton said.

Josh saw a dim ray of hope. "You ever hear any talk about it?" he asked Hodgins.

"N-no, but it might be," he said lamely, thinking there might be a dim hope of living out the day if the wild American raced off in search of the Edgewater woman.

"How far to this place?" Josh asked Michael.

"With fast horses we can make it in four to five hours."

"Zarenko has Sabrina. He'll remember her from the hotel. We don't have four hours," Josh said harshly. "How isolated is this place? Any roads leading to it?"

"Yes, it's on a decent thoroughfare to Colchester."

"Good. We'll take the Mercedes."

The earl raised his eyebrows. "I scarcely believe it is as reliable as my best horses."

"Can any of them run fifty miles an hour for over two hours?"

"Good God, can your vehicle?" his uncle asked, but Josh was already heading to the door.

"I have to load extra cans of fuel in the trunk and get on the road. Will you guide me, Michael?"

"With Zarenko at trail's end, need you even ask?" Jamison replied coolly.

"I shall deal with our lovelorn fool here," Hambleton said, shoving Hodgins into a chair, where he collapsed in a rumpled heap, trembling as he realized all his dreams of Paris and Tasha were over.

"What of me?" Edmund asked as he trailed along after Josh and Michael.

"No time, Edmund," Josh said dismissively as his long legs carried him out the kitchen door toward the mews where he garaged his automobile.

"B-but it's all my fault that this happened to my cousin. I must make amends. I'm coming along," he huffed, struggling to keep up with them.

Without breaking stride, Josh said, "Right as rain about this bein' your fault. I reckon we could use another man when it comes to handling the petroleum."

Edmund's face brightened as Josh entered the mews and yanked a heavy covering off several large metal drums stored in a stall beside the gleaming automobile.

"Start loading while I crank her up," he instructed his helpers.

Dubiously, Jamison and Whistledown set to work.

* * *

"Hurry up or I shall simply shoot you and say you tried to escape," Natasha said as she observed Sabrina answering an urgent call of nature in the woods surrounding the shooting lodge where they'd imprisoned her last night.

Sabrina took her time. "You cannot kill me without risking your brother's wrath. Remember that I'm a valuable hostage," she replied calmly, trying to believe it herself, all the while her mind frantically turned over ways to escape and warn Josh and the earl about what was going to happen that very afternoon.

"Nicki is a fool to think the viscount would give a fig for an insignificant servant such as you."

Sabrina straightened up, feeling more confident now that she was not subjected to the humiliation of having this spiteful woman watch her squatting in a patch of weeds. She was not as tall as the ballerina, nor as strong. She needed some weapon as an equalizer. Zarenko and Valerian had left her and Natasha with only two brutish guards who spoke nothing but Russian. The men seemed content to remain in the lodge, drinking vodka and throwing dice. Natasha had taken over the role as her jailer and relished it.

La Samsonov had been spurned by Josh and was obviously itching to take revenge on the woman she viewed as her rival, even if she would never admit it. Sabrina thought there had to be a way to overpower her and escape. Thus far nothing had occurred to her, but she knew her best opportunity would be when they were alone like this. As they made their way back to the lodge, she scanned the surrounding woods for weapons and hiding places.

"Don't dawdle in the hot sun. It will ruin your wonderful English complexion," Natasha said snidely, shoving Sabrina toward the steps.

That was when Sabrina saw it off to the side of the weed-infested path, half hidden in the shadow of the sagging porch. The Russians servants were apparently allowed to remain indoors and drink rather than see to the upkeep of the place. But considering that the entire lot of them would shortly be leaving England, that was scarcely surprising. Her find was a rusty hunting knife with a broken blade. Certainly not her first choice for self-defense, but it would have to do. The thought of stabbing the jagged edge into human flesh made the bile rise in her throat.

Would you rather die?

The sadistic Russian woman would delight in killing her. And Sabrina intuited that Natasha Samsonov would not be at all merciful about it.

At five feet two inches in height, weighing barely a hundred and three pounds—and seven of that hair, as her mother always said—Sabrina knew she could never match the strength of a woman half a head taller and a good twenty pounds heavier. Besides, while Sabrina spent her days pouring tea and instructing debutantes, the ballerina honed powerful muscles in the rigorous exercises of the dance.

It was now or never. Sabrina deliberately stumbled when she reached the first step, toppling sideways toward the place where the blade lay hidden. As Natasha cursed and reached down to grab a fistful of hair to drag her up the steps, Sabrina slipped the blade in the folds of her skirt.

Somehow she would have to conceal it on her person before her next "call of nature."

Chapter 20

"I say, Josh, that rising needle? Is it perchance a temperature gauge?" Michael Jamison asked warily, nodding toward the dash panel of the speeding Mercedes.

"Yup," Josh murmured. Even though he'd checked the radiator and knew it still held plenty of water, the heat was climbing way too high. Small wonder. In the past hour and a half they'd traveled at breakneck speeds.

Edmund leaned forward from the back seat and yelled over the noise of the engine, "Crikey, does that mean we can go even faster?" He sounded delighted at the prospect as he gazed curiously at the various knobs and gauges on the complex piece of machinery.

Michael just sat stoically, his hands braced against the dash panel as the wind whipped his straight black hair about his face. Oddly enough, the coolly imperturbable spy was more frightened than the timid Edmund by hurtling along at speeds nearing fifty miles an hour. *Then again*, Josh thought, *Eddy's such a fool kid, if he fell down, he couldn't hit the ground.*

"No, we can't go faster. As it is, we've been pushing too hard without giving the cooling system time to rest," he explained in terms he hoped both men could understand. And a tone that would not unduly upset poor Michael.

"Does that mean the whole bloody thing could explode?" Jamison asked sharply.

"Unfortunately, yes, but I think we'll make it," Josh replied with what he hoped was confidence . . . and accuracy.

They had followed the main roads out of the city heading northeast, with Michael giving directions for turns and checking landmarks as they progressed. By the time they had to make the first stop to refill the fuel tank, the engine was already so hot that the cap to the cooling system's water supply could not be removed without special tools and the risk of scalding anyone who performed the task. Josh figured his beautiful automobile would soon be a melted-down piece of scrap metal. If his beautiful woman was safe, it would not matter.

Sabrina. He could not lose her this way. He could not bear the thought of losing her in any possible way. No woman had ever seized hold of his heart as she had. Now he recognized it and knew he never wanted to live without her again. If only he had the chance to tell her that.

"How much farther?" he asked Jamison, who was squinting at the roadside searching for landmarks.

"If you'd slow this bloody hell machine down, I might be able to see something," Michael snarled. When Josh removed his foot from the gas pedal, Jamison leaned out the side and peered at a tall stand of oaks clustered around a turn-off. "I believe that's it," he said.

Josh emitted an oath that drew a sharp intake of breath from Edmund, who still leaned forward by his shoulder. "Unpaved roads. The Mercedes isn't going to cotton to that," Josh said as he turned the wheel sharply. The tires hit the loose gravel, skidding in a half circle before he regained control of the wheel. Edmund was pitched headfirst against Michael, who cursed and yelled at him to stay the hell in the back seat where he belonged.

Jamison had not wanted the boy along, and Josh had to concede he had a point. Whistledown was purely a magnet for trouble, but he did provide another pair of hands for hefting the petroleum keg and holding the funnel to the fuel-tank opening, always a tricky maneuver. Also, they might be able to use him as a decoy to lure the Russians into an ambush in the woods. Until he saw the lay of the land, Josh had formulated only the loosest sort of plan with Michael. But there was one thing on which they agreed—no way would either man turn Edmund Whistledown loose with a gun.

The bumps and ruts carved by rains and carriage traffic over the years, perhaps centuries for all Josh knew, had made the narrow trail nearly impassable in an automobile. He downshifted but still went as fast as he dared. The vehicle endured horrible jarring as the wheels bounced from rut to rut, struggling for purchase on the dusty, rocky ground.

"Damnation, that was a cow you almost hit! Slow this bloody thing down." Michael's voice had lost any semblance of British stiff upper lip. Indeed, he sounded on the verge of panic.

Edmund, on the other hand, was in his glory. "Have no fear, sir. Lord Wesley is at home racing across the range, weaving in and out of herds of cows, swerving around prairie hogs—"

"That's prairie dogs, you idiot," Jamison snapped. "Now shut up!"

"Please, sir. There's no need for rudeness. In any case, we have slowed drastically. Crikey, a horse would be much faster than this," Edmund ventured, disappointed now that the thrill of speed was over.

"Find me a horse and I'll ride it hell bent for leather," Josh said through gritted teeth, fighting to hold on to the wheel and keep the Mercedes on the road while he watched the heat gauge climb into what he knew was a danger zone.

Edmund sighed. "We wouldn't have got this far nearly so fast on horseback, I'll concede."

"How much farther to their hidey-hole?" Josh asked Michael.

"I'd say about four or five miles, over the rise," he replied, his calm returning in direct proportion to their decline in speed.

"Good," Josh said, braking to a halt.

"What are you stopping for?" both men asked.

Edmund looked at the viscount as if he'd taken leave of his senses when Josh jumped out of the car and withdrew his Colt from its holster. Michael's expression cleared when he realized what his companion intended to do.

"The engine's going to blow if you don't relieve the pressure?" he asked.

Josh nodded as he took careful aim at the very top of the grille so as to avoid the engine. He fired a single shot. Whistledown held his hands over his ringing ears. "Not the engine, the radiator—or boiler as you'd call it on a locomotive or steamboat," Josh said. "That bullet hole should act as a steam vent . . . until the engine runs dry. At least we're out of earshot of the Russians."

"But not me," Edmund said, rubbing his ears. He positively hated the noise firearms made.

The men ignored him as Josh jumped back inside and revved up the engine, which started with a swift lurch that sent their rear passenger tumbling against the plush leather squabs. They took off in a trail of dust, spraying gravel in their wake. "Tell me when we get close enough to worry about the noise carrying," Josh said to Jamison.

"Deuced hard to judge. I've only been here twice, and one time was after dark. On horseback," he added unnecessarily.

They bounced along for another quarter hour as Michael peered through the greenery and open fields ahead. The area was deserted except for a few badly frightened deer and small game that bounded as far from the noisy, evil-smelling vehicle as possible. Then they reached a level stretch where the dirt road was relatively unrutted and free of large rocks. Josh shifted into higher gear . . . for a few hundred yards.

The horrible squeal of metal grating against metal began as a low whine and grew to an unbearable cacophony of clanking. Josh did not even bother changing gears. The whole engine locked up, and the automobile rolled to a halt.

"I was afraid of that," he said, jumping out of the car. "How much farther? I'd reckon about a mile."

Michael nodded.

Josh pulled his Winchester 76 rifle from the trunk and checked it, stuffing extra ammunition in his pockets.

Jamison did likewise with his Lee-Enfield. Both men were armed to the teeth.

"I say," Edmund ventured timidly. "Might I—"

"No!" each of them chorused, and he subsided.

"Then what am I to do?"

"Guard the Mercedes," Josh suggested.

"B-but it's . . . dead," he replied, hurrying to keep up with their long strides as Jamison led the way through a stand of trees toward the crest of a hill.

"Quiet. Voices carry," Michael whispered as he neared the top.

"No way we leave him wandering loose. He'd likely set the woods on fire," Josh whispered to Jamison, then turned to Sabrina's cousin. "Just stay behind us and do exactly what we say. Not one word of sass, you comprende—er, understand?"

Nodding, Edmund followed, picking his way very carefully through the high weeds. He positively hated snakes.

It was nearly noon and both of the Russian servants were growing exceedingly jovial, slapping each other on the back and upending bottles of vodka, having given up the bother of pouring it into glasses. Sabrina had heard rumors of the Texas viscount's prodigious capacity for liquor, but surely he could not have kept up with these beastly men. Then again . . .

"All men are drunken sots," Natasha said contemptuously.

And hypocritically, to Sabrina's way of thinking. She watched the ballerina take a dainty sip of tea, normally not her beverage of choice. Not understanding English and probably too inebriated to care, the servants did not respond to their mistress's insult. Natasha stood by the window, looking out at the isolated countryside, a bored expression marring the perfection of her features. One elegantly booted foot tapped impatiently on the rough planks of the floor.

Sabrina had waited for her opportunity, hoping the men would pass out, but they seemed to possess boundless tolerance and continued to throw dice and place wagers. She had no idea how much longer it would be before Zarenko and Valerian returned.

Time was running out. Steeling herself, she cleared her throat and said, "I drank too much tea. I need to go outside again."

"I'm not a nursemaid," her captor snapped, restless and impatient for the men to return, their mission accomplished, so they could sail for France. "Soon I shall dance in Paris . . . and you shall be dead," she added maliciously.

"I shall burst before you can shoot me if I do not visit the necessary," Sabrina replied, refusing to give the nasty witch the satisfaction of showing the terror she felt.

"Very well," the Samsonov woman said angrily. "All I need in addition to smelling those filthy serfs is to have to endure you soiling yourself." She led Sabrina to the rear door, saying something to the men in Russian. One fellow nodded, but his companion continued to toss the dice without looking in their direction. "When Nicki and the rest return, I shall kill these two serfs myself," she muttered in French.

Sabrina did not doubt the woman was capable of it. The question now was whether or not she herself could be equally ruthless. *Think of Josh and his uncle, of the international diplomatic repercussions, the embarrassment to His Majesty's government . . . the surety that you'll die.* She held on to those disconcerting thoughts as they walked toward the trees, feeling the heavy handle of the broken knife as she clamped her fingers tightly around it.

There would be only one chance.

Josh and Michael lay at the top of a small rise, studying the cabin below them. "I make out two men inside," the Texan said, handing the binoculars to his friend, who focused them on the large window fronting the lodge.

"Difficult to tell if there are more. The men aren't familiar. They have the look of servants about them."

"Drunk as hoot owls," Josh noted.

"That will simplify our work."

"Don't count on it. I've seen these Russians drink. Falling down, they're still cussed mean if you cross them. I only wish there were some sign of Sabrina."

"Or La Samsonov," Michael added.

Just then a loud scream followed by virulent cursing in French and Russian echoed from behind the lodge. The clear soprano of Sabrina's voice now blended with the guttural sounds of her antagonist. Uttering an oath of his own, Josh jumped up and started to run, with Michael right behind him.

"You take care of those drunks. I'm going after Sabrina," Josh said as he veered around the log structure.

"I'm with you, m'lord," Edmund said, panting heavily as he attempted to keep up with Josh.

The Texan far outran him, desperate to reach Sabrina, whose voice he could hear under the curses of the ballerina. Hell, that bitch was twice the size of his little darlin', feisty as she was. Natasha could break her neck! Keeping an eye out for any other Russian men who might burst upon the scene, he put on the brakes when he saw the bright colors of women's clothing writhing on the ground. The sight was so incredible that he had to blink twice before he could get a handle on what was happening.

Sabrina was straddling the much larger and stronger woman, holding the jagged rusty relic of a skinning knife to her throat. There was blood smeared over both of them, but it appeared to be all the Russian's, since she was the one cradling an arm against her chest. Sabrina's skirts were ruched up around her hips, revealing the delectable curves of her slim, stocking-encased legs. Even a garter peeked out on one creamy thigh. Peering around the area and deciding that no enemies lurked in hiding, Josh leaned against a tree trunk and admired the view.

"Make one more sound and I swear my next cut will be to that pretty white throat . . . or perhaps your face," Sabrina hissed through gritted teeth. She had intended to catch the larger woman off guard and place the knife to her throat, threatening to kill her if she did not turn around at once. Then all she would have had to do was cosh her over the head with the heavy handle of the knife.

However, things had not worked out quite so easily. The Russian had twisted away and nearly disarmed her—would have if not for the accidental slash of the knife across her arm when the two of them tumbled to the ground. Fortunately, the Russian had been taken in by Sabrina's feigned docility and had not even brought her pistol along.

The sudden spurt of her own blood had had a surprising effect on the woman, who enjoyed inflicting pain on others but became hysterical when it was she herself who bled. That was when Sabrina had seized on the notion of threatening disfigurement unless her foe quieted. It had worked, but not before they'd made enough noise to awaken the dead. Where were those two inebriated "serfs"? She dared not take her eyes from Natasha to see if the men were crashing through the brush to rescue their mistress. Then she heard a familiar drawling voice and jerked about in shock.

"Well, now, after all I sacrificed to get here, I reckon you don't even need my help."

She looked up at Josh disbelievingly. As she suddenly became aware of the spectacle she must look, all thoughts of Natasha's cohorts fled from her thoughts. "How did you get here?" she asked idiotically.

"Darlin', that's a long, sad story," he said, holstering his Colt and reaching down to assist her so she could climb off the sobbing, cursing ballerina.

He pulled her into his arms, and she went willingly. "Oh, there are two men—"

He shushed her, brushing her tangled hair from her face. "Michael has them hogtied by now. Are you all right?" he asked, inspecting her to be certain the blood was indeed none of her own.

"I'm uninjured, but I suspect Madame Samsonov will require some medical attention," she said with a bloodthirsty relish that immediately appalled her.

Josh laughed heartily, kissing her with a sudden surge of gratitude that made his eyes sting. How close he'd come to losing her forever! "Woman, I am never again letting you out of my sight," he whispered as his lips brushed hers. Lordy, she tasted sweet.

The look in his eyes made her dizzy with longing. He acted as if . . . as if he loved her—but of course that could not be. Should not be. He was a viscount. "Josh," she said softly, her blood-smeared hand daring to caress the bristly black beard growing on his jawline.

The tender interlude was interrupted by a panting

Edmund, who rushed toward them, calling out, "Coz, crikey, I'm that glad to see you're—" He pitched headlong over Natasha, who was trying to crawl on all fours into the brush to escape. She let out a curse and kicked him soundly in the ribs. With a moan, he rolled to Josh's and Sabrina's feet.

"Whoa, there, princess," Josh said, giving the ballerina a meaningful look.

Natasha subsided, sullenly flopping onto the ground and cradling her bleeding arm as if it were a compound fracture instead of a superficial cut.

"I've tied up those two louts inside. Where are Zarenko and his companions?" Jamison asked as he arrived on the scene.

"Gone back to London," Sabrina said with sudden alarm. What was she thinking, mooning over Josh while the fate of Anglo-Japanese relations hung in the balance? "They intend to assassinate Count Hayashi as he arrives at the Court of St. James's for a ceremonial dinner this evening!"

"Crikey, how can we make it in time with the automobile dead?" Edmund asked.

"The Mercedes? You rode it here?" Sabrina asked Josh.

"Rode it and shot it dead," Michael said with a hint of relish in his voice.

"Shot it?" she echoed, puzzled.

"To vent the radiator so the bloody—er, my pardon, Miss Edgewater—so the engine wouldn't blow us to kingdom come," Michael replied.

"Not the engine—the radiator. Then the engine finally locked up and quit on me. I was pushing her so hard her piston rods and cylinders plumb melted together from overheating," Josh explained, although no one understood one word.

But Sabrina understood one thing. "Oh, Josh, you shot your Mercedes for me?" she exclaimed. Suddenly giddy, she flung her arms around his neck.

"Sabrina, darlin', I had to make a hard choice—you or my Mercedes. Now, she was a good ole gal, but I can buy me a dozen fancy automobiles. You're the one and only Miss Sabrina Edgewater."

With that, he kissed her. Edmund turned away, uncomfortable watching his proper cousin's most improper behavior.

Michael rolled his eyes over Josh's Texas-sized flattery. "We will need horses for a hard ride to London, unless you've forgotten the mission your president sent you to England to accomplish," he said dryly.

Flushed with embarrassment, Sabrina broke away from Josh's embrace. "Oh! There is a stable of sorts down that way." She pointed to a faint trail through the brush. "That awful Zarenko and his friends took the carriage, but I believe there are more horses inside."

"Do you want to add her to your collection inside the lodge while I scout out a remuda for us?" Josh asked Michael.

Jamison reached down and pulled Natasha Samsonov to her feet. She let out a yelp of anger at his cold professional handling, which he ignored, saying, "Come on now. Some agents will come calling in a few hours to collect you."

While he secured the three captives, Josh, Sabrina and Edmund made their way to the stable, where they found half a dozen fresh horses. All of good quality, Josh decided after inspecting them. He examined the tack, whistling low. "Some fancy rigging, to match up with prime horseflesh. Make yourself useful and throw a saddle over that gray for Michael," he instructed Edmund.

Whistledown's face turned bright red. "Uh, I-I, that is . . ."

"Eddy dislikes horses, except for wagering on them. He never learned to ride, much less saddle one," Sabrina supplied as she set to work bridling the gray. "If you'll assist me by throwing Natasha's sidesaddle over the mare, I can do the rest."

"Now, I don't mean to clabber up and churn all over your picnic, darlin', but Jamison and I are going to ride these critters till their legs near drop off getting back to London. We can't wait for a lady on a sidesaddle," Josh said in his most placating voice.

"I've been riding since I was a girl. I can keep up with any man alive," she said stubbornly.

"I'd never doubt it . . . only not on horseback, darlin'."

Sabrina gritted her teeth and ignored the gibe, striding over to the tack bench after she'd expertly bridled the gray he was saddling. Pointing to Natasha's saddle, she commanded Edmund, "Please swing this over that mare's back after I put the blanket on." She pointed to a sturdy dun.

"She's bested all three of her brothers on a fox hunt," Edmund put in as he grunted, lifting the saddle from its resting place.

"This is a skunk hunt, not a fox hunt," Josh said as he tightened the cinch on the big gray gelding.

"No one could be more aware of that than I," Sabrina said sweetly as she smoothed the blanket on the dun mare and helped her nervous cousin position the saddle.

As she worked, Josh stopped what he was doing

and reached for her busy hands, pulling them free. He raised one and kissed it, sighing in defeat. "There'll be no stopping you, will there?" She shook her head, and tangled bronze hair shimmered around her shoulders. Bits of twigs and leaves were caught in it. She looked endearing . . . and very determined. "All right, Sabrina. I reckon you've earned the right to see this through, but at least make one concession. Ride astride."

"Astride?" she echoed, aghast.

"You act like I was asking you to go stark naked like Lady Godiva . . . come to think of it, that's not a half bad—"

"Wipe that lascivious grin off your face, you rogue," she said in her sternest schoolroom voice. "I have no suitable clothes. My skirt—"

"I think I can fix it," he interrupted, extracting a wicked-looking knife from his belt. When she blinked and jerked back a step, he laughed. "I'm not gonna scalp you, just give you some leg room. Edmund, why don't you mosey up to the lodge and see if you can help Michael with the prisoners?" It was not a suggestion. Eddy nodded, eager to get away from the contretemps brewing in the stable, not to mention the horses.

Josh knelt in front of her and seized the limp fabric of her skirt, slicing it up the front. Then he turned her around and did the same for the back. "Now your petticoats should cover what's in between, and the skirt will rest over those beautiful legs."

"What will Mr. Jamison think?" she whispered, nearly undone when Josh stood so close and spoke of limbs no gentleman should ever mention in a lady's presence.

"If you show a bit of leg, I'll threaten Jamison with a pistol whipping if he so much as glances your way."

Well, that certainly solved that.

Michael strolled into the stable just as Josh and Sabrina finished saddling the third horse. "I dispatched Edmund on foot. With the map I drew for him, he should reach the Colchester constabulary about the time we're rounding up the Russians. Good heavens! I'm starting to speak in your peculiar cow-smasher's vernacular." Jamison looked appalled.

"Cowpuncher. And I'm not one anymore. I'm a stockman."

Sabrina let out a tiny chuckle, and all three burst into tension-purging laughter.

"Considering your cousin's penchant for trouble, I felt it best to get him as far removed from Madame Samsonov as possible, lest she somehow induce him to release her," Michael said to Sabrina.

She nodded. "Eddy is quite gullible, I fear." Then she noted the way Jamison's eyes strayed to her ruined skirt and felt her face suffuse with heat. "This was the viscount's idea. He insisted I ride astride."

Jamison's sangfroid deserted him again. "You can't come with us. I expected you to remain here with the prisoners until help arrives."

"You lose on that one, pard," Josh replied.

"Especially considering all the information I overheard about the assassination plot before Zarenko and his friends departed this morning," she said.

Both men stood with their jaws dropped as she bounded into the saddle. Her brothers could have told Josh that Sabrina never required a gentleman's assistance to mount a horse. As she waited for her bit of vital information to sink in to two befuddled male brains, she arranged the petticoat and skirt flaps strategically to cover her legs.

"We can discuss a plan for countering them while we ride. Well, what are you waiting for? Time is of the essence," she declared.

Like two attendants to the late queen, they mounted up and dashed after her.

Chapter 21

"All I know is gleaned from the bits and pieces I overheard at the lodge. Since they never expected that I'd escape, they spoke freely, but the plan had been formulated some time ago. I fear I don't have exact details, such as who this marksman is who'll be positioned in the park." Sabrina outlined the gist of Zarenko and Valerian's conversation with Natasha.

The three riders had ridden their mounts into the ground after leaving the cabin in Essex. Slightly past the halfway point to London, they had stopped to change to the three fresher horses they'd brought from the Russian's stable. As Michael and Josh switched the saddles, Sabrina talked.

"I'd feel better if we knew who this sniper is," Michael said as he tightened the cinch on a big roan. "St. James's Park affords a splendid view of the Mall for quite a distance, and it's so overgrown, an entire regiment of Russian cavalry could hide in it. How the devil are we going to find one man with a rifle before he shoots that idiot Hayashi in his open carriage?"

"They never mentioned him by name, but apparently he's considered their finest marksman for long distances. From what I could ascertain, he, not Zarenko, is the one responsible for this mission. Even Natasha did not quibble over who was in charge, although she acted a bit oddly about the mystery man."

"What d'you mean, 'oddly'?" Josh asked, giving the black he would ride a pat.

She shrugged. "She seemed to think it was . . . droll, for some reason," she replied, groping for a better word, finding none.

"Droll?" Josh echoed, scratching his head.

"You know, old chap, amusing?" Michael supplied as he swung onto his new mount impatiently. Now that she'd told them what she knew, he had made it clear that he felt it would be better if she remained behind.

But as long as she could keep up, Sabrina stubbornly insisted on riding with them, and Josh had reluctantly backed her, not wanting her wandering around the countryside alone. He looked up at Jamison with annoyance. "Far as I can see," he said, giving her an assist into her saddle, "this is about as funny as a yellowjacket in an outhouse."

Sabrina gave him a censuring look for his vulgarity, but he winked at her and mounted up without apology. "At least we know where Zarenko and his pals are going to set off the diversion," he said as they resumed their grueling pace once again.

"I mislike the presence of explosives in a crowd, especially in an area as large as Trafalgar Square. That could bring on unforeseeable complications," Jamison muttered, turning over in his mind various possibilities about how to handle the situation and net the conspirators.

"The explosion will be set to go off at half past four, if they proceed as they said they would," Sabrina assured him. "That is supposed to put Count Hayashi's progress halfway down the Mall to St. James's Palace."

"We have to get there in time to stop half the police and agents assigned to protect him from rushing off to the explosion site," Michael replied grimly.

"I bet Uncle Ab's fit to be hogtied over the route," Josh said.

"Lansdowne was no happier, I can assure you," Michael said. "But Salisbury insisted upon it. It would seem that our new allies in the East have very set notions about being received in a manner befitting their imperial status. If they aren't given the full treatment afforded Europeans, they will, as they put it, 'lose face.'"

Josh snorted. "Face. If those Russians start shooting, Hayashi'll lose a hell of a lot more than his face, he'll loose his as—"

"Ahem," Sabrina interjected with a meaningfully raised eyebrow at the viscount's slip into vulgarity.

He subsided.

The Japanese delegation had insisted on a procession from Downing Street up Whitehall and then down the wide thoroughfare to St. James's Palace, where a formal state dinner with King Edward would set the stage before the Anglo-Japanese treaty was signed. Although the Prime Minister had informed the Japanese government about a potential Russian plot, there was no diplomatically acceptable way for Salisbury to once again cancel the ceremonial honors the emperor's government expected.

To further complicate the situation, Lord Salisbury and Lord Lansdowne would be in the open carriage with Count Hayashi. Josh hoped, whoever this sniper was, that the fellow was a decent shot and wouldn't hit the English ministers instead. But it was his and Michael's job to see that the shot was never fired . . . if they could find the assassin in over ninety acres of heavily wooded, hilly park alongside the Mall.

The sun continued its descent toward the westward horizon as they rode. Jamison pulled his pocket piece out now and again to check the time. Josh could not imagine how the Englishman could read it from the back of a bouncing horse. After spending a lifetime on the Texas plains without the luxury of timepieces, he'd learned to use the sun to reckon time quite accurately. He figured they had no more than an hour to reach St. James's Park.

How the hell was he going to do his duty for the colonel and Uncle Ab—and see that Sabrina was out of harm's way at the same time? What a pickle.

As it turned out, Michael Jamison solved the dilemma for him when they reached the bustling crowds along the Strand. When they were forced to stop in the press of traffic, Michael scribbled a note on a scrap of paper and gave it to Sabrina.

"I want you to take this to that shop," he instructed her, pointing to a rather run-down-looking men's haberdashery just off the Strand. "Ask for Mr. Parker. He's always there. Certain to be today, as he's the chap who keeps track of all the agents' assignments during state visits. Explain everything you know about the situation, and he'll deal with the diversion Zarenko plans at Trafalgar. Tell him the viscount and I are going into St. James's Park to try to locate the sniper. Parker will have to seal off the whole of the park."

Sabrina nodded, stealing a quick look at Josh, uncertain about showing him that she was fearful for his safety. He took the decision out of her hands by leaning across his saddle and giving her a swift, serious kiss, before releasing her. "We'll talk after this is over, darlin'," he murmured.

"Be safe, Josh," she murmured, unable to look at Jamison, knowing what he must think of their relationship. Clutching the note tightly in her fist, she turned her horse and headed to meet Mr. Parker.

"Can this Parker fellow really find that dynamite in Trafalgar and seal off this place?" Josh asked dubiously as they approached the park.

"I fervently hope so. Miss Edgewater's information was most helpful about the conveyance. They can easily search for a wagon loaded with turnips," Jamison replied.

"She had more information than a mail-order catalogue, that's for sure. We'd be up the creek without a paddle if not for her," Josh replied.

"You care for her."

Michael's tone was neutral, but Josh knew enough about the way the English mind—not to mention the class system—worked to realize what his friend was thinking. "I don't just care for her, I'm fixing to marry her," he surprised himself by saying.

Jamison's eyebrows rose. "My grandmother, as I may have mentioned, was American. Also possessed of quite a scandalous reputation as a libertine before she married the Earl of Lynden. Considering how very properly English and properly proper Miss Edgewater is, I don't imagine she'll have any difficulty being accepted in Society."

Josh looked at the twinkle of amusement in Michael's eyes. "You mean Society'll accept her a hell of a lot faster than it did me," he said with an answering grin.

"Quite. We'd best split up here," he said as they rode in sight of the park. "I'll approach by the Mall, since they probably won't recognize me. You slip in from the eastern side."

"Watch your backside," Josh called out as his friend rode away.

The park was beautiful, rambling and hilly, lush with tall trees and dense shrubbery allowed to grow into a natural-appearing wild habitat right in the middle of the smoky, overcrowded city. In short, a perfect place from which a keen marksman could pick off a target and vanish without a trace before the police and Foreign Office agents could respond.

Josh surveyed the lay of the land, trying to remember any clear views of the Mall from high elevation. He'd been through it a few times, but not nearly as often as Hyde Park, which was larger and offered more open space in which to ride. As he recalled, there was one rise on this side of the artificially created swan pond that might offer a good vantage point.

He approached as close as he dared on horseback, then dismounted, finding a youth who sold meat pies to passersby and offering him some coins to watch the winded black gelding. He might still have need of a mount before this afternoon was over. Josh squinted at the sun. It must now be getting on a quarter past four. Not much time to find one varmint in a ninety-acre wood.

Going on pure instinct, which he'd learned to trust during the war, he made his way past flower beds now spent in the warm autumn sun, shoving spirea bushes aside as he climbed through the most densely overgrown part of the park. Having learned to hunt small game as a boy, he moved silently, his Colt clutched in his hand. Josh peered through the still green shrubbery toward the hill overlooking the Mall.

It was then he saw a figure lying flat on his belly, aiming a Remington-Creedmore .44/100 on the Mall below. In minutes the Royal Horseguards would proceed ahead of the targeted carriage.

Just like Sabrina described it. Josh eyed the sniper's weapon. The rifle was the finest weapon made for such a difficult shot. In the hands of an expert marksman, it could blow Hayashi's head clean off his shoulders. Josh drew closer, preparing to get the drop on the sniper. When he recognized the man, Josh understood why Natasha had thought it so amusing that he was the mastermind behind their schemes. Damned if he hadn't been taken in just like everyone else.

Feeling betrayed, although he knew that was a damn fool attitude, he raised his Colt, but before he could order the other man to drop his rifle, the sound of a twig snapping behind him made him crouch and pivot, to confront a knife blade that would have slit his throat in another instant.

"I would suggest you drop your weapon," the sniper said conversationally, rolling over and aiming directly at Josh's back.

Sabrina stood at the edge of the crowd, observing the commotion as half a dozen agents assisted by bobbies removed a sizable bundle of explosives concealed beneath a load of turnips. The two men on the wagon were in custody. She recognized neither one of them, but both were babbling in Russian.

Now if only Mr. Jamison and Josh could capture Zarenko and Valerian . . .

Her thoughts were interrupted by a harshly familiar whisper. "I might have known you'd be responsible for this." She felt the cold pressure of a pistol pressed into her ribs as Nikolai Zarenko clamped one elegant hand around her arm and began leading her away from the crowd.

"You'd be best advised to release me," she said with considerably more bravado than she felt. "The government knows everything, and agents have your companions in custody now, including your sister. There will be no assassination."

"All the more reason you'll be useful . . . if what you say is true. But give me leave to doubt our sniper in the park has been taken," he purred. "Even without this little diversion, we'll succeed—with a proper English hostage or two. Perhaps the viscount? I imagine Lord Hambleton would move heaven and earth to obtain his release in exchange for my sister."

"Don't be foolish," she said, trying to wrest her arm free of his punishing grasp. "How do you expect to capture Jo—the viscount?"

He pressed the gun harder against her side. "Why, with you as bait. I know he's one of the men prowling the park. And he's your lover." He tsked mockingly. "Servants do gossip, especially English servants. In Russia we'd cut out their tongues if they were so loose."

"You, sir, are an animal," she said coldly, trying to gather her racing thoughts to form some kind of plan. She would never allow this viper to use her to trap Josh.

Ignoring her insult, he dragged her toward a closed carriage parked across the street. The driver was one of the men she'd seen at the lodge. If she got inside, all would be lost. Willing herself to use every ounce of strength her already aching body had left, she twisted free of Zarenko's grasp and started to scream, but he raised his pistol and clubbed her over the head before she could utter a sound.

Everything went black.

He quickly handed the gun to a man inside the carriage, then glanced around to see if anyone had noticed. Fortunately for him, all eyes remained fixed on the excitement across the square. He scooped her into his arms and handed her to his servant before climbing aboard himself. The carriage took off with a lurch, headed toward the park.

"I figure we have what folks back home call a Mexican standoff. You can't fire or you'll give away your position," Josh said, his Colt aimed at Sergei Valerian's heart. He backed around so he could see both men. "I reckon I savvy why Natasha thought you being the brains of this outfit was so funny, Alexi."

"Alexi, the good-natured drunk. Everyone loves a jovial buffoon—even you, my American friend. I have fooled your arrogant British spies as well," Alexi Kurznikov said conversationally.

"Maybe," Josh replied, waiting for an opening as Alexi started to leap to his feet in a surprisingly supple motion for one so rotund. Small wonder he had the capacity to drink a dozen men under the table and still stagger upright. What appeared to be fat was in reality thick, well-conditioned muscle. When the barrel of the rifle moved fractionally, Josh dived to the ground, rolling as he fired at Kurznikov, grazing his arm, but the Russian did not relinquish his hold on his weapon.

Before Alexi could sight in on his target, Josh was partially concealed behind a thicket of overgrown boxwoods. "Dispose of him," Alexi snapped in Russian to Valerian, then turned back to observe the parade on the Mall. The open carriage continued to draw nearer, although several soldiers at the rear had pulled abreast of it to offer protection as soon as Josh's shot rang out.

He got off another shot at Alexi, but Valerian threw himself across the space separating them and spoiled his aim. The Russian landed on top of him, knocking the Colt from his hand even as he brought the deadly blade up, intent on silencing his foe permanently. They rolled in the thick brush, thrashing as Josh fought to hold on to Valerian's knife hand. The wickedly gleaming steel nicked his throat before the Texan was able to force it away.

Sweat beaded their faces as they struggled. Time was running out. Alexi was going to take that shot, and if he hit the Japanese minister, it would be an international catastrophe. Josh used his leg as he'd learned to do "Injun rasslin' " back home and hooked it over Valerian's leg, then bent it quickly, throwing his opponent off of him. The Texan followed, never relinquishing his grip on his enemy's knife hand. Now he was on top and used the leverage to lower the blade toward Valerian's throat.

Suddenly Michael burst into the clearing, winded from his run across the bridge and up the hill. Ignoring the life-and-death struggle between Josh and Valerian, he yelled at Kurznikov, "Drop the weapon or I'll kill you where you stand."

Alexi did not comply. His sights were in alignment and his finger squeezed the trigger. Jamison's shot rang out, plowing into Alexi's shoulder an instant before the Russian's Remington went off. Kurznikov's shot kicked up dust at the hooves of one of the parade soldier's horses, causing the animal to shy and rear up, but no harm was done once the frightened animal was back under control.

The carriage full of dignitaries continued on to St. James's Palace.

Josh used the interruption to good advantage, pressing the knife closer to Valerian's throat, but at the last instant, the Russian grabbed a fistful of dirt with his free hand and threw it in the Texan's face, then rolled over again as Josh, coughing and blinking away the stinging pain in his eyes, tried to regain control of the fight.

Michael sighted his Webley down on Alexi, who had lost his purchase on the rifle and lay, defeated, clutching his ruined shoulder, which was bleeding profusely. The British agent moved closer and picked up the sniper's rifle. "A fine weapon," he said. "Pity you missed with it." Then, satisfied that Kurznikov was no longer a threat, he turned to see how Josh was faring.

"I could use a mite of help, ole chap," the viscount drawled as he punched blindly at the Russian's face. One fist connected with a glancing blow just as his vision started to clear. He rolled up on top again and put all his weight onto Valerian's arm so the knife blade pressed into his throat. "Drop it or bleed," Josh said.

The Russian let the knife fall from his grasp, glaring up at the grinning Texan.

"Much obliged for your help," Josh said dryly to Michael, who was hauling a pale, stoic Alexi Kurznikov to his feet.

"Think nothing of it, old chap," Jamison said. "My first priority was to protect Count Hayashi. You are, after all, merely a viscount, and England already has a surfeit of them."

"But only one Texas viscount," Josh countered as he recovered his Colt from where it lay hidden in the brush and motioned for Valerian to stand. "That ought to mean something."

"We have a saying in jolly old England. A viscount by any other name is still a viscount," Michael replied cheerily as they herded their prisoners down the slope.

"Will Shakespeare was talking about roses," Josh groused.

Ignoring the gibe, Jamison looked around. "Where the deuce are our agents? The place should be swarming with them in response to those shots."

"It's a large park, and I arranged for one of my servants to take them on a bit of a wild goose chase, I believe you English call it," Nikolai Zarenko said conversationally as he stepped into their pathway with a pistol. When Josh and Michael started to turn their guns toward him, he added, "I would not advise shooting me, else Yuri will be forced to break Miss Edgewater's interfering neck."

Josh swore as a bear of a man appeared beside him carrying an unconscious Sabrina in his arms. "If you've hurt her—"

"Not yet. But I would advise you to drop your weapons, lest she come to a swift and ugly end."

"You have no hope whatever of escaping, Zarenko. Give yourself up, and your diplomatic immunity will see you safely back to Mother Russia," Jamison said coolly.

"Forgive me if I place little faith in your government's 'immunity,' " Alexi wheezed, struggling to stand upright as he broke free of Michael's hold.

Valerian stepped away from Josh at the same time. Sabrina, who had returned to consciousness just as she was being hauled from the carriage, had overheard Zarenko instructing his men to carry out this escape plan. She knew she had to do something, but, held fast by such a brute, all she could do was feign unconsciousness, praying for inspiration as they made their way toward the assassination site to locate their leader.

Now Josh and Mr. Jamison were here, and the Russians might kill them. She allowed her lashes to lift just enough to see where everyone stood. Both her love and the British agent were armed. She had to move before they dropped their weapons. Zarenko stood close beside her, his pistol aimed at Josh. In one sudden movement, she kicked out as hard and fast as she could, aiming for his gun arm, while at the same time sinking sharp little teeth into the hairy throat of the bear who held her.

With a startled oath, he dropped her. Zarenko's weapon discharged as the toe of her boot connected wickedly with the bones in his elbow. The shot skimmed by Josh, who dived toward his nemesis, unable to fire for fear of hitting Sabrina. Still, his Colt made a formidable club, and he smashed it into the side of the Russian's face as they went down together. The servant who had been carrying her made a guttural sound as one meaty paw rubbed at his throat where she had drawn blood. His other hand lashed out, connecting with the side of her head and knocking her to the ground.

Sabrina literally saw stars as the earth came up to meet her and everything around her whirled in dizzying circles. On all fours, she shook her head to clear it as the sounds of life-and-death struggling surrounded her. *I will not be used as a bargaining chip again!* That was all she could think of as she saw Josh and Zarenko punching each other bloody.

Alexi was too weak from his injuries to make it more than three steps before he fell to his knees. Ignoring him for an instant, Jamison fired at Valerian, who had seized the pistol Zarenko had dropped when Sabrina kicked him. Valerian went down, hit point-blank in the heart. Zarenko's servant reached for her, knowing that she was the key to ending the fight before help arrived for the English, but she kicked and struggled, engaging his attention until Jamison could reach them. When she twisted away from the Russian's grasp, Jamison dispatched him just as he had Valerian.

"Josh, watch out!" Sabrina screamed, looking past Michael to where Josh had just knocked Zarenko unconscious. Alexi, still on his knees and white as the cliffs of Dover, had picked up Valerian's pistol and was taking aim at Hambleton's heir.

"My last act for Mother Russia," he said with a sigh.

But Josh's instincts were honed by years of bar fights and backroom brawls. He dived behind Zarenko, who was struggling to get back up. Alexi's bullet hit his compatriot an instant before Jamison put a second shot into the ringleader.

Peering across the carnage, the Texan grinned. "About time you did something to help me," he said as he stood up, dusting off his torn and bloody clothes.

"Happy to oblige now that diplomacy's been served," Michael replied coolly.

"Are all men idiots?" Sabrina asked rhetorically,

swallowing her gorge as she tried not to look at the dead Russians littering St. James's Park. Instead, she fixed her eyes on Josh, who was striding toward her.

"I can't rightly speak for all the members of my gender, but when it comes to you, darlin', I reckon I'm one," he said, picking her up and whirling her around in a circle.

"Put me down," she hissed as the sounds of men approaching were quickly followed by the appearance of a phalanx of bobbies and Mr. Parker's agents.

Josh ignored them and her command, holding her fast as he let her curvaceous little body slide down his. He kept one arm around her waist and cupped her face with the other hand, gently caressing the angry red swelling where the Russian had struck her. "Can't you ever stay out of trouble?" he asked, planting soft kisses on her injury.

"Josh, we have an audience," she whispered as the officers of the law began to haul away bodies while Michael Jamison calmly related to Mr. Parker what had transpired.

"Appears to me half of 'em is past caring and the other half is too busy to pay us any mind," Josh said, silencing her next protest by lowering his mouth to hers and kissing her soundly.

"Whatever am I to do with you?" she asked in a dreamy voice when he relinquished her lips.

"Marry me?" he supplied.

"Josh, don't be absurd. You're Lord Hambleton's heir and I'm—oh!" She realized the deadly Mr. Jamison was standing directly beside them now, grinning as he listened to every word they said!

"You can't possibly be as unsuitable as Grandmother Beth was when my great-grandfather Blackthorne forced my grandfather Derrick to marry her,"

Michael said. "The Countess of Lynden was reputed to cavort naked with Italian artists, and even lived in an Algerian seraglio for a time."

Sabrina blinked. "You're jesting," was all she could think to say.

" 'Pon my honor, it's the truth." Michael raised one hand solemnly.

"And a spy would never prevaricate," she replied dryly.

"More ten-dollar words," Josh said. "I reckon I'll have to buy a dictionary just so I can palaver with her once we're married." By this time the three of them were alone. He winked at Michael.

"Oh, Josh, you don't realize what you're asking," Sabrina said softly as she met his laughing green eyes. "I'm the daughter of a country squire, a—a nobody compared to a viscount, much less an earl."

Josh scratched his head. "You know, I've been studying on why Uncle Ab hired your fool cousin and then you. Now I know the reason. Clear as sunrise."

She had been wondering about that herself. "And, pray, what could that be?" she asked suspiciously, not daring to hope this wonderful dream could ever work in the real world.

"We'll just go and ask him right now," he said resolutely.

Sabrina swallowed for courage. How could she dare to face the Earl of Hambleton with such an audacious proposal? But Josh appeared so determined, so certain. After all they had been through together, she knew, for good or ill, that she would brave the old man's wrath. "I shall go with you, but I fear you're going to be given a sharp set-down."

"Would it bother you to marry a plain ole Texas

stockman—who happens to be a millionaire? 'Course, you'd have to come live with me in America."

Now his certainty appeared to waver. "Oh, Josh, you cannot abdicate your family duty," she protested.

"Hel—I mean, shucks, darlin', the only reason I agreed to a viscount in the first place was because President Roosevelt asked me to." He remembered how Uncle Ab had pulled strings to bring that about and grinned, his confidence once again rising. "No more balking. Come on," he said, taking her hand and practically dragging her to where the boy watching his horse stood dutifully waiting.

Josh paid the youth a sum sufficient to cause the lad's eyes to widen in astonishment. "Thank ye, gov, thank ye!" He gave a crude bow and scampered off.

Josh swung up into the saddle with that fluid horseman's grace she'd always admired, then reached down and pulled her into his arms. As he kicked the horse into a good trot, she suddenly realized that he was smeared with blood and dirt and had bits of grass and twigs clinging to his torn clothing. If he looked that bad, how much more disreputable must *she* appear?

With dismay, she glanced down at her slashed skirt, petticoats hanging out in plain view. After hours on horseback, she reeked of equine perspiration, not to mention her own. Her hair was a welter of tangles, with pins undone and the whole mass falling about her shoulders. The earl would be appalled almost as much as she. "Josh, my unmentionables are showing!" she cried, trying in vain to smooth her skirt over the white cotton that billowed out stubbornly all around it.

He threw back his head and laughed joyously. "I won't mention 'em if you won't."

Before she could retort, he kissed her, silencing her protests.

"Please allow me to make myself presentable first," she hissed as Nash, without so much as a raised eyebrow, led them toward the earl's office.

"When I tell him what you've gone through to save the treaty, he won't care if you're wearing nothing but a ring and a sneeze."

Red-faced with mortification, Sabrina allowed Josh to lead her into the earl's presence. The sooner Josh was disabused of his romantic notions, the less painful it would be for everyone. Seeing her in this condition would certainly exemplify for Hambleton how impetuous and impractical Josh's plans were.

The old man's face was enigmatic as they stepped into his office. He stood up, his keen gray eyes sweeping over their rumpled appearance. If he was upset by a woman whose petticoats hung out from her slashed skirt, he did nothing to indicate it. "Mr. Jamison just departed after giving me the particulars of your adventure. I commend you both on work superbly done, although I certainly apologize to you, child, for having placed you in such danger," he said as he walked around the desk and made a courtly bow before her.

That caught Sabrina up short. "It is I who must apologize for my most unseemly appearance, my lord, but Lord Wesley insisted that he speak with you at once." There was nothing for it but to stand up straight and face the consequences.

"Oh, and what is it that 'Lord Wesley' "—he stressed the title with a bit of humor twinkling in his eyes—"wishes to say, hmmm? Allow me to speculate, if you please," he added quickly as Josh opened his mouth to speak. "Indulge an old man's fancy." He looked from the belligerent stance of his nephew, who held Sabrina Edgewater's hand in a deathgrip, to her pale, proud face with those worried blue eyes fixed on her love.

His smile broadened. "You wish to marry, and I, of course, give my blessing. After all—" He paused, thoroughly enjoying the looks of incredulous joy on both of their faces, then proceeded. "I went to considerable trouble bringing you together."

Josh sighed with relief. Uncle Ab had come through. "You knew I'd never go for one of those snobby, blue-blooded females who can't pick up a hankie without asking for help."

"That is why I paraded the most oppressive of the lot before you."

"Lady Eunice?" The words popped out of Sabrina's mouth before she could stop them. She reddened again. Curse her wayward tongue! Ever since she'd met Joshua Cantrell, her decorum had fled along with her heart.

"Quite so," Hambleton replied delightedly.

"He wanted a woman with some gumption for me—oh, and with enough spit and polish so a little would rub off. You were made to order for me, darlin', and all the while neither of us knew it." He turned to the earl. "But Uncle Ab did."

"Yes, I most certainly did, most especially after she planted that facer on you at the fountain. Well done, my dear. Young Whistledown's potential was not at first nearly as apparent as yours, but now that Hodgins is gone, I suspect I can whip him into shape, with a bit of help from you," he said to Sabrina.

"You are more than kind, my lord. I shall see to it that my cousin lives up to the trust you have placed in him."

Fixing his eyes sternly on Josh, the earl said, "The only concern I had with your potential was getting you to give up your libertine way of life. I'm delighted that Miss Edgewater has made you see the error of your ways."

"I reckon she'll keep working on my errors . . . for the rest of our lives," Josh said with a rueful grin.

"Get on with you, then. I suspect you have more to say to each other in private," Hambleton said, shooing them from his office. "I have a mountain of paperwork from the Foreign Office to address."

Josh took Sabrina out into the garden by the fountain where they had first kissed with such disastrous consequences. Now that they had his uncle's blessing, he had to be certain she understood what she would be taking on by getting hitched to him. "I may be a viscount but I'll never make a real English gentleman." He shook his head, searching for the right words. "What I mean is, I reckon you can take the boy out of Texas but you can't take the Texas out of the boy."

"Josh, I was hired to teach you manners—and at times I may still chide you—but you have more fine qualities than any stuffy Englishman I've ever met," she said earnestly.

He felt warm as a Texas sunrise when he saw the glow of unconditional love in her eyes. "Then you won't mind coming to America with me—just to check on my businesses and to visit a few special friends now and then."

"Your 'aunts' who helped Miss Gertie raise you?" she asked with a smile. "I would love to meet them and to see if your Texas is half as grand as you've always bragged it is."

"What a woman!" he exclaimed, picking her up and whirling her around by the edge of the fountain. "Uncle Ab got the pick of the litter for me, he surely did. I reckon he's the smartest fellow ole King Eddy's got working for him."

A slow grin tugged at her lips, matching his. "King Eddy?" she echoed teasingly. "I believe that's lese majesty."

"There you go with more ten-dollar words . . . and in French, even."

"Then I suppose I shall have to start teaching you French in addition to deportment," she murmured, letting her arms glide around his neck.

He chuckled. "Darlin', the young gals at Gertie's already taught me enough French so *I* can give *you* lessons."

"Joshua Cantrell, I suspect you're being bawdy again," she murmured.

"Naw, darlin', just in love," he protested innocently.

She slid slowly down his long, lean body, holding fast as his mouth slanted over hers, sealing their love with a kiss. They'd start the French lessons after the wedding. . . .

•

Epilogue

Five years later

Trunks were piled high in the foyer as Nash fussed over assigning his most reliable footmen to load the wagons. The viscount and his family were making their annual trek to the wilds of America tomorrow, and everything for a three-month stay had to be safely stored aboard the ship by morning. Young Master James and his sister Abby came racing down the hallway of the city house, filling the air with squeals of glee when they saw the mountain of luggage.

At once, like a pair of monkeys, the four-year-old boy and his three-year-old sister commenced to climb atop the highest pile. Distraught, the butler was forced to snatch the two squirming children from near disaster before their nurse came rushing into the foyer.

"I'm that sorry, Nash, but I turned my back only long enough to fetch a toy box for the maid who was packing and they were off and running," the breathless woman said.

"Quite all right. A propensity for mayhem runs in the family," he replied in resignation as he handed the giggling children over to her. Oh, for the days when only His Lordship the earl was in residence here. He would roundly enjoy several months of peace and quiet, with only spies and Foreign Secretaries coming and going!

Josh stood at the top of the stairs, observing the pandemonium below. His children were growing fast as Texas tumbleweeds in a high wind. So was young Maggie, now down for her afternoon nap in the nursery adjacent to their bedroom. Being raised a lone boy surrounded by older females, he had never imagined how much he would enjoy being a father. His three children were the light of his and Sabrina's lives, not to mention the earl's, who now felt the Hambleton succession was secure.

Just then Josh's wife and Dru walked through the front door. As always, his face lit at the sight of Sabrina, who had a smudge of chalk dust on the shoulder of her dark blue suit. She and Lady Drucilla Whistledown had a great deal to discuss, since Edmund's bride was taking on the considerable responsibility of administering The Cantrell School for Young Ladies while Edmund and Sabrina were in America.

His viscountess had made quite a success of the venture, with financial backing from Uncle Ab and himself, but it was Sabrina Edgewater Cantrell who was the driving force behind everything. Over the years, hundreds of girls had been rescued from the slums of London. She and her staff taught them the same stern values of education and independence she herself had exhibited as a twenty-year-old from the Berkshires facing the vast harshness of a city that often left such girls no options save starvation or prostitution. Now they were given the opportunity to become self-sufficient young women, entering service as upper household servants, clerks, nurses, governesses and teachers.

As Edmund Whistledown strode confidently down the hallway and bussed his wife lightly on the cheek, Josh had to admit that the damn fool boy who'd barely escaped prison or death for treason had done amazingly well for himself. After two years as Uncle Ab's secretary, he had been encouraged by the earl to begin the study of law. This past year he'd been admitted to the bar. Now he used his considerable talents, not the least of which was play-acting, to win over juries on the behalf of unjustly accused clients.

The Chiffington clan had been delighted to see their second—and as far as they were concerned, unmarriageable—daughter wed. Even if her husband did not possess a title, he was connected to the Earl of Hambleton. The good offices of the earl had soothed the old marquess, but the money Edmund earned as a barrister went a long way toward sweetening the bargain. Being a self-made man himself, Josh took pride in seeing Edmund succeed so spectacularly, especially considering that it meant "polluting" the snobby Chiffington bloodlines.

When the Whistledowns had announced that they were expecting their first child at dinner last night, Josh had proposed a toast using words to that effect. Sabrina had kicked him so hard under the table that he grunted. But the earl had joined Edmund and Dru in a hearty chuckle.

As Edmund and Drucilla departed, Sabrina ignored the pandemonium around her and looked up, feeling her husband's eyes on her. She could always tell when her Texas Viscount was watching her. He was ecstatic over their return to his ranch in Texas. Of course, they would make obligatory stops in New York for business meetings and in Washington so Josh could confer with his old friend the president before heading for Dallas. She had a bone to pick with him about what was to occur when they reached the ranch.

Determinedly she made her way up the stairs to where her tall, grinning husband stood waiting for her. She could tell by the gleam in his eyes that he had another matter entirely on his mind. Sabrina was determined not to let him distract her. But when he reached out and pulled her into his arms, she could not resist a warm kiss hello.

"I missed you, darlin'. Uncle Ab's kept me hopping faster than a one-legged man in an ass-kicking contest—"

"Another folksy analogy, you silver-tongued devil," she said, placing her fingers over his lips. "Josh, what ever shall I do with you? You're incorrigible."

He nibbled on her fingers as he led her down the hall. "Oh, I have an idea or two," he murmured in a husky voice.

"None of that until we talk," she said in the sternest voice she could muster.

In answer, he brushed the chalk dust from her jacket, deliberately running his palm across her breast, knowing how that would affect her. "Not sporting," she protested softly.

"Sporting is exactly what I have in mind," he murmured as he pulled her inside their bedroom and closed the door.

The lock clicked. "Now, what were you fixing to say?" he asked as he began unfastening the frog closures on her jacket.

"There is a serious matter—"

"Only an hour before Maggie wakes from her afternoon nap, and you know she sets up a holler like a treed bobcat. Now, *that's* a serious matter," he crooned, nibbling her earlobe as he eased her jacket off and tossed it on a nearby chair.

"You intend to present James with a horse when we reach the Circle C, do you not?" she persisted, placing her hands flat against his chest.

He shrugged, knowing she would not be distracted until they talked it over. She could be stubborn as one of those Missouri mules when she had a cud to chew. "He'll be five this spring. In Texas a boy rides before he learns to walk. Not a landowner in the Berkshires would let his son go this long without riding, either. Your daddy agreed with me."

"Papa! I might have known the two of you were conspiring about something last weekend," she said, feeling miffed that her father would take Josh's side over this, although, considering how horse-mad the squirearchy as a whole was, it was hardly surprising.

"Hell, darlin', it's only a pony, not a full-grown horse. He's a blood bay, the same color as Comanche. Jimmy will be crazy about him, and he's gentle as a lamb."

She scoffed, ignoring his use of profanity. At least he was careful not to use it around the children . . . most of the time. "What would a cowsmasher know about lambs, anyway?" she asked with a saucy grin.

Josh sighed and rolled his eyes heavenward, ignoring her use of Michael's favorite expression. "For your information, we are now also sheepsmashers. I just bought two sheep ranches—in Australia. I figure next January we'll head down under and check 'em out." He started nuzzling her throat as he bared the skin beneath her now unfastened blouse. "We could use a change from the cold drizzles of English winter."

"I understand the seasons are reversed in the southern hemisphere. Lovely and warm in January . . . but climatology can wait," she murmured, getting into the spirit of the seduction. They actually had less than an hour until Maggie would awaken screaming for her afternoon feeding.

"Any time we're together, it's more than warm, it's hot as—"

"Don't you dare say it," she interrupted playfully, kissing him full on the mouth as she started to work on the studs holding his shirt closed.

"How'd you know what I was gonna say?" he murmured, cupping a breast swollen from nursing their three-month-old daughter.

" 'Hot as the hinges of hell' is one of your favorites. Oh! Joshua Abington Charles Cantrell, you are a terrible influence," she said, but the conviction in her voice faded as he lowered his head and took a bared nipple in his mouth. All that remained of her reprimand was a low, satisfied moan of pleasure.

"I sure hope so. Somethin's got to counter all that propriety you've beaten into me."

"For all my success, I might as well have tried beating crumpets into a stone wall," she said while he unfastened her skirt and petticoats, letting them drop in a pouf at her feet.

"Now, that's not true," he averred. "You reformed a hell-bent—er, heck-bent hell-raiser." By now her blouse had joined the growing pile of clothing on the chair.

As she slid his shirt from his shoulders, Sabrina chuckled, shaking her head in resignation. She would never change Josh. And she never wanted to. Instead, she reveled in the dark skin and hard muscles of his shoulders and arms. Carelessly he shrugged the garment off and tossed it. When they were in residence at their country estate, he insisted on working in the stable yards without a shirt. But only she was privileged to see the sharp line of demarcation at his waist and the much paler skin on his hard buttocks, long legs . . . and other places. She began unbuttoning his fly, eager to free that thick, hard proof of his desire and take it in her hands.

"You always forget," he said in a voice made raspy with desire. "Boots first." With that he scooped her up and tossed her gently on the bed, sitting on the edge to tug off his footgear, then turning toward her. "Now . . . where were you?" he murmured.

She completed her task with delicacy and skill, eliciting groans of pleasure from him as he kicked his trousers over the foot of the bed. When he started to caress her legs and peel down the silk stockings and garters, she murmured dreamily, "I seem to recall a prudish miss who was ever so embarrassed to have made love while wearing these. What a twit she was."

Josh considered for a moment. "Well, she was . . . but I loved her anyway," he said, adding, "You've always been the best part of me, darlin' . . . always will be."

"I believe you, my lord." She helped him slide her chemise and underdrawers off, loving the way his eyes swept over her body. Although the birth of three children had put extra pounds on her, he always assured her that they were distributed in the best possible places. Seeing the hunger in his eyes as he caressed her breasts, she sighed in bliss and arched up, offering them to him with a soft murmur, "Leave something for Maggie . . ."

He licked and teased the extra-sensitive nipples, gently cupping the fullness of her pale, sweet flesh, then nibbling his way downward to her once again flat little belly. His tongue flicked inside her navel, then moved lower toward the golden bronze mound, where he buried his head.

Sabrina cried out and dug her fingers into his hair, urging him on eagerly. The first time he'd done this, she'd been shocked at such an unimaginable way of making love, but once he'd insisted, she'd been shocked at the unimaginable pleasure of it. With unerring skill he found the tiny nub and mouthed it until she moaned his name. This never took long, but he paused, leaving her gasping for more, drawing out her keen hunger until she pleaded for release.

Then he gave it, and all the stars of the heavens exploded behind her fluttering lashes. As she came back to earth, he kissed the insides of her thighs and used his hands to cup her derriere and knead the soft flesh. She moved her hands from where they had gripped the sheets and reached for his shoulders, pressing him onto his back as she rolled over beside him. "Now it's my turn," she whispered, stroking the proud erection as he lay with his fists clenched at his sides.

"Any . . . thing . . . you want," he finally managed to get out.

"I should hope," Sabrina murmured.

She knelt and looked at him, her powerful lover, made utterly helpless by her touch. His bronzed skin and night-dark hair were in stark contrast to the whiteness of the sheets. With her free hand, she traced a pattern from the stubble on his jawline down through the forest on his muscled chest, following the narrow line of black hair that arrowed down his belly to the bush at his groin. Then she took him in her mouth and applied the most ladylike pressure with her lips and tongue, until she had him arching and bucking helplessly, crying out her name.

When he knew he could hold out no longer, Josh reached down quickly and pulled her up to him, rolling on top of her. "Not this time," he said breathlessly. "I owe you this." As he plunged deep inside her, he remembered all the times she had made love to him while recovering from their children's births. It was his greatest pleasure to even the score afterward.

"We owe each other," she whispered, clutching his shoulders, drawing him into a deep kiss.

They moved rapidly at first, then slowly, prolonging the pleasure. Each time he could feel her begin to peak, he would stop, panting and eager as she, determined to make the beauty of their joining last. Then just when they both mindlessly believed the ecstasy could go on forever, a sharp squall sounded from the nursery door.

"Maggie," Sabrina murmured through the haze.

"Time to go," Josh said on a sigh, increasing their rhythm until he could feel the contractions of her velvety sheath. As she arched up in culmination, he spilled himself deep within her, shuddering and collapsing on top of her in utter satiation.

They lay together for a moment, tangled in the sheets, still panting and damp with perspiration in spite of the cool spring air. He nibbled kisses across her face, planting one on the tip of her nose. "I thought we had an hour," he said. "That little gal is as insatiable as her mama."

"You misjudged the time. And who is her father to condemn her for being insatiable? She comes by it from you."

"All my children have Texas-sized appetites," he said with a proud chuckle.

"You once told your uncle my good manners should rub off on you. I rather believe your hungers—for good or ill—have rubbed off on me."

"Aw, darlin', as long as we keep on rubbin' together, who cares?"

Their daughter demanded attention. Sabrina gave a joyous laugh as she slipped from his arms and reached for her robe to attend to another Texas Cantrell.

Author's Note

Historical events often provide the framework for a story. There were two treaties between Great Britain and Japan directed against Russian encroachments in the Far East. During negotiations over the first alliance, Tadasu Hayashi was the Japanese minister to the Court of St. James, Lord Salisbury was the British Prime Minister and Lord Lansdowne was Foreign Secretary. President Theodore Roosevelt supported the alliance as a means of using the Royal Navy and the Japanese military to protect American interests from Russian aggression. The Siberian Transcontinental Railroad was completed in 1901, giving the Russian Empire access to the Pacific.

However, I took some literary license in writing *Texas Viscount*. Minister Hayashi was only presented with the final draft of the treaty in the fall of 1901. It was not signed by his government until January, 1902, but since I wanted warm weather for my story, I fudged the date. Roosevelt had no direct involvement in the process until he negotiated the end of the Russo-Japanese war in 1905, for which he was awarded a Nobel Peace Prize. Nor, as far as I know, did any Russian agents attempt to assassinate Tadasu Hayashi or disrupt the diplomatic process leading up to the Anglo-Japanese Alliance of 1902. But considering how much was at stake in the Far East, it is not inconceivable that some disgruntled Russian faction would have plotted to scuttle the treaty.

I had a ball creating Josh and Sabrina, the third and last pair of lovers in my American Lords Series after Jason and Rachel in *Yankee Earl* and Brandon and Miranda in *Rebel Baron*. As always, my husband Jim refined the dialogue. If you laughed at Josh's bawdy humor and Sabrina's sassy retorts, I owe that in large measure to his able assistance.

Michael Jamison's family history may have sounded a bit familiar because his infamous grandmother was the heroine from Wanton Angel, the last book in my Blackthorne Family Trilogy. Perhaps somewhere along the way he'll get his own story. Like his cool spymaster grandfather Derrick, Michael deserves a happy ending, too. Let me know what you think. Happy reading!

Shirl Henke
www.shirlhenke.com

REBEL BARON

SHIRL HENKE

Wealthy widow Miranda Auburn hides her femininity behind a facade of cold calculation. Her only womanly emotions are reserved for her daughter, whose fondest wish is to marry a peer.

Brandon Caruthers hopes to put the lost cause of the Confederacy behind him when he travels to London to become Baron Rushcroft. But the only way to salvage his impoverished estate is to marry an heiress.

The transaction Miranda proposes seems to suit all involved—a huge loan in exchange for making her daughter a baroness—until Brand finds himself craving the mother instead. . . .

YANKEE EARL
SHIRL HENKE

Jason Beaumont, brash American privateer, is now Earl of Falconridge, and the Honorable Miss Rachel Fairchild could not be more horrified. Until she finds herself making the brute's acquaintance lying flat on her back in the mud, gazing up at a particularly fascinating portion of his anatomy. She grows still more flustered when the arrogant colonial proceeds to set London's tongues wagging with his daring exploits, and challenge her own cutting wit with his outrageous innuendoes. But most shocking of all is a surprise betrothal ball where she learns her own father has conspired to see her leg shackled, for better or worse, to the Yankee earl.

ATTENTION BOOK LOVERS!

Can't get enough of your favorite **ROMANCE**?

Call **1-800-481-9191** to:

✳ order books,

✳ receive a **FREE** catalog,

✳ join our book clubs to **SAVE 30%**!

Open Mon.-Fri. 10 AM-9 PM EST

Visit **www.dorchesterpub.com**
for special offers and inside
information on the authors you love.

We accept Visa, MasterCard or Discover®.
LEISURE BOOKS ♥ LOVE SPELL